Sando:

An Accounting for Evil

Part Two

V.F. Porzio

Published by:

Vincent Porzio

Porzio_V@Yahoo.com

Published by: Brooklyn Publishing

ISBN-13: 978-1492103899

Printed in the United States of America

First Edition

Acknowledgments

I am indebted to the following people for their support and contributions to this book:

To my first readers: Koreen, Justina, Nicole, B.J., Becky, Katrina, Vera (best mom), Zia Janet, Laurie, The two Maria's, Miriam, Mariah, Phil, Theresa, Stephan and finally, David Kelley (a fine author in his own right). To all of you from the bottom of my heart, thank you for your love, inspiration, support, and the constant question that kept me motivated the whole time, "when are you going to finish?" Words could never express my feelings. I love you all.

To my family: My parents, thank you for life. My wife Koreen, your faithful support had you laboring over every page, proofing and re-proofing time and time again. My daughters, Justina and Kaitlyn, who encouraged me to never give up. My dogs, Baxter and Chance, thank you for making me laugh every time I picked my head up from the computer. Thank you all for giving me the opportunity to go on this great journey of adventure and capture the story that was in my mind. Your never ending patience, support, laughter and much love kept me moving towards my goal. All my love.

To the great museums and galleries of Florence: The Uffizi, the Accademia, and the rest who are home to the real heroes of the arts. The giants who sleep at night, but come alive when mere mortals like us gaze with wonder and awe at their silent beauty.

To the real Antonio, Tomasso, Maria, Countess, and Giovanni Solasso, (Drew, Tom, Maria, Miriam and John.) You have been a constant pillar of strength, support, and an undying friendship to me that is so enduring...we truly are a family. Thank you for giving me the inspiration to bring my characters to life.

To Diane at "Righting the Write" Editing Services: A big, wonderful thanks for advising me and helping add clarity and polish as you made my story come alive.

To Aunt "Zia" Janet: It was you who took the "older Vincent" on a walk down the halls of the spectacular Uffizi on the journey of a lifetime. On that day, Sandro and Ernesto came to life. The prologue in this book is dedicated to you.

To Tink: Thank you for helping me remember what it feels like to put my imagination down on paper.

...and finally, this book is dedicated to the "grand" woman of Florence: my late grandmother, Eugenia Palazzo.

At a young age when I would "mutilate" the beautiful Italian language, she would patiently teach me the melodious sounds of her native tongue. She was indeed a beautiful Renaissance woman and none better to be my inspiration for "Sandro."

For Baxter

Chapter One

The terrified heartbeat was loud. Loud enough that it hurt the eardrums of the poor captured soul. A bloodied rag stuffed into the mouth, muffled the cries for help. Like a caged animal, the hunted prize thrashed about in the rear of the Medici guards' wagon…panicking.

Hearing the commotion behind them, Lippi turned and sneered, "Wait till he sees who we kidnapped! I'm sure there's a big reward for this one." The hostage stared at the man. In seconds the initial shock gave way to overwhelming anger. Groaning in disbelief, the prisoner fought to loosen the bonds. Panic set in as searing pain overtook the frightened soul.

"Shut up, Lippi," the man's angry voice hissed. "Just drive the wagon and keep your voice low." Lippi recoiled in anger, his blistering gaze fixed on a bottle of wine. Pulling a cork out of it with his teeth, he spit it to the ground and gulped down the reddish liquid. Speeding towards their destination, Ciro Devoto hit every rock in his path, almost breaking the wooden vehicle into pieces.

My God, where am I? That question raced through the captured soul's mind.

I have to escape…NOW!

Slowing down, every rock they hit almost tipped the wagon over. A loud belch came from Lippi as the wagon stopped by a grove of Boboli trees.

"Now?" Ciro's eyes bulged. "Are you crazy?" Twisting his neck sharply, Ciro looked around and spied their surroundings. "We're going to get caught!"

Lippi's brow furrowed in anger. "You worry too much." Jumping from the wagon, his eyes darted across the landscape back and forth, looking…listening.

A grin flashed across his face as he loosened the sash around his pants and walked towards some bushes that dotted the landscape. His body swayed slightly from the wine. "I'll be back in a minute," he shouted.

Ciro frowned. *Drunken fool!* he thought. He wished Lippi would hurry so they could be on their way with their prized catch. Hearing the muted cries behind him, Ciro turned and smiled, exposing his rotted teeth. "Relax. We're not going to kill you…at least not today." His words mixed with his foul breath filled the air. The sudden dread in the prisoner's soul made it hard to lay still. Eventually, Lippi made his way back to the wagon. Attempting to climb back in, he paused a long moment to think. He ran a meaty hand through his greasy hair and flashed a sadistic grin towards Ciro.

"What are you doing?" Ciro whispered. "Lippi, get in here, we have to go."

Lippi grumbled something in Italian and walked towards the rear of the carriage. Studying his helpless victim, he pulled out his sword that he kept around his waist and very skillfully, angled the piercing tip of the blade to the heart of their prisoner. With a sudden, quick flick of his wrist, he tore a long gash on the prisoner's clothes. In breathless silence, he stared at the prone victim. Running his tongue over the front of his decayed teeth, he wiped salvia that ran down the side of his mouth. He placed his filthy hand on the knee of his victim and sneered. After a long moment, he made his way back into the wagon, grabbing the reigns.

Ciro drew a seething inhalation, "Why did you do that?"

Lippi's dark eyes seemed to scorch the earth below him. "Shut your mouth." After giving a sharp tug of the reins, he looked into his Ciro's eyes and threatened, "Never ask me about the things that I do...no one asks me!"

The uncomfortable silence between the men was quickly interrupted when muted screams of terror were audible over the loud noise of the wagon. "Relax, *Signorina*," Lippi muttered, "we will be there soon enough." His sinister laugh that followed was not convincing at all to Fioretta who began kicking her legs against the side of the wagon in protest.

"Go ahead, make all the noise you want. Nobody can hear you," Ciro laughed, feeling confident that they were not followed.

Again, the repulsive Lippi turned to look at Fioretta. His leering eyes scanned the curves of her body. Not much longer and I will make her mine, he thought. The man's excitement was reaching a fervor when a small amount of drool began to form, which he slowly wiped on his sleeve. "She's a pretty young thing, isn't she?" Eager to fulfill his lustful desire, he asked Ciro, "Do you think they'd mind if we stopped for awhile? You know what I mean. I can take her back there…back in the bushes. Nobody would have to know."

"Tend to the wagon and leave her alone! Our orders are simple. Deliver her safely. Keep your perverted thoughts to yourself," Ciro barked.

Fioretta's body went rigid as she listened to their conversation. In the back of the wagon, she agonized how she got here and who these men are. Slowly, she was able to replay in her mind the last few moments that she could remember.

I was in the church and I saw a man. I don't remember who he was, but he was yelling. I remember him shouting at Giuliano and then....

Closing her eyes, she pressed herself harder to remember.

Men were running with swords and knives.

They...they...they tore each other's flesh...mutilated each other. MY PARENTS! My God...what happened? Are they dead?

A nauseous feeling came over her instantly when something jogged her memory.

An angel! I remember it now! It had to be an angel. Her heart began to race reliving the recent events. I was standing in an aisle in the church. The angel and Giuliano were in the same aisle. I ran towards them... running through men slaughtering each other. Blood...blood was everywhere. My dress, splattered in blood! OH MY GOD!!!

Fioretta's eyes bolt open in fear, reliving the horror that she experienced. Tears welled up in her eyes. The air was scented with the blossoms of Linden and Mimosa trees. Her eyes were fixated on the hanging branches that were gently bent in submission, almost touching the wagon. The early morning birds began their daily chatter while the sunlight's rays filtered in through the trees.

Fioretta's mind wandered when a sudden violent jolt from a large rock in the path jarred her back to her senses. Her eyes hardened when her sporadic memory returned. I can't breathe!!! Panicking, the last thing she remembered was being trampled outside the church.

How am I alive? she wondered.

Trying to remain calm, she focused in on her breathing to slow it down. Her eyes studied the backs of the two men while she tried to make sense of things. *Did they save me?* For a brief second, she caught glimpses of the two, when they turned to check on her every so often. *This is a mistake! They think I'm someone else…it's all a big mistake. But…where are they taking me?*

The brightness of the rising sun made it difficult to see when she thought she saw a white light coming towards her. Closer it came to her when she shut her eyes and she remembered it…the angel. I remember!

Running out of the large wooden doors of Il Duomo, there it was, an angel. Its appearance was a dark brown figure but with the sunlight streaming in through the doors, it gave a heavenly aura around itself. As she reached out to the light, she was knocked violently backwards to the ground by the mob of people who were fleeing the church. Her breath was being sucked out of her as the terror-stricken churchgoers trampled her, suffocating the young woman.

How am I alive?

Fioretta snapped back to reality when the wagon suddenly came to a stop. Squirming her bound body closer to the edge, she overheard a third voice joining the other two.

The conversation quickly turned angry. From her view in the back of the wagon, she watched as Lippi picked up his wine bottle. Thinking he was going for a drink, he instead hurled it outside the wagon. Hearing a painful scream, Fioretta's eyes shot up to a face that suddenly appeared. The stranger had a freshly bloodied gash across his forehead from Lippi's thrown bottle. He smiled warmly at her, calming her for a moment.

"Go," the strange man shouted, "get this wagon out of here." Pulling away, the man shouted, "And Lippi, this is not over. I swear...one day I will kill you."

Sneering at the bleeding man, Lippi cursed and spit in his direction.

What in God's name is happening? she wondered.

The morning sun warmed her face as Fioretta closed her eyes for a moment.

Within a few minutes, the wagon make a sudden stop as a man's voice began to shout, "You two fools...you morons! What did the Pazzi's ever see in you? You both better watch your step, especially you, Lippi," barked the threatening voice. Studying what was before him, he asked sharply, "Lippi, what have you done? This is the wagon of the Medici guards."

Jumping off the wagon, Lippi stared the man down. Then quickly, his heels spun in the dirt and he began to walk away.

"Do you hear me, Lippi? Why this wagon?"

Lippi stopped and slowly turned to face the man. "Who put you in charge that you can bark orders around here?"

"Jacopo Pazzi did! Do you have a problem with that?"

Disgusted, Lippi mumbled, "Pazzi brought you a gift...a friend, he said. She's in the wagon." Lippi turned and walked away into the brush, looking for food and drink with Ciro closely following him.

Fioretta's green eyes flashed fear hearing the interchange of words.

"Silvio, what's all the commotion about?" a voice rang out as Fioretta's ears perked. "Who were they?"

Silvio's voice was cold. "His name is Lippi and that other one is his relative named Ciro. Don't ask me how, but they're friends of Jacopo's, but I can't see how that is.

"Why are they here?" The young man looked around and shrugged his shoulders. "Really, who are these others that are here?"

"Jacopo knew that the killing of the Medici's would be more intricate than planned, so just in case, he had twenty of us positioned around the church. Unfortunately, with the people storming the door to get out, we couldn't get in. We were pushed out, like Jacopo was."

The young man's gaze was sharp. "Jacopo's alive?"

"He should be…I yelled out to him as everyone was fleeing the piazza. He told me to get the men together and meet out here." A slight worry showed on Silvio's face. "But he should have been here by now."

"I'm sure he'll be fine. He's probably with his brothers now making their way here." Turning his stare back to the brush, he asked, "So tell me…that man, Lippi. He's a friend of Jacopo's and yours?"

"He's no friend of mine!" barked Silvio. "Somehow, years ago, he saved Jacopo's life and so Jacopo has given him some small jobs to take care of. You know… to show his gratitude."

The young man's eyes widened. "Jobs?"

Silvio's broad jaw tightened. "Jobs! Just like yesterday's job. I guess Jacopo had them meet out here as well. I just hope those two fools weren't followed stealing that Medici wagon. Now, let me see her."

"Her?" he asked, startled.

"Lippi said she's in the back of the wagon…a gift from Jacopo."

Frightened, Fioretta heard the whole conversation. The voices became clear as they approached the wagon. Holding her breath, Fioretta trembled in fear. I'm dreaming, she told herself. It's all just a bad dream.

Heart pounding, her line of sight was hindered by the intense morning light, jading her vision. Laying there in horror, she strained to lift her head to see but all she could make out was the silhouette of a man climbing into the cart. The stranger came closer towards her when she was shocked to hear her name.

"Fioretta! She's alive!" the man screamed loudly.

Overtaken by fear, Fioretta quickly regained her composure. They know me?

The blinding light gave her a glimpse of the face of the man who was only inches from her body. Suddenly, her eyes lit up and a small smile began to form around her gagged mouth. As he gently untied her and removed the cloth from her mouth, she let out an exhausted gasp.

"Antonio!" she screamed. "You're alive!"

"Tomasso," he shouted to his cousin."Hurry up. It's Fioretta."

Fioretta glanced up at her young captor. "Tomasso's alive as well? I don't understand. I saw the both of you at the church. I assumed that you…you died along with the others." Confused, she sat up in the wagon and rubbed her eyes. Tears began to gently roll down her cheek. "Where am I? What day is it?" she asked.

"It's Monday," Tomasso joined in. "And let me help you out of this wagon."

Extending their hands, they helped her down. In stark contrast to the bloody massacre that she witnessed the day before, her eyes opened up to the beauty of the thick lush forest. Still in pain from the trauma that her body received on the steps of the church, she walked alongside Antonio and Tomasso slowly but felt somewhat safe.

As they walked deeper into the woods, the April morning grew cooler. The beautiful white and pink buds blooming on the trees were gently lifted off by the breeze, filling the air with its sweet aroma.

Fioretta gently picked up a blossom and inhaled, smiling as she marveled at the beauty in this secret location. It reminded her of the fragrant fields where Ernesto first told her that he loved her. Her conscience troubling her, she gave a grim sigh, missing the days when life was simpler, days when she was with Ernesto.

Lowering her head again for one last whiff of the flower, she glanced something up ahead that caught her attention. They approached a clearing in the brush, and she was surprised to see a group of men cutting trees and building shelters. "What is this place?" she asked. "All I've seen are men…no women." A worried look appeared on her face. "Tell me where we are? What has happened?"

"Come with us," Antonio smiled. "There are things you need to know."

With her two friends leading the way, they walked through the makeshift camp. Confused, men stared at her, never expecting to see a beautiful woman out in the middle of the forest wearing a torn, bloodied dress. Passing two priests tending to the wounds of some of the men, they turned and extended her a blessing.

"Why are they blessing me?" she gasped. "What happened to those men?"

"We'll explain everything, but just follow us," Tomasso answered.

Up ahead, the flames of a small fire caught her attention as she quickly walked to investigate. Startled, her eyes grew wide in fear when she saw blood stained clothing, as wounded men tended to their injuries. Others scurried around trying to help those who were crying out in pain. Her memories instinctively went back to the day before, back to the killings at Il Duomo.

Fioretta felt a sudden surge of uneasiness as the sight of blood sickened her. Feeling a wave of panic overtaking her, Fioretta grabbed hold of Antonio's arm, to help steady her. The young man gave her a reassuring smile. "We're almost there."

"Antonio, please," she pleaded, "I feel sick; please take me away from here."

Tomasso gently whispered, "Look…look up ahead."

Through the small wisps of smoke coming from a fire up ahead, she noticed two people sitting around it with blankets covering their heads, warming themselves.

Chapter One

Fioretta cautiously approached the fire. An old man who was warming himself stood and smiled saying, "*Signorina*, it's nice to see you doing better."

What does that mean? she wondered. Confused, she watched the old man walk away with a feeling like she had seen him before.

"Here, sit down by the fire with us," Antonio said.

Feeling the soothing warmth of the fire on her face, she relaxed but soon wanted answers. "Okay, so where am I?" she asked, her voice sounding hollow.

Both Antonio and Tomasso remained quiet. Awaiting their response, she gazed into the fire and saw another man sitting alone, his head down, staring into the flames, his clothing drenched in blood. Livid by their silence, Fioretta glared at her friends in disbelief. "Look," she said, dangerously defiant. "I want to know how and why I am here. Where are my parents and who are all these men? If they're friends of yours, then why was I bound and tied?"

"Some are friends," Tomasso snapped back. "But most we just met last night."

Antonio stared at the woman for several moments. "Do you remember anything about yesterday?" he asked.

She shrugged. "Absolutely nothing."

"You have to remember something," Tomasso argued. "Anything…"

"An angel," she mumbled. "I guess I saw an angel."

Stunned, Antonio looked over at his cousin and frowned. "Fioretta, think harder."

After a long pause, she bowed her head, staring down at the ground. "Bits and pieces…that's all. People, there were lots of people. They were coming at me, pushing me to the ground. I…I couldn't breathe."

"Yes," Antonio said. "That's right. Yesterday outside of the church, you were, you were being trampled. You almost died!"

Jumping to her feet, her anger blazed. "How do you know that?"

"Because," Tomasso fired back, "some of these men escaped from the guards and were ----."

"Escaped?" Fioretta interrupted. "These men…here? Escaped from what?" Fioretta's voice escalated, "Tomasso, my God! Are these men killers?" Fioretta felt herself losing touch quickly. She stared at the quiet Tomasso who remained speechless. Their eyes met for a split second then he lowered his head to the ground.

"Tomasso, just who are you? A killer? And you?" she hissed, turning her attention to Antonio, "are you involved in this as well?"

Antonio stayed quiet, processing the question when she yelled, "I can't believe this! Why would you get me involved in this by bringing me----?"

"WHY?" Tomasso shouted, cutting her off, "to pull you out of there before you got killed…that's why."

"Fioretta," Antonio reasoned, "you would have been dead in minutes! That old man who just walked away saved your life! He was running out of the church and saw you get pushed from behind. He risked his life pulling you out from the thousands of people who ran out!"

Realizing now why that man's face looked familiar, Fioretta's tone softened. "I guess I saw his face right before I blacked out."

"You're here. You have bumps and bruises, but you're alive, that's what's important," Antonio said. "And that old man? His name is Alberto and he lost his brother yesterday. As he was pulling you out, his brother bent down to help and was dragged back by Medici guards. They killed him right there on the steps of Il Duomo."

Fioretta heard the words but they made no sense. "But then why was I tied up?"

"Incompetence!" Silvio's booming voice broke the conversation.

"Excuse me, *Signore*? But I was treated like a thief. Kidnapped and taken to…to this place with murderers. You call that incompetence? I call that a crime! Who are you people?"

"I'm sorry, *Signorina*," Silvio expressed. "Yes, you are correct. We do owe you an explanation. What happened at Il Duomo does not concern you but if we did not act and act quickly, you would not be talking to us now. I apologize for you being treated like a criminal. Please, sit by the fire and let me explain." As they both sat, the older man's voice was caring and warm. "When I said incompetence, I was referring to the two fools that roughed you up and brought you here. After Alberto carried you to safety, you were put on a wagon carrying wheat that was going to get you to safety. I'm not sure if you knew this but in the last few weeks, Giuliano had threatened to have you killed."

"And how do you know that?" she sighed.

"Because," Tomasso interrupted, "Arturo Bracciolini told Jacopo that he wanted you dead. He was planning it!"

"Bracciolini? Jacopo? These are more friends of yours? Murderers, I assume?"

"*Signorina*," Silvio tried to edge a word in. "You were hidden for your own safety. My friend Jacopo saw the Medici guards watch as you were placed in the wheat cart. He grabbed two men that he had waiting to get you out of there safely. Unfortunately, they stole a Medici wagon. The fools decided to tie you up and gag you in case you tried to run. I apologize for their actions."

"Fioretta, be honest with yourself. Do you really doubt that Giuliano would have had you killed? He was a raving mad man who deserved to die."

Antonio's words crashed down on her heavily. She lowered her head and softly wept. "You should have left me to die. I don't deserve to live after what I've done to him."

Confused, Silvio asked, "Done to whom? *Signorina*, who are you talking about? What have you done to wish your own death?"

"I killed him, *Signore*, it's all my fault. I knew he was going to be killed, yet I didn't try and warn him. He's dead and it's all my fault." Fioretta's voice trailed off to a whisper. "He was there. I saw him there at the church. Some form of spirit or apparition. He came for Giuliano and he was coming for me as well. He is coming to kill me! For what I have done to him, he is coming." Upset, she stood up and paced in front of the fire.

"Fioretta, please remain calm," Silvio begged. "No one here is going to kill you. Sit down and let's talk."

"No…I won't sit," Fioretta's voice grew surprisingly stern. "I don't want to talk. I want to run from here. Just leave me alone!"

"No," Tomasso grumbled. "You cannot leave."

Fioretta's brow furrowed in apparent confusion. "Are you saying that I'm a prisoner here?"

Antonio opened his mouth to speak when from the other side of the fire another voice from under a blanket, resonated loud and clear, "No *Signorina*, you are not a prisoner here."

Through the smoke, she saw a figure facing her, but was partially hidden due to the flames.

Fioretta looked troubled. "*Signore*, please. Are you also are saying that I can't leave?"

Standing, the stranger slowly removed the covering off of his head and through the small amounts of the billowing smoke, Fioretta's eyes met his.

"OH MY GOD!" she screamed. "You're...you're alive. You're not a ghost," she said throwing herself into his arms. "You're real...you're flesh and blood and you're alive!"

Chapter Two

An updraft of cool mountain air whipped over the top of the bluff that the four friends stood on, overlooking the makeshift camp. The stiff late afternoon breeze sent a chill through Fioretta. Her body began to shiver when Ernesto offered her the outer vest on his body, which she quickly declined. She felt so alive that her body was actually burning up.

As they stood on a small hilltop in the dwindling daylight, Fioretta wanted to know what had happened to him. So many questions plagued her about Ernesto. Where was he? If it wasn't him who was killed, then whose body was it that was found by Sandro and *Signora*, and what actually happened in Il Duomo the day before?

"Ernesto, I need to know, and um…I understand completely if you did…but did you kill Giuliano?"

An awkward silence hung in the air for several moments. "He didn't do it!" Antonio's eyes went wide. "Ernesto didn't kill Giuliano. He only wounded him. Bracciolini did it. He killed Giuliano and Lorrenzo."

"Bracciolini? You said that name earlier today." Fioretta's muscles tensed. "Wait a minute, now I remember that name. The night of the party, Giuliano hit me across the face, knocking me down. Bracciolini offered to help me up but Giuliano warned him to let me lie there in my blood." Fioretta stared at Antonio. "So he was spying on the Medici's?" Still unsure, she looked into

Ernesto's eyes, "but that was you walking up the aisle to meet him, wasn't it?"

With a quiet smile, Ernesto gave a slight nod of his head. "Good," Fioretta whispered, "I really thought I was seeing a ghost…your ghost. That's why I ran out after you."

Fioretta gazed blankly at the camp below them. "So, the three of you waged this private war against Medici's and a friend of yours named Bracciolini killed for you? Is this what you're telling me?"

"Fioretta," Ernesto paused, pondering his next words, "if I told you who was involved, you wouldn't believe me."

Her eyes remained focused on the camp. "So, there are more people involved?" Her tone turned cold.

"Fioretta, now's not the time to talk about this," Ernesto said.

"No, Ernesto, you're wrong," she insisted. "Now is the perfect time."

Ernesto winced. "The Pope," he said softly.

"I'm not joking, Ernesto…tell me the truth!" she demanded.

Ernesto eyes his friends for a moment and then looked at Fioretta. "I am telling the truth."

A chill quickly raked her flesh. "You take me for a fool, don't you? All of you do."

"He's telling the truth," Antonio said.

Fioretta turned to look at Ernesto who concurred with a nod. His words sent the woman staggering backwards. Her face was grim. She pondered, "You mean the Holy Father wanted to kill all the Medici family?"

"Not the Medici family," Tomasso interrupted. "Just Giuliano and Lorrenzo. The Pope owns Lord Medici and he'll do whatever he says. It was his sons who were a threat to the Vatican…and that's why they had to die."

Fioretta's head was spinning. She didn't know whether to laugh or cry. "This is the truth?" she asked.

Fioretta stared at Tomasso a long moment and then turned to Ernesto. "How did you get mixed up with this? Fioretta looked overwhelmed. "Oh my goodness….Sandro, does he know? He's devastated. He thinks that you were murdered!" Turning away from him, she stopped suddenly. "So then, whose blood was found in the house and whose body was burnt in the pit?"

Tomasso was grinning smugly. "Giuliano's cousin. He was nothing but a whining coward who stood behind his family's name. Don't worry about it…he won't be missed," he chuckled.

"So," she shot back in anger, "killing innocent people is funny to all of you?"

"No" Ernesto yelled. "No, it's not funny, but would it have been alright for them to kill me? Was it all right if they killed me?"

Fioretta expression turned to one of deepening concern. "No, it wasn't alright but they were out of control. They were sick…twisted."

Ernesto took her soft palm into his and found himself instantly fixed in her gaze. Her brilliant green eyes sparkled as they did years ago. "They tried to get rid of the church in Florence. If they succeeded, they would have spread into other cities. Unfortunately, innocence was lost for all of us…including you."

"Me?" she retorted angrily. "Are you including me in what you have done?"

Chapter Two

"You knew that Ernesto was going to be killed," Tomasso argued. "People saw you in the palace with Giuliano. They verified that he told you that he was planning to kill Ernesto. Is that true?"

Fioretta's blistering gaze fixated on Tomasso. "I love Ernesto," she hissed. "I always have. Giuliano was drunk and he just talked. He always just talked. He never followed through with anything. That's why I'm surprised he was really going to do the things you say he was. Kill me? He was too scared. He would never follow through with anything."

Antonio shook his head. "But yet you were going to marry him anyway?"

Fioretta looked stunned, her eyes giving way to tears. "I really didn't know what I was doing," she whispered. "I lost myself. He told me about how bad Ernesto really was and then…well, he enticed me with his family's wealth and I guess…" she said, swallowing hard, "I…I just got caught up in it all." Her emotions were stripped raw in front of the men as she broke down. Distressed, she pleaded with Ernesto, "I never meant to hurt you. Honestly, I never did…."

The sun was setting, as the oncoming night grew cooler. Ernesto looked at Fioretta, her eyes filled with tears. "Fioretta," he paused, a knot growing in his throat. "I know you didn't."

She reached out and touched Ernesto's cheek. "I love you."

Ernesto was lost in her eyes. He pulled her close, cradling her body close to his. "It's over now. The Medici's are dead. Now we can go live our lives in peace."

"HE'S ALIVE!!!" The shout of a rider coming into camp broke the stillness of the quiet evening. "MEDICI'S ALIVE!!!"

Ernesto's muscles turned rigid. "Lorrenzo!" he gasped. "He's coming."

The rider caught his breath and forced the words out again. "Lorrenzo is alive."

"That's impossible," shouted one of the men. "I personally saw Arturo cut him down before he was killed. I saw him down on the ground dead!"

"Are you positive he was dead and not just wounded?" Tomasso asked the man.

Silence hung in the air as the man's face nervously twitched.

"Are you positive?" Tomasso asked, louder.

"I know what I saw," the man said, "and it looked like he was dead."

After catching his breath, the rider shouted over the loud voices. "My brother saw him. He was standing on the street when Lorrenzo walked out on the balcony to calm the crowd."

"He is going to come after us. Lorrenzo and his guards will hunt us down," another man anxiously admitted.

Ernesto's eyes widened. "I have to leave here," he mumbled to Fioretta. "It's me he wants. We have to get you out of here."

Trembling, Fioretta whispered, "What do you mean?"

"I can't be with you. Not now. Not with Lorrenzo still alive." Fioretta stared at him in disbelief. "Fioretta, it's time…you have to leave."

"NO," she interrupted. "I'm staying here with you. I thought I had lost you once before and I'm not doing it again."

Ernesto looked surprised. "If Lorrenzo knows that I am alive, he will hunt me down and will not stop until I am dead and if he finds out that you are with me, he'll kill you too. I know what he is capable of, please," he pleaded, "please go back to your parents. I will find you. Trust me…after he's dead, I'll come for you...I promise."

"Yesterday, as I ran out of the church chasing after you, it seemed like a dream…like a horrible nightmare." Fioretta seemed overwhelmed. "Ernesto, it was terrible. I saw bodies being hacked apart in front of my eyes," Fioretta's voice dropped to a whisper now.

Ernesto's expression was grim. "You know, I wasn't supposed to be in the church yesterday. I wasn't supposed to face Giuliano. The Pazzi's were assassins. It was their commission from the Pope for all of this to happen." His heart began pounding. It's been over thirty hours and the Pazzi's, Arturo, and the others have not met them at the designated meeting place. "I fear something bad has happened to them. When we found out that Giuliano hit you, they wanted to go in and kill him right then, but they had to follow orders. Antonio told them about my feelings for you and it was those men who said I had to stay away or I would compromise the plan."

"But you couldn't stay away, could you?" she whispered into his ear. "Ernesto, I know you hated him. Honestly…I hated him too. Deep down, I hated him. He was cruel and I was such a fool to think that I could marry him and be happy. Ernesto, please tell me…how were you going to kill him?"

Ernesto's eyes moved heavenward. "I made a wooden knife from the stick that he beat me with years ago. I wanted to kill him so badly. I never stole that ring from his father. I never stole anything. He stole from me. He stole everything that I had." Turning his palms over, he studied his broken, mangled hands.

"He stole the one thing that I was good at, my art and then he stole you! I wanted him to pay like I did. I wanted him to die…he deserved to die!"

Fioretta ran her hands through Ernesto's long, unkempt hair, down over the growth of hair forming a beard and saw the pain deep in his eyes. Feeling the rage churning in his body, she held him in her arms. "I know you are not a killer, but at this moment, I wish you did kill him. I wish that it was your dagger that took his pitiful life and not from the sword of another man."

As they stood silent in front of the fire, Ernesto sighed…his mind was made up. Walking over to Tomasso he asked a favor, "Please, I need you to take Fioretta to the edge of the city and let her off there."

Overhearing his request, she shouted. "NO! I told you already. There is no way I am leaving you. Not again."

"Fioretta," he pleaded. "Please listen to me. Right now, I have no home, no family. I have no place to go but stay out here in the forest. You have your family, go to them. We are all wanted men and they will hang every one of us if we are caught. You need to be where it's safe and when the time is right, I will come for you. When we are free to live our lives, then we'll marry."

A second rider furiously rode into camp. The exhausted man barely made it off his horse before he collapsed into the arms of the men.

"Are there more coming behind you?" someone asked.

Catching his breath, the rider gasped, "We're on our own…they're all dead!"

"Dead?" Silvio asked. "That's impossible…who's dead?"

"Everyone. The Pazzi's, the priests…everyone who was in the church."

"No…you're wrong," a man shouted over the others. "I saw Jacopo escape. He got the girl out. I saw him walking out of the piazza."

"Well I saw him hanging from a noose," the rider answered back. A sickening feeling raced through his body as he felt the bile rise in his throat. "I saw their bodies hanging from buildings. The wild dogs…they, they ate their flesh in the street as they were cut down. Everyone is gone. Everyone except Lorrenzo.

Silvio gazed upward at the stars now shining overhead. He glanced around at all who were with him and then took charge. "Tomasso, take the girl to the city gate. Leave her there and quickly meet us back here. The rest of you, we need to re-organize and continue the plan. Our friends the Pazzi's would want us to. Somehow, we need to get in touch with Rome for our next move. For now, we have to keep Ernesto safe and out of sight. We'll stay here and wait for the right time to avenge our friends. The right time to kill the Medici!"

Chapter Three

Picking up the corner of his painting, *The Birth of Venus*, Sandro frowned. "Hypocrite!" he mumbled, remembering Savonarola called his painting a pagan masterpiece.

Sighing, he looked across the room and saw the painting of Ernesto's mother he did as a gift for the boy many years earlier. Sandro's deep brown eyes clouded with pain as he picked up the work. His thoughts went to Ernesto. I wish I could meet the man who killed Giuliano, he thought. I would thank him for taking the life of the one who took my boy from me.

Sandro eyed the portrait for several moments then took a deep breath and exhaled, "I miss you, boy."

Sandro's head was spinning. Life was now a chore. Things in which he once found pleasure in doing, he now lost interest. The Il Duomo murders changed people. His thoughts had become jaded in who he could trust. Rumors swirled about the Medici's, about Pope Alexander and about his friend, Pope Sixtus, who they say was murdered from someone inside the church.

As he ran his fingers across the surface of the painting, he felt the brush strokes on the canvas as a tear developed.

The artist was silent for several seconds when a sudden knock on the door startled him. "*Signore* Botticelli, are you in here?" Ignoring the visitor, the knock became more persistent as did the person's urgent cries, "*Signore*, please answer!"

Chapter Three

Sandro's eyes went wide. *A young woman's voice?* he thought. *Who would come here?* "Please, *Signore*...I need your help," came the woman's plea.

Opening the door, he was shocked to find one of Lord Medici's daughters with tears rolling down her cheeks.

"I don't know if you remember me, *Signore*, but my name is Bianca Medici. You painted my family's portrait years ago," she cried.

The artist peered closely at the girl, as he exclaimed, "Why yes...yes of course I remember you. What's wrong child?"

The young woman stood before him, still catching her breath from running. "We need your help. If...If you can, please help us."

"Slow down...who needs my help?"

"My father. He needs to speak to you right away. His health is failing quickly. Please, I beg you, will you come, *Signore*?"

Sandro felt apprehension. He flashed back to when he found the body of Ernesto, burned in the pit, years earlier. In his mind, the Medici name brought up thoughts of both admiration and of hatred. Hatred for Giuliano and Lorrenzo, but although stern, Lord Medici gained Sandro's respect by being a fair man. He gave a curt nod, "Yes, of course I will come with you. What does he need?"

"I will tell you on the way, *Signore*. Please, we must hurry."

"I have asked all of you here to discuss a matter of special importance," Savonarola began his sermon to a large group of altar boys. "The Lord High God is very displeased with the actions of the people in this city. The lust for wealth and power has made us a city of greed." Testing the children's memory, he asked, "Do you remember the story of Lot and his wife? She was a lover of greed. She turned back to see the riches that she was leaving. Young men," he said, his voice rising in an impassioned plea, "she turned around to see her possessions and God destroyed her, turning her into a pillar of salt."

Droplets of sweat poured out from Savonarola's forehead onto his outstretched hands. "You are his children. You are his young disciples and it's time to take matters into your own hands. God spoke to me this morning and his words were simple…rid Florence of its lust for riches, for vanity, for power and for prominence. This, I swear, I will do with you as warriors of the almighty." The young children were mesmerized by his words. "The holy city of Rome has sent us two men of faith who are going to help us conquer this evil once and for all." Looking behind him, he gave a brief smile. "This is Fra Domenico da Pescia and Fra Silvestro. They will assist us in the spiritual cleansing of Florence."

Father Giorgio Conti, a priest in his late seventies, was sweeping in the back of the church when he became increasingly troubled by Savonarola's message. After catching bits and pieces of Savonarola's stinging tirade to the young boys, the older man walked up to the front of the church and asked to speak with him in private.

Chapter Three

"Private?" Savonarola shouted. "Father Conti, you should know better. There are no private matters regarding our heavenly father." Pointing to the young boys, Savonarola urged. "These young boys are agents of our God in heaven and they will hallow his name, do you understand?" he screamed as his angry tone spiraled out of control.

By the time Savonarola finished his words, the older priest looked ill. "Hasn't there been enough hatred? Hasn't enough blood been spilt? Couldn't we----"

"Murderers!" Savonarola screamed, interrupting the man. "That's what they are, murderers and that is why we are going to take back our city! Can you understand that?" Turning his attention away from the older priest, he stood on the front of the grand altar and raised his eyes heavenward. "Myself, Fra da Pescia and Fra Silvestro and all these young warriors will take our city of Florence back from the wicked…one item at a time." Turning to the huge cross behind the altar, he vowed, "Father in the heavens, you have commanded me to do this work and with your help, it will be done."

As a priest, Conti had served nearly fifty years in Florence and had never seen anyone speak such hateful things as Savonarola. Knowing his message was one of evil hidden behind the name of God, the older man slowly backed away and questioned, "What are you talking about? Take back what item of greed?"

"You will see!" Savonarola loudly bellowed. "All will see! He is going to use me to cleanse this city. Both God and I wish this city to burn in hell. Fra da Pescia and Fra Silvestro, the time is right to fulfill your commission before God."

Father Conti had no doubt that something was terribly wrong. As he quickly left for the door, he stopped to take a final look at the crazed priest. Their eyes briefly met when he saw the evil that was about to consume the entire city.

Sandro felt an eerie quietness as he walked through the big doors of the Medici palace. Consumed with memories of the past, he immediately thought back to when Ernesto ran through these halls with Giuliano and Lorrenzo. Once, these halls were filled with loud, playful children and now, the grief of the Medici family is evident. Looking to his side, his painting, *Madonna of the Magnificat* is now displayed in the hall.

Sandro frowned inwardly at the painting, realizing that this painting could have been the defining moment that turned the friendship between Ernesto and Giuliano. Because of *Madonna of the Magnificat*, he was able to paint frescos at Il Duomo and the Vatican, but its cost seemed too high…the life of his best friend. Lost in his thoughts, he continued to walk down the lavish hallway. "In here, *Signore*," Bianca cried out, her voice echoing through the halls. "In the study…hurry please."

Maybe he wants another portrait? Sandro wondered as his eyes caught sight of the ailing man. Lord Medici sat in the middle of the room surrounded by all of his books stacked neatly in a row, just like they were years ago. Propped up in his chair, the gravely ill man was covered in blankets, very strange Sandro thought for the hot July weather. For a moment, Sandro considered turning around and leaving, then thought about offering condolences for his son's death, but quickly changed his mind. No Medici offered any condolences to me for Ernesto's death. Feigning a smile, he walked up to a chair and grabbed the man's hand. "Lord Medici, I'm here...what do you wish of me?"

The older man struggled for air, adjusting his body into a more comfortable position to speak. "My old friend Botticelli, please sit with me." His weakening, sullen eyes looked into Sandro's. "It's been many years since I had you here. A lot has happened to us in these years. It seems that we both have lost our sons." Sandro nodded absently as he detected a sense of grief for not only his son, but for Ernesto as well. Sandro gazed up at the paintings that furnished the Medici room, many which he himself had painted, as he listened to Lord Medici talk about what a good son Giuliano was and that he simply was misunderstood. "Alessandro, I want to apologize for how I treated your boy, Ernesto."

Swallowing his apprehension, Sandro sat in a chair next to the dying Medici, confused why he was apologizing now. "I believe I was too hard on him," he said in a weak, struggling voice. "I am sorry for what I did to him and to you, my friend."

Sandro's eyes were wary, but finding compassion in his heart he sat quietly, taking in the man's admission of guilt. "My lord," he asked, "I'm confused. Did you summon me here to apologize?"

"Sandro...my old friend, yes, yes I did. To apologize and," he said as he closed his eyes, reserving what little strength he had left, "I also do have a few favors to ask of you." After a long sigh, Medici began his words when a loud knock on the door startled him.

"Father, I need to talk to you," Lorrenzo shouted as he charged into the room.

With a wave of his hand, Medici dismissed his son. "Not now, Lorrenzo. Leave us."

"Well," the young man said smugly, "if it isn't the famous artist himself…*Signore* Botticelli."

Sandro gave an awkward smile as he rose to his feet. He bowed before the young Medici. "My lord, I'm glad to see you up and about. I heard your health has improved very quickly."

Ignoring Sandro's words, Lorrenzo's voice was cold, "So, what have you come here for? Money perhaps? Haven't we paid you years ago for your worthless pieces of art?"

"Enough! I said leave us." Lord Medici's hoarse, gasping words silenced his son. Lorrenzo defiantly sneered at the artist and marched out the door, slamming it behind him.

Sandro felt the hatred in Lorrenzo's voice. Watching the door slam shut, he shook his head in disbelief as he thought, after Giuliano's death, he still has so much hatred.

Sandro's eyes moved back to Lord Medici. "So what do you need me to do, my lord?"

In a pained voice, Medici whispered something into the artist's ear. Appalled, Sandro fell back down in his chair. Curiosity fueled his expression, as he could not believe what was just asked of him. He looked at the dying Medici and asked again, "Excuse me, my lord, but you want me to do what?"

"Paint a portrait of Giuliano." Medici stared at the artist. "Please, Sandro…please do this one thing for me."

"But," Sandro swallowed hard, his pulse thundering, "my lord, your son is gone."

Chapter Three

Lord Medici's feeble shaking hands gently clutched the artist's hands as he pleaded, "I beg of you. I had a plaster mask made of his face right after his death. If you can, paint from that. It's the only memory of him that I have to look at."

Having never painted anyone from a death mask before, Sandro was flabbergasted by Medici's request. Normally, he would turn down this demand immediately, but the man still had a place in Sandro's heart. A quick nod of his head had Sandro agree to paint the portrait…but at a heavy price. Sandro's conscience was sorely troubled knowing that Giuliano was the assumed killer of Ernesto. To Sandro, Giuliano was the enemy…he was a murderer!

Dumbstruck, Sandro inquired, "What is the second favor that you wish of me, my lord?"

"Finish the portrait, then I will tell you," Medici said, his voice trailing off weakly.

As he stood to leave, in an instant, Sandro felt a puzzling mix of respect and duty fall into stark focus. The artist gave a quiet wave as he disappeared into the darkness.

"Alessandro," Medici whispered, "please hurry…I don't have much time left."

Just before the break of dawn, Tomasso left Fioretta just outside the city walls, fleeing back into the safety of the forest. Missing for days, she shocked the guards as she entered into the city, still in her bloodied white dress. Put on high alert due to the assassination of Giuliano and the execution of the captured conspirators, the confused guards stared at the young woman.

"Name?" the one guard asked.

"Umm, Lu…Lucrezia. Yes…Lucrezia Postano."

"Postano? Where were you, *Signorina* Postano? You're all bloodied."

Phony tears ran down her cheeks as she explained that she feared for her life. She was in church and then… Her sobs got louder. "Then, I saw horrible things so I ran and hid. I ran out of these gates and hid behind the tress on the other side of the gate. I…I guess I fell asleep and lost track of time. Please…is it safe to go home, *Signore*? I'm frightened."

One slip-up, one false word could bring death to Ernesto, her friends and herself. The guards studied her for a long moment, and then told her to go home.

A few days after her return, she knew of the funeral for Giuliano. Her heart raged with hatred. She wished that she could have gone just to spit on his rotting corpse, which lie in the very church where his life ended.

Every day grew harder and harder for her patiently waiting for a signal that she could be re-united with Ernesto. As she watched and waited, her parents were concerned for her health. Agonizing over Ernesto, it took a toll on her health as she became more and more despondent as days turned into weeks that turned into months.

Worried about her daughter, Isabella Gorini watched as she hardly talked anymore. Locking herself in her room, she remained a recluse, not wanting to see anyone since coming home.

Chapter Three

"Fioretta," her mother pleaded to her, "your father and I were so happy when you came home months ago, but you still refuse to talk about it."

Both parents feel her reluctance to talk about the atrocities of human bodies that she saw mutilated in Il Duomo and assumed that it is the reason for her being so tight-lipped. "We can't help you if you refuse speak to us," her father said.

Fioretta remained distant. Her eyes remained vague as she gazed out the window. Also plaguing her thoughts were the fear that if Lorrenzo knew the truth about Ernesto, the repercussions would be immense, putting his life as well as her own and her family at risk.

Roberto straightened his vest, his eyes riveted on his daughter. Every day that passed, Fioretta's mood seemed to worsen. "You're very quiet." Roberto said, gazing across the room at his daughter. "Please tell me what happened?"

Fioretta squirmed in her seat. "Father, if I told you I saw an angel, would you believe me?" she asked.

Roberto eyed his daughter carefully. "An angel?"

Fioretta stared out the window. "I saw an angel in the church…I saw him, Father. He was there…I was there…I spoke to him." She turned suddenly to her father, her eyes welling with emotion. "I was with the angel, Father…he touched me, kissed me."

Roberto struggled to hide his emotion, but yet, he could not believe what he was hearing. "Fioretta," he said quietly. "You've seen horrific acts. I understand, but you're not thinking clearly. An angel didn't kiss you."

His words seemed to strike a nerve in his daughter. Her body was cold as she stared blankly into the void outside her window. His brow furrowed as he looked out the window with her, gazing off into the distance. A thin trail of dust off into the horizon caught his eye as a fast approaching horse headed towards their home. Hearing the man shouting something, Roberto's bushy eyebrows arched with intrigue.

Leaving Fioretta's side, he raced downstairs and out the door to meet the rider. Upon returning to the house, he looked stunned.

"Roberto," Isabella asked, "what happened? What did that man want?"

Roberto winced. "They just hung a man. Supposedly, they say he was one of the assassins who were hiding out in the forest. Right now, his body is hanging outside the city gates," he said, shaking his head in disgust. "They tortured the poor soul until he told them where the rest of the conspirators were."

Wagging her finger at her husband, she shouted, "I told you before that this city is pure evil… my God, will this ever end?" Isabella asked sadly.

Roberto cleared his throat. "Tomorrow night, they're going into the forest to flush them out and hang every single one of them."

Standing atop the steps out of sight, Fioretta heard her parent's conversation, when she released a blood-curdling scream. "No…oh my God no…they can't be caught." Running down the steps, she pleaded with her parents. "We have to warn them. Please, Father…Mother, the angel…he can't get caught."

Chapter Three

Isabella felt a shiver. She grabbed onto her daughter's dress, "What's wrong?"

Fioretta's screams cut the air, "No, the angel…he can't be caught. Please, we have to save him!" Unable to restrain their daughter, Fioretta quickly collapsed to the floor.

Isabella already looked troubled. A chill rose through her flesh when she felt an unexpected apprehension. "Evil, I tell you, plain evil. I don't understand any of this."

Isabella Gorini looked beautiful walking towards the waiting carriage. The sun was creeping higher in the sky as birds swarmed in the skies overhead. Wearing their finest clothes, the Gorini family was heading to Sunday mass at Il Duomo. Fioretta closed her eyes and slowly lifted her head up to the sky, soaking in the sun's rays. Looking behind at their daughter, Roberto and Isabella grinned to see their daughter feeling better. Turning the bend of the dusty road, Fioretta smiled as she saw two horses playfully running in the fields. Suddenly, without warning, the weather changed as the winds began to howl. The darkening skies and the loud clasps of thunder spooked their horse. Black skies threatened to open up at any second with a deluge as the wagon was coming up to the city gate. Violent stabs of lightening lit up the skies, illuminating the surroundings. Stopping just shy of the gates, a limp figure swayed forcefully through the gusting winds. Curious, Fioretta slowly climbed down from the carriage to investigate. Looking back at her parents, their eyes were fixated on the freakish scene. Cautiously, she took slow, deliberate steps as the terrible powerful gusts of wind blew hard against her slight body. In an instant, the heavens opened up angrily as the rain came down horizontal, pelting the frail girl's body. Stopping short of the wind driven figure, she looked up, desperately trying to make out who or what it was. Squinting from the stinging rain, she took her hands and grabbed her long hair from her eyes and pulled it to the side. Lowering them, she noticed the rain dripping from her fingers, changing color. Confused, she slowly raised her palms to her face as she stood in horror. Reddish liquid ran down the length of her arms, soaking her white dress in blood. In shock, she spread her arms out to the side, as the pummeling rain made huge drops of blood drip off her arms, forcing her to stand in a bloody puddle. The intense lightning brightened the sky when she noticed the figure hanging above her. Horrified, she screamed but her parents ignored her cries. Dropping to her knees, she pressed her face into the bloodied dirt, gurgling as the splashing blood forced its way into her mouth. WHY? she screamed…why? Looking up, Ernesto's dead body blew lifelessly in the strong gusts of wind. His neck snapped and his eyes were opened wide, staring down at Fioretta as he hung from the noose.

"NO!!! Help me…help me!" she shrieked as her body shook violently. Her screams for help continued on as her parents ran into her bedroom. Frightened, they woke Fioretta from her hellish nightmare. Her eyes shot open in panic, clutching at her parents. "We have to save him…save all of them. I know where they are…I KNOW WHERE THEY ARE!!!"

"You what? Fioretta, what are you talking about? Save who?" Roberto asked.

"Father, please…please, you must trust me," she said, quivering from fear. "We must go now because it's far away."

Unsure if their daughter's cries were fact or it was a terrible nightmare, Roberto and Isabella knew one thing was certain, their daughter showed signs of life for the first time in months.

"Please," she urged her parents. "I know what I am doing. But we have to leave… NOW!"

"But it's the middle of the night," her father tried to reason. "Can't this wait until morning?"

"Morning might be too late," she said, grabbing her parents by the arms and pulling them outside into the family carriage.

Trembling, Roberto whispered, "No, we can't pass the guards in the carriage. You two need to get in the back of the wagon. I'll cover you both with hay."

"Roberto, what are you thinking?"

"Well, what do you expect me to tell the city guards? We're going for ride in the middle of the night? Just get in the back and don't get up till I tell you." Pulling away from his house, Roberto thought, what are you doing? Think, Roberto, think. What will you say to the guards?

The rocky trail leading out of the city proved quite uncomfortable for Fioretta and her mother, who were hiding in the rear of the wagon. The flames of the torches that were burning at the city walls came nearer as Roberto stopped at the walls by order of the guards.

"*Signore*, do you realize that it's the middle of the night?" the guard asked sharply. "What purpose do you have out at this time?"

Think, Roberto, he told himself…*say something.*

"Umm, I...um, I have a meeting in Calenzano," he said nervously.

"Calenzano?" That's a far trip," the irate guard snapped.

"Yes...yes it is. I wanted to get an early start. So I could get there at sunrise."

"And your business there?" the guard suspiciously asked.

"Oh, I'm...umm, I'm picking up a surprise for my wife. May I leave now, *Signore*?"

"A surprise? At this hour? You said it was a meeting?"

Roberto was not about to argue with a guard bearing a sword, but he needed to leave immediately. "It is, *Signore*. Well, it is business because I am doing something for him and instead of payment, he is making me something special...for my wife, but I really must be on my way."

The guard turned and spoke to his partner in private. Turning his head to the side, Roberto's muscles turned rigid when he saw the dead man the rider mentioned, hanging on the city wall. Taking a deep breath, he closed his eyes and turned away from the grisly sight.

After a long moment, the guard's gruff voice startled him. "*Signore*, you may proceed."

Roberto grinned and gave the reins a slight tug as he started to pull away. "Wait!" the other guard called out. "What is your name...for the record?"

"Why yes, of course. My name is Gorini...Roberto Gorini."

"Be careful, *Signore*. Only ones up to no good are out at this time. Like that poor fellow." He pointed to the dead man.

"I understand...thank you." Thinking for a moment, he asked, "Umm, excuse me...may I ask who he was?"

"One of the conspirators who tried to kill the Medici's. At first light, we're going to flush them out of the forest. We know exactly where they are."

"Thank you. And trust me, I'll be careful," Roberto said as he led his carriage through the gated wall.

Making sure he was a safe distance away, Roberto stopped as his wife and daughter climbed out from under the hay.

Roberto gave the reigns a sharp tug, sending the horses off into a furious gallop. Fioretta braced herself as they sped down the dusty trail, making their way deep into the forest.

"So, who is this angel that we are looking for?" he asked his daughter.

"Ernesto!" she shouted over the deafening noise of the wag-on.

"WHAT?" he replied, totally perplexed.

Ignoring her father's reaction, she forcefully tapped him on the shoulder, "Father, don't ask questions just please go fast-er…his life is in danger."

Shocked, Roberto raced his horses deep into the darkness of the forest, all the while praying that his daughter knew exactly where she was taking them.

Chapter Four

Sandro was seated on a stool at his worktable. The lone flickering candle provided an eerie setting as he stared at the death mask of Giuliano. Sandro groaned as anger flowed through his body simply by running his fingers across the smooth finish of the mask.

His eyes looked away, looking to temporarily ease his pain. Destroy it. Those two words kept playing over in Sandro's mind, reasoning that this would be the final blow to Giuliano Medici. In his trembling hands, he gripped Lord Medici's only reminder of his son. Sandro's eyes twinkled at the thought of crushing the mask…shattering it between his fingers. Shortly after midnight, Sandro began to lay the first strokes of his brush. Alternating between sketching and painting the canvas, he was reminiscing about the brief lives of Ernesto and Giuliano. Effortlessly, his skillful hand applied long strokes with his brush, offering a slight smile as he remembered when the two young boys first met and how they would run and play, becoming the best of friends.

Wiping a small smudge off of the canvas, his mind took him back to when people in the town would confuse the two because they looked so much alike. In the beginning, the boys would love to play this game on others but as they got older, something changed in Giuliano. Perhaps the children's upbringing played a part in Giuliano's sudden change of attitude. As he grew older, he wanted the attention and admiration for himself, not wanting to share anything with anyone. It would be unthinkable for an orphaned peasant boy like Ernesto to share the same identity as one from the noble blood lineage of Medici. While Botticelli sketched the sullen eyes of the deceased, his attention to the mask was evident. Studying the details around the eyes, he decided to make the painted face in the portrait have the same lowered eyelids just as in death.

Sandro caught himself grinning smugly. Years ago, when he switched the boys' faces in his Madonna painting, Giuliano vowed to get back at Ernesto and he carried out that threat. Sandro now can do anything he wants to this painting and not fear any retribution. While adding colors to achieve the proper flesh tone, Sandro's grin quickly turned to a frown as his anger surfaced when he remembered what Ernesto's face looked like after the Medici brothers savagely beat him. Distraught, the troubled artist slumped deep into his chair and stared at the artwork, placing the mask on the table before him. Wearily, he placed his chin into his hands and questioned himself as to what exactly he was doing.

You killed MY boy! Sandro thought as he stared hard at the mask before him. Torn with the guilt of painting this portrait as a favor for Lord Medici, Sandro looked down at the palms of his hands and noticed they are glistening with a thin sheen of sweat.

Sandro looked heavenward and cried, "God, I'm sure you look down on me in shame!" Suddenly, he tossed his canister of paintbrushes to the floor in disgust. His hands trembling, he grabbed the mask and threw it across the room, striking the wall, shattering it to pieces. Sandro's body shook as he fell from the chair. He lay for a moment, gasping for breath when he heard a voice whispering. His eyes darted around the room looking…searching. *Ernesto?* he thought. Closing his eyes, he tried to remain calm. "Why are you doing this to me?" the haunting voice asked. Looking up at the ceiling, Sandro extended his hands, his fingers grasping the air, groping to where he heard the voice coming from.

Suddenly, there was silence as he was left lying on the floor. The sting of loneliness for his young friend Ernesto has left him with nothing more than painful memories. Remaining very still, he heard the voices once more. Frightened, he closed his eyes and cupped his hands to his ears to muffle the voices. Wincing in pain, he summoned all his strength to gain control of his thoughts. When the voices stopped once more, he slowly opened his eyes and turned his gaze to the shattered pieces of Giuliano Medici's death mask on the floor, staring at him.

Gianni woke slowly. A loud voice disturbed his sleep. "Wake up, someone's coming!" Slowly, the fog began to lift. "Are you awake? Gianni, please hurry, someone's coming."

"Luca," he shouted, "leave me alone! I'm tired."

"Gianni, keep your voice down. I tell you…someone's coming."

Irritated, the sleepy man mumbled, "It's probably an animal, now let me go back to sleep." Turning his back to Luca, Gianni lay back down under the tall Cypress.

Luca's blistering gaze was fixed firmly on Gianni. "Wake up and get over here, I said! Look at this."

Chapter Four

Perched high on an embankment, Luca and Gianni were overlooking the thick forest. Any intruders who stumbled this far into the woods were not an accident. Dawn was breaking as Luca's eyes were fixed on the horizon. A silhouette of a horse and wagon approaching towards them concerned him.

"Gianni…for God's sake, wake up!"

His eyes shot up at Luca. "All right…I'm coming." Irritated from being woken, Gianni wiped the sleep from his eyes. "So? What's the problem? Who's coming?"

"Look…over there!" he exclaimed, pointing off in the distance. In the early morning shadows, slowly, a figure came into view heading towards them. Luca's frightened voice stirred Gianni to action. "Quick, go ride to the camp and wake everyone, we might have to leave here now!"

Gianni obeyed the order and left to warn the others. While Luca watched his friend take off, he quickly turned his attention back to the mysterious wagon rumbling through the forest at dawn. Luca drew a deep breath as he mumbled, "Alright…we'll be ready for you."

The early morning breeze had picked up, sending spiraling dust into the air. The rough ride had been a most uncomfortable one for the Gorini family, especially Fioretta who was almost thrown from the carriage a few times. The sun's rays stretched across the landscape. Fioretta stood in the wagon, trying to remember. Disoriented, she quickly yelled to her father, "STOP!"

Roberto pulled back on the reigns, slowing the horses down. "What's wrong?"

Fioretta gazed blankly at the landscape. "I…I'm not exactly sure where I am."

Roberto noticed the shimmering water from the sun's rays up ahead. Guiding the horses to the water for a well-deserved drink, he turned towards his daughter and barked, "You've been here before, and now you don't remember? Fioretta, look around…we're in the middle of nowhere!"

Ignoring her father, she jumped off of the carriage to look for landmarks that she saw when Tomasso brought her out here a few months ago.

Luca's eyes flew open in surprise. "A man and two women?" he gasped. Watching the intruders, he relaxed and smiled. Fools, he thought, they're lost in the middle of nowhere. Taking one more look, Luca was smart enough to know that Lorrenzo and all the Medici guards were after them, so he mounted his horse and quietly made his way through the thick forest to get a closer look at these uninvited guests.

Gianni rode furiously through the woods making a sharp turn into the narrow opening in the trees where their camp was. Still early, most of the men lie sleeping around the dwindling fire. His screeching voice cut through the stillness of the new morning, "Wake up! They're coming!" Gianni frantically pulled back on the reigns, drawing his horse back onto two legs before dropping down to a complete stop. Jumping off his horse, he doubled over to catch his breath.

Chapter Four

Ernesto raced out first and ran towards the rider followed by Antonio with his sword drawn. "What did you see?" Antonio shouted.

"Medici's men…have your weapons ready."

"Where's Luca? Tomasso asked.

"Taking a closer look," Gianni wheeled, anger brimming. "He should be right behind me."

Tomasso gave a wave of disgust. "It's been three months and they finally found us." A slight growl strangled in his throat. "Just be ready…either for a fight or to run, but after three months of hiding out here, I'd prefer a fight right about now. I'm tired of waiting for them. I say we go after them and end this."

"They don't know we're here yet!" Antonio shot back. "Luca, how many men did you see?"

"Plenty!"

Tomasso glanced at his cousin and grinned. "I like our odds."

"There's plenty of them and they are probably well armed. Let's stay put and see what they do. We're still waiting for plans from Rome to get here so we can finish off Lorrenzo."

"Really, cousin?" Tomasso sharply answered. "Is there a plan or are we stuck out here with no help from anyone? Answer me. Are we stuck out here to die?"

Antonio scowled, "My understanding is that the Pope has a plan. The church won't abandon us out here…not after what we did for them!"

Antonio glared at his cousin. "We just need to keep the Medici guards away until we get our plans…is that understood?"

Knowing that the enemy is not far from them, silence overtook the camp as the only sound that was heard was that of a gasping Gianni, still trying to catch his breath.

Fioretta bent down on one knee, cupping water from the stream. Moistening her forehead, she stood and surveyed her surroundings again. "I don't understand," she said, her voice faltering. "I could swear that this was the way…I know it. Father, I think I've gotten us lost."

Roberto lowered his head and slumped back into his seat in the wagon.

"I don't understand. This just doesn't look familiar at all," Fioretta mumbled.

"Think quickly, Fioretta. We're in the middle of nowhere, trying to save someone who we believe is dead."

"We are trying to save Ernesto and he's alive!" she screamed.

"Ernesto is dead, Fioretta," he shouted, his words echoing throughout the empty forest. "Please, for your sake and ours, you need to get over it. This is crazy! Making your mother and I leave in the middle of the night to chase after what? A Ghost? It's daybreak and we've found nothing…seen nothing!"

"Roberto, please don't yell at her," Isabella demanded.

Remaining quiet for a few moments, Roberto remembered how his daughter was when she was a little girl, very playful…very energetic. She was so curious about every little thing. As she got older, she had a fierce determination to do what she wanted and now, her parents wish she had that back. But he also knows that she has gone under severe anguish in what she saw so he calmed down and gently tried to reason with her, "Fioretta, please try to understand. Your friend Ernesto was killed months ago and we still don't know who killed him. You probably just dreamt that you saw him. Please, let's go home. I beg you…let's end this silly chase now."

Fioretta spun, clutching her father's shoulders and burying her head into his chest. "Ernesto's alive, Father! I'm not crazy. I swear to you that he is alive."

"What business do you have out here?" The deep booming voice sliced through the trees.

Isabella stifled a gasp. Stunned, Roberto turned his head to a patch of thick trees. "Who's there? Show your face." The stranger's deep voice sent cold chills through the Gorini family. Protecting his family, Roberto shielded them and pleaded, "We are unarmed, please *Signore*, can you help us as we're lost out here."

Staring into the direction from which the voice came, Roberto inched forward to the trees, trying to get a better view. "*Signore*? Can you hear me? Please help us."

Suddenly, the shiny tip of a sword was visible.

The low bushes surrounding the trees parted, a tall man with his sword drawn appeared. "Explain your business out here in the middle of nowhere."

Roberto nervously flashed an awkward smile. "*Signore*, please, my name is Roberto Gorini. We're simply lost and mean you no harm. My daughter, Fioretta, thought she had----."

"Fioretta?" the stranger interrupted. Carefully he moved closer, sword poised, ready for action. "*Signorina*, a few moments ago, I thought I overheard you shout out the name Ernesto. Is that the name?" She slowly nodded her head in agreement.

The stranger's voice softened. "Come out from behind your father, child. I will not harm you or your family."

Slowly, she stepped in front of her parents for the man to clearly see. Within moments, the edges of his lips turned upwards and a smile slowly grew across his weary face as he lowered his sword back to his side.

"So it is you!" the man exclaimed. "My name is Luca. I never was formally introduced to you the last time."

"The last time?" Roberto whispered to his wife. "My God…She has been telling us the truth all this time?"

"God only knows how you found your way back here," Luca said, pointing to all the trees that surrounded them. "*Signore*, I overheard your conversation moments ago and trust me your daughter has something to show you."

Roberto gulped as his eyes opened wide in curiosity. "Something to show me?" he whispered.

Luca nodded. "Tell me…did you notice if anyone followed you?"

Roberto shook his head. "No, nobody. We left in the middle of the night."

"Luca…they're coming tomorrow. At dawn…all of them, everyone has to leave," Fioretta said, her voice waning, "They're going to kill everyone here."

Slowly, she picked her head up as Luca noticed tears forming in her eyes. "What?" he asked. "What else?"

Chapter Four

Roberto interrupted his daughter's response, "Luca, there was a man hanging from a noose on the city walls. We passed his body on the way out of the city. They killed all the conspirators three months ago…well at least they thought they did. Yesterday, a man…a rider, came by and told us about the hanging. I thought he mentioned a name, but I can't seem to remem----."

"Pino," Fioretta interrupted, remembering the horror of what she saw only hours ago that was seared into her brain. "His name was Pino."

Shocked, her father turned and asked, "How could you possibly know that?"

"I was peeking up through the hay when you were talking to the guards; I saw the body hanging there. His eyes, they...they were staring at me," she said as if in a trance. "Father, I…I couldn't look away. I was mesmerized in fear that this would be our fate as well. When you started to pull away, I pulled the hay back on top of me and then I saw it. I saw a name scribbled on a piece of wood under his body. It said, Pino, the traitor."

Saddened, Roberto turned to Luca."Did you know the man?"

Luca stood silent for a moment, then with his head back, he closed his eyes and took in the aroma of the trees and flowers deep in the woods. "Do you love the smell of the trees? It's alive…it's beautiful." Breathing deeply, he exhaled and looked at Roberto. "Yes, I knew Pino. I knew him quite well. He was like family to me, but he never listened. He died because he wanted to be something that he was not. He wasn't asked to help us kill the Medici's. He overhead me talking to a man named Jacopo Pazzi about it and asked if he could help. I told him no but he kept insisting and kept running his mouth about it. The fool probably told people that he helped and he was hung. He was just a stupid innocent fool."

A stiff breeze whistled through the trees breaking the silence. Luca took another deep breath that seemed to hang forever, and then slowly released it. "Well, that's that. There is no time for mourning now. Fioretta, you might not realize it but you saved a lot of lives. *Signore*, you should be very proud of your daughter, she is very brave."

"Of course her mother and I are very proud of her, but what do you mean a lot of lives?"

"Come," Luca said. "Follow me, we only have hours."

Chapter Five

"What is this place?" Roberto gasped as the carriage made its way into the camp. A group of men in ragged clothing stood bearing weapons, staring in disbelief at the visitors.

Dumbfounded, Silvio approached the carriage. "Where's the Medici guards?"

"Guards?" Luca asked.

"Gianni told us the Medici guards were approaching. There were at least twenty of them."

"Did he?" Luca asked to which Gianni took a few steps backwards, hiding behind some of the men. "Fool! You frightened everyone."

Roberto's heart pounded. "Who are you people?"

"My name is Silvio, and I'm sorry that we startled you, *Signore* Gorini."

Roberto recoiled; a look of bewilderment was in his eyes. "How…how do you know my name?"

"From the young maiden that is behind you. Are you not Fioretta's father?"

Fioretta jumped out of the carriage and threw her arms around Ernesto, the tears flowing faster.

"I know this may be hard to understand, *Signore*, but we are hunted men. Our only crime is trying to end the tyranny started by the Medici's," Silvio explained.

"You're the killers?" Roberto gasped. "But…but, I thought you were all dead. I'm sorry…I mean I'm not wishing that you were all dead. What I mean is…well, I'm glad you're all alive."

"Relax, *Signore* Gorini," came a voice from behind, startling the man. "We know what you mean." Spinning around, Roberto stood face to face with a vaguely familiar face. The young man took a few more steps forward as Roberto studied his face. Roberto reached out and carefully pulled the long strands of hair away from the young man's face.

"I know you!"

"You did. You met my cousin and me years ago. We've been to your home as well."

Roberto leaned over and whispered in the man's ear. "Antonio?"

The young man nodded, "And do you remember my cousin Tomasso?"

"Welcome, *Signore*." Tomasso's firm hand embraced Roberto's.

Shocked, a tired smile was all he could offer. Standing next to Silvio, Roberto listened in mute astonishment while he was told the story of what happened on that day, months ago, and how they had been living out in the wilderness.

A firm hand landing on his shoulder got Roberto's attention. Turning, he found his daughter standing next to the man whom he threatened a year earlier.

"My God. How is this possible? I was told that your body burned outside your house… you were killed over an argument."

Isabella was stunned. Her voice fell to a whisper, "Did the Medici's really attempt to kill you?"

"They did," Ernesto explained. "They thought it was their men who killed me but we tricked them. It's a long story, *Signora*. Perhaps one day I can tell you."

Ernesto drew a short breath and stared at *Signora* Gorini. His painful memories haunted his soul. "I would like to start over, *Signore*. I would like to try."

"I'm, I'm sorry," Roberto stuttered. "I'm sorry for what I thought about you, about what I said to you."

"I understand why you did the things you did…you needed to protect your daughter. I understand that you were lured by the power of the Medici's power and fame."

"I beg your pardon?" Roberto growled, his eyes piercing Ernesto. "I did no such thing. I was not lured by anything. I was acting on information that was provided to me."

"Provided?" Ernesto looked incredulous. "Provided by whom? Perhaps in the future, *Signore*, you should check your sources of information first.

The awkward silence between the two was cut when Roberto extended his hand out to Ernesto. "I will take note of that in the future," he sheepishly grinned.

The morning breeze picked up as Ernesto stood with Fioretta. Listening as the men talked with Roberto Gorini, Lippi eyes were riveted on Fioretta. "Look at her," he mumbled under his breath. "He doesn't deserve her…he's weak, a coward."

"Shut up, Lippi," Ciro whispered.

"Why should I?" he replied, leering at Fioretta like she was a prize ready to be given away. In breathless silence, he lustfully thought about her. "Yes…Ciro I have a plan, but I need your help."

"NO!" Ciro muttered under his breath, "I'm not going to help you. I don't owe you any loyalty."

Lippi recoiled in disbelief. "You'll do what I say…do you hear me?" His blistering gaze quieted Ciro instantly.

As Roberto addressed the men, his eyes were filled with fear. "There will be Medici guards searching the forest for you tomorrow. You need to flee."

"*Signore*, all of us owe you our lives," Silvio said.

"No," Roberto said his voice firm, "it was Fioretta." Pointing towards his daughter he explained, "She knew how to find her angel."

"*Signore* Gorini," Antonio said. "Lives are at stake. Ours and now yours. Please, you must never let on that you saw any of this." Antonio stared at the older man for a few moments. "We didn't want to get involved in any of this. Trust me, we're not killers. All we were asked to do was watch the doors at Il Duomo and make sure the assassins got out safely. Everything else just happened." Stunned, Gorini listened as Antonio explained their predicament. "The Medici's tried to kill Ernesto for some time. Giuliano was being groomed to take charge of the family and he made sure of three things. Kill Ernesto, marry your daughter and take away power from the church for himself and his family. *Signore*, the Pope commissioned a group of men to kill the sons of the Medici and also the priest Savonarola. Again, it was an accident that we're here.

"So who really killed Giuliano?" Roberto asked.

Tomasso cursed, spitting fiercely on the ground, "I wish Ernesto had done it…I wish he had cut his heart out."

Chapter Five

"Bracciolini did it," Antonio said. "Arturo Bracciolini...he's the one who killed him. He and the Pazzi's and others were the real killers. We heard that they were all caught and hung. I suppose we are the lucky ones, if you call hiding out in this desolate forest being lucky. We just want to get out of here alive...all of us. We want to go back to our lives."

"*Signori*, I had no idea what was going on in the city. I really don't know what to say to you men." For a moment, Roberto considered questioning why Ernesto would pull his daughter into this danger but thought the better of it. He saw the expression on his daughter's face. Despite staring possible death in the face, she seemed happy to be with Ernesto. Roberto's voice caught when he looked at Ernesto. "You were right. The power and fame...all of it blinded me. I almost let my daughter marry that monster. I was a fool." Gorini eyed the men in front of him. "Is there any way I can be of assistance?"

Silvio confessed. "We probably can't get out of this alone. We are going to need some help. Hopefully, his Holiness didn't forget us. I pray he will be sending more men to finish what was already started."

"More men?" gasped Roberto. "You're not going to continue with this plan, are you? It's suicide, I'm sure you know that." Roberto felt a cold sweat breaking across his forehead. "Your secret is safe with us, but I am taking my wife and daughter and we are leaving now. I promise, we will not tell a living soul of what we saw."

In the silence of the woods, Fioretta's voice cut through the air, "I'm not leaving, Father."

Roberto shot her a startled look. "What did you say?" he demanded.

"I'm not leaving Ernesto. I will not lose him again."

"NO!" he fired back, tired and frustrated. "You will leave with your mother and me."

Ernesto stared. "Fioretta, your father is right. You must leave. It's not safe out here."

"Is that so? Well, *Signore* Palazzo, my mind is already made up…I'm staying."

Ernesto took her soft palm in his and felt himself lost in her strong gaze. "Fioretta, please…listen to reason. You can't stay with me. I will not have you die out here with me. I love you but I'm ----."

"And I love you," she interrupted, "and I want to spend my life with you, but you must understand something. Because of my stupidity, you were almost killed. I will not allow that to happen again. I will stay with you till the end…our end if necessary."

Ernesto looked troubled. "I said NO! I will not allow it."

As she stormed over to her parent's carriage, all Ernesto could do was watch in silence. The stars were now just starting to appear and looking up, he saw the light of the rising moon snake its way through the branches.

"I'M NOT LEAVING!" Wiping her eyes, Fioretta trembled as she shouted, "Father, I love you and Mother dearly and I would never do anything to hurt you, but I love Ernesto too and I won't hurt him again. My mind is made up!"

"WHAT?" Roberto roared. "That is impossible. You are leaving!"

"I won't," she protested, her tone icy. "Father, I will not be treated as a child…I'm an adult, so please treat me as one." Her expression turned to sadness. "Father, I will always be your daughter, but I need to grow up. You need to let go. I'm a woman and I can make my own decisions and I've made mine. I'm staying here with Ernesto."

Roberto's eyes welled up. "But where will you stay…with these men? Be reasonable, some of them are murderers."

"No, Father! I know these men. They are honorable; I know they won't hurt me."

Roberto shook his head. "No! It is wrong. I'm sorry but I cannot let you stay here!"

Stepping from the shadows, Lippi feasted his eyes on the woman. "Let the girl speak, *Signore*." He took a deep breath. "She is a grown woman. She can make her own decisions."

Roberto scowled at the ill-timed intrusion.

Slowly, Fioretta pulled a petite necklace from under her dress. "Father, you gave me this when I was very young. I'll cherish it always, but I need to do this. Ernesto needs me and I will be here with him. I am going to stay out here with these men and if I must…I will die with them."

Roberto looked vexed. "You'll be on the run…like a hunted animal. If these men get caught…they will hang. You will hang!"

"Then we won't ever let that happen, Father. You must trust us," she said.

Night was beginning to fall in the wilderness. Preparations were under way for the men to leave and find a new hiding area. Soon, the forest would be crawling with Medici guards. Only the Gorini's and Ernesto stood by the fire.

"Your mother and I wish you would reconsider this course of action," Roberto explained in a voice choked with pain.

Fioretta's voice fell to a whisper. "I'm sorry but I can't."

Roberto's mouth fell open. He had no idea how to respond.

"Ernesto," *Signora* Gorini asked, "Does your teacher Sandro know that you're alive?"

"No. Both he and *Signora* Mangini can never find out."

"What? That's very cruel. They've been suffering all this time thinking that you were killed."

"What's worse? Being cruel to them now or taking the chance that the Medici's would kill them? Trust me, *Signora*, Lorrenzo would have them killed in an instant if he ever found out that they knew I was alive. When the time is right, then I will go to both of them. Please try to comfort them as much as possible, but never say anything about any of this. Please, I beg you."

Through his tears, Roberto hugged his daughter, then he turned to Ernesto. "Not long ago, I thought you were the enemy…but I see now that you are that angel, the angel that Fioretta spoke about…her angel. Please protect her. Keep her safe.

Fioretta threw her arms around both her parents in a tearful goodbye. "I hate to leave you here," Roberto said, "but it's time to let go. You've never been apart from your mother and me and this is so hard for both of us. We realize that this is what you want. We love you so much and know in our hearts that we will see the both of you again soon."

Roberto felt a deepening sadness. "Run away. Run far away. Leave Italy if you must, but get out now. You're not killers, so then why keep running…keep hiding?"

Chapter Five

"Because the job is not finished, *Signore*. We can't go back until Lorrenzo is dead. God willing, this will all be over soon. Do you remember how to get back?"

A whimper rose in Isabella's throat. "We made our way out here in the middle of the night; I guess we can do the same thing.

Roberto grabbed the reigns and hesitated, his eyes focused on his daughter. Through her tears, Fioretta nodded. Suddenly, Roberto charged his horses back deep into the forest in the blackness of night…never once looking back.

A short while later, the small band of wanted ones were ready to leave. Ernesto helped Fioretta up on the horse and gave her a confident smile. "We'll be fine. Do you trust me?"

Fioretta's words were a choked whisper. "With all my heart." With her final word, she immediately thought of her parents…the sound of their voices echoing in her head.

"Where to?" Ernesto yelled.

"Baruffi!" Silvio shouted.

"Baruffi? We're heading south?"

"It's a few days ride, they'll never look for us down there. Besides, people hate the Medici's there. Jacopo once told me about this place. He would go there to rest."

"If Gorini was correct, then the guards should be here in a few hours. Once we get to Baruffi, we'll send a rider to Rome to try and make contact with someone in the Vatican. Jacopo told me that Alexander has been grooming one of his Cardinals as his personal confidant.

"A confidant?" Tomasso asked.

"Yes, a man named Greco. He became Cardinal very quickly and now is the Pope's envoy. If we can't make contact with the

Pope, then this Greco is our man. Let's just stay alive until the church can finish what they started."

Sitting on their horses following up behind the men, Lippi and Ciro watched as one by one, the others made their way deeper into the forest to their new destination. Lippi didn't take his eyes off of Fioretta. Studying her from a distance, her beauty captivated him. "That one," he said pointing to her. "That one has a lot of life in her…I like that. I wonder how she will be when I take her."

"Have you gone mad? She belongs to Ernesto, leave that one alone," Ciro cautioned.

"Why? Ernesto is supposed to be dead. If that's the case, I guess she's fair game. Besides, she will look good in my bed," Lippi pondered, saliva dripping from the corner of his mouth.

"I said leave her alone. Your thoughts can get us both killed."

"Really?" Lippi grunted. "I was thinking of someone else being killed."

Ciro's eyes flashed fear as he quietly followed the others.

Dawn's light broke over the horizon, as a weary Roberto approached the city walls of Florence. Making sure his wife was fully covered under the hay in the rear of the wagon, he slowed the wagon down as they neared the gates.

"Name?" the ill-tempered guard demanded. Looking down at the scribbling on a piece of paper, the harsh voice pressed, "I said NAME!"

"Gorini. I'm sorry, *Signore*…I'm a bit tired. I just returned from ----."

"What business did you have out of the city, *Signore*?" the guard interrupted.

Nervous, he stumbled over his words, "Well like I said, I was----."

"Wait a minute. Gorini? Roberto Gorini?" Thumbing through his papers, he looked up to make eye contact with Roberto. "It says you went to Calenzano, to pick up a gift?" Looking in the rear of the wagon, "I see no gift."

"Oh, yes, well he said that it wasn't ready yet. He told me a few more days."

"Hmmm, I see." The guard carefully eyed the wagon.

His voice soft, Roberto asked, "Excuse me *Signore*, but we never had this kind of questioning before…why now?"

"Since the assassination attempt on the Medici's, we want to know who is coming in and going out of the city."

Roberto feigned a laugh, changing the subject, "Oh, well I'm sure you know who I am. My daughter was to marry Giuliano." Eyes closed, he shook his head and mournfully said, "She's devastated…the whole thing is so sad."

Uninterested, the guard commanded, "You may leave, *Signore*."

"Oh, thank you…thank you very much," Roberto replied, still very wary of this encounter. Pulling away, he slowly rode past the dead body that still hung on the wall. Stopping his wagon, he turned back to ask the guard, "Did Pino have any family?"

The words quickly processed in the guard's mind. Eyeing Roberto suspiciously, he asked, "How did you know that his name was Pino?"

"That piece of wood has his name on it."

"*Signore*...we removed that last night."

A chill raked his flesh. "Yes, of course...but I saw it when I was leaving."

The guard scowled as he turned to look at his partner. "You say you saw that little piece of wood?"

As Roberto nodded, the guard complimented him, "*Signore*, for an older man you have very sharp eyes to be able to see that from where you are sitting in the wagon."

Roberto hesitated for a long moment as he thought what to say. Sweat trickled down his forehead. "Hot, *Signore*? It's very cool this morning. Are you feeling alright?" the guard asked skeptically.

"Yes...thank you, but yes, I'm fine."

"So, you were telling me how you saw his name?"

"Just lucky to have good eyes, I assume."

"Luck? Maybe. Like I said...you may leave."

The guards watched as Roberto slowly made his way down the road. "There's something suspicious about that Gorini. Keep an eye on him when he leaves and see how long he is gone."

That one is hiding something, I'm sure of it and I'm going to find out what it is! the guard thought.

Chapter Six

Botticelli looked troubled. His blistering gaze was fixed on the canvas before him. Gazing at the finished painting, he felt like he was just kicked in the stomach. In shame, he lowered his head in disgust. The death mask portrait of Giuliano had made his health deteriorate. A sporadic numbness in his left arm and blinding headaches had been plaguing him as of late. Weakly, Sandro shook his head. Walking to a water basin, he splashed the liquid on his face and stood there staring into the water. What have I done? he asked himself. He was always overly critical of his own work, but this one was different. He felt like spitting on the finished piece. He had painted for the most renowned churches of Italy but he cursed himself every day for agreeing to do this for Lord Medici. Acting on impulse, Sandro grabbed the painting and bolted out of the door for the Medici Palace. The irate artist's heart pounded as he made his way across the city to deliver the detested artwork. Sandro frowned as he lifted his hand to knock on the massive palace doors. He looked closely and noticed that they were left ajar. Before he could think about it, he slowly entered very quietly. Sandro was wary as he walked through the hallway when he suddenly heard screaming coming from the upstairs.

Still feeling the effects of his sustained injuries, Lorrenzo slowly made his way down the grand staircase when a voice shouted from one of the rooms, "We have guards searching now!"

Enraged, Lorrenzo turned and screamed in the direction of the voice. "I don't care if they're searching. This time I want them found immediately. I want them to hang by their necks for what they did. Three months ago you said you had them locked in the church. Then you said that they were hiding right here in the city. Stop telling me stories, just get them…and get them NOW!"

Making his way back down the steps, Lorrenzo was startled by the unexpected appearance of the artist. The young Medici scowled at the artist for his ill-timed intrusion.

"What business do you have here, Botticelli?" he demanded, his voice brimming in anger.

"I brought the portrait that your father requested, my lord."

"Portrait?" Lorrenzo snatched the painting out of Sandro's hands and tore off the cloth covering. Lorrenzo's eyes were riveted to the artwork. "My father requested this? his voice growled. In a burst of anger, the Medici threw the painting to the floor and pulled a dagger from the inside of his vest. "I should kill you right here…like a dog. The way your boy killed my brother."

A fearful bewilderment swept across Sandro's face. His eyes were glued to the weapon pointed at his heart. "My...my boy?" he stammered.

"Yes…don't play dumb, Botticelli. We all know who killed Giuliano! Ernesto butchered my brother in the church."

Sandro slowly raised his eyes away from the dagger. "Excuse me, my lord," Sandro said softly, "but Ernesto is dead."

"Liar!" he screamed. "He killed my brother and now I will kill you-----"

Chapter Six

Standing in the darkness of the hallway, Lorrenzo heard his mother's voice echoing through the palace. Medici cursed under his breath and mumbled, "If you say a word to her, I will cut your heart out. Do you understand?"

Sandro's muscles seized with terror. "My lord, I think ----."

"Down here, Mother," he shouted, interrupting Sandro. "Do not utter a word."

Sandro drew a breath, about to protest.

"There you are," *Signora* Medici said from the top of the stairs. Lorrenzo quickly slid the dagger inside his clothing. "Oh, *Signore* Botticelli. What a pleasant surprise. I didn't know you were coming."

Lorrenzo laughed coldly as he spun and limped away from the artist. "Where are you going? Lorrenzo, I need to speak to you," she called.

"Don't bother me now, Mother," he shouted as she was walking down the stairs. Turning back towards Sandro, he flashed a menacing glare, threatening, "Remember...say nothing!"

Taking a deep breath, Sandro stood silent as he watched Lorrenzo hobble out the door.

"*Signore* Botticelli."

Sandro seemed oblivious to the woman's voice, which now accelerated...louder, faster.

"*Signore*? Are you listening to me?"

Sandro glanced at the woman. Shocked, only five words replayed in his head, your boy killed my brother.

Sandro felt as if his tongue was on fire. He couldn't speak to the woman. His thoughts raced wildly.

"*Signore*, are you listening to me?" she demanded.

What in God's name is he talking about? He and his brother had Ernesto killed. I was there...I saw his burned body, was it Ernesto's ghost that he saw?

Gazing absently at the woman, Sandro watched as her mouth moved but ignored her words.

"*Signore...Signore*, please?" she said loudly.

After several minutes, as if suddenly sensing her loud voice, Sandro shook his head and made eye contact with her. "What? Oh, oh yes. I'm...I'm so sorry, *Signora.* What is it that you need?"

"Need?" she chuckled, "I don't need a thing. What is it that you need? You're in my house, so you must need something."

"Oh, yes *Signora*, I'm sorry. I have the painting that your husband asked me to do. It is a gift and if I may, I wish to present it to him."

"Botticelli, my husband is very sick." The woman frowned. "I don't think it is a good idea."

"Please, *Signora.* It would just be a brief visit. I promise."

The big expressive eyes of the artist revealed much to the older woman. She's only known him to be a kind, gentle man. Studying his face, the deep lines grooved into his forehead, she doesn't see the monster that both her sons portrayed him to be. *Signora* Medici looked wary. "I will let you see him, *Signore*, but please be brief. He needs his rest. He is in the library, but remember, be brief."

Picking up the painting that Lorrenzo threw down, Sandro quickly covered the work with a cloth and thanked the woman and started to walk down the long corridor as he had done countless times before.

Chapter Six

"*Signore*, Botticelli...wait a minute please." She walked up to Sandro. "Your work has always brought a smile to my husband's face. He needs that smile once more. Please, what did you bring him this time? May I see it?"

"*Signora*," he politely responded, "you don't want to see this. It would bore you. It's just a little something that Lord Medici asked me to do for him."

"Nonsense," she scolded. "If my husband requested it, then I'm sure it is for me also. Now show me what you brought."

Sandro, not moving a muscle, frowned as he stood before the woman.

"*Signore*...I command you to show it to me!"

Removing the tattered pieces of cloth that Lorrenzo tore apart in his fit of rage, Sandro hesitantly turned the painting towards her. The woman's demeanor suddenly turned frosty.

"Why?" she gasped. "Why would you bring this...this horrible reminder into this house?"

Sandro gave a weak nod. Her pain was obvious. "*Signora*, it was a request," he politely responded.

"Of all the beautiful things that you have created for us in the past, he now asks you to do this? This is just plain cruel. God has put a curse on my family."

She stared at the artist a long moment then turning her back began to climb the steps up to her bedroom.

Sandro never flinched and continued down the hallway until he reached the library. After giving a few gentle raps on the door, he heard no movement from inside. Sandro slowly opened the library door and found Lord Medici motionless, sitting in his chair staring out the window. Knowing the man for years, Sandro felt saddened as the one time strong leader of the city prepared to die. So as not to alarm him, Sandro gently cleared his throat, getting the attention of the terminally ill man.

"My Lord…I'm sorry to have disturbed you, but I have come with the painting you requested."

The dying man weakly lifted his arm and motioned Sandra to enter. When his eyes caught sight of what Sandro was carrying, his voice trembled. "Alessandro, please let me see." His expressionless face was stone. Devastated by the loss of his son, the portrait touched a nerve as his eyes began to well up. "You were far too young to die, son," Medici mumbled softly. "Why did you do it?"

Botticelli lowered his head and slowly walked away, leaving the man alone to grieve. "Stop," Medici whispered. "Alessandro, come here…there's something I must tell you." His lungs, filling with fluid, made the man lower his head into his hands, and wheeze violently. Seeing the distress that Lord Medici was in, Sandro ran to his side. At times, Sandro felt only distaste for Lord Medici who in the past had let it be known that Sandro was just an unimportant peasant, but now, as their eyes met, he felt pity for the stricken ruler.

Reaching out for the artist's hand, he whispered, "I asked you for two favors, my friend…the last one I need right now."

Sandro glared at Medici. An inner conflict struggled inside of his body. Feelings of anger, hatred, and of uncertainty troubled the artist's soul. For him, it was like giving an absolution to the family that killed his boy. Wondering now if Lord Medici wanted something that possibly he could not give, he bent down closer to hear the man's instructions. "There…up on the bookshelf.

There is a book of papers. Bring it to me please." Medici pointed up to the hundreds of books in his collection.

The bookshelf covered the entire length of the wall in the library. Sandro started to thumb through the hundreds of books on the shelves. As he looked up and down the books for a clue, he remembered years ago when he first came into this library. Thinking back, he told himself that some day he would read books like these. Overwhelmed by all the titles, he was growing impatient looking for this one certain book. "Is there a title for this book, my lord?"

The corners of the man's mouth turned upwards a bit producing a weak smile. "It's a book on Alchemy," he replied.

Sandro frowned, "The book of what?"

"*The Book of the Composition of Alchemy*," Medici sighed. "My memory is not what it used to be. If I remember…that is the title. It's very old and has a red spine."

Sandro looked skeptical. "Lots of books have red spines on these shelves," Sandro replied, annoyed at this silly request. Thumbing through book after book, Sandro asked coldly, "Have you really read ALL these books?"

"Yes," he whispered. "Now keep looking…you're in the right area. My children might have moved some books around."

Sandro moved through the countless numbers of books on the shelves, until finally, something that fit Medici's description came into focus sitting high up on one of the shelves. Gazing triumphantly, Sandro blew off the dust and gently placed the pile of papers bound together into the lap of the man, whispering, "Here you go, my lord. *The Book of the Composition of Alchemy.* I hope you enjoy reading it."

Sandro placed his hand on the old man's shoulder and smiled at him, wondering if this would be the last time that he would see him alive. Just as Sandro was ready to leave, Lord Medici's eyes raised up from the book. "Sit down, Botticelli. There is something I want to share with you. Something that I wanted to do for a long time."

Without a word, Sandro sat next to the man. "Alessandro, I was a coward for many years."

Sandro drew a startled breath. "You? A coward? Lord Medici, I never viewed you as such."

As Sandro looked on, the old man's feeble hands fumbled through the papers. "I am. I have been a coward for a long time," Medici sadly confessed. "Here it is," the old man mumbled as he grabbed loose papers from the binding.

Sandro turned his attention to the papers that Lord Medici held in his hand. "I need you to read these for me."

Taking a deep breath, Sandro shook his head. "This is the favor that you wanted? Read to you? Lord Medici, couldn't your wife read this for ----?"

"READ, BOTTICELLI!" Medici interrupted, his voice angry.

Sandro felt ready to burst. He grabbed the papers from Lord Medici's hand and shuffled them in some form of order. His eyes scanned the pages, reciting the written words in a low undertone. Confused, Sandro looked up at Medici. "These are love letters addressed to you from someone signed only with an E."

"Alessandro," the sickly man whispered, "please, keep reading."

Shuffling the pages, Sandro's eyes suddenly opened wide, "Piero…the love of my life," he read aloud. The artist looked up at Lord Medici. "Love of my life? When were these written?"

"Twenty three years ago," he mumbled.

"Twenty three years?" Sandro gasped. "But you were already married."

The color drained from his face. "*Signora* Medici knows nothing of this?"

Lord Medici was silent. He never moved his eyes from the floor.

Sandro's brow arched. "Why are you telling me this?"

"I'll be dead soon," Lord Medici whispered, "and I needed to tell someone. You're involved, Alessandro."

"Me?" Stunned by Lord Medici's statement, his eyes seemed to go right through the man. "I'm involved? But…but, I've done nothing."

"No, you're wrong. Keep reading."

Sandro looked vexed. His stomach was knotted as he continued to read…

Piero,

When I first met you I was young, too young for a man of your position, but now I am a woman. Oh my love, I am with child, your child. I realize that you have a wife who is also with child at this time. I am not asking you to leave her for me. All I ask is to please tell me you will be there to help with our child. I know the scandal that this would mean for you but you can trust me, my love. I will not tell a soul. My response will be that the child's father died in an accident.

My love is for you always,

Eugenia

Sandro's eyes grew bigger than florins. "Eugenia," he gasped. Thumbing through more of the pages, he quickly devoured the material until something else caught his eye.

My beloved Piero,

He is absolutely beautiful. He has your curly hair and your eyes. He is our little precious gift from God. I hope you can make your way to me to see him. I heard that you had another son and you named him Giuliano. That is a beautiful name. Maybe one day they can meet. I do long to see you, my love, and for you to hold your new son. I have named him Ernesto.

Please come to me, my love.

Eugenia

"NO! This is impossible. It's a lie, all just a terrible lie," he screamed in disbelief. "Eugenia was Ernesto's mother. I painted a picture of her as a gift for the boy."

Alarmed, Lord Medici raised his hands, trying to silence his visitor. "Alessandro, please…please be quiet and listen to me. It's not a lie. I'm Ernesto's true father."

Stunned, Sandro sat upright, "So that's why Ernesto never knew his father…all he remembered was his mother." Within seconds, the artist lashed out at Medici. "You knew he was your son and yet you threw him out of your house? I found the boy freezing, living on the street begging for food. He was starving,

Signore...starving while your other children lived here in this palace like royalty!"

Lord Medici buried his face in his hands. His confession, his guilt that he held in for so long, finally unburdened him as he began to sob. "I would visit him from time to time," he said in between sobs. "I had no idea that Eugenia was so sick. I would have helped her. Believe me...I really would have."

"No, you wouldn't have!" Sandro declared. "You were too ashamed to have your name tarnished with scandal, so you hurt an innocent boy who is now dead at the hands of his own brothers."

"Giuliano is dead, yes that's true. But Botticelli, here's a question you must ask yourself, is Ernesto really dead? I am not so certain about that."

Shocked, Sandro winced. "This is a cruel joke you are playing on me, isn't it? I have been a faithful servant of yours for all these years and now you insult me and insult the memory of your son? NO...not your son...MY SON!" he screamed. "How dare you! I'm the one who found Ernesto's body in the fire. It was your two sons that had him killed. Do you know that Giuliano and Lorrenzo almost killed Ernesto when he was a boy?" Sandro's pulse was raging. "Ernesto didn't fall off a roof like people said. My goodness, are you that blind? Open your eyes and look what your sons have done!"

Lord Medici only heard the faint murmur of Sandro's voice. He was lost in his own memories. A place where his past actions have resurfaced from the shadows and have now created pain for all. The grief stricken Medici took a rag and blotted the tears from his eyes. "He's not dead," Medici cried. "Alessandro, he's not really dead. Ernesto's ghost lives…It lives and it kills…he kills."

Sandro felt rigid staring down at the man. "I don't believe in ghosts!" he shouted. "Ghosts and holy men. It's all a made up story to scare people into worshipping a God that I'm not even sure exists."

"Never say that, Botticelli." Medici's voice faltered. "There is a God."

Sandro gathered his thoughts for a moment and lowered his voice. "After what you've done, the damage that you and your family created, do you think that God really cares about you and your family? I hope he never forgives you for what you've done!"

Ignoring the artist's words, Medici clenched his teeth, "I tell you that he's alive and he is a killer."

"So, you're telling me that the ghost of Ernesto came back and killed Giuliano in the church…in front of all those people?"

Medici took a weak breath and slowly nodded his head.

"These ancient religious teachings should be outlawed once and for all," Sandro hissed. "They're far too dangerous!"

"You step on dangerous ground, *Signore*," Medici warned. "Do not mock God!"

"God?" Sandro countered. "I don't mock God. It's you who frighten people, making them believe that God is just hellfire and anger. No, *Signore*…the God that I want to believe in is a loving God, not the one your priest Savonarola threatens us with!"

Medici closed his eyes. "May God forgive me for what I have caused. Alessandro, please…please forgive me for what I've done. My time has run out and I need to tell you this. Listen carefully," the man whispered. "One of the guards who was at the center of Il Duomo during the Easter mass said that when the fighting began, he saw someone or something that looked like Giuliano, almost like it was looking at his twin. The morning light streamed in through the glass and this ghost or whatever you want to call it had a heavenly glow around him, just like a spirit creature." Wincing in pain, Medici began to have a violent coughing attack. Gasping for air, he summoned all his strength and whispered, "Ernesto lives and he will haunt me until I'm dead."

Turning towards the window, Sandro gazed outside. Studying the beautiful landscape that he loved to paint, he contemplated the irony of the situation. Why am I now hearing about the ghost of Ernesto and who actually killed Giuliano?

Chapter Seven

The raids began early in the morning. In place, Savonarola and his young warriors of God were ready. Teenaged altar boys paired with younger ones. While many of the townspeople of Florence were still sleeping in their beds, they stormed into their homes, taking with them any material possessions that Savonarola viewed as sinful.

Savonarola's army took at will whatever they deemed necessary. Mirrors, cosmetics, fine clothing, musical instruments, books, even paintings of art were all loaded onto horse drawn wagons.

Sandro stared up at the ceiling lying in his bed when his door flew open and the marauders ran in. "Thieves!!! Get out!" Sandro shouted, racing from his bed.

The artist reached for one of them when he abruptly stopped, trapping the two in the corner of his home. Sandro shook his head. "Why…you're only children. Why are you robbing my house?"

"We're not robbers, *Signore*," the young boy scowled. "We were sent to take objects that God hates."

"Sent?" Sandro asked. "Sent by whom?"

"Savonarola," the boy quickly replied.

Sandro's brow furrowed, "So Savonarola is stealing from me?"

"No, he's not stealing…he's saving you, *Signore*."

Chapter Seven

"Get out...NOW!" Sandro yelled as he turned his back on the boys and headed for the door. From across the room, the older boy noticed a large canvas that the artist had completed. "This is exactly what we're looking for!" The two boys converged on the painting. Sandro reached for the other end of the canvas and fought them for the painting.

Suddenly, the older boy grabbed a candleholder and smashed the artist in the back of his head. Sandro hit the ground hard. Watching the young vandals remove painting after painting, he tried to speak but couldn't form the words. In the distant recesses of his groggy mind, somewhere nearby, children were talking. "Look at what you have painted, *Signore*...what mockery!"

His vision blurred from the vicious blow to the head, Sandro traced the outlines of the boys throwing his valuables around the room. Sandro drifted in and out as the boys' laughter was getting louder. His skull ached. As Sandro's vision began to clear, he found himself staring at the boys leaving his house with his paintings.

Sandro caught sight of the chair that Ernesto used to sit on. Grabbing it, he ran towards the door. The older boy did not see it coming. Out of nowhere, a crushing blow to his back from the chair knocked the boy to his knees.

Sandro stood over the young man holding a splintered piece of wood from the broken chair. Memories of Ernesto were haunting him. His muscles began to tighten as his mind replayed to when he found Ernesto's body, burning in the fire. Holding the wood over the prone boy, his memories of intense hatred surfaced like a crazed monster. Staring at his hand, he realized that it was almost the same weapon that the Medici's beat

Ernesto with when he was young. The burning hatred of Giuliano surfaced as he raised the stick high up over his head, wanting desperately to shatter the fallen boy's body.

"Alessandro!" *Signora* Mangini's voice shrieked. "Don't do it!"

Sandro remained silent, standing over his captured prey, ready to strike in an instant.

"Please…I beg you. Put the wood down."

Sandro shook his head. "No…Giuliano must pay for what he's done. He took Ernesto's life and now I will take his!" he yelled.

"No, Alessandro. That's not Giuliano! He's been dead for months. Please, please drop the wood."

Tears rolled down his cheeks looking down at the helpless boy sprawled on the ground.

"Alessandro…please!" she screamed.

Sandro scowled at the young man lying at his feet. "Why shouldn't this boy pay for what happened to Ernesto? A life for a life…that seems fair to me."

Signora Mangini walked over, her voice soft. "Sandro, this is wrong. Please put it down. Let the boy go." She placed her hand on his arm holding the weapon, gently lowering it.

Sandro ran his fingers through his hair trying to ease his overwhelming sense of fear and desperation. He took a deep breath and exhaled.

The frightened boy slowly got back to his feet, still shaking from fear. Neither spoke a word as they locked eyes for a moment. The boy quickly turned and ran for the wagon, his tone was defiant, "Pagan…you will pay for this! You will suffer at the hands of Savonarola."

Chapter Seven

Signora Mangini stood with Sandro watching as the wagon pulled away. "You're bleeding. Are you alright?" she whispered.

Adrenaline coursed through every vein in his body. "A terrible headache but I guess I'll be fine."

Watching the wagon make its way over a hill off in the distance, they walked back into the house. *Signora* gasped, "Oh my God."

"What's wrong?" Sandro asked.

"Two different boys came to my house a little over an hour ago and they made a mess like this," she said looking at broken glass on the floor. "They just barged in and took the most unusual things." *Signora* drew a heavy sigh. "Nothing makes sense to me anymore. Ernesto's death, Giuliano killed in the church and now the church sending young boys to steal from us. It just makes no sense at all. What is happening here?"

"Gisella, what did they take from you?"

"Nothing of value really…just a few books, an old garment, even my old mirror. What's so important about those things?"

Sandro scowled. "Savonarola's behind this and this time he's gone too far!"

When the old woman saw the large canvas on the floor, she bent over and grabbed a corner of it, inspecting it for damage. "This is so beautiful. What did you name it again?"

"Beautiful?" Sandro was looking closely at the canvas. "Apparently, the church has their opinion about that as well."

Gisella turned to Sandro. "Why is that?"

"I fear," Sandro said, "that it all has to do with paganism. I think that's why they took those things from both of us and who knows how many more homes they went to."

"And you think he's doing this for God?"

"No. Just for himself. It's ridiculous. Jewelry, clothes, even art is evil…pagan."

Signora ran her hands over the texture of the canvas. Admiring the beauty of the painting, she asked again, "You never did tell me. What do you call this?"

"*The Birth of Venus*," he said, "but I should have just called it the birth of the pagans."

Gisella frowned. "With Lord Medici on his deathbed, who is going to stop Savonarola's madness?"

Sandro shrugged. "He called me pagan because my paintings don't reflect God's glory, but what is God's glory?" he asked. "The stars, the sun, the sky? My goodness, WE reflect God's glory and by me painting that, I am viewed a pagan. I'm telling you…he's the pagan."

Gisella looked troubled. "Sandro, look at this," she said, reaching for a torn canvas painting that Sandro had done of Florence. Her expression turned to one of deepening concern. "There is a rumor that is spreading around the city."

Sandro's brow furrowed in confusion. "Rumor? What are you talking about?"

"Sandro, they're saying that the church was responsible for Giuliano's murder. They wanted to kill both of the boys. I don't want to believe such nonsense but there's a lot of talk about it." The woman shrugged. "What is happening to this city?" *Signora* stared into the weathered eyes of the artist. In their silence, she saw the pain that he harbored against the Medici's and towards life. Thinking of her pain, it took her a long time to get over the anger that she had when the terrible earthquake took the lives of her husband and son, many years ago. Sighing, her eyes gazed at the small house that Sandro lived in. It seemed like an eternity ago when her only problem was Sandro not paying his rent. The sudden dread in her soul worried her about the events swirling around them these days.

The sun rose high over the Tuscan hills as Savonarola's army of young men pillaged the homes in the city at will; taking whatever items they viewed as a distraction to worshipping God. Following Savonarola's orders exactly, one by one, they each took turns in unloading all of the stolen items into a big pile in the middle of the Piazza della Signoria. Immediately, word spread of where the stolen goods were taken. Angered and curious onlookers came to see what Savonarola's grand purpose was.

Luca's voice was anxious when he questioned Tomasso. "Why are we going this close to Florence when they're still out hunting us down?"

High up on a bluff, Ernesto, Antonio, Tomasso and Luca headed to their home city to see what the truth was about Lorrenzo's health and about the rumors about Lord Medici being on his deathbed. After a two-day ride from their new location in Baruffi, the city walls of Florence loomed in the distance. Luca felt a wave of horror when he saw the walls come into view. Ernesto felt that same feeling but was somewhat eased as Fioretta was safe back in Baruffi with the others.

Fioretta felt utterly at ease when she left the camp to wash at a small lake a short distance away. The white and yellow Cypress trees were in bloom, their sweet odor filling the air. Walking down the path, she suddenly sensed an uneasy feeling in the pit of her stomach. At the water's edge, she quickly spun around, and to her relief, she saw nothing. You're being silly, she told herself.

She dropped to her knees and reached her hands into the cool water. A smile appeared on her face as she splashed the refreshing liquid on her face. Fioretta stared into the water a long moment. Waiting for the ripples to clear, she looked at her reflection and frowned. The harsh conditions of the wilderness had taken a toll on the young woman.

"*Signorina*," a voice echoed across the water. "I didn't know you were coming here. I would have escorted you had I known."

Startled, Fioretta quickly glanced up and noticed Lippi sitting on a small pile of rocks a few yards away.

"The water feels good, doesn't it?" he said.

Fioretta stood up. Looking surprised, she instinctively took a few steps backwards. "I suppose."

Lippi winked. "What is such a beautiful young woman doing alone down here by the water? You never know who is lurking through the forest."

A shiver ran down her body as Lippi climbed off the rocks and started to walk towards her. Taking a few more steps back, her voice trembled.

Chapter Seven

"What do you want, Lippi?"

"Ahh, you remembered…very good, my dear. Now, do you also remember that it was me who saved your life…do you remember that?"

I know who you are," she said angrily. "You stare at me every chance you get."

Lippi reached out and placed his hand on the side of Fioretta's face. She gasped, jerking her body away from the man's touch.

"You didn't save my life," she shouted. "An older man did… Alberto. He saved me. His brother died saving my life. Yes, *Signore* Lippi, I know you. What is it that you want from me?" she demanded.

Lippi's dark eyes studied her for a moment. "Alberto? Well, there seems to be a discrepancy in who is telling the truth, but it truly doesn't matter. *Signorina*, you're here with me and you're very beautiful.

Lippi slipped his hand into hers. "Don't touch me!" she said, her voice shaking.

"*Signorina*, there's no reason to be alarmed. I mean no harm. Do I frighten you?" his haunting voice asked.

"Yes…yes you do, so please leave me alone."

"Of course I will. Has anyone told you that your eyes sparkle like emeralds?"

Fioretta turned her back on the man, ignoring his question and walked away. "You were engaged to Giuliano Medici, weren't you? Maybe it was he who told you about your lovely eyes?"

Remaining quiet, Fioretta's back was towards the man.

"*Signorina*, I do believe I asked you a question that deserves an answer."

Fioretta's tone was cold. "Yes…yes, I was engaged to him."

"And did you love him?"

Her heart pounded. Remaining silent, she closed her eyes, disgusted as she lowered her head.

"*Signorina*?"

Fioretta hesitated. "What? NO…no, I didn't love him."

"And yet you were going to marry him? I would say that you're somewhat confused."

"I LOVE ERNESTO!" Fioretta screamed. "I love Ernesto and I am going to marry him. Now please, *Signore*, please leave me alone!"

"Ahh yes, Ernesto…the young man who miraculously came back to life. Very lovely story if I do say so." His sinister tone sent a wave of panic through her. "My dear, let me ask you a question. Giuliano is of course dead, but what would happen if Ernesto by chance would wind up dead? What would you do?"

Fioretta drew a seething inhalation. She turned towards Lippi. Her blistering gaze was fixated on the man. "What kind of sick question is that?" she screamed. "Are you threatening him?"

"Never…never would I do that," Lippi replied, falseness evident in his voice. "What I want to know is what would happen if he were not to come back?"

Fioretta reached the end of her patience. "You frighten me, *Signore*. Leave me alone…never speak to me again, do you hear me? I am going to tell Ernesto about this, do you understand?"

As Fioretta spoke those words, a smug smile crossed Lippi's lips. "Of course, *Signorina*, of course. Please tell him…tell him about you and me." Staring at her as she walked out of sight, he licked his lips mumbling, "Do tell him…do tell him."

"Lippi." Ciro's voice came from behind the bushes. What are you doing?"

"Fool…you startled me!" Lippi said.

"I thought I was clear when I told you to stay away from her, wasn't I?" Ciro demanded.

"Sure…sure you were, but I'm confused as to what girl you are referring to? I never did talk to Fioretta now did I?" Ciro remained quiet. "Did I?" Lippi shouted. "You never saw anything, did you? Do you remember that I was with you all day? We were hunting, do you remember? We hunted all day. Stay by those words Ciro because it could save your life."

Luca simmered with rage as the group of men stopped just shy of the city walls. "Now what?" Luca demanded. "You're going to get us all killed! We can't just walk in through those gates, you know."

Antonio and Tomasso surveyed the fortified city walls and wondered if they made the right decision to come as well.

"We can't get in this way," Luca said.

Ernesto's eyes locked in on the walls. "We're not going in through those gates," he whispered.

Tomasso shot Ernesto a startled look. "What? You have a plan?"

"I do," he grinned, "and it's not through those gates."

"Then where?" Antonio smirked.

"When I was young, I used to play outside those gates with Giuliano and Lorrenzo. We would pretend that the guards were chasing after us." The three listened, as Ernesto's childhood game now became their plan. "We need to stay behind the shrubs and rocks for cover. On the opposite end of the city is an old cemetery. I followed Sandro there one time. The back of the church leads to thick woods. They never did finish building the gates back there and that's where we'll go in."

"Alright, but we need to be quick." Antonio nodded. "Check on the Medici situation and let's get out of here. I don't feel like hanging from a rope today."

"If Lorrenzo is alive," Tomasso proclaimed, "he won't be for long…I'll take care of that!"

Antonio arched his eyebrows. "We get in and we get out, I said." He growled. "No hidden agendas."

Tomasso gave a curt nod as they prepared to skirt the outside of the city. The four followed the trail around the city until they came to a large crag of rocks that gave a partial view of the walls. Looking up, they noticed the strange sight of swarming birds high overhead the center of the city. Ernesto's eyes widened. "This is strange…very strange. Usually you would see people coming in or out of the city; there's been not one person. And take a good look on the walls."

"I don't see anything," Luca said, eyeing the gates.

"Exactly…there's no one there. No guards!" Ernesto said.

Bewildered, they trotted their horses through the thick brush until a clearing up ahead was visible. A thin veil of light trickled past the lush trees when they came upon tombstones.

Chapter Seven

"Is this it?" Luca asked.

"It is." He smiled. "The Church of Ognissanti. In front of this church is a small winding trail that we follow. It will lead us right into the Piazza della Signoria. If we're careful, we can get in, get some information and get out quickly."

They moved silently into the shadows of the trees, making their way into the center of the city. A bittersweet smile grew on Ernesto's face, thinking of when he secretly followed Sandro here to find that his old love, Simonetta, was entombed inside. As they slowly approached the center of the city, Antonio's voice broke the eerie silence, "That's strange," he said. "Look at that black smoke." All four stopped and watched the thin trail of smoke quickly get bigger. "Something is very wrong. It's never like this."

"Wait…listen. Do hear that?" Tomasso's hoarse whisper cut the air.

A low roar echoed through the forest. Cautiously, they made their way through the deserted streets. Nearing the piazza, the sounds of people shouting got louder. Turning a corner, the four found themselves standing on a cobblestoned street that gave them a clear view into the piazza.

Ernesto felt panicked. "Oh my God!" he gasped.

Shocked, the young men witnessed the chaotic scene unfolding before their eyes. Mobs of screaming people surrounded a huge fire that a priest and his altar boys were standing besides. Next to him were piles of clothes, musical instruments, books and paintings.

All four froze. "What did we just walk in on?" Antonio whispered.

At that moment, Ernesto remembered the conversation that Sandro had with him years ago about priests who would do things their way, not God's. His expression remained uncertain. To get a better look, he squinted his eyes, bearing down on the man wearing a long black robe, when he gasped out loud.

"WHAT? What is it?" Antonio blurted.

"It's the priest Savonarola and…" Ernesto drew a startled breath. "Oh my God!"

"What else do you see?" Antonio shouted.

"SANDRO!" Ernesto howled. "I see Sandro. He's there!"

He instantly dug his heels into his horse hard and shouted, sending the animal galloping dangerously close into the Piazza della Signoria.

"NO!" Antonio cried out in shock. Wild panic gripped him as he and the others took chase to catch their friend.

Ernesto pulled back sharply on the reigns, bringing his horse to a skid and jumped off rushing through the mob of people. Doing the same, Antonio caught up to him right before he reached the piazza.

"Hey!!! Antonio screamed over the roar of the crowd. "What do you think you're doing? We were supposed to get in and out…remember?"

"Leave me alone!" Ernesto mumbled, his attention fixed on finding Sandro. Brushing Antonio's hand off his shoulder, he lunged deep into the sea of people. Unable to grab him, Antonio looked back at the other two and frowned.

Horrified, Luca shouted, "We're making a big mistake. With that fire, we're walking directly into hell."

Chapter Seven

Ernesto tightened the rope around his waist and raised his hood, covering most of his face. His head lowered, he carefully made his way through the shouting mob when the sound of a thundering voice stunned him, silencing the crowd. Savonarola, the tall man of God with a long sloping nose, climbed onto a platform in full view and gestured for silence. Dressed ominously in a flowing long black robe, he wore a large cross that decorated his chest.

"Sinners!" His loud resonating voice echoed through the crowd. "You know who you are. It's your abhorrent love of vanity that makes you that way."

Gesturing to the pile of stolen goods, he shouted. "This is the fruits of your labor?"

The frenzied crowd rushed the platform. He quickly grabbed a lit torch and held the crowd at bay, threatening to set fire to their belongings.

"GOD commanded me in a dream to burn these pagan relics as a symbol to all who are sinners and to all who put their hope in possessions. You people are unholy blasphemers of God! You laugh at me and mock me but it is you that will be mocked…By GOD!" Savonarola's eyes moved heavenward as his voice escalated to a fervor pitch. "Stand and watch as I give you but a taste of what God will do to your souls if you don't change your ways."

The crowd held their breath as Savonarola's torch inched closer to the pile that was dumped in the center of the Piazza della Signoria.

Lord Medici's weak voice was hardly heard over the shouting of the incensed mob. "Stop here." His carriage stopped just short of the center of the piazza. The dying man looked up at the platform where Savonarola was standing and a chill ran down his spine. He was summoned immediately from the palace when word of Savonarola's intentions was discovered. Helpless, he sat in his carriage, too ill to walk. He watched in horror as Savonarola condemned everything as vanity. Being a lover of art and books, his heart sunk to see such a mockery of religion. Making their way through the violent crowd, Sandro and *Signora* Mangini got close to the platform and were instantly appalled by the priest's behavior. Without blinking, Sandro lunged towards the platform, cursing, "Hypocrite! You're a hypocrite!"

"This is not the church that I remember," *Signora* shouted over the noise.

Through the vicious crowd, Sandro spotted Lord Medici's carriage. Making eye contact with the man, he tipped his head in respect and wondered what could be going through his thoughts as he is witnessing the end of all things that were once beautiful in his city.

Savonarola repeatedly antagonized the crowds, spewing more hatred, prompting screams for his blood. Violence broke out between those who supported Savonarola and those against him. Amidst the chaos, many struggled to get their possessions back, only to be beaten with heavy clubs being used by followers of the priest. Emboldened by his protectors, Savonarola bellowed. "Like Moses and the Egyptian armies, you will now witness the anger of God. You must pay for the errors of your ways. Prepare to see God's illuminated glory!"

It was late afternoon and the sun began its descent behind the Tuscan hills. Savonarola, with his arms stretched heavenward felt energized as he stood on the platform ready to burn the valuables. Several moments passed. Finally, Savonarola ran his hands over his forehead, pulling back his long hair and gave a single nod to his young army of boys. Out of nowhere, they produced lit torches that joined in the circle around the pile.

The crowds watched in horror. "Don't do this, Savonarola," some shouted. "Give us back our things!"

"Your things?" he screamed. "Let's watch as God takes away all of your things which truly belong to the devil!" Savonarola's dark eyes studied the boys. He raised his hand and on command, they took their torches and held them upright, staring at him, waiting for his signal.

Time seemed to freeze, while all watched as if in slow motion. Sensing fear in the young boys' eyes, Savonarola offered a silent prayer and screamed aloud, "Young children of God...you will burn in the flames of hell if you disobey me." For a full second, Savonarola did not breathe. Suddenly, he looked heavenward as if for approval from God, then lowered his hand, commanding the pile to be lit. Sinister laughter pierced the night as the tumultuous crowd charged the burning pile, attempting to no avail to snuff out the flames. Savonarola's followers beat people away with clubs as the flames shot higher into the already darkening skies.

Sandro watched as the scene turned into utter chaos. A sickening feeling overcame him. From his carriage, Lord Medici watched in horror. Tears slowly ran down his cheeks as he was witnessing the end of his beloved city. Ernesto moved through the middle of all the pandemonium, looking for his teacher while Antonio was not far behind, trying to stop him.

Savonarola trailed a few fingers across his sweating brow as the flames shot higher. Horrified people watched as their books, jewelry, clothes, sculpted pieces of art and paintings were mercilessly, one by one, tossed into the raging inferno.

Lord Medici noticed one of the young boys carrying the portrait of Giuliano that Sandro had recently painted. Too weak to shout, he ordered his driver to get one of the guards. "I don't know how they got that out of the palace…stop them." The quick acting guard grabbed it out of the boy's hand before he threw it into the fire. Other Medici guards joined in and fought Savonarola's supporters over the painting. Instantly, another boy picked it up off the ground and ran towards the intense fire. On command, a Medici guard drew his sword and took chase after the boy. Savonarola was screaming like a madman for the Medici painting to be consumed in flames. Within yards of the fire, the guard caught the boy and plunged his sword deep into his back, sending the boy spiraling into the stone pavement, tearing his body open.

"NO!" Savonarola cried out, trying in vain to stop the killing. He seemed stunned to see the guard standing over the dead boy with a smile on his face. Savonarola wiped his face with the fold of his smoky tunic, his anger blazing. He pointed his finger at the guard and instantly his supporters pinned the man down and savagely kicked him. The guard cried out in agony as the blood poured from his wounds until he fell deathly silent…payment for the killing of one of God's young warriors.

Coaxing his followers to further feed the flames, they threw more of the "vanity" possessions into the fire. Due to the extreme heat, people collapsed as the tension proved too great for some.

Antonio's raging eyes scanned the mob, finding his target. "We need to get out of here…NOW!" he yelled. "If we get caught here, they will throw us into the flames." Antonio looked Ernesto in the eyes. "There's no time to waste." He stammered, overwhelmed. "We have to be careful…you told me that!"

Without blinking, Ernesto spun away from Antonio and ran into the middle of a shoving match between a few of the guards and Savonarola's men. In one fluid motion, a wayward elbow from a guard smashed into Ernesto's mouth, sending him to the pavement in a thundering crash. Afraid of getting crushed by the mass of people running everywhere, Antonio reacted quickly. He grabbed his dazed friend by his jacket and pulled him out of the mob before they were trampled.

Blotting Ernesto's bloodied lip, Antonio pleaded, "We have to leave now."

"But I need to find Sandro!" Ernesto yelled over the loud commotion.

"NO!" Antonio shouted. "This is madness. Let's go!"

Helping Ernesto back to their horses, something quickly passed in front of Ernesto that caught his attention. "Wait!" he screamed to Antonio. "Not yet!" His heart soared as his eyes were riveted on something.

Antonio gasped as his friend ran once more, into the fracas that was ensuing before them. Getting dangerously close to the flames, Ernesto was drawn to a painting that one of Savonarola's boys was about to toss into the fire. Ernesto sounded horrified. "Oh my God, NO!"

Only feet away from Ernesto, Sandro noticed the same painting that the altar boy had in his hand. In a sudden rush, Sandro shouted in desperation as he lunged for the painting. "Don't do it! That was Ernesto's."

Fighting his way through the crowds, Sandro chased after the painting, within minutes, having it in his sights. The young boy held it high over his head and with a mighty thrust, threw the painting into the fire.

I can grab it! Sandro thought as his body reacted on instinct. He hurled himself towards the pile of burning rubble.

Landing on top of a group of people standing by the fire, Sandro knocked several to the ground. The Medici guards quickly grabbed Sandro and pulled him off of the people and pushed him away from the flames. Tears streamed from his eyes as the artist condemned Savonarola's boys, screaming into the night, "Thieves! That was Ernesto's. Do you hear me? It was his mother. I hate you…I hate all of you! It was Ernesto's…Ernesto's."

Lying on the bottom of the pile, Ernesto lay motionless. The sound of running footsteps around him echoed in his head. After Sandro was pulled off of the pile, two others remained on top of Ernesto. Lying there outstretched on the cold stone, he felt his breath returning to his body. Struggling, he was able to push off the two bodies on top of him. Ernesto staggered back to his feet and looked around and caught sight of his mother's portrait, burning in the fire.

Over the deafening noise, Ernesto wandered about listening to his name echo in the night. Ernesto was silent for several seconds, listening to the voice calling his name until he realized who it was. "SANDRO… it's me!" he screamed, "it's me!"

Sandro could not believe what he heard. Through the many sounds of this night, one was clearly audible to Botticelli. He raised his head erect and looked all around, at times, jumping up and down, trying to look over the crowds. That voice…I swear that was his voice, he told himself. His eyes welled with emotion. "Ernesto!" he cried out.

From the corner of his eye, Ernesto thought he saw what looked like Sandro heading towards the flames. With only moments to act, Ernesto darted forward with his fists clenched, swinging wildly at anyone in his way. *My God…it is him…it's Sandro*, he said to himself. Realizing he was only yards behind him, Ernesto stretched his arm forward to grab at the artist. He opened his mouth to yell to him when suddenly, a hand closed over his mouth as he was grabbed from behind.

"Shut your mouth right now before you get us killed," Tomasso screamed, pulling Ernesto to his feet.

Ernesto stared at Tomasso in disbelief. "Sandro was there…I had him in my grasp, and you took him away!"

"I said shut your mouth or I will do it. You're compromising our safety so stop drawing attention to yourself!"

"Are you crazy?" Ernesto shouted. "Look around you. Draw attention? It's chaos here. No one cares what's going on so leave me alone."

Antonio caught up with them, breathless. "We have to hide…look over there!" The three watched as Lorrenzo Medici led the way on horseback followed by ten of his guards. Ernesto's blood ran cold as he saw his enemy. His eyes were glued to the

Medici. A rush of adrenaline came over Ernesto as he hissed, "So it's true…he's not dead after all." Ernesto quickly grabbed the dagger from his waistband, "Now, I can have the pleasure of killing him!"

"NO!" Antonio reasoned. "Not now. I want Medici dead too but this is suicide. Wait…wait just a little longer and I promise we'll get him. I promise, just not now."

Ernesto's eyes went wide as he watched Medici's horse trot by him. Crouching low to stay out of sight, he knew Antonio was right. Knowing that any attack on his part would mean death to them all, all he could do was shake his head in disbelief.

"Tomasso," Antonio's voice intruded. "Somehow find Luca in this madness and meet back at the camp in two days."

Tomasso gave a grim sigh. "That could be almost impossible."

The three watched the chaos ensuing before them. They had never seen such a thing in their home city of Florence. Riots were breaking out all around them. The Medici guards mounted on their horses stood their ground, circled around the raging fire, when Savonarola's thunderous voice rose above the screams of people.

"Children of the demons. Look. Look before you and see. This is your fate in these flames of hell. This is your future. All here tonight…all of you will suffer just like these possessions of Satan."

Ernesto's eyes remained fixed to the swelling crowds for one last glimpse of his teacher. Holding his breath, he felt a sense of foreboding that something terrible was going to take place.

His eyes welled up with emotion, as he stood hypnotized, gazing into the fiery inferno. He was so close. Sandro was gone…wandering through a sea of people, looking for one young man.

As Ernesto and Antonio left the piazza and the city for the safety of the forest, Ernesto's mind remained locked on the face of his teacher. *I'll be back, Sandro. I'll be back*, he thought to himself on the long ride.

Standing in the middle of the insanity, Sandro watched as the last bits of the portrait he painted of Ernesto's mother was consumed in the flames. Hearing his voice tonight brought back painful memories. *I heard his voice*, he told himself. *Ghost? Could Lord Medici be right?*

The sounds of his name being called echoed in his mind again and again until finally, it faded off into the night.

Chapter Eight

Lorrenzo felt hollow as he carefully maneuvered his horse through the scorched rubble of Piazza della Signoria. He nervously tapped his finger against his teeth as he surveyed the carnage.

A man stopped from picking through the burned debris when he noticed Medici on his horse. "*Signore* Medici…excuse me, but may I speak with you?"

Outraged, Lorrenzo's cold stare terrified the man, "You dare call me *Signore*? Don't you know who I am?"

"I…I do," the voice trembled.

"Well then you should know that I am not your *Signore*…is that understood?"

"You are the son of Lord Medici."

Lorrenzo growled, "I AM Lord Medici now. You give your allegiance to me!"

The frightened man quickly bent to one knee. "My apologies, my lord. We saw you here last night. You saw what he did." The man's voice lowered to a choked whisper. "Why would he send innocent children to steal from us, just to burn everything? Please, my lord, are we not allowed to have anything of our own? Have we displeased God? Have we displeased you? He is your priest. Please help us."

Lorrenzo sneered outwardly at the man. "He's NOT my priest!" he fumed. "Can you understand that? He's not my priest!" Medici's eyes scanned the people picking through the rubble. Everyone froze. They shook their heads in disbelief as he reviled the man.

"What do you people want from me? Go pray to God...pick up your belongings, but leave me alone!"

Lorrenzo turned to leave when the thundering sound of hooves smashing down on flagstone echoed throughout the piazza. Captain Rafael of the Medici guards voice was rigid. "Excuse me, my lord, action must be taken against Savonarola. What do wish me to do?"

Lorrenzo eyed him carefully. Taking a deep breath, he surveyed the charred piazza around him. "That priest is finished," Lorrenzo scowled. "Man of God or not, he will pay. I swear to you...with his life, he will pay for what he did to my city!" Kicking sharply into the muscular flesh of his horse, Lorrenzo took off in flight after the embattled priest.

As the mid-afternoon sunlight slowly crept up the main aisle of Il Duomo, Fra Domenico da Pescia and Fra Silvestro were busy lighting candles and offering up prayers. Savonarola knelt before a large crucifix, praying silently to God. The silence of the church was shattered by Lorrenzo's screaming voice. "Savonarola, how dare you make a mockery of my city!"

Savonarola jumped to his feet and with his two priests, charged down the aisle to confront the angry Medici. "NO! How dare YOU and your captain come into my father's house with your hostility!"

Lorrenzo's eyes bulged. His blistering gaze settled on the large cross, worn around Savonarola's neck. "Who are you to steal from people and then tell them it's what God wanted?"

Stepping in between them, Fra Silvestro grinned at Medici, making his hatred for his family evident.

Lorrenzo drew a seething inhalation. "Back away, Silvestro, or else you'll find yourself praying in a jail cell."

A phony smile grew across the priest's face, "You have no authority here in God's house, so go back home, boy. Go be with your family. They tell you what to do anyway."

Captain Rafael recoiled in disbelief. He quickly drew his sword and placed the cold steel tip onto the priest's neck, making a small impression on his throat. "Men of God should not speak with the devil's tongue, Father," he said calmly.

Silvestro could feel his own heart pounding as he stared down the blade. Medici quickly put his hand up and placed it on his captain's sword, lowering it. "Enough blood has been spilled in this building…in this city, do you agree?" he said.

"And whose fault is that?" Silvestro asked. "Ever since you and your brother tried to take control of the church…"

"Silence!" Savonarola screamed.

Silvestro paused a moment, his eyes glaring at Medici. "You brought this upon yourself," he said. "You are dead in our eyes, Medici."

"Really?" Lorrenzo was thunderstruck. "We shall see about that!"

Medici turned his eyes towards Savonarola. "This is not over between you and me. We'll return and you'll pay for your crimes." Medici sharply turned on his heels and he and Captain Rafael made their way down the long aisle of Il Duomo. Under his breath, the captain whispered. "You should have let me kill that disrespectful—."

"No," Lorrenzo stopped him. "There will be a time and place for all three of them. Trust me, Silvestro will pay for his remarks."

Rage coursed through Lorrenzo's veins as he climbed onto his horse. "They all will pay." He smiled, gently patting his sword.

As Lorrenzo headed back to the palace, he rode his horse out in the countryside. He could already feel his muscles relaxing. The sun was starting to set over the hills when he stopped his horse to view the beauty surrounding him. He watched horses run wild through the tall grass as he closed his eyes, inhaling the sweet fragrances of the flowers. *How did Father keep things from spiraling out of control?* he wondered.

The shrill of children's laughter quickly caught his attention. Three small boys were running through the tall wheat that was swaying in the breeze.

A small smile formed across his lips as he thought of his brother Giuliano. In these very fields, they spent hours running and playing. It was just the two of them, side by side.

One day, a third boy showed up. This boy was smaller and weaker but soon became their friend, a good friend until something went wrong. Instantly, his smile vanished from his lips as he thought of the boy. Without warning, Lorrenzo's hands shook; his lips trembled as he tried to control his emotions. Without warning, his mouth opened wide as he screamed. "Ernesto!" His voice echoed throughout the valley. Cursing the name of his enemy, Lorrenzo realized that the laughter of the children had stopped. They stood frozen in fear. As he tried to apologize, they ran away crying. Embarrassed, he kicked his heels hard into his horse, sending his mount galloping furiously towards the palace.

The pathway to the main entrance of the palace was lined with blooming flowers. Before Lorrenzo could burst through the doors, the prim, elegant servant had swung them open when he caught sight of the young Medici furiously riding his horse down the path.

Lorrenzo scowled when he saw Captain Rafael waiting for him in the foyer. "My lord, I've been here for a while, where have you been?"

"Out riding! Why? What business is it of yours?" Lorrenzo snapped.

The captain's eyebrows arched with concern. "After you left, I got word that one of my guards was killed last night." The captain shook his head. "He was killed by one of our own. Savonarola coaxed him into doing it. He called it a mercy killing. He told him God commanded him to do it."

Lorrenzo remained silent, sickened by this news. After a long, uneasy pause, he looked up and frowned, "Thank you, captain, you may go."

Rafael headed out of the doors when he abruptly turned, "My lord, through all the chaos last night, I forgot to mention that we did make one arrest. A local man was trying to steal a couple of horses, what should we do with him?"

Lorrenzo's jaw dropped. "A priest burns our city, one of our guards was killed and now you have to ask me what to do with a horse thief?" Medici smirked. "Kill him if you want...I don't care!"

Spinning on his heels, Rafael ran from the palace.

Why would someone steal horses if they live here…we would spot them instantly. After thinking a quick moment, he shouted to his captain. "Wait!" Lorrenzo ran outside as Rafael readied his horse to leave. "Don't kill him, I want to meet him."

Lorrenzo hurried into the jail, his eyes urgent. "Where's the horse thief?" The guards immediately snapped to attention, their swords and daggers polished bright. One of the guards led Medici down the stone stairwell. Opening the cell for the corridor, Lorrenzo dismissed him.

"Lord Medici? I don't understand," the young guard questioned. "I will stay with you."

"No! Lock the door behind me and I will call when I'm ready to leave…that's an order!" Lorrenzo barked.

A few lit torches fastened to the wall gave Lorrenzo sufficient light to see. He followed the ancient cobblestone pavement towards a small flickering of light coming from the furthest cell. As he approached it, Lorrenzo placed his hands on the cold iron bars, gazing down at the man sprawled out on the stone floor.

"You there…horse thief. Get to your feet. I want to ask you a few questions."

The prisoner, his back towards Medici, did not budge. "I said I wish to ask you some questions, so get up…now!"

"I hear you, guard. If you want to talk, well then talk. But be quick, I'm sleepy."

"I'm not a guard!" Lorrenzo shouted. "My name is Lord Medici, and I order you to face me this instant!"

"Order? You're ordering me?" The prisoner never flinched. "Look…I don't care who you are." The prisoner's eyes opened wide. "Wait…you say you're a Medici?"

The man spun on the floor, rolling over to his stomach. "My God…so it is the great Lorrenzo Medici. And here I thought it is only your father who's called Lord Medici?"

"You're arrogant for a man who was caught stealing," Lorrenzo said.

A smirk played across the prisoner's face.

"You find this amusing? I can have you whipped for stealing our horses."

"Those horses weren't yours. Your name wasn't on them," he said grinning.

"Don't play games with me!" Lorrenzo demanded, "As your lord, you will answer my questions or else!"

"Yes…yes," the thief laughed. "I heard you say who you are. I think everyone in Italy knows who the great Medici is."

Lorrenzo looked vexed. He placed his face up to the narrow opening in the bars and through the dim light, he saw the man pull his long hair back, exposing more of his face.

Taking a deep breath, a perplexed Lorrenzo stared at the prisoner a long moment. "We've met before, haven't we?" he asked.

"Have we?" he replied, toying with Medici.

Lorrenzo's eyes grew wide in disbelief. "My God! I know who you are," he gasped. "We were children and you…you were friends with Ernesto…you and another boy." Medici eyed him carefully. "I'm curious, why haven't I seen you in the city since you were a boy. Why is that?"

"I keep to myself. That's not a crime, is it?"

Medici felt uncertain how to proceed. Squinting his eyes, he looked deep into the man's eyes. "A crime? No, no it isn't, but the guards said that you were caught trying to steal horses and that is a crime, my friend," he said, remaining calm.

"Steal? Oh, I'm very sorry, your majesty, but stealing is such a harsh word, don't you agree? Honestly, between you and me…it was really just a simple mistake."

Slowly lifting himself off of the floor, he walked to the iron bars that imprisoned him. "You see, Lorrenzo," he reasoned, "I thought they were wild horses that got spooked from the fire, so I thought I would rescue them."

"Rescue them?" Lorrenzo asked. The prisoner's words seemed to strike a nerve, so Lorrenzo gave him a moment. "Rescue them?" Medici repeated his answer deliberately.

"Yes, your majesty, that's what I said. Rescue them. That's not too hard to understand, is it?"

Medici's anger began to grow hot. "You will address me as Lord Medici, not your majesty. Is that something that YOU can understand?"

"Yes…of course. Please, you must forgive my manners," he said with a chuckle, "they're simply deplorable…LORD MEDICI!"

"Listen carefully," Lorrenzo said. "You know my name, but I don't remember yours, so please refresh my memory, you know…for old time's sake."

"My name?" the prisoner snickered. "Come now…you truly don't remember?" The man playfully ran his fingers up and down the iron bars, smiling as Lorrenzo's frustration rose.

His patience worn, Medici screamed, "WHAT IS YOUR NAME?" A few seconds of silence went by. "I'm waiting!" Lorrenzo gulped hard. "Fine, if this is what you wish. I will have the guards whip you and then you might be more inclined to talk to me."

The prisoner laughed as he motioned Lorrenzo to come closer to the bars. "Just a little closer Lorrenzo and I will tell you… just a little more."

Without his guards in the dungeon, Medici exercised caution but curiosity took over as he slowly rested his face on the bars, just inches away from the prisoner. The man's eyes were aglow when he whispered, "My name is Tomasso Solasso. Do you remember me now?"

Tomasso's laugh filled his cell and bounced off the walls, echoing throughout the entire dungeon. In shock, Medici froze for a moment, his eyes glued to the man.

Lorrenzo grabbed hold of the bars that separated him and Tomasso. "I don't understand you. You're in my prison for stealing, and this is all a joke to you?" he hissed.

While Tomasso ran his hands through his unruly long hair, Lorrenzo locked eyes with him, wondering if he really was crazy. Medici slowly backed away from his cell and walked down the corridor. Shouting for the guards to let him out, as he climbed the steps, he could still hear Tomasso's voice echoing from the basement.

An hour later, the sound of clanging iron began to make its way down the steps to the jail cells. Tomasso's insistent laughter continued, ranting that he beat up Medici when they were young.

Chapter Eight

Through the darkness of the dimly lit dungeon, Lorrenzo came into view. Medici glanced over his shoulder at the guard who followed him. "Release him," he mumbled.

The heavy iron door creaked when it swung open. Tomasso stepped out and grinned. "Letting me go so soon?" he questioned. Standing inches away from Medici, he looked deep into his eyes. "Now I see it. It is certainly you." Without hesitation he added, "And if I remember correctly, you also have a younger brother, don't you? Where is he? Upstairs perhaps?"

Without blinking, Medici's dark eyes settled on the haughty Tomasso, his blood boiling in his veins.

Tomasso reached behind Medici and patted him on the back. "Lorrenzo, this was fun…we must do it again." Then he turned and began to walk down the long corridor to the stone steps leading upstairs. Before taking the first step, he turned and again offered a mock apology. "Again, I've forgotten my manners. When you do see your brother, please give him my regards, as well as the regards of my cousin Antonio and an old friend of yours…Ernesto Palazzo."

Before he could take another step, Medici asked. "Tomasso, I was just curious, since you do live in the city…did you not hear that my brother was killed months ago right across the street in the church?"

"Really?" Tomasso grunted. "What a shame. I didn't hear a thing about it. I've been traveling out of the city," he replied coldly. "I guess I'm sorry to hear about your loss."

"Sorry?" he said shaking his head. "People from all over Italy had heard about it. I'm surprised you didn't."

"Well, like I said, I keep to myself. I don't pay attention to trivial stories."

"Before you leave," Medici asked, "I need to ask you something. You did ask me to give regards to my brother from your cousin Antonio and Ernesto Palazzo? I believe that is what you said, correct?"

Tomasso nodded his head.

"Forgive me, but please humor me with one last question. If I'm not mistaken, wasn't my old friend Ernesto Palazzo killed about a year ago?"

Tomasso glanced up, surprised by the question. Quickly realizing his error, he backtracked his story, changing his timetable with no success. Fumbling over his words, he replied, "Oh yes, Ernesto…of course he's dead. What I meant to say was that if he were alive, he would send you his regards. And again, I apologize for the loss of your brother." Tomasso's expression clouded. "Am I done here, Lord Medici?"

Medici adjusted his thick leather belt that harnessed his sword. Smiling, he walked towards the steps to answer his question. "Yes, my friend, of course you are free to go but please do me a favor."

Tomasso nodded blankly.

"Please give Ernesto my regards, will you, *Signore*? Even better, please give him regards from both myself and my brother."

Tomasso's crooked smile flashed as he quickly ran up the steps and out of the building. A chill raced up his spine as he walked onto the road, nervous of what just took place.

"Why would you release him, my lord?" the guard asked. "He's a thief."

Chapter Eight

"No, he's not a thief." Lorrenzo grinned. "He's not a thief at all. He is exactly what I thought he was…a murderer."

"Murderer, my lord? And we're letting him go?"

"Yes, yes…I know what you're thinking. Listen to me closely. I want you to go after him, but he cannot see you, understood? I don't want him arrested. I just want to know where he goes." Dismissing the guard, Lorrenzo ran up the steps with a smile, delighted by the turn of events of the afternoon.

Medici couldn't tear his eyes away from the window of Captain Rafael's office. He grinned watching the silhouette of Tomasso furiously riding out of the piazza. Lorrenzo shared with his captain what just happened when one of the Medici girls, Bianca, burst into the room crying. "Lorrenzo! You have to come home immediately. It's papa…he's dying and is asking for you."

Ignoring his sister's pleas, he continued devising a plan with Rafael.

"Lorrenzo?" she shouted, grabbing the material of his jacket. "Didn't you hear what I said? Papa's dying! Please, we have to leave now."

"Bianca…I'm busy. I'll be home later."

"Lord Medici," Rafael said. "Perhaps it's best that you go. Your father is waiting for you."

Lorrenzo felt his teeth clench in rage. "Right now, I don't care about my father and I don't care about horses that were stolen. That man who just walked out was part of the group that killed my brother. I am so close to avenging Giuliano's death!" He grabbed his sister by her shoulders and hissed, "That man who just left killed OUR brother…and I know who he is! I know who he is!"

Overhearing the conversation, one of his guards approached Medici. "Excuse me, my lord, but we arrested all those men and put them to death months ago. This Tomasso is nothing but a common horse thief. Let's just throw him in jail for awhile and let him think about his actions."

Lorrenzo heard only the faint murmur of the guard's voice.

"PLEASE, Lord Medici…your father!" the captain pleaded.

Lorrenzo was talking in rapid bursts now. "Rafael, do you know what this means? He's alive...Ernesto Palazzo is alive! Do you hear what I am saying? He lives and his friend Tomasso is going to lead us right to him."

Rafael couldn't believe his ears as Lorrenzo continued. "I just sent one guard to follow him. Now, I want four more of your best men to follow him…now." A sadistic grin broke across his face.

Shaking her head in disbelief, Bianca ran out of the room, back to the palace. She wanted to be with her father for his last few breaths of life. Lorrenzo's eyes went wide as he screamed for all to hear, "Palazzo will stand before me for the killing of my brother! Ernesto will surely die…this time for real!"

"Look at you," *Signora* laughed, "you're a sentimental old fool."

"Old fool?" Sandro asked as he continued thumbing through a pile of old paintings that he had done.

Seeing the frown on his face, *Signora* explained, "He treated you so poorly and now that he's dying, you're fawning over him. I'm sorry," she said callously, "I'd just let him die and be done with it. It's no great loss."

Sandro was shocked. "Gisella! I've never heard you talk like this before."

"That man took advantage of you all these years and for what? Heartache? Misery? Admit it, that's all you ever received from that family. Can you deny it?"

Sandro looked up at Gisella, locking eyes with her. "No, but it's something that I have to do…I must do." Turning his attention back to the pile of paintings, a smile suddenly formed on Sandro's face as he found something perfect. Fortunately, Savonarola's boys missed this certain pile of paintings that were hidden away. It was one Sandro did a long time ago. Long before the Medici children, long before Savonarola, long before the trouble in his beloved city…long before Ernesto came into his life. The proud artist blew the dust that settled on the painting to show *Signora.*

Confused, she looked at Sandro. "Florence? Why give him a painting of the city?"

"Because this is his city," he said staring at the painting. "He's always loved it. I want this to be the last thing that he sees before he passes on."

"That's it?" she snapped. "Sandro, he's taken credit for everything great about this city. It's the people, Sandro…the people. You…me…everyone who has lived here, worked here and raised families here. Medici did nothing for us, absolutely nothing. All he did was give us rules. HIS rules!"

The artist shrugged. "At times he did make burdensome rules, but deep down he's a good man and for some odd reason, I consider him a friend." He carefully wrapped the painting in some old rags.

"FRIEND?" Gisella shrieked. "His sons killed Ernesto! That's your friend?"

Sandro stared at the older woman for several moments. He let out a sigh then took her by the hand and sat with her. "Do you remember years ago when you threw this chair at me? Ernesto was just a little boy."

"Sandro…stop," she answered wearing a sheepish grin. "You know you deserved it."

"Ha! Then you threatened me, calling me a no-good drunkard who would amount to nothing."

Gisella closed her eyes from embarrassment and looked away, "Sandro, please stop bringing those things up."

"No, Gisella, you're going to listen to me. It's no secret that I didn't care for you. Honestly, I really didn't care for myself either." Rubbing the top of her hand, Sandro sighed heavily. "When Simonetta died, I wanted to die as well. But I lived and went on a life of destruction. I painted and drank and that was it but then something wonderful happened to me. That something was Ernesto, that beautiful little boy I found living in the street. He changed my life…he changed both our lives. We both cared for him and raised him…he was a wonderful boy."

Tears formed in *Signora's* eyes as Sandro reached over to hug the woman. "Thank you," she whispered. "We both should be proud. He brought us together."

Sandro struggled with his next words. "You're all I have, Gisella. With Ernesto, we were a family, but you and I," he paused, "you and I are a family as well."

Signora kissed Sandro on his cheek. She was still for several seconds, until a knowing smile crossed her lips. Suddenly Sandro's face brightened. "You were always there for me, prodding me along, and not very gently may I remind you."

His boisterous laughter brought a smile to her face. "I also thought of you as my family. Even when I was yelling at you, for some reason, you always were like the son that I never had a chance to see grown up. When my husband and son died in the earthquake, I thought my life was over, but you moved in and as much as I disliked you, well…I guess you just grew on me." Her face grew serious now. "Sandro, I'm sorry for complaining about your friendship with Lord Medici, but be honest with me. After all he's done to you, what can you possibly feel for the man?"

Sandro needed a minute to find his words. "Pity maybe? I'm not really sure."

Something in his response sparked her curiosity, "Is that it? Be honest with me. Why do I get the feeling that there is something more, something you're not telling me?"

Sandro gave a tired smile. "Gisella, I found something out recently that I think you should know."

Sandro stood from his chair and walked over to *Signora.* He explained that he was at the Medici Palace a short while ago and Lord Medici had asked him to read some old letters. He then told her about one very special letter. While he was telling the story of the letter, she impatiently cut him off, "Sandro, get to the point. What is this big secret you found out?"

Sandro fell silent, feeling the weight of her question. Turning his eyes towards Gisella, he felt himself flush.

"Can you tell me?" she asked.

The artist cleared his throat.

The woman sighed with mock exasperation. "Sandro, what's wrong with you? Why can't you tell me?"

Sandro immediately placed his head in his hands and sat down for a moment. A blinding sharp pain raced through his body making him dizzy and momentarily he lost his speech. *Signora* jumped to her feet trying to comfort the artist. His gaze was distant and his tongue fell lazily to the side.

"Sandro! Can you hear me?" *Signora* cried. "What's wrong? Answer me."

Sandro strained to understand. After a few minutes, he seemed to wake up. Shaking his head, he groaned. "What happened?"

Concerned, she stood next to him, holding his hand. "You seemed to fall asleep. You just fell asleep. Are you in pain? How do you feel?"

"Tired and my…my tongue feels too big for my mouth." Trying to ease the older woman's fears, he winked. "And you know how big my mouth is."

"That's not funny, Sandro…I'm really worried about you. Ever since Ernesto has been gone, you never eat. You hardly sleep. I just worry."

"I'm fine, Gisella. Just a little tired, I guess."

After some time had passed, Sandro seemed back to normal. He picked up the painting for Lord Medici and was preparing to leave.

"Wait…what was that secret of yours that you are keeping?" she asked. "What evilness did Lorrenzo do now?"

"Not Lorrenzo," Sandro replied sadly. "His father."

She stared at him. "I don't understand."

Botticelli sighed heavily. "Lord Medici is Ernesto's father."

Stunned, Gisella felt a gnawing in her stomach. "Have you gone mad?" she asked. "I don't believe it! Who told you this story? Medici?"

"It's true," Sandro pressed. "I believe the man, and besides, why would Lord Medici lie about something like that? Gisella, he confessed to having an affair with a woman named Eugenia. Remember? That was Ernesto's mother's name. Then the boy was told that his father was dead. That's all he knew."

Recalling past events, he gazed into *Signora*'s eyes. "I never understood Lord Medici's odd behavior when Ernesto was in the palace. Gisella, everything makes perfect sense."

"It could be true," she mumbled. "In the back of my mind, I always found it curious that Ernesto and Giuliano looked so much alike…the same father."

"But there's something that's bothering me that I'm not really sure about."

Her eyebrows arched with intrigue. "Oh? What's that?"

Sandro remained silent a long moment. "Lord Medici swears that it was Ernesto who killed Giuliano."

"WHAT?" *Signora* screamed. "No, Sandro. I don't believe that. Ernesto is dead! You know he is. We saw his body, his hair and his…his blood!"

As he put his arm around the old woman, she looked up at him, her face pale. "We were there, we saw him. Sandro, he is dead…isn't he?"

Time seemed to freeze. "Yes, Gisella. He's dead." Sitting back down next to her, he explained. "Medici said that Lorrenzo saw a ghost in the church that day. He said it was Ernesto's ghost that stabbed his brother in the heart." Sandro shook his head in disgust. "It's all just foolish stories. I don't believe in ghosts and in my heart, I know that Ernesto is dead. Like I said…foolish stories."

The old woman gasped. "So Medici thinks that it was brother killing brother?"

Sandro's face turned white, his voice shaky. "It doesn't matter now. Both are dead…there's nothing anyone can…can…" Sandro grabbed his head in pain, staggering about the floor.

"Sandro!" she cried. "Is it the same pain?"

"I…I don't know. My head…I have blinding pain in my head. It hurts." Sweating profusely, he stumbled onto his bed. "Everything hurts, my arm, my face. I don't understand." *Signora* sat silently at his bedside holding his hand. After a few moments, Sandro was unconscious. *Signora* dropped to her knees and prayed fervently to God to spare her dear friend.

Sandro awoke with a start. In the distant recesses of his groggy mind, he remembered having that blinding pain in his head earlier today. Gently, he turned his head to the side and found Gisella fast asleep in her chair.

Sandro stirred in his bed, waking *Signora* up.

"How do you feel?" she asked.

"Not bad." Sandro's head begged to differ. "How long have I been sleeping?"

"A few hours, I guess," Gisella frowned. "Sandro…I'm frightened."

Slowly, he stood up and firmly planted his feet on the ground. He took a deep breath. "I don't know what happened. It just came so suddenly. A blinding pain shot through my head. I felt like I couldn't use my arms."

"You're probably exhausted. Please…for me, go lay back down in bed. With all this talk about Medici and Ernesto being alive, it's no wonder you feel sick."

"No, I feel better. Just my legs are still a bit wobbly and my arm hurts a little."

Gisella's face was grim. "Sandro, please!"

"Gisella, I'm fine. No need to worry. Look at me. Do I look sick?" he laughed. Quickly grabbing the gift that he had wrapped, he headed for the door. "I am going to bring this to Lord Medici before it's too late. Please come with me."

Frowning, she whispered, "No, you go. He's your friend. Spend whatever time he has left with him. It's a beautiful painting. I'm sure he'll love it."

He smiled and left for the palace.

The brilliant sunshine coming in through the window looked inviting to *Signora.* Worried from seeing Sandro in pain, she moved a chair towards the window to close her eyes. The warmth of the sun made her sleepy. Her eyes fluttered as she dozed back off to sleep. The last thing she remembered was thinking, *Ernesto…alive? That's impossible.*

Darkness permeated the palace as *Signora* Medici covered the windows to keep daylight from entering. The servant gracefully ushered Sandro upstairs. With each step of the grand staircase, his thoughts were of his dying friend. There were times that he hated him. At times, Lord Medici forced Sandro into doing work for him, but in hindsight, it made him a better artist. Replaying the recent conversation that he and Medici had, he concluded that that was why Medici gave him steady work, so he could keep Ernesto fed.

Reaching the top step, Sandro heard voices coming from one of the rooms. Through the dimly lit hallway, he noticed that one door was cracked open. In the darkness, a woman's soft whisper invited him in. A moment after his eyes adjusted, he caught sight of Lord Medici's wife, Lucrezia, and their three daughters standing around the bed of Lord Medici.

"*Signore* Botticelli," *Signora* Medici whispered. "Please come in. Piero was just asking for you."

Sandro was stunned not to see Lorrenzo there. He approached the bed and his heart sank deep into his chest to see his friend gasping for air. How he remembered the man when he was vibrant and healthy. Stern at times, but fair.

Sandro looked Medici in the eye.

"Come… come closer," he whispered. All of his strength was consumed in relaying those few words. His eyes communicated with his wife. Finally, summoning whatever strength he had left, he gasped to Lucrezia, "Leave us."

Wearing a brave smile, she looked down at her dying husband and tenderly kissed his forehead. "I love you and I always will," she whispered in his ear. Tears began to roll down her cheeks. "Girls, let's leave your father and *Signore* Botticelli alone to talk."

The three daughters hugged their father, knowing he was in his final moments.

"*Signore* Botticelli," Lucrezia said softly, "what did you bring us?"

"A small gift from me to Lord Medici."

"For Piero? May I see it please?"

Pulling the wrapping off of the canvas, she held it up and smiled. "I love it. Thank you, *Signore*. I know he will love it as well. When he feels better, you can give it to him." Sighing, she whispered, "He loved this city." The woman placed her hand on Sandro's cheek and gave a weak smile. "I know sometimes it was rough, but thank you for being his friend."

Sandro had a faint smile on his lips as he took Medici's hand in his. "You were a great man. This city…all of us who live here are much better because of you." Sandro bowed his head and muttered a prayer.

Father in the heavens…
In your mercy, overlook his shortcomings…
The sins of which he knew; the faults he was unaware of…
Grant him forgiveness for his sins…
God is good…God is merciful…

Sandro's dark eyes studied the man a long while when suddenly a gripping pain shot through Lord Medici's body as his face and body contorted violently. Clamping down on Sandro's hand in desperation, Lord Medici took one final breath, heaving his chest forward and painfully gasped his last words on earth, "Sandro, forgive me................"

Lord Medici was gone.

Tears welled in Sandro's eyes as he took the painting and placed it into Medici's hands.

Several moments passed when he finally looked heavenward...Amen.

Alessandro Botticelli breathed a heavy sigh then slowly walked out of the room...out of the palace and finally walked out into the darkness of night.

Chapter Nine

The mist rose from the Tuscan valley shortly after sunrise. Out of the haze, the sound of pounding hooves filled the air. The lone rider recognized his surroundings when he slowed his horse down to a trot.

There it is, he thought as he maneuvered his horse through a large gathering of trees, when he saw them. "Luca!" the man shouted. "Where have you been? Ernesto and Antonio got back days ago."

Luca frowned. "Never mind that, where is Tomasso?"

Puzzled, the lookout asked, "He's not behind you?"

Luca's heart raced as he took off down the trail. He snaked his way through the trees when he saw his friends running to meet him.

"Thank God you've both made it back," Antonio said. "We've been worried." Looking around, Antonio gasped. "Where's Tomasso? Where's my cousin?" Antonio spun and looked down the trail only to see no one coming. "Luca, what happened? Where is he?"

Breathless, Luca replied, "He didn't return?"

"WHAT? You don't know where he is?" Antonio shouted.

Hearing the commotion, Silvio ran over to investigate. "What's wrong?"

Antonio glanced over at Silvio, locking eyes with him. "This fool left Tomasso behind!"

Luca gulped hard, "He…he was supposed to meet me. I guess I left without him."

Silvio's face filled with rage. "You guess?"

Fumbling over his words, Luca defended his actions. "Tomasso told me to stay where I was. There was so much noise. The fire was raging. People were screaming. A young boy was killed. It was scary." Getting down off his horse, he yelled, "Look…he said he was just going to take a couple of horses. Nobody was watching. I figured he would get them and be right behind me."

"Idiot!" a distraught Antonio screamed.

Startled, Luca spun towards Silvio. "He said if we got separated, start back and eventually we would meet up."

"And?" demanded Silvio.

"I waited a day wandering out here," Luca scowled. "I even backtracked but then I figured that maybe he was in front of me."

Antonio was dumbstruck as he paced in front of the two men. He rubbed his hands across the back of his neck and glanced back to Silvio. "I knew it was a bad idea to put Tomasso with this idiot!"

"I'm not an idiot!" Luca shouted. "I was obeying orders. You should know that, Antonio."

"ORDERS?" Antonio shouted, his blood boiling. "Leaving someone in all that chaos is obeying orders? It's foolish…it's deadly."

In the distance, Ernesto saw the two men arguing. Moments later, Ernesto's pulse was racing when he bolted to stop what he was seeing. Antonio grabbed Luca's shoulders, shaking him violently. "We've been back three days worrying about where the two of you were!"

"Antonio, stop it!" Ernesto shouted. "It could be anything. You know your cousin. He's the most impetuous person I know. Give him a little more time. If he's not back, then we'll go after him."

Antonio's anger blazed. Ernesto's words made sense to him, but he was sorely troubled. Ernesto gave him a weary look. "Take a walk with me."

In the silence of the woods, Ernesto took a deep breath. "Antonio…what is it? There's something that you're hiding."

Antonio remained silent.

"Trust me…he'll be back. Tomasso is probably selling those horses he stole."

Antonio nodded, his expression serious. "It's not just that," he said. "It's all of this…it's everything, Ernesto, everything that's happened to us over these last months. Face it…we're not killers. I mean look at us…we're all just trying to survive out here."

"Antonio, I promise you…we'll get through all of this. We all will and soon, we'll have our normal lives back."

Antonio's deep brown eyes looked tired. His body, weary from being chased by the Medici guards, longed for some of the simple pleasures in life…warm bread and good wine. Instead, he and the others were forced to hide out in the forest, eating what they catch, eating moldy bread and spoiled wine.

Antonio gave a grim sigh. "What is normal? I've forgotten what that is. Ernesto, we're killers now…royal family killers…remember? Nothing will ever be normal again," he said, his voice trailing off. "For what we've done, we all could hang from a tree tomorrow, our necks snapped by a noose."

"You lose your faith too quickly," Ernesto replied. "Like I said before, we will get through this…all of us. You'll see. Tomasso will get back and when he does, we'll leave. We'll head to the mountains…to the city of Turin. We can start a new life there where nobody knows us...I promise."

Antonio gave no response. He stood motionless as if offering a silent prayer for deliverance.

The two lookouts were fast asleep nestled up against a tree in the early morning hours. Unaware of his presence, Tomasso grinned as he grabbed a handful of dirt and let it slowly trickle onto their faces. One of the snoring guards brushed his hand across his face while he slept. Tomasso's eyes lit up as he poured more dirt on them, some of it finding its way into their mouths. Choking on the dirt, the startled guards looked up to see Tomasso laughing loudly. "Aren't lookouts supposed to be doing something, like…well, you know…looking out?"

Jumping up, the angry lookouts brushed the dirt from their faces. "Where have you been?" the one barked. "Luca got here yesterday."

"I got captured by Medici guards trying to steal horses."

"Medici guards?" they mocked. "You're no horse thief. Really…who captured you? Perhaps the old woman who owned them?"

Ignoring their comments, Tomasso jumped back on his horse and shouted. "Fools! This place could be swarming with Medici guards and you would sleep through it!"

After he took off for the camp, the one guard boasted, "I hate him. I should go slit his throat!"

"You won't have to," the other replied. "Silvio is fuming about his disappearance that he just might do it himself." The lookouts smiled at each other and quickly got to their horses, not wanting to miss that fight.

Less than a quarter of a mile away, Lorrenzo's guards watched through a clearing in the trees. Smiling when Tomasso left with two lookouts following him, the one guard asked, "Lookouts…all the way out here? *Signori*, I think we have found the rest of our conspirators."

Holding their position, they decided it best to wait until dark to pounce on their prey.

"You're all under arrest by order of the Medici!" Tomasso's voice bellowed. Startled from their sleep, the men fumbled for their weapons when Antonio ran to where the commotion was with his sword drawn.

"Are you going to kill me, cousin?" Tomasso grinned.

"Don't tempt me, cousin," Antonio's anger was brimming. "Now where were you?"

"Why so hostile? I'm back. That's all that matters."

"Answer the question," Antonio repeated.

"It's nothing…Medici guards arrested me for trying to steal some old horses."

"Did you see Medici?" Antonio asked.

"Oh of course…the great Medici came to my jail cell and stared at me…angry. He kept asking me about this and that, but I let him know who he was dealing with," he said as the others laughed.

"So, you spoke to Lorrenzo and he let you go just like that?" Ernesto asked.

Tomasso took his sword out of his holster and ran his hand down the long blade. "Yes," he said with a confident grin. "Just like that."

"And did he recognize you?" Ernesto asked.

"What? What are you talking about?"

Stunned, Antonio yelled, "Answer the question! Do you think he recognized you?"

Tomasso backpedaled. "Does it matter? So what if he did…so what? Honestly, I told him who I was. I reminded him when you and I beat him to a pulp…he and his brother. Everyone relax, it doesn't matter. He'll never find us out here," Tomasso assured. "We're safe!"

Ernesto looked distressed. "And what makes you think that?"

Tomasso smirked. "Trust me…all of you. Just trust me."

Shaking his head, Silvio cursed. "My God, Tomasso. Medici let you go intentionally. Do you realize that you probably were followed?"

Tomasso brushed off Silvio's charge, laughing. "Followed? Honestly, do you think I'm that stupid not to realize if I was being followed?" He turned to Antonio immediately, his face stone. "Trust me…I wasn't followed!"

"But you don't know that for sure," Ernesto blurted. "Since you told him who you are, I have to agree with Silvio. He let you go intentionally." Ernesto took a deep breath. "Did he mention me?"

"Sort of," he mumbled.

"Oh my God…what did you say?"

Hanging his head low, Tomasso whispered, "I told him that you send your regards."

"What?" Antonio screamed. "What were you thinking? Is this all a game to you?"

"You put us all in danger," Silvio warned.

"No!" Antonio shot back. "He just dug our graves."

Fioretta waited for the right time. Seeing Silvio head down the path to a small lake, she quickly ran after him.

"Silvio," she said, "May I speak to you about a problem that I'm having?"

"Problem with Ernesto?" the older man asked.

"No…not at all, but when he finds out about it, I fear there will be trouble. I need your advice."

Fioretta respects the older man. Silvio Pacitti was in his sixties. A thin tall man with classic Italian features; strong chin, long nose with silver hair that's slicked back away from his face. Fioretta knows Silvio as a kind, gentle man, very considerate and fair. She's grateful to him, as he was one of the first men who greeted her when she was brought to their hiding place.

"What kind of trouble are you having?"

"How well do you know Lippi?" she asked.

Silvio's voice turned cold. "Lippi? Why? What has he done to you?"

"He's always following me, looking at me. Sometimes I catch him just staring at me. He makes me uncomfortable. If I go anywhere, do anything in the camp, he always has a way of being right in front of me wanting to talk." Lowering her voice to a whisper, she confided, "The other day when the others had gone to Florence, he approached me…scared me is more like it. He asked what I would do if Ernesto died. I asked him if that was a threat. He never replied."

"When he's around me, he usually keeps to himself or he's with Ciro."

"He frightens me! He hides behind trees and shrubs. He watches everything we do…especially ME! I tell you, I'm afraid of that man."

"Well, if it makes you feel better, I don't trust him either. Let me tell you how he wound up here, but first, did Ernesto ever tell you about a man named Jacopo Pazzi?"

"I remember hearing his name," she said.

"Jacopo and his brothers were contacted by envoys of Pope Alexander to bring an end to the Medici rule in Florence. Alexander knew that Medici's boys were going to take over for their father and their views differed from Alexander's. Those two wanted to rid Florence of the church."

"*Signore*," she said quietly, "in case you didn't realize, I was engaged to Giuliano and I knew what he was doing but I was too weak to say anything to anyone."

"It's alright," he whispered, his eyes reassuring. "We stopped them. Well, almost. Lorrenzo is still in power but not for long."

At the end of the path, it opened up to a small lake. Wanting to rest a minute, Silvio sat on a rock as he dipped his hands into the water to wet his brow. "I'm sorry…I must be boring you."

"Not at all, *Signore*. Please, go on."

"Well, I'm an old man as you can see, much older than Jacopo or his brothers. I worked with their father, Vittorio in the vineyards for years. It was hard work but we enjoyed it. We both saved and bought a nice vineyard outside Florence many years ago. It was around that time when that dog, Piero Medici, became the Gonfaloniere of justice in the city. His family history was in the business of banking. They put him in charge and he came on our land and told us if we didn't pay him this new tax, he was going to take our land away. This was no little tax. He tripled it knowing we couldn't afford to pay him. Our soil was the most fertile all around Florence and he wanted it for his family."

"So what happened?"

"What could we do? We gave over our land. His guards…many of them, came with their swords pointed at our hearts. Mine, my wife, my children." Silvio took a deep breath and gazed absently at the water. "It was different for the Pazzi's. It happened on the day when we were leaving our land. We packed what little belongings we had in our wagon and left. Vittorio Pazzi and his three boys, Jacopo, Francesco and Renato were in the fields gleaning whatever grapes they could into sacks.

Vittorio's wife, Rosa, was gathering their belongings. One of Medici's guards, a young man from the country as well, didn't think that she was moving fast enough. Out of anger, he pushed her out the door of their home. Her leg got caught on a piece of wood that had come dislodged on the house and she fell hard to the ground." He remained silent for a moment. "Rosa's neck snapped back when her head smashed into a rock, killing her instantly. She was a beautiful woman. Anyway, when Vittorio came back from the vineyard with his boys, he found Rosa lying dead. In the distance, he saw a Medici guard sitting on his horse watching him. Vittorio went after the man, catching him not far from their home. With the boys watching, the guard cowardly defended himself saying the woman started the trouble. Vittorio accused the man of killing his wife and out of anger, the guard spit on him. Vittorio looked at his boys and told them that their mother was gone because of the Medici. In one swift move, the elder Pazzi removed his sword and plunged it deep into the young guard's chest. 'I curse the Medici family to hell…Death to them all,' is what he screamed till the day that he died.

So, now you can understand Jacopo Pazzi's intense hatred of the Medici family. He and another man named Arturo Bracciolini and others vowed that they would kill the Medici's anyway they could."

"Is Lippi related to the Pazzi's?" she asked.

"That fool?" Silvio laughed. "He and Jacopo fought in the early wars about twenty years ago. Rico Lippi was put under Jacopo's command and the man couldn't do one thing right except get drunk. The man let his wife and children starve, drinking his money away. Jacopo stepped in and had him do work for money but the money was to go to Lippi's family. Jacopo told me about the plan to kill the Medici's and asked if I would help. For their father…for old times' sake…for the death of the Medici's, I agreed. Lippi was outside the church that Sunday. He and Ciro, one of Lippi's relatives, waited in a wagon in case we needed another way to escape. You're the only one who Jacopo got out into that wagon. He told Lippi to get you safely here but as for that fool, I wouldn't trust him one bit. Jacopo isn't here to check on him and he has no loyalty to anyone. I'll keep an eye on him, but Ernesto should know how you feel as well. It will be all right. Let me handle it."

On their way back from the lake, they noticed a lone person coming their way. An uneasy feeling gripped Fioretta as she grabbed onto Silvio's arm.

"Good afternoon, Silvio," Lippi said as he walked by. Stopping for a moment, he turned to look at Fioretta. "And good afternoon to you, *Signorina.*"

She felt herself bristle instantly.

Lippi waited for no reply from her and kept walking until he cleared the lush thickness of the trees toward the water. Silvio and Fioretta stood silent, looking at each other trying to understand Lippi's strange behavior.

Hours later as the sun was just setting, Lippi was at the water's edge. He noticed five men coming through the trees. Being careful not to get caught, he crept into the bushes and snuck up behind the men.

Medici guards, he smiled. Being very quiet, he climbed onto the rocks behind them. "Hello, friends!" he called out. "And who might you strangers be?"

Scrambling to get their weapons, they drew their swords and surrounded the man. Smiling, he put his arms in the air. "My friends…I mean you no harm. Look, you see…I have no weapons."

Knowing exactly who they were, Lippi played along, trying to understand their plan. As he leapt off the rocks, he walked up to the guards with his arms still raised. A single lone guard placed the point of his sword over Lippi's heart. "Who are you and whom do you side with?" the guard commanded.

"Side with, my lord?" he asked. "I side with no one. Please, allow me to introduce myself. My name is Rico Lippi and I am at your service."

"Well, Rico Lippi, in the name of Lord Medici, you are arrested as a conspirator against the Medici's," the guard said.

Lippi shook his head. "Conspirator is such a strong word, don't you agree? I view myself as more of an informer. I assume you are here for those murderous vermin running around the forest?"

"And you are not one of them?" the guard declared, his eyes narrowing with anger.

"*Signore*, you insult me with that accusation, and please point your sword elsewhere."

The guard glanced at the others as he lowered his sword away from Lippi's heart.

Lippi smiled. Clearing his throat, he asked, "Now, do you think I am one of them? Please…I am coming to you in good faith. You are not capturing me; I am here to help you capture them. Trust me…I hate all of them."

A guard stood across from Lippi, looking pale. "Careful, it's a trap! They're probably watching us now through the trees. Draw your weapons, men!"

Lippi cursed quietly as the guards drew their swords as he found himself with the sharp edge of a blade pressing against the soft flesh of his throat.

"Conspirators…come out or else this man dies," a guard shouted. The only sounds that were heard were that of a few birds flying in the air getting ready to nest for the night.

"*Signori*, I told you I am here alone. Even if they were watching, they would have you slit my throat and leave me for the animals because they're a hateful bunch. They hate everybody." Lippi paused a moment. "Can I let you in on a little secret? You men are greatly outnumbered and need me to overtake these…these, animals."

The guards pondered Lippi's words and slowly began to lower their weapons, all except the one on Lippi's throat.

"*Signore*, please, if you don't mind." Lippi put his hand on the edge of the blade and slowly lowered it for the guard. "Now that's so much better…don't you agree?"

"We only came for one!" a guard grumbled. "That's what Lord Medici ordered…just one man."

"One? That's it? Well, that can't be too hard. Tell me, which one are you looking for, maybe I can help?"

"Ernesto Palazzo!" the guard demanded.

Lippi's eyes widened. "Ahhh, yes…Ernesto, the sworn enemy of the Medici, so I've been told." Pondering the guard's order, Lippi made a request of the men. "Perhaps your Lord Medici would be thrilled if instead of one, you come back with ten?"

"Our orders are for one. Palazzo."

"Of course, of course…your orders. But perhaps, if you take me to this Lord Medici of yours----"

"He's your Lord and you will address him as such!" the guard shouted. "He is ruler of Florence!"

"Yes, of course, I apologize, please forgive me. As I was saying…perhaps if I can sway OUR Lord Medici into taking all of these murderers, think how you men will be viewed…heroes! Honestly, if you do what you were commanded, not only will you fail to get Palazzo, but you'll wind up dead as well…cut to ribbons by those killers. It's your decision, my friends." Lippi slowly turned his back on the guards. "I'll just be sitting on those rocks over there until you decide. Oh, and *Signori*, know this…if you say no, I will scream for help and all ten will rush out with their swords drawn and put every last one of you to death! Sad to say…that is a promise."

The guard paused, looking more confused every minute. "*Signore*, I thought you said they hate you?"

"Oh trust me, they do…but it seems they hate the Medici's far more than me. It would be such a pity to see your body parts strewn around this beautiful countryside."

Scratching the stubble on his chin, the guard looked suspiciously at Lippi. "What do you get out of this, *Signore*?" he asked.

"It's not what I get…it's who I get. Live or die, *Signori*. You decide."

Chapter Ten

"What crime have I committed? I demand you release me immediately."

"*Signore* Lippi, we told you before, when Lord Medici has time, he will talk with you," the young guard explained.

"So…I'm to rot in this cell until his greatness decides he's ready to see me?"

A booming voice echoed down the hall. "That is correct, *Signore*. Do you have a problem with that?"

The young guard nervously watched as Lorrenzo came out from the darkness of the hallway. "Unlock the cell," he commanded.

The flustered guard fumbled for the key on the heavy iron ring. "My lord? You're wishing to go in there with this…this criminal?"

Medici's silent gaze quieted the guard as he opened the cell. Slowly, Medici let his eyes trace the outline of the man from head to toe. "You do know who I am?"

Eyes wide, Lippi stared at the man, nodding.

"So, you do know that I am not addressed as 'his greatness,' is that clear?"

Lippi gave him a dubious look.

Lorrenzo pursed his lips. "You are *Signore* Lippi, correct?"

Lippi gazed blankly at the floor. Silent.

"Very well then, I see that I am wasting my time with you. Stay here and rot until you have something to say." Turning away from the man, Lorrenzo stepped outside the cell door and began closing the iron door.

"Can I trust you?" Lippi's asked Medici through the bars.

Lorrenzo turned to face his prisoner. "Trust me? Trust me regarding what?"

"They are going to kill me…I need protection!" Lippi confessed.

"Who? Who is going to kill you?"

Lippi stared at Lorrenzo and couldn't help but smile.

"WHO?" Medici screamed. "Very well…let the people who want to kill you, kill you. If not…then I will."

Lorrenzo slammed the cell door shut, ordering the guard to lock it.

He was almost out of the building when he heard a name…a vile name, echo throughout the cells. "PALAZZO."

Medici stopped. A chill ran through his body. His face red, he turned and briskly walked back to the occupied cell.

"What did you say?" Medici whispered.

"Palazzo…Ernesto Palazzo, my lord. I fear he and his friends are going to kill me."

Medici looked surprised. "Why would he kill you?"

"Because he's a murderer…they all are murderers. I heard what they did. I wasn't in the church that day, but I heard the stories." Putting his face close to the bars, Lippi whispered, "I heard he killed someone!"

"MY BROTHER!" Lorrenzo screamed. "It was my brother he killed!"

"My apologies, my lord. If…if I've struck a nerve, I'm very sorry."

Medici's dark eyes settled on him. "Stop wasting my time, Lippi. What is it that you want?"

"Oh, it's not what I want, my lord…it's what you want. It's what I can give you. The head of Ernesto Palazzo. He and the other murderers as well."

"I don't care about the others. Kill them if you want. I just want Palazzo!"

Lorrenzo looked more troubled now. "Wait…this is too easy. What is it that you really want, Lippi? My men say that you're one of the conspirators against my family."

"Conspirator? Oh, my lord," he chuckled, "you insult my intelligence. I am, what you can call an enterprising man looking just to survive in these tough times." A big grin formed on Lippi's face. "A handful of Florins, my lord. Yes, a handful would be enough and, oh, if I may ask for just one other small token of your generosity, I would greatly appreciate it."

Lorrenzo glanced at Lippi's fake smile. "You will receive your Florins…after I have Palazzo in this cell. He will hang for my brother's murder."

Medici turned and began to walk away, when Lippi cleared his throat loudly, "Ahem…my lord? You seem to have forgotten something."

Lorrenzo never flinched. His eyes were riveted on the stone floor. "I don't believe I have. The coins are what we agreed on."

"Ahh, but my lord, my second request from your generosity of course, will not cost you anything. Let's just say it's… charity."

Medici fumed, "What is it that you want, Lippi?"

"It's WHO I want my lord. Who…I…want."

Medici was stunned. "You want a person? Who is he?"

"She, my lord. It's a she and I believe you know her, quite well at that. The way I've heard it is that she was engaged to your brother."

Lorrenzo Medici was livid, glaring at Lippi in disbelief. "Fioretta?" he gasped. "I haven't seen her in months…since my brother's funeral. Lorrenzo took a menacing step forward, placing his face against the iron bars. "How do you know her?" he growled.

"Oh, she gets around, my lord. As we speak, she is planning to marry Palazzo. My lord, my request is simple. Please, all I ask for is that you don't kill her. After you have Palazzo, I will take her away…with your permission, of course."

"She's a traitorous whore and deserves to die," Medici raged.

"She didn't kill your brother, my lord. Palazzo did. Kill him and end this. Leave the woman for me…I beg of you."

Lorrenzo had no doubt that she wasn't involved in his brother's murder, and yet he sensed another emotion as well. She will take me to Palazzo, raced through his mind.

"Lord Medici." The voice was loud. "My lord, are you down here?"

Lorrenzo felt his teeth clench in rage. "I'm busy!" His tone was sharp.

Medici turned to see Captain Rafael and one of his guards walking briskly down the darkened hallway.

"There you are. You've been down here for a long time. We were getting concerned."

Chapter Ten

Medici ignored Rafael's voice as he turned back to Lippi and nodded his head in agreement. "Take the girl. I don't care if she lives or dies. You will have my guards to take with you." Turning his attention to Rafael, he commanded, "Let the prisoner go. Send eight guards with him. Kill the men. Lippi takes the girl and bring me Palazzo…ALIVE!"

Lippi's eyebrows arched. "Only eight guards? My lord, there are ten men."

Medici's eyes bulged at Lippi's demand. "They're a band of misfits running in the forest! All the real assassins were hung months ago. Palazzo is not a fighter. He never has been. He surprised my brother in that attack before he stabbed him. Trust me, he is not a killer nor are those friends of his. Old men and a few boys don't frighten me, Lippi. Eight guards are all you get. Guard, take Lippi with you upstairs and wait while the captain handpicks his men for this assignment. I want no mistakes. I expect Palazzo to be here in a few days. Understood?"

The fresh-faced young guard nodded his head. As they turned to walk upstairs, Medici held his arm out to stop Rafael.

"My lord? Is there a problem?"

Waiting until the others were gone, Lorrenzo gave his captain strict orders, "I don't want to waste good men on a few lone criminals. Send one good guard for Palazzo. Let him take inexperienced guards with him, like that young one. If they die…too bad."

Rafael took a deep breath. As he started to walk up the steps, Lorrenzo called out one more order. "Rafael, I want Lippi dead. Let him lead us to Palazzo then, I want you to have him killed. He's a liar!"

"We're killing him because he's a liar?" the captain asked.

"No…we cut out liars' tongues…we kill traitors and that's what *Signore* Lippi is...a cowardly traitor. KILL HIM!"

Chapter Eleven

"*Ponta. Ponta*," Silvio instructed. "Like this…thrust...thrust!"

Tomasso's head whipped around. "You want me to charge?"

Silvio moved in closer. "No, I want you to thrust…*ponta*, like this." Silvio demonstrated by lunging forward with a stabbing attack and quickly retracting. "Now try it again. Antonio, I want you to try it as well."

Antonio and Tomasso had been learning the art of fighting from Silvio. From his experiences fighting in the wars, he realized that the young men needed to be able to defend themselves, especially being thrown into the conditions that they've been living in.

Silvio frowned when seeing Ernesto and Fioretta walk across the wheat fields. "What happened to him?" he asked. "There are days when he wants to learn and then he loses interest."

Antonio shrugged. "The Medici's stole everything from him. His life. He's been forced to have people think he was killed. Giuliano had Fioretta fooled into marrying him…it almost worked too, but you're right, it's getting too dangerous. I told Ernesto once before…kill or be killed."

Silvio nodded blankly. "So, the bad blood between the Medici's and Ernesto is really over Fioretta?"

"No…it started when they were young. He and Giuliano were the best of friends but it changed quickly when Giuliano became jealous that people would confuse the two. To him it was an insult how a poor young boy could be confused with the bloodline of the Medici's. They almost killed him a few times, but Tomasso and I were there to help."

Silvio frowned as he listened to Antonio's words. "I wonder when it will end? Apparently, the Medici's have declared war on that young man."

"And the church declared war on the Medici's," Tomasso sighed.

Silvio scowled when his eyes met Tomasso's. "Alright, it's time to get back to training. Tomasso, grab the bow. Let's see if you can hit a target with these arrows."

As the day progressed, Antonio and Tomasso picked up some rudimentary skills of defense used against an enemy. "Watch this!" Tomasso shouted, "I'm going to shoot this arrow straight up to the heavens." Pleased with his new acquired skill, he pulled back hard on the bowstring, releasing it with such force that it sent the arrow sailing high into the sky, losing its sight against the thickening dark clouds.

The four horses pounded their hooves into the dirt, emitting a loud snorting sound. Overlooking the meadows, the Medici guards sat high on their horses, making their way to where the conspirators were hiding. One seasoned man, Flavio Alessi, led the three young inexperienced guards. Alessi, a tall man in his late thirties, had a frightening look with long flowing blond locks. His jaw was set in a hard line and his narrowed eyes were steely blue.

Forming a circle on a high bluff, Rico Lippi sat on his horse next to Alessi. "You are positive that the other four will be close to their camp by that lake?" Alessi asked.

"Trust me," Lippi answered. "We will surround them. If we come in from this side, and the others from the other side of the lake, they won't be expecting a thing."

Alessi gazed up at the frightened look on his young guards' faces as a storm was moving in. Winds whipped through the wheat, swaying it back and forth when a lone arrow soared through the air, finding its mark perfectly, its point buried in the ground not ten feet from them. Terror filled the eyes of the inexperienced guards as they quickly looked for a sign of anyone. After a long moment, their eyes focused in on something bouncing up out of the swaying wheat.

Rain started to fall as Silvio followed the flight of a buzzard soaring low over the fields. Rubbing the stinging rain from his eyes, something strange caught his attention off in the distance. A darkish shape bounced up and down in the light tan wheat stalks coming towards them. Wanting to get a closer look, Silvio cautiously walked in its direction with Antonio and Tomasso following. Reaching a small incline of a hill, Silvio shook his head laughing. "It's Ernesto…it's his hair that we're seeing. It's bouncing up and down."

Standing erect, Silvio followed Ernesto's body running down the hill when suddenly he gasped, "Oh no! Quick, get down."

"What…what is it?" Tomasso whispered.

"It looks like Medici guards," Silvio said as he pointed off to the distance.

Antonio pointed a shaky finger. "Out here in the middle of nowhere? No! I knew it…they followed you Tomasso. They followed you here."

"Keep it down," Silvio cautioned. "Strange, they're not moving. I guess they haven't seen Ernesto."

"This is my fault," Tomasso told the two men. "I'll be right back." Crouching low, Tomasso ran up the hill towards Ernesto. As he closed in on his friend, Tomasso lunged at Ernesto, tackling him to the muddied ground.

"Hey! What are you doing?" Ernesto shouted as a loud thunderclap rocked the fields.

"Shhh…shut your mouth. Medici guards… on the hill, behind you. Stay low and follow me."

On their stomachs, they crawled back through the mud until they reached the others. "Now what?" Tomasso asked.

Silvio never flinched. "We kill them."

"WHAT?" Antonio's hoarse whisper cut the tense silence. "Us? We have to go back and get the others! We can get ----."

Silvio cut him off. "There's no time. Remember what you told me earlier? Kill or be killed? Well, it's us or them." Picking his head up slightly, Silvio took a quick glance. "There are four of them and four of us. We can do this but we don't have much time…they're heading towards us."

Ernesto's eyes grew wider than florins. "Silvio, we…we have no weapons?"

"We have a few swords, a bow with some arrows. That has to be enough," Silvio replied with a brave smile.

Antonio glanced over at Ernesto. "Kill or be killed!" Reaching in his belt sash, he pulled out a small dagger and tossed it to his friend. "You were handy with this before…you need to do it again!"

"Spread the line out!" Flavio Alessi commanded the young guards. Through the driving rain, he scanned the meadows, forming his plan. "That arrow came from down there so take your swords and start swinging at that wheat. Don't think, just swing at anything that moves…slice them to pieces."

One by one, the guards went slowly down the hill, stabbing fiercely into the stalks.

"Look at that…he has guards not much older than you. They've probably never been in a fight," Silvio mumbled.

Looking at his three inexperienced young men, he spoke slow and clear. "Alright, we are going to surprise them. Antonio, you follow me. Tomasso, go get that bow you had and whatever arrows are left. We're going to draw them in close so you can at least hit somewhere on their body with the arrows."

Ernesto gave an uneasy smile. "What about me? What should I do?"

"Yell!" Silvio replied, sensing urgency in Ernesto's eyes, "Yell. I want you to jump up and down, scream, do whatever, but draw them into this area. Antonio and I will hide in the high stalks and when they're on top of us, we'll strike." Silvio wheeled to Tomasso. "Within ten feet, start shooting those arrows…and don't miss!"

Silvio took a deep breath. "We will have one shot at this, so let's make it count. Medici wouldn't send only four guards, so be sure that there are not more in the area."

Silvio's eyes narrowed. "Make sure when you kill a man, get his weapon…we'll need it."

Antonio and Silvio crawled towards the riders. Waiting for them to arrive, Antonio studied the older Silvio. He had killed men. He had killed with weapons and his hands. Can I do that? Can I take another man's life? His heart was beating wildly while these thoughts filled his head. Antonio picked his head up quickly to see. "They're almost here," he whispered.

"Quiet!" Silvio ordered.

The Medici horses slowly made a swath towards them. The nervous guards swung their blades, slicing tops of wheat off cleanly, looking for anything that moved below them.

"Ernesto…get ready!" Silvio said under his breath.

Ernesto nodded his head. His voice trembled under his breath, "One…two…three." Ernesto's blood went cold.

"HERE!" he screamed, jumping up through the stalks. "Over here!"

Led by Alessi, the guards charged towards Ernesto.

A growl of rage ripped from Silvio's throat as he and Antonio lunged up, swinging their swords high and tore their blades into any flesh they saw. Silvio's sword tore into one of the guard's legs pinning him to his saddle. He moved with lightening speed to free his sword and thrust upwards when Tomasso fired an arrow from close range that ripped deep into the guard's back. Trying in vain to pull his sword free, the guard's horse galloped away taking Silvio's trapped sword with it. As he ran for his weapon, the slick, ground prevented Silvio from gaining solid footing, sending him headfirst into the mud. Tomasso warily kept an eye on another guard who came after the defenseless Silvio. From his back looking up, Silvio saw the guard's blade ready to crash down when Tomasso whirled and fired his last arrow that found its mark dead center of the guard's back. His lungs aching, the brave young guard pulled his sword and slid off the horse to kill the weaponless Silvio. The relentless rain pelted both men, making it difficult to see. The guard slowly made his way towards Silvio when Ernesto ran to his aid.

"You don't want him," Ernesto shouted. "I'm Palazzo…I'm the one you want."

The wounded guard looked to his side to see Flavio Alessi nod approvingly. "Kill Palazzo first, then the old man."

The burning in the guard's flesh gave way to the warmth of his blood flowing from his body. Pulling the arrow from his back, he past the prone Silvio and limped angrily towards Ernesto.

"Use the dagger, Ernesto!" Silvio screamed.

Antonio ran towards him. "Ernesto…the dagger I gave you! USE IT!!!"

Ernesto suddenly froze. His eyes were riveted to the blade of his assailant's sword that was coming at him. "Ernesto!" Silvio repeated.

The Medici guard's sword glistened as it sliced through the air in a crisscross direction as he cut off Antonio's path towards Ernesto. With limited knowledge of swordplay, the guard advanced towards Antonio who briefly offered up a silent prayer. With an explosive lunge, he threw his body in a low arch at Antonio, his arm slashing out viciously. The guard was satisfied to hear Antonio scream and see him drop his sword, clutching his lower leg in agony.

The mud made the guard briefly lose his footing as he stumbled backwards momentarily, giving Antonio the seconds he needed to recover and pick up his sword but was only partially standing before the attack was launched again. The guard's blade tore across Antonio's shoulder, ripping his shirt, exposing a fresh gash. Stumbling backwards to the ground, Antonio quickly raised his sword in defense. A smug looked played across the guard's face.

"Wait!" Alessi shouted. Dismounting his horse, he stared down at Tomasso who was scrambling, looking for a weapon.

Walking up to the fallen Antonio, he looked down and snickered. "Tell me, boy, do you really think you can win your little war against the Medici's? You're nothing but commoners…criminals." Sensing the fear in Antonio, the guard laughed coldly. "Before my young pupil runs you through, please allow us the honor of knowing the name of the one he kills."

Chapter Eleven

Antonio suddenly felt his teeth clench in rage. His nails dug into the ground, scooping up a handful of dirt he threw it at the man. Alessi smirked as he slowly paced his way closer towards Antonio. Standing over the prone Antonio, Alessi quickly pierced his leg as Antonio let out a cry of pain. "Stand up and die like a man," Alessi commanded.

Stumbling to his feet, Silvio charged towards Ernesto's direction. Throwing his body into Ernesto, he sent the young man tumbling. While they were on the ground, Silvio grabbed the dagger from Ernesto's hand and quickly got to one knee as the guard charged. In one swift motion, Silvio launched the dagger downwards with all his strength. The guard dropped like a stone, the dagger piercing his throat, killing him instantly.

"He's mine for the kill, *Signore*," the confident guard said.

"You can handle this?"

"Yes…with pleasure."

"Very well. I am going to the lake to re-group with the others. After you finish this one off, these misfits have no more weapons. Kill him then meet up with us there."

Flavio Alessi mounted his horse and watched to see the execution through.

On wobbly knees, Antonio's wounded body painfully held his sword before the guard. The guard quickly snapped his wrist and sent Antonio's sword from his hand, harmlessly falling into the muck. "Is there anything you would like to say before you die?" the guard asked. Suddenly, Antonio dropped to his knees. His eyes only blinked momentarily while off in the distance behind Alessi and the guard, Tomasso pulled the arrow from the body of the guard he had killed and ran to Antonio's defense.

Exhausted and numb from the cold rain, a slow grin creased Antonio's face when he noticed his cousin's eyes look down the sight line of his bow. The guard placed the tip of his sword over Antonio's heart and was ready to plunge the weapon deep into his heart. Undetected, Tomasso pulled back a shaky arm and fired an arrow straight at the young guard, dropping him with the arrow clean through his chest. The spray of blood arched in the air, covering Antonio's face. Antonio grinned when he looked into the guard's eyes. The guard lowered his gaze slowly down to his chest where Tomasso's arrow came cleanly through his body. Still leaning on Antonio, the guard's legs finally gave out, collapsing him into the mud. Quickly, Antonio stumbled to his feet and took the arrow jutting from the guard's chest and tossed it to Tomasso who charged in his direction. A horrified Flavio Alessi froze as he watched. Turning his horse, he kicked in his heels hard, sending the horse into a gallop for help. Tomasso took aim but Alessi was far out of range.

With weary eyes, Silvio pulled the dagger from the dead guard's heart. "Take a good look at his face," Silvio screamed, "next time that will be you!"

He dropped the bloodied knife into Ernesto's hand. He stared at the red liquid dripping off of the knife. He watched in silence as it ran down the handle and pooled neatly into his palm.

"That guard said he was heading for the lake," Silvio recalled. "Pull whatever arrows you can from the dead. We need to warn the others… NOW!"

"The lake? Ernesto asked. "That's where Fioretta was headed. After our walk, she said she was going there."

Silvio growled. "MOVE NOW!"

Chapter Eleven

The rain had let up for a while as Fioretta placed her hands into the water. Swirling her fingers in it, she dabbed some of the cool water against her brow. Sitting back on the water's edge, she smiled, listening to the sounds of birds as they called to each other. Closing her eyes, in the distance she heard water cascading from a small waterfall. Refreshed, she placed her hands back into the water. From her knees, she cupped her hands so water would pool to get a drink. As the ripples in the water got smaller, she looked at herself in the water's reflection. A frown grew at her image. Her beautiful features were showing the signs of stress from hiding in the woods. Fioretta let out a deep sigh as her fingers coursed their way through her hair and eventually across her lips.

Unhappy with her reflection, she frowned, and splashed the palm of her hand back in the water, distorting her reflection. After the ripples had settled, she leaned in for another drink when suddenly she was horrified.

Her screams sent echoes off of the water. Her reflection had taken on a different image. What she saw sent a shock through her body. Turning her head sharply, she screamed, "WHAT ARE YOU DOING HERE?"

Rico Lippi loomed behind Fioretta with an eerie grin on his face. The evil in his eyes frightened her as he licked his finger and slowly ran it across his pasty lips. "*Signorina*, your beauty puts me at a loss for words, but yet, I cannot understand what possibly attracts you to someone like Palazzo?"

"Why are you here?" she hissed. "I want you to leave me alone!"

Lippi's demeanor suddenly changed. "You're in no position to make rules," he shouted. "Shut your mouth or I will take other measures!"

A chill raced through Fioretta's body as loud claps of thunder were rumbling around them.

"Er…Ernesto will…he will be here shortly. He'll be here with others!" she stumbled.

Lippi smiled, scratching his chin. "Really…and how do you know this?"

"I hate you!" she screamed.

"What a shame, my *bella Signorina*." He smiled. "Hate is such an evil word and I hate to be the bearer of bad news, but I feel I should be honest and let you in on a little secret."

"Secret? What secret?"

"Oh well, if you must know. By now, your beloved Ernesto should be in chains getting ready to be handed over to Lord Medici. As for Ernesto's little band of murderers, well let's just say that the guards are rounding them up as we speak. It will be so much fun to watch as they hang from these beautiful trees…snapping their necks in two. Don't you agree?"

"You're a liar!" she protested.

"Am I?" he asked, his scowl deepening. "Your young man is gone and now you're all mine. Lorrenzo Medici has spared your life, but be very careful because I may not!"

Chapter Eleven

Fioretta jumped to her feet when she felt the forceful hands of two men clutching her body. Subduing her, two Medici guards wrapped chains around her wrists and tried to pull her towards the thick covering of trees. She screamed instinctively only to have Lippi's hand cover her mouth, muffling her cries for help.

In desperation, she bit down hard on his hand, allowing a scream for help to get out. The rain became a torrent as the winds howled through the trees.

"That's her voice! That's Fioretta!" Ernesto shouted. Even as he ran through the forest, Ernesto's mind remained focused on rescuing the love of his life. He led the charge through the trees with Silvio, Antonio and Tomasso behind him. They barreled through the clearing of trees in time to see Lippi dragging Fioretta from the water's edge along with four Medici guards.

With the fierce storm raging, Lippi grew fearful seeing the four men charge across the shallow lake after him. "They're the conspirators," he screamed to the guards. "KILL THEM!"

Flavio Alessi's horse arrived in a fury. With a roar he screamed, "You fools! What are you doing?" They recognized the deep, growling voice. The guards spun their heads around quickly to face him and appeared shocked when they realized that he was alone. "Lippi…leave the girl. You men, they're not armed…follow me. We are going to send all of the conspirators to hell."

"NO!!!" Lippi screamed. "Get these men here. Get Palazzo!" The confused guards hurtled their bodies into the lake after them.

Silvio was the first to reach the water's edge. Running into the waist deep water, he raced to the other side where Lippi was holding Fioretta. Having two arrows left, Tomasso quickly placed it on the rest and pulled back hard on the string, taking aim at the lone Medici guard running in front of the line.

The arrow found its home buried deep into the chest of one of the guards. Killing him instantly, he fell face first into the mud.

Tomasso gazed up ahead as a guard took to flight after him. Getting within striking distance, Tomasso saw the determined look in the young man's face coming at him brandishing a sword. His quick eyes darted back and forth at the man, trying to figure out how he was going to take him down.

Tomasso curled his lip and snarled then shouted obscenities at the man who smirked, realizing Tomasso had one arrow but it wasn't on his bow. Swinging his sword high, the guard brought it down towards Tomasso's neck. With lightening speed, Tomasso quickly slid into the mud, winding up beneath the guard. From his sash he pulled out the dagger he had taken from one of the dead guards. In one deep slash, Tomasso cut the guard's hamstring muscle from below. White hot pain surged through his body.

Antonio charged after his cousin. In full stride, he pulled the last knife he had and cocked his arm back high, releasing the weapon that spiraled into the abdomen of the guard. Doubling over in agony, he staggered, bleeding profusely from his wounds until he made it to the water's edge where he fell face first in the water, unresponsive.

As Silvio made it to the shallow side of the lake, Alessi's horse cut him off from getting to Lippi. Jumping off into the knee-deep water, Flavio Alessi stared at the older guard with spewing hatred. "Are you ready to die, old man?"

A growl of rage rose from Silvio's throat. "I'll see you in hell, Medici dog!"

Swinging his sword high, Alessi brought it down towards Silvio's neck but the older man moved quickly to deflect it as metal met metal.

Moving his sword from hand to hand to conserve his energy, Silvio realized that he was being backed up towards deeper water, which would make his movements sluggish. Alessi lashed out viciously with his sword, cutting the older man across his shoulder. The stronger Alessi saw uncertainty in Silvio's face and launched his attack, driving him further back into the water.

Alessi whirled just in time to see the injured Silvio leap at him with a terrifying scream. Knocking the Medici guard backwards into the water, Silvio's fist crashed against the guard's jaw making stars leap before his eyes as he held tightly to his sword and counter punched up hard under Silvio's chin. Silvio dropped his sword in the water and brought his fist up hard against Alessi's nose, once, then twice. The crunch of the bone being shattered was loud as blood spurted over both of them. Silvio kicked out with his foot and knocked the bloodied Alessi off his feet, driving him face first into the water.

"Ernesto!" Fioretta screamed, trying in vain to push Lippi's hand from her mouth. Trying to pull her from the water and back into the forest, Lippi pushed her but the added weight of the chains wrapped around her wrists sent her splashing into the shallow part of the lake.

Seeing Ernesto charging after him, Lippi had seconds to act. He pushed Fioretta down into the water and stepped on her back, submerging the woman. "Palazzo…stop there or she will drown, right here…in front of you! Her blood will be on your hands."

The sound of splashing water turned Lippi's attention away for a moment. Spinning his head, he saw Tomasso and Antonio closing in on him.

"Don't do it. Don't be a hero…you'll kill the girl!" The two immediately stopped. Fioretta struggled to raise her head to the side for air, prompting Ernesto to lunge closer towards Lippi. "Palazzo, I said stop there or you'll be with her in hell."

Fioretta struggled to get air as the gurgling sound was slowing down.

"Let her go, Lippi," Ernesto pleaded, seeing her slowly drowning. "You don't want to kill her…it's me. It's me you want to kill."

After a long moment of holding the three men at bay, Lippi screamed. "Of course I want her. I could care less about you. Medici wants you. He wants you alive, but if you die…even better."

As the three men surrounding Lippi moved in closer, Lippi reached down and placed his hand on the back of Fioretta's neck. He used his full weight to hold her under until the struggling began to cease and air bubbles were no longer rising to the surface. Tomasso knew there were only seconds left before

Fioretta drowned. Her feet thrashed about as water washed over her head and entered her mouth.

"Lippi," Tomasso urged. "There's no way out. Give us the girl and we'll let you live."

"WHAT?" Lippi roared. "LET ME LIVE? Tomasso, you stupid fool…it is you that I will let live…all of you. Now drop your weapons and leave. There's no way you can win against our guards."

"Lippi," Silvio shouted from across the lake. "You don't want to kill her. Let her breathe!" He realized that if he could distract Lippi, one of them would be able to move in and kill him. Trying to buy time to prevent Fioretta from drowning, Silvio again tried to reason. "Lippi, think about it. You want her, don't you?"

Lippi rethought his actions. "Yes…yes I do want her. She will be mine. Do you hear me, Palazzo? She is mine!" He reached down and pulled her up by her hair. She broke through the surface coughing and spluttering but alive.

All eyes turned towards Fioretta as Silvio began walking through the water towards Lippi. Flavio Alessi came up through the water sputtering and gasping for air, his mouth wide open. His lungs burned from the abuse of holding air for so long. Raising his sword in the air, he looked around and saw Silvio walking away. "You should have killed me when you had the chance, old man. Let's end what we started."

Silvio wore a tight smile as he turned to Alessi. "Old?" he sneered. "It seems that I am not that much older than you, *Signore*. Perhaps you would like to try your swordsmanship against this old man then? Well, what do you say? Soldier against soldier."

The loud crack of thunder was overshadowed by Antonio's scream. Pain shot through Antonio's left leg sending him into the mud below. He clenched his teeth and forced himself up to his elbow to look around. He drew a deep breath, shouting. "I thought he was dead!"

Antonio shifted to his side, groaning as he inadvertently drove the arrow deeper into his flesh. He remained still, taking in deep breaths to force down the nausea in his throat and fire in his leg. Tomasso quickly dropped to his knees to pull the arrow from the back of Antonio's leg.

Tomasso looked up to see the guard, with the dagger still protruding from his abdomen, hold up a bow. His hands shaking badly, he loaded another arrow and took aim at both Tomasso and Ernesto. "I have two arrows left," the young guard said in a weak voice. "Now…the two of you will die."

"Very well," Lippi said abruptly. "Things seem to be slanted in our favor so if you don't mind…I will be taking the girl and leaving." Grabbing Fioretta by her hair, he dragged her through the mud to be next to him. "Don't do anything stupid or I will kill you. Make no mistake about that."

"Alessi!" Lippi shouted. "Kill the old man and then I want the heads of those three lopped off and put on stakes for Medici. I don't care what he says…kill Palazzo! KILL THEM ALL!!!"

Lippi's deep, rumbling voice sent shivers down Fioretta's spine. He grabbed the back of Fioretta's hair and lifted high, making eye contact with her. "You little fool," he snarled. "You don't need Palazzo…you need me!"

In desperation, a sudden rage coursed through her veins. As Lippi yanked her hair, whipping her head around, she noticed the dagger that was tucked in the sash of his tunic. While her body was being dragged through the mud, she lifted up the heavy chains wrapped around her wrists and reached for the blade. Fioretta caught Lippi turning away from her when she thrust the dagger with a short, stabbing stroke that went clean into Lippi's foot, severing tendons and breaking bone. Enraged, she lifted the blade high and plunged the knife deep in the top of his foot, pinning him to the ground. As he gasped in shock, Fioretta pulled the dagger out and began hacking at both feet with the weapon, eliciting a string of curses. Feeling a taste of blood run through her body, Fioretta yanked out the knife and quickly thrust her right hand and stabbed at the man, under his tunic where it pierced the soft flesh of his stomach and sank in deep.

Lippi roared in agony. Stunned, Lippi could only stare wordlessly as blood began to bubble from his mouth. Fioretta slowly withdrew the knife as the man teetered but did not fall. Fioretta jumped up and stood directly in front of Lippi's glazed eyes. In a flash, she got behind the man and taking the slack from the chains, she wrapped it around Lippi's throat…pulling hard.

Flavio Alessi slashed wildly with his sword, tearing Silvio's flesh at will. Lunging at him, Silvio back peddled in the water, when a bellow of pent up rage rang from Silvio's mouth, cursing Alessi. With a mighty swing, Silvio's blade sliced a deep gash across Alessi's shoulder. Both proceeded to swing their blades wildly towards each other. Bloodied, Alessi's cold dark eyes, had death written in them.

Silvio looked up just in time to see a sword above his head descend quickly in the direction of his neck. He swung his left arm up hard and the two weapons collided sending Silvio's sword through the air and into the shallow water. Spinning quickly, Silvio frantically used his hands to push water to catch sight of his weapon. Catching sight of it, Silvio turned quickly to retrieve it when Alessi lunged in and thrust his blade deep, piercing his lower back.

Grabbing his side in pain, he put his hand over the hole to stop the flow of blood. "Have you had enough, old man?" Alessi grunted, wiping the spattered blood from his face.

Silvio turned, a frown puckered his brow. "Enough?" he asked. "I'll have had enough when I see you floating dead in this water."

Bloodied and beat up, the older Silvio screamed with rage. "MEDICI!" Suddenly, Alessi froze as his sword lashed out at will, stabbing the guard in both his chest and shoulder. "Medici guards aren't supposed to be this sloppy, are they?" Silvio smirked.

A wave of dizziness swept over Alessi. A quick glance revealed a hole in his chest, close to his heart, that was running red with blood. Alessi clenched his teeth in rage, throwing his body at Silvio, who quickly splashed water into Alessi's face. In one final thrust, Silvio buried his sword into Alessi's gut. The shocked guard dropped to his knees. Blood poured from his wounds as he lowered his head for an honorable death.

Lippi's eyes filled with terror as the chains cut off his air. Choking Lippi, she squeezed until his eyes bulged…until his tongue dangled loosely from his mouth…until his face turned purple.

Desperately trying to get air, he noticed someone standing in the water. With one last gasp, he screamed, "Kill the girl!"

Exhausted, Fioretta pulled back with all her strength, when she heard the crack of Lippi's neck breaking. Fioretta, stained with blood, stood staring at the carnage, her chest heaving with exertion.

From twenty yards away, Tomasso turned in horror to see the young guard who shot the arrow at Antonio. He was standing knee deep in the water, staring down the line of the bow that Tomasso left on the ground. His hands shaking, the guard took aim at Fioretta.

"I should have killed you when I had the chance!" Tomasso shouted.

A weak smile formed on the guard's lips as he pulled the string of the bow back hard, yelling, "Die, you stupid bit—."

From the corner of his eye, Silvio caught sight of a guard ready to fire the arrow. He jerked his head around to see who its target was.

"FIORETTA…NO!!!" he screamed.

Wounded and kneeling in the water, Alessi instinctively grabbed his sword and thrust it deep into Silvio's heart.

Unsteady on his feet, Silvio's eyes slowly filled with tears. He stared down at Alessi, sneering. Silvio lowered his head and watched the water around him turn crimson red. Letting out a heavy sigh, a feeble laugh came from his mouth as Alessi pulled out his sword from Silvio's body. The blade slid out with a gurgle as Silvio slowly slipped to his knees, his dead eyes open and staring until he fell face-first into the muddied water.

The arrow honed in on its target as Tomasso tracked it in its flight. At the last second, he threw his body directly into its path, taking it deep into his chest.

"TOMASSO…NO!!!" Antonio screamed.

Ernesto charged the young guard from behind and used the bloodied knife that Silvio had given him. Mouth open in a silent scream, Ernesto viciously tore into the guard's flesh. Plunging the knife deep into the guard's back with no remorse, Ernesto hacked at the guard until his lifeless body fell forward with a splash.

Chapter Eleven

Stunned, Fioretta released the chains around Lippi's neck. Frantic, she ran through the water to be with Tomasso and gasped when she saw the arrow swaying from Tomasso's chest. Antonio was too stunned to move, looking at his cousin with his eyes wide open. After a long moment, Antonio limped through the mud to get his cousin. He looked down with tears in his eyes at Tomasso's body lying slumped at his feet. Badly wounded, Antonio dropped to his knees besides his cousin. Tomasso's breathing was shallow as Antonio reached in the lake and cupped water from his hands, gently dripping it into his cousin's mouth.

"I'm sorry…I can't see this through with you," Tomasso whispered.

"Be quiet…save your energy," Antonio cried, cradling his cousin's head. "You have to live…do you hear me? You have to live."

Antonio pulled the arrow with a gurgling sound as air rushed through the gaping wound.

Exhausted and numb, Antonio knelt in the water staring at his cousin. From behind, he heard Fioretta scream Tomasso's name. Immediately, she ran to him and began to sob as she gently pressed against his wet, cold body.

Antonio looked into his cousin's eyes and saw his fear. "NO…you can't die!" Antonio's eyes were fixed on Tomasso's as they fluttered.

"Ernesto," Tomasso hoarsely whispered. "I need Ernesto."

Ernesto knelt next to his friend and clutched Tomasso's trembling hand.

"I'm here, Tomasso…I'm here."

"Ernesto," he gasped. "Kill or be killed! Live Ernesto…stay alive."

Ernesto fought off the smothering emotion and pulled himself back to his friend. Looking down, he was hit with the emotional pain that was so fierce…he was about to vomit.

Tomasso looked up and struggled to get his last breath. With every ounce of strength, his breath left his body saying, "Ernesto, stay alive…"

Tomasso's life ended, his eyes open, staring at his three best friends. Ernesto gently ran his fingers across his friend's eyes and closed his eyelids. A raw sob escaped his throat. "No! No!" he screamed. "I hate this place! Do you hear me? I hate it all. I hate the Medici's. I hate all of this…this running. Tomasso died, for what? FOR WHAT?" he shouted. "He's dead. He's dead and I killed him!"

Ernesto's expressive brown eyes narrowed, blazing intense fire. He turned his head and saw Silvio's lifeless body lay still in the water. "We can't keep running like this! It has to end…I have to end it."

Ernesto walked through the murky red water to Silvio's body. He remained silent as he walked past Flavio Alessi, still on his knees, gasping for air. Carefully, Ernesto placed his hands on Silvio's waterlogged coat and began to pull him to dry land.

"Tell me," Alessi's weak voice struggled to say, "was it all worth it?

Ernesto's pulse thundered. Laying Silvio's body carefully on the shore, he stormed over to the guard and dragged his broken body through the water and left him next to Silvio.

Chapter Eleven

Ernesto picked up Silvio's sword and placed it over Alessi's heart. "This is for Silvio…this is for Tomasso!" he screamed.

"What are you doing?" Antonio grumbled. "Leave it alone, Ernesto…It's over! Just leave it alone."

"NO!" Ernesto bellowed. "He needs to pay…THEY ALL NEED TO PAY!"

"Don't you see? We paid…we paid. Isn't it enough now? When is it going to end?"

Ernesto pressed the sword deeper into Alessi's body, bending the blade. "He won't care if I do it!" gasped Ernesto, then he clamped his teeth shut to still his sickening stomach.

"Please," Fioretta moaned. "Ernesto, let it end."

Ernesto finally cried out, "It ends when this scum dies!"

"Then who's next? Antonio shouted. "Who else has to die? You? Fioretta? Me? Where does it stop Ernesto? Please listen. Put the sword down. I beg you."

After a long moment, Ernesto looked down at Alessi. He shook his head and frowned. "They're right. I should kill you right now, but I have a better idea."

Throwing the sword down, Ernesto grabbed Lippi's body and dragged it next to the Alessi's. Grabbing one of the Medici horses by the bridle, he led him to the bodies.

"Ernesto, please," Fioretta urged. "Listen to Antonio. Please, I love you but I can't do this anymore…you can't. It will kill us!"

"Palazzo," Alessi whispered, gasping for air. "Pick that sword back up and finish me off. Let me have my dignity…let me die with honor."

Ernesto was suddenly filled with rage. "Honor? You call this honor? Look at all the dead…where's their dignity? WHERE IS IT?" he screamed. "SHOW IT TO ME!"

Antonio's eyes widened in utter disbelief as Ernesto picked up Alessi's body and placed him into the saddle of the horse. "Have you gone completely mad?" he asked.

Alessi screamed in agony as he slumped forward on the horse's mane.

His eyes glazed over, Ernesto picked up Lippi's body and threw him across the horse's hindquarters.

"What are you doing?" Alessi moaned.

Ernesto turned an icy glare to the guard. "Go back to Medici. Tell him I spared your life. Tell him that Lippi is a gift from me."

"Palazzo," he gasped. "It's a two-day trip to Florence. I'll die along the route!"

"Then I suggest you ride quickly." Ernesto slapped the horse's hindquarters, sending it on its way.

Ernesto watched him fade off into the distance. "Tell him Ernesto Palazzo lives!" he screamed. "Do you hear me? Tell him he lives!"

Chapter Twelve

Kill or be killed. The words replayed constantly in Ernesto's mind. While standing at the water's edge skipping rocks, he replayed each step of those few horrific moments from three weeks ago…the day that Tomasso and Silvio were killed. Silvio was a new friend and teacher, an older man he met after the assassination in Il Duomo. He helped them in these woods, helped to keep peace among the men. He was training others to be able to fight…to defend themselves…to kill or be killed.

Sadly, his thoughts raced of how he first met Tomasso many years ago. They were like brothers, Tomasso, Antonio and himself.

The corners of his lips turned up a bit as a weak smile broke across his face. He recalled how Tomasso and Antonio saved him from being beat up by the Medici brothers on more than one occasion. *Tomasso was always so brave*, he thought to himself…*so impetuous, so hot tempered.* Watching as the rock skipped across the surface of the water, he realized that Tomasso never had a woman to love. He would occasionally talk of some of the girls he found pretty but never experienced a relationship with any of them. *He died too young…too young*, he told himself. *Tomasso wasn't a killer, none of us are.*

Rock in hand, he studied the ripples dance across the surface of the water from the skipping stones. *I'm not a killer, but now I am,* he justified. *I had to. I had to save the others.*

The sun rose quickly over the horizon while Ernesto watched as birds swooped down for a graceful landing on the water. *I've got to get us out of here…end this nightmare for good or we'll all wind up dead.*

His follow through was perfect as the flat rock left his hand and skipped numerous times, dancing across the surface of the water.

"Nice throw," Antonio said, picking up a stone.

"What? Oh…you startled me!" Ernesto grumbled.

"Really?" Antonio sounded surprised. "After what we've been through, I wouldn't think anything could startle you or any of us anymore."

"I suppose," Ernesto nodded watching his friend's rock skip across.

"How is Fioretta? She's been very quiet since that day…too quiet. She doesn't acknowledge me at all."

"I know, she hardly talks to me either. She says only a few words here and there."

"It takes time. You know…healing."

"I don't know. It's different now…she's different. She just seems so distant. I guess we're all going crazy here," Ernesto frowned.

"I can see that," Antonio said. "Do you remember what you said to me not long ago? We'll go hide…go off into the mountains. Start a new life where no one knows us. Remember?"

Ernesto nodded blankly, "Yeah I do, but I never thought we would wind up like this. My God, Antonio, look at us. We're no better than the Pazzi's…the Medici's or whoever. I can't live my life like that. If we did go and hide in the hills, they'll keep coming after us. Medici won't stop. He won't stop till we're all dead. It has to end and I have to be the one to end it."

Antonio's lips turned upward a bit. "I still laugh when I picture you being bullied by the Medici's and then Tomasso punching Giuliano in the nose."

"That seems like a lifetime ago," Ernesto said, thinking back.

"They deserved it," Antonio said. "The Medici's were bullies then and Lorrenzo is a bully today."

Seemingly uninterested, Ernesto picked up another stone and skipped it across to the other side.

Antonio looked at his friend and frowned, "Are you listening to me? They're bullies…all of them."

Oblivious to his words, Ernesto turned to Antonio. "What? Did you say something?"

"Yes I did. I say we do something about the bully."

"We?" Ernesto glanced over.

"Listen to me," Antonio said, "for all of this to end, Lorrenzo needs to die. Either he dies or we will be hunted like dogs. Is that what you want?"

Pointing across the other side of the lake, Ernesto drew a deep breath. "Right over there is where Tomasso and Silvio were killed…"

"And they didn't die in vain," Antonio snapped. "Look, I miss them too, Ernesto! Tomasso was my family…my blood, but we can't bring him or Silvio back." Placing his hand on Ernesto's shoulder, he tried to reason. "Listen to me, Lorrenzo will send more guards to find the ones we killed. Soon, these woods will be filled with them…all looking to hunt us down and kill us."

"No!" Ernesto shouted. "They won't kill us. It's me they want. Eight guards dead? Lippi? Antonio, this is my battle. He wants only me. I will not have blood on your hands any longer. If Medici has to die, then it has to be by my hands alone!"

"He hates all of us," Antonio vehemently protested. "He hates us for what we've done to his family and it never will be over till he rots in hell. Do you understand that?"

Ernesto looked into his friend's eyes. "Antonio, listen to me. I told you before…it's me he hates. It has nothing to do with you or anyone else. This is my fault. Because of jealousy…because of Fioretta, this whole thing started. No, Antonio, no…I will face him alone."

Antonio feigned a laugh. "So what's your plan? Just walk right up to him and kill him? Right in front of all of his guards? They'll hang you the minute they see you!"

"I don't believe that. Yes, Giuliano would. He was hot tempered, but Lorrenzo wasn't like that growing up. He followed his brother's lead. Perhaps if I come to make peace, he'll listen. Antonio, I know this sounds strange, but somehow I feel a connection with him…like he won't hurt me."

"You have you gone mad, haven't you? Ernesto, he'd be satisfied seeing you hang from the city walls. Do you think you're special?"

"No, but I have to try something. I'll never get close enough to kill him, but maybe he'll listen to reason."

"So you're just going to walk right into the city with your hands up in surrender?"

Ernesto arched his eyebrows. "It might be the only way that the rest of you can lead normal lives again."

Staring at his friend in disbelief, he chuckled, "What the hell…might as well die a free man instead of running and hiding. Is that what you think?"

A faint smile broke across Ernesto's face. "It's been too long since I've been free. I would love my life back…Sandro and *Signora* and now Fioretta. I am going to marry Fioretta and I won't have her living like this anymore."

"And if he kills you? What will Fioretta do then?"

Ernesto picked up a beautifully smooth stone and with one quick flick of his wrist, sent it skipping across the water. He looked at Antonio and shrugged his shoulders, "Let's just hope it doesn't come to that."

The two friends spent the rest of the morning skipping stones, discussing their future without Tomasso and talking about the complicated strategy of dealing with Lorrenzo Medici.

"That's impossible, he can't do that!" Lorrenzo roared at his guards. "How…how did it happen?" Annoyed at the blank expression on the faces of his guards, he barked, "I want answers. Get me Captain Rafael…NOW!"

Rafael, the oldest of the Medici guards walked into the palace library dressed in full military attire. For a man of his years, Rafael was handsome and rugged. A thatch of grey hair gave him a very distinguished appearance. Deeply set hazel eyes, a well-shaped nose and big bushy brows rounded out his face. Being in the service of the Medici family for over twenty years, he watched the

Medici brothers grow up. It deeply saddened him when Giuliano was killed in the church but it didn't surprise him that someone would eventually take the younger Medici's life. His arrogance and ill temper was his quick downfall.

From under bushy eyebrows, the captain asked, "Yes, my lord?"

"Rafael, these papers say that Savonarola is thinking of stopping all business trade in Florence. Did you hear about this?"

"Just earlier today, my lord. The merchants have complained to me about it already. Please Lord Medici, remember…act calmly. Don't rile the church because it will just lead to bigger problems."

Lorrenzo's scowl deepened, "Rafael, remember who I am and who they are. I will rile the church…shake it off its very foundations if I must. Nobody makes rules for my city!" he bellowed. "Do you understand?"

The captain's lips tightened into a horizontal line. He remained silent as he remembered Giuliano's intense outbursts.

"So, the merchants are up in arms because Savonarola wants to rid Florence of free trade? Fine. Now this is what I want. Raphael, I want you to send one of your guards to kill him. No! On second thought, I want YOU to cut his heart out and throw it on his own altar!"

"My lord!" Rafael cried. "Think of what you're saying. He's a man of God."

"He's a lying priest and no more! He has no Godlike power. He's out of his mind if he thinks he can dictate to us how we do business here. I am dispatching an envoy to Rome immediately to end this now and if I must…to end him."

Rafael let out an incredulous gasp. "My lord? You're sending someone to talk to Borgia? Think about your actions. Rodrigo Borgia is the biggest criminal ever to be elected Pope."

Unbeknownst to both men, *Signora* Medici was lying down in a nearby room. Trying to nap, she lay on a couch and closed her eyes but she could hear their voices quite clearly. Her brain soon numbed and she drifted into a state somewhere between wakefulness and sleep.

"Lord Medici...please listen to reason. Don't go down the same path Giuliano did. Please! It can only end up in disaster."

"Nonsense!" Lorrenzo scolded his captain. "Rafael, set up a meeting. I want Savonarola out of this city and if it means killing him, so be it. Like my brother, I will not let the church tell me what to do! I want them out as well!"

Signora Medici's eyes snapped open and she lifted her head off a pillow, wondering what words had penetrated her drowsiness enough to startle her. As she listened carefully, the plan she overheard frightened her. She hardly slept and when she did, she awoke many times during the night, horrific dreams plaguing her rest. Would the terrible pain of Giuliano's death ever lessen? After hearing enough, she rose quickly and ran to the next room. "EXCUSE ME?" she screamed, "I cannot believe the words I just overheard. Have you not learned anything from your brother's death? Leave the church alone!"

Lorrenzo's tempered flared. "Mother! Leave here immediately!"

"How dare you speak to me that way?" *Signora* Medici was furious and unleashed her full wrath on her son. "Remember your place. Your father may be dead, but I am the parent and you are the child…it is not the other way around!"

Lorrenzo gave a disgusted snort and mumbled an apology before bowing his head in respect.

Her flash of anger lessened, she turned to Lorrenzo and tried to reason with him. "Don't turn against the church like Giuliano did. God will punish you as well…he'll punish you. Please, please don't. I can't do this again."

Signora Medici turned her attention to the captain. "We won't be needing you any longer this afternoon, captain. Lorrenzo is not going through with these foolish ideas of his. You may leave."

Lorrenzo reddened with fury and leaped up to face his mother. "I make my own decisions! I am in control of Florence, not Savonarola, not the Vatican and definitely not you!" Lips pressed tight in anger, Lorrenzo turned to Rafael and shouted, "This message will be delivered, regardless of what my mother says…do you hear me? I'm tired of the church meddling in my affairs. I don't care who it is, Borgia or whatever he calls himself now…"

Weariness was etched in his mother's face as she stared across the room at her last living son. Her voice was grim. "If your father were alive today, he would slap you across your face, you foolish child!"

"CHILD?" he lashed out. "Mother, leave us. You have no idea what you're talking about."

She sighed heavily. "I beg you…please reconsider your actions."

Chapter Twelve

Lorrenzo turned to Rafael, frustration tightening his voice. "You have your orders. Leave."

Disgusted, her eyes closed into tiny slits. "You have such a hatred for God."

"Oh, it's not God I hate, Mother," he said with a grin. "It's just imposters that want to play God, who I hate."

"God have mercy on your soul, Lorrenzo," she said walking out.

Seeing the frightened look on *Signora* Medici's face, Captain Rafael realized the potential for disaster unfolding before his eyes as he pleaded one last time. "Lord Medici...Lorrenzo, please, I've known you since you were a child. Please reconsider your actions. Please, for your own safety I implore you to think about----"

"Rafael!" he screamed. "You worry about your guards. Let me worry about the Pope." Fumbling through the papers of Savonarola's cease of trade decree, Lorrenzo mumbled, "How dare these hypocrites try and bully me. They will pay. They all will pay for what they've done to my family!"

Hands on his hips, he walked around the library. His eyes were drawn to the many books his father had read about Florence and Rome. His eyes froze when he saw a few books about the church. Shaking his head in disgust, he was startled by the loud voices outside the palace doors. Running out to investigate, Captain Rafael was trying to calm the fears of a frightened guard.

"What is all the commotion about?" Lorrenzo shouted. "Rafael...what's wrong with him?"

"Something has just happened, my lord."

Lorrenzo gritted his teeth, "What now?"

"My old friend, Flavio Alessi. They found him dead!"

"Dead? How?" Lorrenzo hissed.

"Stab wounds. He was found hunched over on his horse. That criminal Lippi is dead as well."

Shocked, Lorrenzo snapped, "Palazzo. It's him…I know it. He's with the others." Glancing over to the captain, he barked, "Rafael, we sent out guards and only one returned…DEAD? Ready your trip to go meet with the Pope." Lorrenzo growled and stormed out of the palace doors shouting, "I'll take care of the others."

Anger was etched in the face of Pope Alexander. "I thought our problem in Florence was going to be fixed. You promised me that you would take care of it. It was simple. You said we'd send two priests to deal with Savonarola and at the same time, get rid of these cursed Medici's, and still nothing… WHY!"

The priests sat upright, their faces drawn. "Your Eminence," the priest sighed. "We have two that are in place and I assure you, they are quite competent in taking care of this small inconvenience."

"Small inconvenience?" Alexander's voice bellowed. "This is no small inconvenience. We have a madman running the church and a pesky young Medici who is hungry for power. That spoiled fool actually sent one of his guards asking me to help him. HELP HIM!!! He wants my help but at the same time, he refuses to acknowledge my right to rule in his beloved Florence." Alexander's pulse raged, "I guess he's learned nothing by the death of his brother. These Medici's don't know how to keep their place."

A frighteningly clever man, Alexander closed his eyes, lowering his voice. "Honestly, I really did like their father, Lord Medici. He was a good man and knew how to show respect for the church and this office, not like his sons."

Alexander raised his eyebrows and sighed. "Savonarola is a thorn in my side. Anywhere I put him, he'll be a thorn in my side. Kill him and I want this Medici problem to go away. Do you understand my words? I want both of them dead and I want it done NOW!"

One of the priests bowed before the chair of his Holiness, assuring him, "Please, Your Eminence, give the men a little longer, they will not fail you."

Alexander's eyes glared down at the men. "Their time is running out and if I see no movement soon, time will be running out for you as well. Do it quickly or both your bodies will wind up in the Tiber river. Understood?"

Cowering before the man, the two priests promised. "It will be taken care of immediately, Your Eminence."

Slumping back in his ornate chair, Alexander dipped his hands into the cool water basin next to him and ran them through his thick long silvering hair. The Petrine Cross, roughly hewn in the back from ancient wood, served as a reminder to him of his position and power. He placed his jaw squarely in his fist as his mind raced of how he will take over Florence.

Hungry for power and wealth, Alexander would take any steps…any means that were necessary to get what he desired. After Florence was transformed to his liking, his papal office would take over cities throughout Italy, doing away with any opposition from its leaders.

The sullen priest entered a small room, his face dripping with sweat. With his silence and dismal stare, another priest took quick notice. "What happened to you?"

As if he'd seen a ghost, the priest picked up a small cup of wine and threw the entire drink down his throat. After wiping his mouth, he looked at the much younger man. "His Holiness, Pope Sixtus was never like this man. This cruel…this power hungry. I miss him."

The naïve, fresh-faced young man who was new to Rome was eager to learn about the deceased Pope. "He died when I was in France studying. What happened?"

In a hushed whisper, the priest confided. "Kind men don't keep the office of His Holiness very long."

"I don't understand."

The priest said under his breath, "Follow me."

A few moments later, they arrived in a dark room, lit only by a few candles. A few cups for wine were left out as well as a small bottle filled with the delicious liquid. Pouring some in the cup, the priest whispered, "Do you want to know how Pope Sixtus died?"

Staring into the flickering candle, he stammered, "I…I thought he was a sickly man."

"Sickly?" he chuckled softly. "No, he wasn't sickly. He was strong and healthy." A warm smile came across his face. "He loved life." He sipped his wine and twirled the stem of the goblet between his fingers.

The gloominess of the room posed fear in the heart of the younger priest as he asked, "And what happened?"

"Murdered," he said in a hushed whisper. He slowly set down his wine glass and turned away slightly to stare at the dancing flames of the candles on the heavy wooden table.

The flickering light played across the young priest's face, emphasizing the look of horror etched across his face. "Who would want to murder the Pope?"

The priest placed his elbows on the table and leaned towards his younger friend. Danger was evident in the tone of his voice. "Rodrigo Borgia."

The younger man's eyebrows rose quickly. His face went ashen. He stared into the eyes of his older counterpart. Making sure that he understood correctly, he silently mouthed, "Borgia?"

Wax dripped further down the sides of the melting candle as the flickering flames began to dwindle. The young man looked down at the cross he wore around his neck and closed his eyes. Terrified, he lowered his head and exhaled deeply. His faith in the church temporarily shaken, he offered up a silent prayer to God, wondering if he was even listening.

A large gathering filled Il Duomo, the largest since the assassination took place. Poised to condemn, Savonarola stood at the grand altar, ready to give his strongest message yet. "God spoke to me again last night. His words were a stinging reminder of what I see every day. All in this city are lovers of money!"

An uproar of voices filled the church, condemning his words.

"Merchants!" he singled out individuals, "your lack of faith in God is tiresome. Must you make secret pacts of business with others instead of trusting in him for your needs? Does he not feed the birds? Does he not take care of the lilies in the field? God hates those who covet riches…who covet money and God hates the way that you are living your lives."

Laughter erupted among many of the people. "Fools! You dare mock God? You question his word?"

"We're not questioning God," their shouts grew louder, "we're questioning YOU!"

A sudden explosion of rage came over Savonarola. "Sinners! All of you will suffer eternal torment from the hands of God." Looking up to the heavens, Savonarola dropped to his knees, screaming, "His anger will blaze against every one of you for your countless greed!"

A torch was quickly pulled from its holder and thrown onto the altar, setting fire to the hand carved wooden chairs that sat behind the elevated pulpit. Sweating profusely, he lashed out at the worshippers. "Starting now, all commerce, trade and places of food and drink will be shut down. Put your faith in the Lord high God and he alone will rescue you."

Screams flooded the huge church as people tried to storm the altar. Savonarola stood defiant, even taunting ones. Afraid of a repeat of the past violence, people raced in all directions looking to escape the church while others wanted death to come to Savonarola. Fearing violence, Fra Domenico da Pescia and Fra

Silvestro stood behind Savonarola, grabbing at his robe to pull him back towards the rear of the pulpit.

Frantically looking for a way to escape, they found a small passageway that led to outside as the violence intensified. The two priests knew they had only a short time left to act. Seeing the madness in his eyes, a deep chill raced through their bodies, agreeing that Savonarola had indeed reached the breaking point…his time was up.

Chapter Thirteen

"Hold him down!" the deep booming voice told the others. His massive calloused hands formed a tight grip around the young man's neck. Terror filled his eyes as the little bit of precious air he had left in his body escaped. In the background, dark ominous shadows approached him.

A single tear formed in the young man's eye, knowing his life would soon end. Suddenly, ghastly, hulking figures dressed in priestly red robes, stood around him in a circle. "Release him!" a loud voice commanded. As soon as the stranger's hands dropped from his neck, the young man gasped desperately for air. Gaining his composure, he discerned his predicament.

Surrounded by a few dimly lit candles, the young man found himself prone on a wood splintered table. To his dismay, a hideously scarred man studied him up and down. With an evil grin, the man produced a long, wicked looking dagger. The gleam off the point of the knife was blinding as the blade angled down on the young man's bare chest. Wiggling the blade a bit, it tore deeper into the young man's skin as a small trickle of blood began to spot.

"Deeper!" the strange voice called out loudly. "I SAID DEEPER"! Pain started mildly at first, then, in an instant, the knife began to borough a deep hole in the stranger's chest. Enduring the pain, the captured soul thought the voice sounded oddly familiar when it screamed, "DO IT NOW!"

Chapter Thirteen

Startled, the man's booming voice was right above him. Coming into focus, a grotesque looking figure was gazing down at him. Bloodied, deep gashes filled the man's face when suddenly, a strange birthmark appeared. "Don't be so surprised. You do remember me, brother, don't you?"

Hatred instantly filled the young man's eyes. Opening his mouth to scream, his voice was hollow. His eyes darted back and forth to see others come into view, all wearing hooded red robes. Their chanting, which began as a low, dulling hum, now escalated into a loud ritual chanting. Their faces guarded, at once their bodies rocked back and forth as if evoking some form of a religious ceremony.

Suddenly, the chanting stopped. An eerily long pause took place with no one making a sound. Slowly, the hideously scarred figure reached inside his robe and pulled out a tattered canvas sack and placed it over his prey's head.

At once, the screams were deafening. "KILL HIM! KILL HIM!"

The knife thrust into his young, muscular chest with intense force. The scarred man grinned as he looked up to the others. In anger, he plunged his hand already holding the knife, deeper into the boy's chest cavity. After a moment, a sucking noise was heard when the sharp weapon was pulled free, allowing air to pour into his chest. Again, the massive hands grabbed the victim and threw his body to the floor with a loud thud. One by one, the hooded men took turns brutally kicking his body, as it lay motionless in a pool of blood.

A roaring fire was started outside as all the hooded men carried their prisoner to the edge of the fire and waited for their orders. Only the crackle of the intense fire was heard, as the prisoner's body was held high over the heads of the men.

Cutting the silence of the night, the scarred man screamed, "THROW HIM IN!"

The young man's lifeless body was tossed into the burning fire. All jeered as his flesh began to smolder. While his flesh was roasting, a few of the men grabbed sticks and poked at the burning body. One stick caught the edge of the canvas shielding the victim's face. In one upward thrust, the stick pulled off the burning canvas.

An older man passing by saw the raging fire and heard the jeering. Curious, he walked closer to investigate. The air was scented with burning flesh as the older man moved closer for a better look. When the smoke began to dissipate, the charred face of the dead man came into view.

Horrified, the old man gasped, "ERNESTO…NO!"

Sandro's terrifying scream filled the room. He bolted upright from his bed in shock. Holding his breath, his eyes darted around the room only to realize that he was alone. Drenched in sweat, his body was filled with rage. Trying to remain calm, his pulse raced uncontrollably as he sat in his bed staring at the walls. His heavy breathing finally slowed down enough so he lay back down in his bed to rest only to be startled by a loud knock on his door.

"Sandro, What is it? What's wrong?" *Signora* screamed. "Sandro…let me in!"

Dragging his body to the door, he turned the lock and the door slowly opened. *Signora*'s eyes traveled up and down his body looking for an injury. Seeing none, a frown appeared on her face. "Sandro, what happened?"

Chapter Thirteen

"Every time I sleep, I see him. I see priests, murderers, I see cruelty… and then I see Giuliano…torturing him…killing him!" Sandro's eyes welled with emotion.

"Giuliano?"

"He murdered him!" Sandro bellowed. "He murdered him and threw his body in that fire, in that pit where we found him. Do you understand what I'm saying? They murdered the boy and I wasn't here to save him."

"How long have you been having these dreams?" she asked.

After a long pause, Sandro stared blankly at the woman. "It's been so long, I'm…I'm really not sure anymore."

"You've lost weight and you seem to be walking funny…bent over a bit. Have you been eating?"

"A little." He reached for the small canvas and a few brushes that he was looking for. "I've been eating a little and sleeping a little."

The woman knew something wasn't right about Sandro's recent behavior. His body seemed to be trembling, his breathing forced.

She watched as he put a few dabs of paint on the canvas. His eyes seemed glazed over and his hands began to shake. "Sandro…are you alright? Sandro?"

"Every night I pray to a God. Not the God of Savonarola…a hateful God, but the one who Sixtus prayed too…a God of love. I pray that he take my life. I ask him every day…take my life. It's my fault that the boy is dead. If I didn't go away…."

His trembling hand stabbed at the canvas, spattering paint all over. Frightened, *Signora* quickly grabbed his arm and helped him back down on his bed while his body jerked violently. Suddenly, she noticed something odd about his face. Rather than his usual smile, Sandro's appearance now was contorted and twisted. "I'm going to get help!" she cried. "Don't you dare die on me. I'll be back soon…I promise!"

After a long moment, his shaking ceased. Sandro's arm dropped to the side of his bed with no mobility. Opening his mouth to get *Signora's* attention, it was empty…his voice had gone silent. Frustrated, Sandro shut his pale eyes and lay very still on the bed.

Signora's expression was grim as she nervously fumbled around getting ready to leave. Frantically, she moved things on a table only to find a canvas buried under rags. Clearing it off, her reddish brown eyes filled with tears. It was a self-portrait with Sandro and Ernesto together. She studied the painting for a moment then gently placed it in his arms. "Sandro, you're not going anywhere. I lost my husband and my son…Ernesto too, but I'm not losing you. Do you hear me? Not now! Please hold on, I'm going to get help."

Chapter Fourteen

Under steel-blade colored skies, the early morning cool mist beaded the green grass like shimmering jewels. The evening fire was dying out when Ernesto watched Fioretta going to the lake to wash.

"It's been a month and you hardly speak to me anymore. You've just been so quiet to everyone."

Avoiding the question, she kept walking towards the water, not saying a word.

"I know you're hurting," Ernesto grumbled. "Tomasso was like a brother…it hurts me too."

"WHAT?" Fioretta spun, her voice angry. "Ernesto, don't you understand what's going on? I killed a man. Do you know what that means? I took a life…a sacred life and God will have me burn in hell for it. He hates me!"

"He doesn't hate you! You defended yourself, and God knows that. Yes, you killed him but it was that or he would have killed you."

Looking incredulous, she exclaimed, "Really? I don't believe Lippi would have killed me."

"None of us trusted him, Fioretta. You said yourself you were frightened of him!"

"That's true…I was frightened of him, but I notice none of you told him that after I expressed to you how I felt."

Ernesto snapped. "He would have eventually killed you, Fioretta! He was a sadistic letch. Lorrenzo was just using him to find us."

Fioretta ignored his response. "I now understand a new word…murderer."

"Fioretta, please listen to your----."

"NO! she yelled, cutting him off. "I'm leaving! I have to get out of here. Get out of this…this, wooded hell. I want to go home, Ernesto. I want both of us to go home. I can't live like this any longer." Outstretching her palms in front of him, she cried, "Take a good look, Ernesto! Do you see my hands? They have blood on them…Lippi's blood."

Frustrated, Ernesto grabbed her shoulders and looked deep into her eyes. "My hand too," he screamed. "I have blood on my hands as well, but I can't worry about that now. Fioretta, I need to get both of us out of here. We need to stop being hunted."

Trembling, she closed her eyes and fell into Ernesto's arms, sobbing, "Ernesto, I'm a murderer…we all are. We're all murderers!" she cried. "You said we were only going to be hiding out here for a while, that's it…just a short time. Look at me! I was never part of this plan…your plan. I feel like I've been kidnapped!"

"Kidnapped?" he said mocking. "What are you talking about? Nobody kidnapped you."

"YOU DID!" she snapped. "You…Antonio and the rest. You promised to save me...promised that we would get married one day, but look at us…we're running for our lives. Is this what you want? Was this part of your great plan?"

"Of course not!" Ernesto's voice softened. "You know it's not."

"Well it's been a month since I…I killed, since you killed and now all we do is stand around looking at each other, waiting for more guards to come and kill us." Fioretta stomped her foot hard into the earth. "I am leaving, with or without you. I used to be happy. WE used to be happy. Even with all the lies that Giuliano said about you, deep down, I knew it wasn't true. All I wanted was to be happy with you, that's all…just to be happy."

His eyes welled with tears. "I promise you, soon, we'll be happy."

"Ernesto, come with me, there's something I want to show you." There was silence between the two of them during their short walk. The small path they were on finally opened up to the edge of the lake. "Every day I come here and every day I cry…every day, Ernesto. It's my fault. It's all my fault…Tomasso, Silvio, Lippi; their blood is on my hands. If I didn't go by myself down here by the water, then they----."

"Stop!" he cut her off. "It wasn't your fault. They knew the risks…we all did." He gazed deeply into her troubled eyes. "I know it's been a month and I promise you, I will get us out of here and we will be married. I made a promise to Tomasso before he died to stay alive, to keep all of us alive and I am keeping that promise to him."

Pulling his dagger from his sash, he cut a narrow strip of cloth from his ragged shirt and took Fioretta's hand. "And the other promise that I am going to keep is this one." Winding the cloth around her finger, his voice was soft, "Fioretta…will you be my wife?"

Tears filled Fioretta's eyes as she stared down at her finger.

"One day I promise you, it will be of solid gold. A beautiful ring."

"No, Ernesto, I love this one. I've wanted to marry you from the first moment I saw you there on the church steps. You were sketching me…do you remember?"

Ernesto nodded blankly, his thoughts going to his teacher. "I wish Sandro could see us…my mother too."

A warm smile engulfed Fioretta's face. "I'm sure you miss her."

"I do. It's funny but I still can remember certain things about my mother. The way she worked hard cleaning other people's houses. Sometimes she would take me with her. I remember at night, I would watch as she wrote letters and then would cry. I thought she wrote to my father but I guess I was wrong. Her death is just a blur to me now. That day when Sandro found me, I had a new start. He became a father to me."

Ernesto's tone turned angry. "When I saw him at the burning, I wanted to run to him, show him that I am alive. Fioretta, he was only a few feet from me. I wanted to scream to him that I'm alive!"

"Then why didn't you?" she snapped back. "He's a grown man."

Ernesto mutely shook his head. "Because, I will not risk his life. He already saved me once and I am not going to be the cause of his death by the hands of Medici."

"Yes, but Lorrenzo hates him too. Don't you remember?"

"Trust me, if it weren't for Lord Medici, I believe Giuliano and Lorrenzo would have killed him already."

Chapter Fourteen

Fioretta's tearful green eyes stared at Ernesto, thinking back at what she had done to him.

After a deep breath, she sighed, "Well, you don't have to worry about Giuliano anymore. I was fooled by his words and caught up in his lies, how you were no good and didn't care for me. How he almost tricked me into marrying him." As tears began to roll down her cheeks, she placed her hand on the side of his face. "You sweet man…I almost cost you your life. No matter what you say, I know in my heart that God will judge me a murderer, but you're safe…you're here with me. Ernesto, please take me away from here. I want to be married."

"We are going to leave here and I am going to end this war with Lorrenzo, not with fighting, nor with killing. There must be some way to avoid more death and destruction. Maybe his father, Lord Medici, will listen to me. If he will, then we will rush to Sandro. It will be like before, you'll see. I promise to make you happy all the days of your life. I can't give you a palace like ----"

"STOP!" she interrupted him. "Ernesto, I don't want any of that. I only want you. Can you ever forgive me?" her trembling soft voice asked.

He smiled. "I already have."

"Thank you."

Confused, he asked, "You're thanking me for what? Forgiving you?"

"Another time…I will tell you another time," she said.

"Why? What does that mean?"

"When we're old with children and grandchildren, then I will tell you."

Savonarola looked at the paintings hanging on the walls of Il Duomo in disgust. The so-called pagan works of art done by Botticelli irritated him every time he glanced towards them. Arrogance, he would say to himself.

Bowing his head in prayer, his eyes noted the now beautiful marble floor that months ago was stained crimson red from blood. His eyes followed the traveling sun as it crept along the floor, creating beautiful designs from the stained glass windows.

Savonarola's sullen eyes rose from the floor to focus on the huge cross hanging directly in front of him. *What do you think of me?* he thought.

A hardness appeared in his eyes. He gazed up at the painful look on the face of Jesus Christ. His jaw was set in a hard line and his narrowed eyes honed in on the eyes of the Christ. *You saw the violence, saw the killings but yet you did nothing!* he thought to himself. Without warning, Savonarola's teeth clenched in rage. "Are you blind or have you ignored everything here?" he screamed, cursing at the statue. Disgusted, he stormed off to go about his preparations for tomorrow morning's Mass.

Behind the grand altar, large black eyes peered at him from behind the huge hanging cross. Da Pescia and Silvestro quickly went in to a small room off to the side.

"Hurry up, open it," Silvestro whispered. "Hurry before he catches us."

Da Pescia chuckled. "The blind fool. He didn't see the pope's messenger leave." Tearing off the papal seal, da Pescia unrolled the letter and carefully examined it and smiled. "Borgia said we must take care of this now! Savonarola and Lorrenzo Medici's time is up."

"It's a good thing that I've saved this lovely gift for a special occasion." Reaching in a small wooden cupboard, hidden way in the back, Silvestro pulled a bottle of wine out and sat it on the table. A sly grin appeared on both their faces as Silvestro pulled out the cork and poured a small amount into a goblet. "This should take care of our problem very quickly." Grabbing the cup, he lifted it and gave it a small swish. "Very powerful, just one swallow…and it's all over."

Da Pescia lowered his voice to a conspiratorial hush. "That Borgia is a frighteningly clever man. Very neat…very clean."

A short time later Savonarola was lighting candles at the altar, offering a silent prayer when he was startled by the echoing voice of Lorrenzo Medici. "SAVONAROLA! I want to talk to you…NOW!" screamed Medici, standing hard on his heels.

Lorrenzo's threatening tone shook the priest away from his thoughts. "Go away!" Savonarola bellowed. "I have no use for you and your rules. God only asks that I obey his rules. Medici…in his eyes, you are nothing but a worker of lawlessness, a fool who he condemns!"

The thunderous echo of footsteps vibrated the church as Lorrenzo charged up the aisle. Drawing his sword, Medici pressed it firmly into Savonarola's back. "I demand you to turn around and face me or I will personally run my blade through your body if I have to."

Savonarola shuddered. He had hoped never to see violence in his Father's house again. "You will what? Kill ME? In my Father's house?" Appalled by Lorrenzo's order, the priest lashed out. "Go home, boy. You and your brother have made it obvious that you don't fear God."

Medici looked at the priest without emotion, shouting, "Who gives you the right to make laws in my city?"

"Your city?" he said in his lowest growl as he slowly walked towards the man. "You are nothing…an insignificant spec. You fool. God is the rightful owner of everything! Can you understand that?" Savonarola turned an icy glare on Medici when he abruptly turned and headed for the small chamber where Fra Domenico da Pescia and Fra Silvestro were.

Medici charged after the priest. "Savonarola!" he screamed. "Don't you walk away from me!"

The brazen priest turned the handle on the heavy wooden door and entered the room, slamming it behind him, surprising the two priests.

Annoyed, he shouted. "What are you both doing? We've plenty to do before tomorrow's Mass."

"Father, we apologize," da Pescia said. "We were just getting the wine ready for the communion tomorrow. I just tasted it and I believe it soured. I was just about to discard it."

"Nonsense!" he growled. "It is a sin to waste. Let me see it." Silvestro held out the goblet of wine when a loud banging on the door startled the priest, making him spill a little of the wine.

"Savonarola, open this door immediately," Medici screamed, pounding both fists on the heavy door. "I command you to open it now!"

Savonarola's scowl deepened as he grabbed the cup from Silvestro's hand. "Will one of you escort that nuisance of a man out of my church?"

Raising the cup to his lips, Silvestro attempted to stop the man. "Father, no it's sour, please, let me----."

"Silence!" Savonarola barked as he pressed the rim to his lips.

Before da Pescia could open the door, Lorrenzo broke through, slamming da Pescia hard to the ground. "Priest!" he screamed.

Startled by Lorrenzo's sudden outburst, Savonarola spilled wine out of the cup before he could swallow any of it.

"Insolent boy! How dare you barge into this holy sanctuary and scream at me! Do you think I'm just an ordinary man that you give orders to?"

Lorrenzo's blood boiled. "You ARE an ordinary man, you fool! Do you think you're special? I will have you thrown into a dungeon cell for your actions."

Silvestro and da Pescia stood in between the two shouting men, protecting Savonarola.

Lorrenzo's broad jaw tightened as he thrust his finger in their faces. "I warned you two before…don't stand in my way. Is that understood?"

Silvestro shot the young ruler an icy stare. "Leave, boy! Leave and take your prideful arrogance with you."

Medici was astonished to see the smug looks on the faces of these godly men.

"You have no love for God," Savonarola joined in. "The only times you came here to worship was when your father was alive!

Both you and your brother thought you could replace God and look what it did for him!"

Lorrenzo's gaze was blood curdling. He forced himself not to run his blade through the priests.

"What's the matter, boy?" Savonarola asked cruelly. "You know I'm right, don't you? Prove yourself a real man of God and come to Mass this Sunday. Imitate your father's example. He was always here."

Without a word, Lorrenzo spun on his heels and walked out of the room, slamming the door behind him.

"Go!" Savonarola shouted. "Go to your big palace…go to your riches but remember what I told you. I expect to see you here in my palace…God's palace."

Silvestro and da Pescia ran out of the room and caught Lorrenzo walking down the long aisle of Il Duomo. They grabbed his arms and forcibly led him from the church. Standing outside on the steps, Lorrenzo screamed. "This is not over! All of you will bow to me before this is over…do you understand? I will be here to prove you wrong."

Silvestro and da Pescia made their way back into the small side room only to find it empty and that the wine had still yet to be tasted by Savonarola.

"This is perfect," Silvestro said. "That fool practically challenged Medici to show up at Mass. They both will drink the wine and----."

"They both will die right here," Da Pescia interrupted. Silvestro scratched the fine stubble on his chin, sneering, "Dying here in the house of his Father? I guess they'll both be closer to God in a few days."

Chapter Fifteen

Lorrenzo stormed through the palace doors, waking his mother from her afternoon nap. Alarmed, she ran to the stairway and saw Lorrenzo run into the library, slamming the heavy doors behind him. His blood boiling, he threw his body down into his father's chair and stared up at a portrait of Lord Medici. He fumed as thoughts of his late father ran through his mind.

After pouring a cup of wine, he took a fast, hard swallow and threw the cup against the painting. "WHY, FATHER?" he screamed. "Why do these…these peasants think they can tell US what to do? Who do these priests think they are?" His cries were so intense, that he failed to hear the creaking as the door to the library opened.

Hunched over in his chair, his face was buried in the palms of his hands. His mother looked her son over up and down with a deliberate slowness. "What is going on?" she asked.

Lorrenzo drew a deep breath. "How did Father do it?" he whispered. Tired, he pulled his hands back and rubbed his weary eyes. "How did he get the city to respect him? I know of people who never liked him but they obeyed him. Why? What's so different about what Giuliano did or what I'm doing?"

Signora Medici sighed and handed her son a new cup of wine. "Drink…it will calm you." Lorrenzo slowly sipped the wine while his mother walked to the window. Looking for the right words to say, her voice was reminiscent. "It wasn't always like that. Your father had many enemies but nothing like it is now. Son, you and your brother did something that your father never did…he never made enemies with the church. He learned that very early on in life. We both learned the proper respect for the church and how far you can push them. Your father and I both loved the church very much and did whatever we could to help expand its power."

"What?" he gasped raising his brow, "expand its power? Mother, why? Why would he do that? We rule Florence, not the church, not the pope or even God!" he protested.

"And that is why they killed your brother!" she cried. "Lorrenzo, don't you see? Our power is limited. Your father played along with the church and in turn, they let us live like this…in this luxury."

"They let us?" he roared. "Mother, listen to yourself. Both you and father are fools who bowed down to these thieves. That's what they are…liars and thieves. I view things differently. We are Medici's and we bow before no one…not even God!"

"Lorrenzo, I beg you, don't make the same mistake your brother made. I will not lose another son. I can't," she sobbed. "Listen to me, son…please. I know Savonarola is dangerous, but he will wind up getting himself killed. Please go along with what the church says, it would be better for all of us."

Lorrenzo's face flooded with fury, his lips pressed into a thin horizontal line. "How dare you say that to me!" he screamed.

Signora Medici was quiet a long moment.

He stared at his mother in silence. Her flawless skin was like pure cream and her dark brown hair cascaded in thick waves flowing down her back. "I want to help you," she said, her eyes pleading with him. "I remember this room like it was yesterday.

You and your brother were so young. Do you remember when we all sat in that corner when *Signore* Botticelli came and painted that portrait for our family?" The woman paused for a moment and sighed, "I hear he is very ill now. I recently spoke to his friend, that older woman *Signora* Mangini. Do you remember her?" Lorrenzo stared hard at the walls, oblivious to his mother's words.

"Well…do you remember her?" she asked again.

"What? Mother, what did you say…who is sick?"

"You know…the artist, Botticelli. That dear man fell ill a short time ago. Even though your father never showed it, he loved him. He considered him a close friend, right up to the day your father died."

Lorrenzo gnashed his teeth in frustration. "Botticelli…a dear man? Close friend? Mother, he found that begging thief Ernesto in the street and took him in and raised him. Don't you remember when he came into our house and stole?" Bolting from his chair, he shouted, "Both Giuliano and I were happy the day that he was banned from this house. He was nothing but trouble. Father said so himself. That fool had us believing that he was dead. Well, I know where he is hiding, so I am going to ----."

"That's enough!" his mother interrupted. "That's your brother you're talking about. Oh, what am I saying? The poor boy is dead! He's dead…it's just so very upsetting."

"What?" Lorrenzo asked, a confused look on his face. "No Mother, you're confused. I'm talking about Ernesto Palazzo, not Giuliano, and he's not----."

Cutting her son off, *Signora* Medici frowned as her voice lowered to a whisper. "I know who you are talking about, son…please sit down. There are some things that you need to know."

Signora Medici sighed heavily and Lorrenzo could see the tears glistening in her eyes. Her words were hesitant. "Your father never knew this, but I had found some letters that he kept hidden in one of his books in this very room. It was love letters from a woman named Eugenia Palazzo."

Lorrenzo was dumbfounded. "Palazzo?"

Her lips pursed thinly. "Earlier in our marriage, your father had fallen in love with a younger girl from the village." The words stuck in her throat, realizing that the painful memories still haunt her, "He had kept their secret affair from me and right up to his death, he was unaware that I knew anything about it."

Lorrenzo winced slightly. "I don't believe it! Father was an honorable man."

"It's true, Son. As much as I hate to admit it…it's all true."

Lorrenzo's heart sunk. "But why didn't you say anything to him?"

"I'm not sure. Fear maybe? Embarrassment?" Re-thinking her past, she reluctantly admitted, "I guess both. This young girl was with child…his child. He was scared and I saw how it changed him even by the way he treated me. I feared the worst and I had my suspicions. I knew something was wrong and then I found the letter that explained it all."

Lorrenzo took a few deep breaths, struggling for control over his emotions. He realized that he had been hunting his own brother for months. He thought back to that day at Il Duomo when the so-called ghost of Ernesto Palazzo stabbed Giuliano in the heart, killing him…or so he thought. A churning developed in his stomach as he remembered years earlier when he and Giuliano tried to kill the smaller Ernesto. His heart pounding, he let out his breath and whispered, "Are you sure that this is all true? Ernesto really is my brother?"

Pouring herself a small cup of wine, she sighed and closed her eyes for a moment, recalling memories from long ago, "The day that *Signore* Botticelli brought him into this house, I knew exactly who he was. He and Giuliano were almost twins. It was too much of a coincidence and as soon as I heard his name, I knew it was your father's son." She sighed again. "I guess the guilt was too much for your father to bear. After the boy was accused of stealing your father's ring, *Signore* Botticelli was ordered never to bring him back into this house again. It must have pained your father to do that, but the fear of embarrassment for our family, our friends and yes, the church would have tore our family apart." From a desk in the room, she pulled a small stack of papers and held them out. Lorrenzo's eyes dropped to the wrinkled and torn letters in her hand as he raised his eyes to meet her gaze again.

Signora Medici sniffed back tears. "This is difficult for both of us."

Lorrenzo studied the pain on his mother's face. He knew these memories must be painful for her to recall. Drying her eyes, she finally spoke again. "After that, your father never saw the woman again. I never let on that I knew, but he had to live with the pain of not being able to treat his third son, Ernesto, like both you and Giuliano. When he was killed, it took a part of your father's life as well. It was right after that when his sickness took a turn for the worse." She drew a shuddering breath, "That poor boy. I hope he didn't suffer much."

Lorrenzo's mind was reeling. "He's not dead, Mother!" he blurted. Without waiting for a response, his voice was louder now. "He's alive. Ernesto is alive!"

"Alive? No, Son…you're mistaken. His body was burned by those killers."

"No, he tricked us into believing that he was dead. I know men who have seen him…they swear that it's him, and," shamefully lowering his head, Lorrenzo took a deep breath. "Mother, I must tell you something. Those killers were ordered to do so by Giuliano and myself."

Shocked, she screamed, "WHAT? What are you saying?"

Lorrenzo remained silent, his eyes glued to the floor.

"Lorrenzo…speak to me!"

"We wanted him dead!" he shouted.

Grabbing her son's hands, she pleaded with him, "Please…please go to the church. Confess your sins to God and leave this whole thing in his hands. I don't want to lose another child. Please, go and ask God for forgiveness."

His mother looked at her son and hesitated for a long time. Despite her churning emotions, she quietly left the room leaving Lorrenzo alone with his thoughts. After a long moment, he shook his head miserably and sat in his chair, his forehead in his hands. Lorrenzo's hands began to shake as he stared out the window, more frightened than he had ever been in his life.

In the emptiness of the room, memories of young Ernesto, running and playing with him and Giuliano flashed before him. Hearing the sounds of children laughing, he rose from his chair to look out the window. Gazing out into the fields, he saw no one. Turning sharply, he looked around the room as he heard the sounds of children running around him. His hands rubbed his swollen reddish eyes as he sat back down into his chair, brooding.

The sounds of children's laughter would not leave his mind.

Chapter Sixteen

Lorrenzo stirred in his bed as the morning sun streamed in through his window, stirring him awake. His brain still numbed from sleep didn't want to leave the warmth of his bed but he knew what he had to do.

Lorrenzo arrived at the jail early looking for Captain Rafael. Climbing up the ancient stone steps, he grimaced slightly from the injuries he suffered months ago. He sighed heavily as he walked into the small office of the prison.

Rafael noticed the grim look on Lorrenzo's face. "What's wrong, my lord? It looks like you lost your best friend."

Ignoring his comment, Lorrenzo walked past the captain.

"My lord…what is it?"

Lorrenzo addressed him in a pained voice, "Something has happened. I'm troubled, Rafael. Deeply troubled."

"Troubled? Over what?" The captain suddenly broke out in a sly smile. "Oh, I know, it's a woman, isn't it?"

"No," Lorrenzo shook his head. "It's not a woman…it's something more troubling."

The captain laughed, "Something more troubling than women? I didn't think there was such a thing."

Sadness filled Lorrenzo's eyes. "I heard some news about Ernesto Palazzo that is very troubling to me."

"Palazzo?" the captain gasped. "What in God's name is this all about? When we find that scum, I will personally run him through myself."

Chapter Sixteen

Lorrenzo turned a glare on his captain that made Rafael's blood chill. "Why would you say such a thing? Never repeat that again! Is that understood, captain? NEVER!"

Rafael simply stared in amazement as Lorrenzo barked orders at him. "My lord," his voice apologetic, "what's wrong? You and your own brother hated Palazzo! Both of you taught all the guards to hate him. I'm sorry but what changed?"

Lorrenzo could not meet his captain's eyes. "My brother, Giuliano, is dead," he mumbled. "He is no longer in charge. You take your orders from me, is that clear Captain Rafael?"

Rafael shuddered as Lorrenzo's eyes bore down on him. An awkward silence hung in the air.

Turning to his guards, he shouted, "Do you all understand that as well? There will be no more talk about Ernesto Palazzo. No more hate; no more violence. Wherever he is…if he's even still alive, let the man go and live his life in peace."

"And what of my men?" Rafael asked annoyed.

Confused, Lorrenzo had tears forming in his eyes. "What men?"

"My men whom we sent out to go chase that horse thief. Remember? They never came back. Flavio Alessi, do you remember him…found dead slumped over his horse outside the city gates! Do you remember, my lord?" the captain snapped. "Where's their justice? I assume they're all dead. Who will answer for the crimes committed against them? My men…your men?"

Lorrenzo briefly met Rafael's eyes then turned and walked down the corridor, out of the building. Wide-eyed, Rafael threw his sword to the floor in disgust, cursing the Medici name. He felt the sickening taste of bile rise in his throat.

Signora Mangini's voice was breathless as she hurried into the room. "Look what I bought for you at the market." She studied Sandro's face as he looked at the new world that was before him…a new twisted, lopsided world that he doesn't understand.

The contorted expression on his face saddened *Signora* as the words thank you tried to form out of his mouth.

"Sandro, look…look at the beautiful scenery that the artist painted. It's almost identical to your style."

It pained the woman to see her friend's health deteriorate. She had known Sandro to be so full of life. She held her breath as Sandro painstakingly lifted up his arm, moving his fingers over the painting to feel the paint daub textures. She let out her breath slowly and whispered, "Look, Sandro. Look at the sky, the different colors of blue. Just like you used to do, just like you taught Ernesto."

Sandro produced a weak smile and closed his eyes, remembering the past.

"I saw your friend, *Signore* Solasso. He said hello and will visit you soon. He prays you that get better. Everyone does, Sandro. Everybody misses you."

Opening his eyes, he stared at the painting. Concentrating, Sandro groaned and blinked, trying to form words.

"What's wrong, Alessandro? What do you need?"

Sandro's mind was reeling but his words were pained…deliberate.

Slowly, each word came out of his mouth. "Who...pain...ted? Who...pain...ted pic...ture----?" Getting impatient, he complained louder. "Who...pain...ted?"

"Hold on." Curiously, she looked for the artist's name. "Here it is." She let out a slight gasp. "M. Giordano. Didn't you tell me that you taught a woman named Maria...in Rome?"

He wanted to jump from his seat. To laugh, to cry and to celebrate, but his body would not cooperate. His eyes would not leave the canvas.

"That's her, isn't it? That's your Maria!" she whispered in his ear.

His head nodded slightly. "She...she." He stopped to formulate his words.

"She? She what?" *Signora* asked. "Sandro, look at me...she what?"

He sighed heavily and closing his eyes. He whispered, "Love."

Chapter Seventeen

The brilliant yolk-colored Tuscan sun rose high above the sloping hills. Roberto and Isabella Gorini brought their carriage to a halt at the orders of the guards manning the city gates. Remembering months ago when he went out into the forest at night, Roberto felt a chill run down his spine as he remembered the guard's face.

"Name?" the gruff voice asked.

"Gorini…*Signore*, we are just ----."

"What is your business outside the city, *Signore*…?" The guard studied the Roberto's face. "*Signore* Gorini, isn't it?" he asked.

"Yes…yes, that's correct. Umm, we have no business, my friend. Just a ride through the countryside with my wife, to enjoy this beautiful day."

"And I assume you will be returning in a few hours?" the guard asked suspiciously.

Gorini nodded his head, trying in vain to not look nervous. "I…I…" The words stalled in his throat. "I suppose so."

"*Signore* Gorini, I remember your name. Months ago, our ledger of who comes and goes was very interesting. It said that you rode out into the forest in the dead of night. I wasn't on watch that night but I wondered why it took you a whole day and night to get what you went out for. I find that rather odd, *Signore*. Do you agree?"

Horrified, Isabella listened to the guard's interrogation of her husband.

Chapter Seventeen

"It really is a simple explanation," Roberto quickly reasoned. "It was so dark when I left that I got lost. Yes…I got lost only a few miles from here."

"Lost?" the guard sarcastically asked. "Hmmm, I find that hard to believe. I mean you, a successful businessman here in the city. You've probably been out of these gates hundreds of times. Did you always get lost in the past, *Signore*?"

Laughing, Roberto slapped the palms of his hands on his knees. "Old age, I guess."

"I don't trust you, *Signore*. I didn't when I read that report months ago and I still do not trust you now."

Roberto's quick eyes darted back and forth between the two guards. Beads of sweat formed on his brow caused by the intense stare of the guard.

"Are you nervous? You seem frightened, *Signore*. Are you perhaps hiding something from us?"

Clearing his throat, Roberto stumbled over his words, "What? Umm, no…no, of course not, I have nothing of which to be fearful."

"I didn't ask you if you were fearful…I asked if you were hiding something."

Sensing trouble, Isabella moaned, "Roberto, my head is throbbing, please take me home." Forced tears began to flow down her reddish cheeks. "I do not want to go for a ride through the forest. Another time, but not now!" She dropped her head into the palms of her hands and sobbed uncontrollably.

Annoyed, the guards looked on with unsympathetic eyes.

Quickly, Roberto's voice turned strong. "May we please leave? You seemed to upset my wife. I must take her home immediately."

"You leave when we tell you to leave!" the guard barked. Studying the ledger that he grabbed from the other guard, he stared at it for several minutes, running his fingers through the grayish unkempt hair on his beard. "*Signore* Gorini, did you know that a few months ago we sent out a small group of guards and none returned alive. One man, a friend of mine, was the lone guard who tried to make his way back here. He died along the way. I was standing on these very walls when I saw his horse approach. It was his horse that stopped in front of the gates. I ran down to help him, but he was dead…slumped over the horse's mane."

Roberto gulped down hard, not looking away from the man.

"He was my friend, *Signore*…my friend. You don't happen to have any information about what happened or who could have killed him and the others, do you?"

Shocked, Gorini fired back. "Of course not. I protest, *Signore*. Please allow my wife and myself to go home…I insist."

"You insist? the guard asked callously. "You don't make demands, my friend. Keep up your rude behavior and you will find yourself behind a set of iron bars. Understood?" The guard's eyes sported a reddish tinge in them as his anger was reaching a boiling point. "Gorini? Hmmm, you had a daughter named Fioretta, didn't you?"

"YOU FOOL!" Roberto screamed. "She's dead, do you hear me? DEAD! Killed in this city. Her body, crushed and broken…damn you for bringing the memory of that day back!" he fumed. "Now, if you please, my wife is ill and I am taking her home."

"Your daughter is dead you say? Please, tell me more *Signore* because this really is quite interesting."

Roberto turned glassy eyes on the guard and whispered, "What do you want from me?"

"*Signore* Gorini, do you realize that we have an eyewitness that has seen your daughter with the very criminals who killed Giuliano Medici and attempted to kill his brother Lorrenzo? Would you like to keep talking?"

Roberto's scowl deepened. "Perhaps you are mistaken."

"Perhaps it is you who are mistaken, *Signore.* She is not only living with these killers, but she is with the killer of Giuliano Medici…Ernesto Palazzo!"

"I don't believe you!" screamed Isabella, tears flowing from her eyes. "She's dead. I saw her bloodied body. Please, *Signore*…I beg you. Please let me go home!"

Ignoring her words, the guard grinned broadly. "We are going to hang each and every one of them…including your daughter! Hang them from the city walls." The guard's pulse was thundering. "Go home…both of you! You are forbidden to leave the city. Is that understood?"

Roberto's darkened eyes settled on the guard. Clenching his lips in defiance, he grabbed the reigns of his horse, shouting as they sped away from the city gates back to their home.

The guard drew a deep breath. "If they try to leave again, let them."

"Let them?" the other guard hesitated slightly.

"Yes, let them. Then your orders are to follow them and when you're far enough away from the gates, I want you to kill them."

"The woman too?"

A brief smile fitted across the guard's face. "KILL THEM BOTH!"

Chapter Eighteen

Lorrenzo felt a sudden and unexpected weariness as he finished dressing for something that he hadn't done since the murders at Il Duomo months ago, attend Savonarola's Sunday service. While he was adjusting his jacket, he thought, to live my father's life shall be my destiny. It will be a never-ending road but I know that I can do it. Looking up to the heavens, he whispered to his deceased father. "Please, help me. Give me the strength and courage that you had."

Knowing that the advice given to him by his mother was sound, he was determined to try to be more like his father and make peace with the church. Lorrenzo gave a heavy sigh and looked back into the mirror. "Today," he muttered, "I'll give my allegiance to the church." A cold chill raced through his body as the family carriage came to a halt in front of the enormous church. Looking up, he anxiously wiped the sweat off of his brow. Letting his mother and his sisters out of the carriage, he did the same, slowly placing his feet to the ground. A sickening feeling rose from the pit of his stomach as his knees began to wobble. His memories raced to Giuliano, bleeding to death on the floor, his body cut to ribbons. His leg, still hurting from the attempt on his life, weighed heavily as he dragged his body up the stairs.

Reliving the horror of that day with each step, the pain from his wounds suffered in this very building screamed through his body. With his family already inside, Lorrenzo finally reached the top step but stood paralyzed in fear. His eyes slowly adjusted to the darkness inside the church as the heaviness of the thick, grayish smoke, hung like a cloud that was tinged with incense.

"Shall I take you to your seat, Lord Medici?" the young guard asked. Lorrenzo never heard the man as the loud singing of the choir disoriented him. "Umm, excuse me…Lord Medici…your seat?"

Lorrenzo shot an angry glare at the persistent young guard. "What? Umm, no…leave me. Leave me alone!"

Walking beneath the ancient stone archway, the frightened Lorrenzo walked down the long aisle of Il Duomo, carefully looking around him for signs of danger.

When the choir finished singing, Savonarola rose and nodded to Fra Silvestro and Fra da Pescia.

Paralyzed in fear, a cold sweat came over Lorrenzo while violent images of the assassination reappeared in his mind. Worshippers in Il Duomo whispered to each other, growing fearful as the young Medici stood frozen in the aisle, shaking from fear. His heart pounding, Lorrenzo raised his arms high, grasping in the air. Horrific flashbacks haunted him as he suddenly reached to his side and screamed, "GIULIANO!!! Don't do it…don't follow him!"

"Lord Medici," the incensed Savonarola shouted, "sit down and be quiet."

Lorrenzo's eyes met the priest's. He took a few deep breaths, struggling for control of his emotions, and then suddenly, his hearing went silent. He shook his head and put his hands to his ears but nothing helped. His eyes watched Savonarola motioning, but no sound followed. Frightened, he turned to see all sitting in the pews staring at him in bewilderment. His head quickly darted to the spot where he saw his brother get a dagger plunged into his heart. Was it Ernesto, his half brother that plunged the dagger deep into Giuliano's heart? Hallucinations plagued Lorrenzo as he saw one of the assassins charge Giuliano's lifeless body, hacking him to pieces with his sword.

Seeing the confusion in her son, *Signora* Medici left her pew and ran down the aisle to help him. Reaching his side, her face reflected a mixture of fear and confusion. "Lorrenzo, I don't understand. What's wrong?" Her words strangled in her throat as she watched her son tremble. "Lorrenzo…look at me!" she screamed.

Lorrenzo's chest heaved with anger and his breath was ragged in her ear. Trying to grab hold of her son, he growled. "Don't touch me, Mother. Help Giuliano…he's hurt, Mother. Help him!"

The loud, booming voice froze everyone momentarily in panic. "Young man," Savonarola screamed, "SIT DOWN OR LEAVE! *Signora* Medici, I insist, control your son or get him out of my house!"

Lucrezia Medici's head snapped sharply towards the altar. "YOUR HOUSE?" she screamed back. "Father Savonarola, shut your mouth!" Looking back at her son, she pleaded, "Lorrenzo…Lorrenzo…can you hear me?"

After a long moment, Lorrenzo shook his head and was gasping for air. His mouth wide open and his eyes squeezed shut he mumbled, "What am I doing? Where am I?" He was too stunned to move and his head whipped around to see all in the church staring at him. "I have to get out of here. I'm sorry, Mother, but I can't do this."

Seeing what was happening, Silvestro leaned over to da Pescia whispering, "We'll have to get Medici at a later time, but Savonarola will die today."

Da Pescia swallowed hard and nodded. "But Borgia wants both of them dead…NOW!"

Lorrenzo quickly broke free from his mother's grip and moved swiftly down the aisle to leave.

Savonarola boasted loudly, "I knew it. I knew he wouldn't have the courage to let go of his pride." Disgusted, he screamed so all could hear. "Haughtiness! That's what you display, Medici. Haughtiness. You are a foolish young man who gives himself the title Lord Medici." Rage fueled Savonarola's words, pointing his finger at the Medici. "Go on home, boy. Go home unless you have the courage to kneel before me, the mouthpiece of God!"

Distraught, Lorrenzo ignored his voice and continued walking towards the doors.

"I am talking to you, Medici!" Savonarola screamed. "You're not fit to be a Medici! You are weak-minded…a disgrace to your family."

Lorrenzo stopped right at the door and spun quickly on his heels. "What in God's name do you want of me?" he cried out.

"I want you to come back here. I want you to worship me! Come here and bow before me as you would bow before God himself!"

Lorrenzo groaned in revulsion. "You're not God…you're not fit to wear that collar!"

"No…you're wrong, boy. I AM GOD!!! I am God on earth and you will do as I say." His pulse thundering, he shouted, "What a pity…you're not a man like your father was. You are nothing but a spoiled little boy, running away from your problems. At least your brother Giuliano had the courage to stand up to me, not hide."

Lorrenzo's scowl deepened, screaming, "LIAR! You have no idea what you are talking about."

Hobbling on badly injured legs, Lorrenzo made his way to the altar.

"Come…come up here," Savonarola taunted. "Come up here and drink of the blood of Christ and show your submission to me, your God here on earth…to this church where I reside and show it to God Almighty in the heavens himself." Sweat dripped from Savonarola's grossly contorted face. "Make your choice, boy. Make it known before all here today! Let them be witnesses of your submission to me."

"I show no submission to you, Savonarola," Lorrenzo said, standing at the foot of the altar. "I only show submission to God!"

Savonarola paused, raising his eyebrows. "All here today take note. You are witnesses to the actions of the cowardly Lord Medici. I ask all here today…is he your ruler? A man who won't even humble himself in the house of God and take the blood of Jesus Christ into his body!"

Lorrenzo's teeth clenched in rage as Savonarola challenged, "Medici…are you greater than Jesus Christ? Are you greater than God Almighty?"

"Savonarola, I command you to stop this immediately!" *Signora* Medici's voice screamed. "Enough of your hatred against my family!"

"Quiet, woman! You command no one! This coward came from your womb."

Lorrenzo bristled instantly. "I will kill you, priest!" he roared.

"Good! Yes, very good," Savonarola sneered, his darkened hateful eyes settling in on the Medici. "That's right, boy…come to me, come here, my son. Show your submission to me. Give obeisance to me and I will forgive you…I will give you life!"

Outraged, Lorrenzo hobbled onto the altar, passing both Fra Silvestro and Fra da Pescia and stood before the crazed priest. Drawing his sword, he placed the tip over Savonarola's heart. "I'll kill you right here. I'll butcher you just like my brother was butchered here!" Medici threatened.

"Good," the priest roared. "You obeyed. First, seal your place in heaven by drinking after me this cup containing the blood of Christ." Raising the cup to his lips, Savonarola was taken back when Lorrenzo abruptly snatched the cup away from the priest's mouth.

"The only place you'll be going to is a fiery hell. Do you understand me, priest…to hell." With the sword still pressed firmly into Savonarola's chest, Lorrenzo raised the cup to his lips and quickly gulped down the wine. Licking his lips, he threw the cup to the ground and with the sword still in place, he lunged at Savonarola, his outstretched hand clutching the priest's neck, choking him in front of the horrified churchgoers.

After a moment, Medici dropped his sword and wrapped both his hands tightly around Savonarola's neck, dropping the struggling priest to his knees gasping for air. "You hypocrite! I want you to die like my brother did. Do you hear me? Like Giuliano did, in front of all these witnesses...here, in God's house."

Within seconds, a sharp pain ran through Lorrenzo's body. Intense heat began to course through his veins. His vision faltered as his limbs went numb. He released his grip on Savonarola's neck who fell hard to the floor with a sickening thud, gasping for air.

Savonarola was struggling to fill his lungs back up with air when he heard a sinister laugh come from behind. Spinning his head, he saw Silvestro and da Pescia smiling, gloating in their victory. "Say farewell to the Medici," Silvestro laughed coldly.

"What have you done?" Savonarola hissed. "You committed this…this vile act of murder in my Father's house? You are supposed to be men of God!" he screamed. Hearing Lorrenzo's horrible scream of anguish, his eyes were drawn to the young man staggering about. Savonarola felt anger boil in his stomach seeing what was happening. He dropped his chin and squeezed his eyes shut. Before long his shoulders heaved with the sobs that rose unhindered from his chest.

The young Medici's body lurched back and forth, desperately trying to get off of the altar. Falling off of the edge onto the cold hard floor, Lorrenzo painfully picked himself up, the intense pain making him vomit violently. Dropping to his knees, he saw the horrified look on his mother's face as she ran towards him. She knelt next to him and cradled his shaking body. Tearing a piece of material from her dress, she wiped the sweat that was running into his eyes. Tears of pain ran down his face as he whispered,

"Don't let it take me, Mother…I don't want to die…not here," he grimaced.

Lorrenzo's body convulsed violently as he lay on the ground, his limbs jerking back and forth.

Frozen in fear, Savonarola watched in horror as the Medici, like his brother months ago, was dying before his eyes.

"Damn you people!" *Signora* Medici screamed hysterically. "Do you hate us that much? Damn you!"

A stiff breeze blew in from the open doors, rustling past Lorrenzo as he lay motionless on the cold floor, his life beginning to fade. *Signora* Medici cradled her son in her arms, watching his eyes flutter a few times until his breathing halted. His body stopped shaking, as his lifeless eyes remained open, staring at his mother. A loud wail came forcibly up from her stomach into her throat, echoing throughout the crowded church. From her knees, she rocked her son's lifeless body in her arms, protecting him from the onlookers who tried to help.

Raising her eyes from her son's body, she focused in on Savonarola. She found him on his knees, his face buried in his hands, staring at the dead young man with unseeing eyes.

Distraught, *Signora* Medici just lost three men in her family in a few months. Her face chalk white, she opened her mouth wide, gasping for air but no sounds came out. Her eyes squeezed shut. The movement of Savonarola drew her eyes. He started to walk towards her, crying with his arms stretched outwards towards the heavens as if he were blaming God.

Signora Medici sucked a huge gasp of air and her screams were intense. The sound of her wailing echoed throughout the church, throughout the city of Florence, and her words echoed into the heavens, "*Bastardo*…*bastardo*…*bastardo*!"

Chapter Nineteen

"Murderers!!!" Savonarola shouted. "Mark my words, I promise that I will personally see to it that both of you hang."

Medici guards rushed the altar and in front of all of the horrified faces, they placed their swords on the backs of Fra Silvestro and Fra da Pescia and led them out.

"I want to see them hang," Savonarola demanded the guards. "Do you hear me? They must hang for their crimes!" Exhausted, he lowered his head in prayer.

The guards gently pulled *Signora* Medici away from her son. Captain Rafael pulled the grieving woman into his body, shielding her from the church full of onlookers. As he led her out of the church, she broke free from his embrace and wailed, "Savonarola did this…all of you did this. You will pay…all of you will pay!"

Savonarola looked up quickly when two guards came from behind and grabbed him. "What are you doing?" he struggled. "How dare you! It was those two who killed the boy. I had no part in this…I swear to you. I'm innocent!"

The guards dragged Savonarola from the altar and led him down the aisle. He could not turn away when he passed the dead body of Lorrenzo on the floor. He thought it reminiscent of how both Medici brothers looked as they both met their violent death on the floor in one of the grandest churches in Florence. Savonarola sighed impatiently. "Wait!" Breaking free of their grip, he demanded, "Please, I must administer his last rites so that God will accept him into heaven."

Captain Rafael's voice was laced with anger. "How dare you! You will pay for this with your life!" Spitting into the face of the priest, he swore, "You're no man of God! Guards…take him away for execution…get him out of my sight!"

Savonarola was too stunned to move and the one word that he tried to get out was lost as the guards grabbed him by his neck and whipped him around. Terror was in his eyes when he caught sight of Captain Rafael pulling his sword out. "Captain, I swear, I had nothing to do with this. Those two tried to kill me as well. Hang them…hang them!"

Disgusted, Rafael turned away from Savonarola and looking down at the twisted body slumped at his feet, tears welled in his eyes.

I swore to protect him. Thinking back, he remembered telling him those words. As he grew up with his brother Giuliano, he was such a playful little boy, a good boy. Shaking his head in disbelief, he couldn't believe that both brothers suffered the same fate.

"Captain, I protest!" Savonarola screamed. "Silvestro and da Pescia did this. Hang them, captain. I demand you put them on trial and then hang them."

Rafael whirled around, startled by Savonarola's request. "Hang?" he mocked. "Did you say hang? Savonarola, there will be no trial…there'll be no hanging. All three of you will be tied to a stake in the piazza and you will be burned until all that is left of you are ashes! Exactly where you burned everyone's possessions. May God have mercy on your soul, Savonarola." Addressing his guards, he shouted, "Take him to the dungeon to await execution."

While the three were being led away, Rafael looked down at the body and whispered softly, "I thought you were the one who would bring peace to this city." Getting down on one knee, he gently closed Lorrenzo's upturned eyes and began to pray.

Chapter Twenty

"I have blood on my hands!" Fioretta screamed. "I killed Lippi. I have blood. Look, look at my hands! God will never forgive me…I know he won't, he can't."

The hair on the back of Ernesto's neck prickled. "How do you know?"

Fioretta groped for words to express her thoughts. "What are you saying?"

"How do you know that God won't forgive you, forgive me…forgive all of us? The truth is we're all killers now. We can't change that, but we killed in self-defense. Lippi was going to kill you. It could have been any one of us. We survived and we have to keep surviving so we can get back to normal lives."

"I've heard you ask what normal is in the past. Well…it's time to tell me."

Taking her hands into his, he whispered, "Normal is getting our dreams back and right now, my dream is to marry you and I want to do so right now."

Slightly annoyed, she raised her brow. "Right now? Here? Be serious, we have no priest here. No one to marry us."

"God will."

"God will what? Ernesto, what's wrong with you? You're speaking foolishly."

"I know that in God's eyes he views us as husband and wife. God will marry us. He knows of our love for each other. He knows the situation that we're in. Fioretta, if I'm going to die out here, I want to die knowing that we were husband and wife. Even if it's brief, even one night, it will be worth it knowing that I had you in my life. I can live with that."

"Stubborn man!" she placed her hands on her hips as he took hold of her hands.

"Before God, I promise to love you and to protect you…forever."

Their lips met, expressing their love for each other as the two were united in marriage. Tangling his hands in her hair, Ernesto pulled her head back gently and captured her mouth once more. After, as they lie in each other's embrace in the tall wheat, their silence gave way to wondering about their lives. Fioretta's head lay on Ernesto's chest, the warmth of his body and his steady heartbeat soothed some of her fears. Very slowly and deliberately, she placed soft kisses over his bare chest, leaving wet trails on his skin. She looked at him, her eyes brimming with love. They lie quietly in the high wheat, staring at each other and planning their future away from these woods.

Hours later when they were back at the camp, Fioretta rested her head against Ernesto's shoulder, when Antonio approached them. "Where have you been?" he said coldly.

Ernesto gave him an odd look. "Why? What's wrong?"

Looking grim, Antonio mumbled, "Everyone is restless. They want to get out of here. No more death at the hands of Medici guards. The church lied to us. There was never a plan. They were always going to leave us all out here to rot!"

"No, that's not true," Ciro Devoto spoke in an angry tone. "Lippi had a plan," he said loudly.

Chapter Twenty

Antonio looked at the man and hesitated for a long time. "What plan? Lippi could not be trusted."

Speaking over Antonio's voice, Ciro piped up, "He was going to set all of us free. We could have gone home!"

"No, Ciro," Antonio reasoned. "Lippi's plan was for all of us, including YOU, to die out here! He ambushed us, did you forget?"

"He didn't ambush any of us, only you, Antonio. You, Ernesto, the girl and Tomasso."

"He betrayed everyone here. My God, he had Silvio killed," Ernesto yelled.

"No! Silvio was in the wrong place at the wrong time. Trust me. Lippi would not have hurt any of us…except maybe you, Ernesto."

"Liar!" Ernesto cursed. Everyone here would have been hanging in nooses including you, Ciro…don't be such a fool!"

"My naïve Ernesto, you worry about Medici," Ciro said. "The truth is very clear…the church abandoned us out here to die and it's all your fault!"

Ernesto turned a glare on Ciro that made Fioretta's blood chill.

"Is there a problem, *Signore* Palazzo?" Ciro asked. "Am I not speaking the truth?"

Ernesto lunged at Ciro, pulling a dagger from his sash and held it to his throat. "You're a liar, Ciro," Ernesto sighed impatiently and pressed the sharp weapon deeper into the man's neck.

"Go ahead, Palazzo. Show everyone that you are a killer. You're no better than Lippi. Do it! Take my life in front of everyone here."

Fioretta placed a shaking hand over Ernesto's fist holding the knife. "Not today, Ernesto…not on our wedding day."

"WHAT?" Antonio gasped.

Irritated, Ernesto did not take his eyes off of Ciro. "Nothing…we will talk about it later."

Ernesto allowed Fioretta's hand to pull the knife away from the man's throat. His icy stare made Ciro cringe as he focused on keeping his breathing under control.

"Antonio," one of the men said, "if we have to fight for our lives against the Medici, well then let's fight instead of dying out here."

Intense glares came from both Ernesto and Ciro when Antonio agreed with the man. "He's right. We have to do something. Out here, we're sitting ducks for the Medici guards. We need a plan to attack the guards and once and for all, get rid of Lorrenzo Medici."

The men walked away except Ciro who stayed with Antonio, Ernesto, and Fioretta. After a few moments, he mumbled, "So…which one of you killed Lippi?" His voice was tinged with anger. "He was probably defenseless. Was it you, Palazzo? You never liked him because he looked at the woman here. You knew nothing about him and yet you killed him anyway. God have mercy on your soul. I hope all of you burn in hell."

Fioretta was crushed by Ciro's words. She began to sob as he walked away. Ernesto's anger was still brimming. "Don't listen to him. He has no idea what he is saying."

"No…he's right." Fioretta wiped the tears from her eyes. "I will burn in hell. God will punish me."

Chapter Twenty

Ernesto stared with concern at his wife. He put his arm around her as he held her tight. Feeling unworthy, she pushed his arm off of her. "Leave me be, Ernesto. I want to be alone," she cried, running from the men.

Ernesto's eyes as well as his heart dropped to the floor.

Standing next to Ernesto, Antonio grinned, mumbling under his breath. "You got married? By whom?"

"Not now, Antonio." Ernesto pursed his lips and laced his fingers together. "I hate that Ciro as much as I hated Lippi. I should run him through as well."

"Save it, Ernesto. Save it for those who matter. Ciro is a nobody, we need to get out of here and if it means killing Lorrenzo, then that's what we are going to do."

Ernesto battled against the rage in his heart as he gazed off in the distance. Catching the last glimpse of Ciro walking away tormented him. *He needs to die…*

Chapter Twenty-One

From a safe distance, Giovanni Solasso watched Gisella Mangini as she walked through the city's marketplace. Not wanting to be detected, he carefully walked across the aisle that she was in, studying the old woman's face.

He knew of her past…her pain when her family was killed years ago from the great earthquake in the city. He studied the weathered lines that covered the woman's complexion. How much pain must this sweet soul bear? he wondered. Ernesto, who was like a son to her had been violently murdered and now she was under tremendous strain from taking care of his old friend, Alessandro Botticelli. As she bent over to look at an items placed neatly on the floor, he came from behind and without her knowing, dropped a few silver Florins into her change bag. Undetected, he darted away and went to the other side of the aisle in the marketplace. Picking through the few sacks of wheat and grain, she stood erect and saw her old friend across the way. Her weathered expression brightened when she saw his smile.

"My goodness…Giovanni. It's been a while. How are you, my friend?"

He noticed how tired her big brown eyes looked.

"I'm fine, Gisella. How are you holding up? I hear Sandro has taken a turn for the worse."

As she spoke, Giovanni noticed tears beginning to well up in her eyes. Suddenly, she broke down and collapsed onto his shoulder. Holding her in his arms, he felt the warmth of her tears gently flow from his dear friend's face.

"Giovanni, I don't know what I am going to do," she whispered.

"Well, first thing, let's dry your tears." Pulling a clean cloth from his jacket, he dabbed her eyes to catch the remaining tears. "Better?" He smiled. "Now tell me, Gisella, what can I do to be of help to you and Sandro?"

"He's fading quickly. I feel he only has a short time left...he hasn't eaten in days. He lies in bed, staring up at the ceiling. I don't know what to do. I've tried to get help from the city, but it's useless. It's been three months since Lorrenzo was killed and nothing is happening here. Who is in charge of the city?"

"No one seems to know. Some think the church should take over but ever since the priests murdered Lorrenzo, everyone is wary about taking orders from the church. A lot of people think Savonarola killed Lorrenzo... others say the Pope was behind it. It sounds crazy but they've left us with nothing. It's like the church has turned its back on us."

"Sandro has done so much for the church!" barked the old woman. "Now when he needs them, they abandon him. That sickens me, Giovanni...it just sickens me."

"I know, I know," he replied. "I've asked them numerous times to help find my son and nephew, but nothing. They just ignore me. They've been gone so long now and no one has said a single word to me about them."

"Giovanni, do you think that it's a coincidence that they both disappeared shortly after Ernesto was murdered? It doesn't add up. First Ernesto, then your boys go missing. Giuliano is murdered and now Lorrenzo." She shook her head and muttered, "I just don't understand it."

Solasso looked straight at her. "I know something has to happen soon. One day, the Medici guards are in power and the next, they're not…there's nothing but chaos everywhere. Savonarola and those two priests have been rotting in that jail cell for months, not knowing what is going to happen to them. The captain of the guards said that he was going to burn them at the stake."

"GOOD!!! Let them all die," she snapped. "Savonarola has done nothing but condemn everyone. Let him and the others burn."

Giovanni put his arm around Gisella and stood for many quiet minutes staring at the bustle of the marketplace. He leaned over and whispered, "I know it's bad now, but one day, Gisella, it will get better…it has to. Please let me know what Sandro needs and I will get it for you. He's my old, dear friend and I want him to be as comfortable as he can in his last days."

Chapter Twenty-Two

"For three months I've been rotting in this cell with these two murderers," Savonarola pressed. "Just how long do you plan on keeping me in here?

The lone guard keeping watch over the cell was sound asleep, his chair propped back against the wall.

"GUARD!" Savonarola shouted. "You can't keep me here forever. I've done no wrong."

Savonarola's shouting startled the watchman. His loud snoring turned into choking as he fell forward from his chair, sending the bottle of wine on his lap crashing to the floor. Angry, the short, fat guard wiped the sleep from his eyes. "Quiet down, you are just as guilty as they are."

Weariness was etched in the face of the embattled priest. "That's a lie," he shouted. "Every day there's a different man watching me and every day no one has any answers to my questions. I demand to speak to someone in charge. Three months…can someone…anyone tell me about my fate?" His long boney fingers extended outside of his iron bars to the cell across from his that held Silvestro and da Pescia. "They killed Lorrenzo Medici…those two there. They poisoned him…they probably killed his brother also."

"Shut up, Savonarola," Silvestro grumbled, "We're tired of hearing you whine about how innocent you are. You brought all of this on yourself."

Savonarola glared at the other prisoner. "Did I put poison in the blood of Christ or was it you two! You disgust me. You're both cowards. Both of you are evil and have done unspeakable acts."

Savonarola felt anger boil in his stomach when the two priests laughed at him. "You find this humorous? You killed an innocent man and you have the audacity to laugh about it? You have no conscience, do you? God will see to it that you rot in hell…do you understand?"

Da Pescia chuckled. "Well then, I guess we'll be in excellent company seeing as you will be joining us. I'm sure your God will see to that."

Savonarola reddened with fury and leaped up against the iron bars. "My God IS your God!"

Evening set as the rising moon cast an eerie light that crept along the floor of the cell. Upstairs, a loud knock on the heavy doors startled everyone, including Savonarola. Listening to the echoes of voices upstairs, he thought he heard a woman's voice. Soon, the soft glow of a lit torch made its way down the long hall, giving some light in the cells. Savonarola shot to his feet quickly. Within seconds, two dark shadows approached as he slowly backed away from the bars.

"Savonarola," a voice called from the darkness. Savonarola remained silent in fear. "Don't be afraid, come here…into the light." The soft sound was a woman's voice. The flickering flames of the torch caught his eye, mesmerizing him, as he slowly walked towards it. He faced the prison bars looking curiously at the hooded stranger, when suddenly she removed her covering and revealed her face.

Chapter Twenty-Two

Savonarola gasped. "*Signora* Medici? What…what are you doing here?"

"Don't talk, just answer my question," she whispered. "For months, I've been haunted with memories of what happened to my son. I need to know for sure…for my own sake." She looked at the man and hesitated for a long time. Savonarola's breathing was short, erratic. "Did you poison him? Did you kill my son?"

He froze as her large brown eyes peered at him from behind the iron bars.

Savonarola sighed heavily. "*Signora*, I swear to you in front of Almighty God himself, I did not kill him. I knew nothing of the plans; it was those two across the hall. You have to believe me," he pleaded.

"I don't have to believe anything," she answered, her voice grim.

She studied his appearance, his tired, weary eyes and the long hooked nose that framed his face.

Thinking back, she remembered the look on Savonarola's face. He stared at Lorrenzo in horror, his mouth open in a silent scream. Silvestro and da Pescia had a look of elation on their faces. For the past three months, she agonized over her son's death and those who were responsible. Shadows from the moonlight crept in through a small window opening in his cell, splashing across his body. She raised her eyebrows to indicate that she believed him. "I believe he's telling the truth. Guard, release him," she ordered.

The young guard looked confused. "*Signora* Medici, I am not under any obligation to obey any command you give. I'm sorry, but my orders are----."

The woman fumed, "I don't care what orders you were given, you fool. Must I go to Captain Rafael personally and tell him of your refusal to obey one simple command?" Her voice was deep and throaty. "Guard, you do know that the captain is a very close, personal friend of mine and he will respect my wishes, so if you do not want this to get difficult, please release him…NOW!"

The embarrassed guard unlocked the cell door and Savonarola quickly walked out a free man. With gratitude, he bowed his head to her and kissed her hand in thankfulness.

She touched the top of his head and made eye contact with him. She lowered her voice to a conspiratorial hush. "Is the church responsible for killing my sons?"

Savonarola studied her face and silently nodded. "Certain things make no sense. I don't understand why those two would poison your son. They hardly knew him."

Signora Medici got close to Savonarola's ear. "Leave Florence," she whispered. "Be very careful…the people are restless. No one seems to be in control of the city right now and I'm not sure if Captain Rafael and the few men that he has left can go up against the church. A lot has happened since you've been in here. There are new faces in the church. When you closed the taverns and the gambling houses, you seemed to make the Pope irate. He reopened everything that you had closed. As much as I don't care for you, I do believe you. In my heart, I believe that Alexander is behind all of this." A sob caught in her throat. "They killed my sons so that they could do as they pleased with no interference…for what? Florins?"

Disgusted, she turned and walked down the corridor towards the steps leading upstairs.

"*Signora*," he whispered, running up to the woman, "the Sunday Mass…who has been giving it?"

She furrowed her brow, "A puppet for Alexander, someone who is told what to say."

Savonarola's jaw dropped.

"Remember," she whispered, "get out while you can."

Her stinging words played over in his head while the woman quickly walked up the stairwell and out of the building.

Savonarola looked at his hands and wondered if he inadvertently had Medici blood on them. Walking back to the cell occupying Silvestro and da Pescia, he agonized that men of God like these were capable of doing such ungodly acts of murder.

Silvestro barked, "Don't be such a fool, Savonarola. You knew what was going on the whole time."

Savonarola squinted his eyes down into tiny narrow slits. Spitting on the ground, he hissed, "Evildoers…I'll make sure you both burn until there is nothing left of your bodies. Perhaps then, God will forgive you."

Silvestro walked slowly up to the bars that separated the two. His fingers wrapped themselves around the cold, iron bars. "You'll be back Savonarola, listen to my words very carefully. You'll be back and you will burn at the stake with us…your body as well as ours will burn to ashes. A fitting sacrifice…don't you think?" A loud howl of laughter erupted from the disgraced Silvestro as his laughter reverberated off the cold stone of the jail.

"We're leaving," Ernesto said. "Fioretta and I are heading back. It's been months and we haven't seen or heard anything from Rome or from Florence!"

Antonio nodded but Ernesto could tell by his tight lips that he did not agree. "What if it's a trap? Maybe they're waiting for us to make the first move."

Luca thought for a moment. "Remember when we scouted out the area a few weeks ago? Those traveling merchants who passed through here talked about Lorrenzo's funeral. Could that be right? Could Lorrenzo really be dead?"

"I'm not sure but we've been like sitting ducks here and we're done with it! We are leaving in the morning to head back to Florence, whether Lorrenzo is dead or not."

"And if he's not?" Antonio shouted. "Then you'll be dead. Both you and Fioretta! Is that what you want?"

"No, but that's the chance we're willing to take," Ernesto countered.

"Ernesto, be reasonable," Antonio's tone was urgent. "He blames you for his brother's death. He will come at you with everything because of it. He'll come after you and he'll kill you. Is that what you want? If so, then all of this was for nothing. "

Ernesto's weary eyes settled on Antonio. "Well, I guess we'll find out soon enough. If all we have is overheard words of Lorrenzo's death, well, that's at least something to go on."

"That means nothing!" Antonio shouted back. "Did those men say that they saw him dead? Did they go up to his body and see for themselves?"

Ernesto didn't reply because he honestly didn't know the answer. He turned away and with Fioretta, they readied themselves to leave.

"Fine, go get yourself killed. What about Fioretta? Do you want to get her killed? Is that it? Kill everyone? Is that your master plan?"

Ernesto heaved a sigh. "Is that what you think?" he asked, spinning to face his friend. "Antonio, I won't do this anymore…hiding, running the rest of my life. Tomasso's last words were to stay alive, but this isn't living. We have to end this and if it is just me, so be it. I will end it!"

"End it? You're crazy! Are you going to risk all of our lives?"

"No…not at all. If Lorrenzo is still alive then it's me he wants. He doesn't care for anyone else, just me and it is me he shall get."

"You're a fool, Ernesto. You won't last a minute. As soon as his guards see you, they'll arrest you and put you to death." A cold chill raked his flesh. "You do know that this is suicide, right?" Antonio asked. "Please don't drag Fioretta into this. Think of her, Ernesto…please, for God's sake, don't get her killed."

Ernesto scowled at this ill-timed plea. The words, don't get her killed, hung over his head, like a cloud, as he thought of the ramifications of his actions.

"Fine…I'm going alone. Fioretta stays here with you. If my destiny is death, then it will just be my death."

"Your death?" Fioretta shouted. "I'm your wife, not a child. I'm your partner…we're in this together."

Ernesto's face drew long. "No, Fioretta, please you have to stay."

Numb from his words, she bristled, "STAY HERE? You're not going to leave me in these godforsaken woods anymore. You're not going off to die and leave me to raise this child alone without its father," she fired back, putting her hands over her swollen belly that she had been hiding from the others.

"She's with child?" Antonio gasped, "My God, Ernesto, don't do this."

Fioretta's eyes blazed with anger. "I'm not staying here. I don't care what you say, I refuse to be left out here without you."

Ernesto's eyebrows arched high as he stared at his wife. "I'm disappointed," he paused, "but honestly, not surprised. You've always been a stubborn woman," he said with a grin.

Ernesto walked back and put his arm around his friend's shoulder. "I'm not asking you to come. Stay here with the others and when it's safe, I'll get word to you."

Antonio swallowed hard. "Luca, I'm going with Ernesto. We'll get word to you when it's safe." Antonio smiled at Ernesto. "I saved you from death at the Medici boys' hands years ago and I surely won't leave you now. I will follow you till death. We will end this together. This is my promise to you, to your wife and your child."

Ernesto looked his friend in the eye. "We leave for freedom at first light."

"I want to know who we're really fighting…the Medici's or the church?"

Ernesto remained silent.

Spitting on the ground, Antonio threw his head back and shouted. "To freedom…no matter what the cost!"

"No matter what the cost!" Ernesto replied.

In his mind, Ernesto knew the cost could be steep…the cost would be paid with their lives!

Chapter Twenty-Three

"She did what?" Pope Alexander screamed, his voice echoing throughout Vatican City.

Frightened, a bishop trembled as he spoke, "She…she released him from the prison cell, Your Holiness."

Despite the soft glow of candlelight in his chamber, Alexander's cold, dark, steely eyes pierced the men dressed in priestly garb. "Who does this arrogant woman think she is?" he hissed. "She's fortunate we didn't kill her along with her sons."

With his growing scowl, the obese man bolted from his chair, brooding over this unexpected turn of events.

"It was very simple. This whole plan from the beginning was so simple. We pay a handful of criminals and Florentines to kill the Medici's…they get caught and they die. Simple, don't you agree?"

"Your Holiness?" a strange voice fumbled from the back of the room. "Pardon me, but I did hear about your plan when I first came here and personally…I had reservations about it."

The Pope did not blink. Nor did he respond. His fierce gaze penetrated deep into the young man's body. The newcomer had heard the stories of the Holy Father's bizarre mood swings, but now he was witnessing it firsthand.

Fear set in for the stranger as he scanned the horrified faces of the others in the room. The Pope's personal chamber was ornately decorated. On the ancient stone walls, gold candle holders were firmly fixed to the walls with lavish candles burning on them. Bright tapestries depicting biblical events lined another wall and stationed in the middle of the room was the Pope's cathedra, his papal chair. The man squinted at the rotund Pope, but his vision seemed blurred by the gold color haze around him. Realizing every eye in the room was fixed on him, he cleared his throat while humbly bowing his head. Still, the Pope remained silent but his intensity in his stare tripled. The uncomfortable silence stunned all in the room. A deep, resonating voice from out of the group of older men finally broke the tension.

"He's new to us, Your Eminence. A while back, you had requested an aid to assist you. This young bishop was sent from Milan a few weeks ago. I was going to introduce you to him after this meeting."

Alexander took a menacing step forward, placing his face inches away from the young bishop. His extreme overweight condition caused his breathing to be loud and throaty. He stood a bit taller than the slightly built younger bishop. Looking down at the man, Alexander smirked, then turned and marched angrily towards a window, with its beautiful stained glass, swung open for the afternoon breeze. Alexander glanced out the open window to the activity going on below. In a seldom seen act of kindness, his Holy Father smiled at his new aide and gestured for him.

"Come here, my son. I want to show you MY kingdom."

The young aide hesitated briefly, then grew a warm smile as he went to stand beside the Pope.

"Look out the window. Do you see those priests below, my son?"

"Yes, *Signore*. I…I mean yes, Your Holiness."

Alexander placed his hand gently on the shoulder of the nervous man. "Very good, my son, very good. Those priests…all priests obey every command I give. Do you understand me? Everyone does. This is MY kingdom. Almighty God has chosen me to be his earthly representative here on earth. I guess you can say that I am like God's own son."

Alexander placed his chubby fingers onto the young bishop's head and proceeded to run them through the bishop's dark wavy hair. Feeling uneasy, the young man took a step backwards, away from Alexander.

"No, no, my son. Please…there is nothing to be afraid of. You and I will become very close. Very close indeed, but first, there are rules that you must obey."

"Rules, Holy Father?" he asked.

"Why of course, my son," he chuckled. "We all abide by rules…MY RULES! No one talks, no one breathes, without first asking me. Can you understand that?"

Speechless, the young man simply nodded his head.

"Good…good. This is good! Silence is good. You see, this is what I want from you. No unsolicited words. No telling me that you had reservations about my plan. That would be a problem, a small one, but still a problem. If not careful, those small ones can turn into bigger ones, can't they?"

The younger man again remained silent.

"Forgive me. You are my aide and I am being so formal. Please…please tell me your name."

"Felice, Your Eminence…Bishop Felice and I will do whatever is asked of me," he offered respectfully.

"Very well, Bishop Felice. Hmmm, interesting name…Felice. If I am correct, I believe in Latin that means lucky?"

Astonished that His Holiness was taking so much of an interest in him, the young bishop smiled brightly and acknowledged Alexander's correct response.

"Why yes, Your Holiness. You know your Latin very well."

"Shhhh," Alexander ordered, placing his thick fingers against the bishop's lips. "Remember what I said? Silence!"

Felice bowed his head in apology and kept his eyes closed.

"Does everyone see this?" he asked those with him. "This is what I am looking for…someone who is obedient."

Alexander took the chin of his aide into his palm and raising the man's head slowly, his eyes met Felice's.

"Very good, Felice, very good. Now, I need my lookout summoned. He is down below with those priests. Do you see them?"

Turning his head slightly, the bishop had a clean view of the priests milling about below.

"Holy Father," Felice asked sheepishly. "May I ask you a question?"

"GOOD!" Alexander boasted, "Good! You're learning quickly. Tell me, what is it, my friend?"

"Well, we are very high up in the tower and he might not hear me. Should I go down to the ground and bring him up with me?"

"No, Felice. It's a good thought, but it would take too long." His ghastly eyes sparkled. "I need to speak to my lookout immediately so just call for him from here."

The young bishop stepped towards the open window and called out to the priests below. Bewildered, he wondered why no one paid any attention to him. He turned back to Alexander with a frown. "No one can hear me," he said sounding dejected.

His Eminence chuckled and looked out the window, surveying the grounds below. "Young Felice, you will learn that around here, there are times that we need to elevate our voices. Here, watch me." Alexander's girth slightly forced Felice back away from the window as the Pontiff leaned out the window and in a loud, booming voice, yelled, "Look out!"

The familiar sound of the Pope's voice got the attention of the priests below as they lifted their heads upward.

The pontiff laughed. "Do you see, Felice? Do you see how they looked up? Try it again, my son, but this time be loud. From down in here," he said, grabbing two handfuls of his fat belly and jiggling it upwards. "Nice and loud."

Grinning broadly, the young Felice said, "I can do that!"

He placed his hands firmly on the stone ledge and in a loud voice, cried out, "Look out!"

"Again," Alexander urged. "Call again, this time louder! Remember…from down below in your belly."

Taking a deep breath, Felice leaned further out of the window and as he exhaled, screamed, "LOOK OUT!!!"

The grossly obese Alexander moved with lightening speed and grabbed Felice's waist and with one deadly move, tossed his body from the large stone window. The older men in the room watching were terror stricken. Young bishop Felice's body slammed hard into the stones below, bursting on impact. The shocked priests ran to check on him but when they looked up, they caught sight of Alexander peering down. In an instant, they quickly went back to their business, leaving the bloodied, broken body on the stone pavement for all to see.

Alexander turned to face the group of horrified men in his chamber, mumbling under his breath, "I truly believe he was a liar…his name didn't mean lucky." Alexander looked his men up and down with a deliberate slowness, a slight sneer on his face. "Learn from what just took place and pray that it never happens to any of you."

Terrified at Alexander's trademark brutality, the men in the room remain silent, fearful of what he would do next. His brute manner intimidated all except his son, Cesare Borgia, who stood with his arms folded, listening.

"That fool Felice distracted me. Now, where was I? Oh, yes…as I was saying, it should have been so easy. All Silvestro and da Pescia had to do was to kill Lorrenzo Medici and Savonarola, like I said…simple! That pesky Savonarola seems to have luck on his side," he said maneuvering his large body to his cathedra and sliding down into the soft cushion.

"Eminence, please forgive me," a close advisor of Alexander's interrupted. "Savonarola is a poor man from the mountains with nothing of value to his name, but we here are filled with many riches."

"WE?" Alexander bellowed.

"My apologies…I meant you, Your Eminence…YOU have many riches." With a wave of his hand, Alexander had the man continue. "Perhaps he can be persuaded by a few of the riches that you have here in this room?"

"No, the man is too stupid for riches, but I have something better than riches."

"Holy Father…something better than riches?"

All eyes were riveted to the rotund Pope. "Prominence! Savonarola is so arrogant. That's how we will trap him…with prominence."

"Your Holiness, what do you have in mind?" one of his bishops asked.

"Again, a SIMPLE plan, but this time…it better work or else others will be getting a better view of my window! From now on, he will no longer be known as Savonarola, the Franciscan monk who became a priest. From this moment on, the priest Savonarola will be known as Cardinal Savonarola."

"And if HE doesn't go along with this plan?" one of the men asked.

"If he doesn't, I have an alternate plan in mind for our friend and trust me, that plan will be worse…much, much worse." An evil grin rose on his face. "Everyone in Florence will turn against him, and then, I will personally see to it that he dies a very slow but very painful death."

Alexander stretched and yawned. "Now, I am very tired and I would like to have some wine and then nap." Alexander's voice suddenly became tinged with anger. "Let's not fail on this. Understood?"

"I don't care if you were sent here by Alexander himself, I will be leading the mass this Sunday," Savonarola told the much younger priest.

"But Father Savonarola," the man tried to reason, "you've been in prison for months. You probably have nothing prepared."

"I have plenty to say, prepared or not. You know nothing of the truth of what's going on. Now, no more talk…all will listen to me on Sunday."

"Please, God," *Signora* Mangini prayed, "please let him hear me. He's been like this for months…I don't know how much longer I can stand to see him this way." The old woman laid her body next to Sandro's and closed her eyes from sheer exhaustion.

The once robust and jovial man was now a former shadow of himself. Frail and incoherent, he lapsed in and out of consciousness. To pass the time, *Signora* talked to him about his paintings, the people he knew and events of the city.

"I heard that Savonarola was let out of his jail cell and back in the church. He is such a cruel man. Remember, Sandro?" she asked knowing there would be no reply. "He was very evil. I heard in the marketplace that *Signora* Medici was the one who released him. She said he didn't kill her son…that the church did it. Sandro, what is happening here? What is happening to our world?"

The exhausted woman picked her head up from his bed. Her eyes darted around the walls of the small house. She longed for the memories that were in this house. Ernesto's bed in one corner, the table where the three of them shared so many meals and stories. In another corner of the room, stacked neatly on the floor were Sandro's paintings. The beautiful colors that once were so vibrant seemed faded and dull now. Her mind wandered until a loud persistent knock on the door startled her. She pulled her tired body off the bed and slowly made her way to the door. A warm smile appeared on the woman's face.

"I hope we are not disturbing you," Roberto Gorini said. "My wife and I heard that *Signore* Botticelli had taken a turn for the worse and we wanted to say our farewells to him."

She embraced Roberto and Isabella warmly and thanked them for coming.

"Sandro, look who is here to see you."

The couple forced a smile, but were shocked by what they saw.

Gisella gently touched her hand to the dying man's face and whispered, "He doesn't have much time left."

The early morning sunlight crept its way into Il Duomo's main chapel, crossing over the altar. Savonarola's eyes sharpened as he prepared to deliver his first Sunday mass in over three months.

While meditating on his words, a persistent knocking echoed from the large front doors. Ignoring it, he bowed his head in silent prayer. It's too early for those arriving for mass, he thought and went back to praying. One of the young choirboys opened the doors, letting the visitor in. Savonarola's eyes popped open when something fell into his lap. Looking down, he noticed a note, wrapped in a ribbon that bore the embossed Papal seal.

"I am Bishop Trentino and I was instructed by His Eminence to deliver this to you and I am to bring a response back immediately."

Fumbling the rolled note through his hands, he studied the Papal seal and quickly placed it down. "You will get my response after Mass today, bishop."

"I will be in attendance but after, I expect a swift response so that I can get back to Rome to speak with His Holiness."

The bishop walked into one of the pews close to the altar.

Shocked that the Pope sent a note to him, he unrolled the letter and began to read it when he quickly turned and settled his darkened eyes on the messenger. His anger suddenly blazed. He crumbled the Papal note and threw it down to the ground.

"How dare he think that I would do something like this!" his voice screamed as he shot to his feet. Hearing the shouting, a younger priest ran out to check on Savonarola.

"What's wrong? Why are you shouting?"

"Alexander thinks that he can reopen the gambling houses and taverns by appointing me Cardinal. The audacity of that man!" he scowled.

By the time the Mass was about to begin, Il Duomo was full. Word spread of how Savonarola was released from jail and now was about to condemn the people for their wrongdoing. The last two Masses that Savonarola gave resulted in two murders, which now had people coming to see what would happen rather than to be spiritually uplifted.

While the thick cloud of incense slowly lifted up towards the ceiling, the altar boys finished their song. Displaying a mix of anger with courage, Savonarola stood before the masses that morning. Taking a deep breath, he glanced at Bishop Trentino for a long moment. After he cleared his throat, the words escaped, "It's been a long time. A long time and what fruits did you offer God? I am like Moses in that when he went up to the mountain, his followers left God and did the works of the devil and YOU people here are the same way."

Savonarola never took his eyes off of Bishop Trentino, as he taunted the crowds further.

"I was away from you for three months and while I was gone, you drank, you gambled, all to make money for whom? For God? Is that what the Holy Father has been telling you? Well I'm here to tell you that the Holy Father is a liar. The Holy Father is a thief."

"YOU FOOL!" Bishop Trentino screamed.

He stormed down the aisle to leave for Rome when Savonarola turned his anger on him, shouting, "Trentino, you tell his Holy Father that I refuse to be his Cardinal. Tell him that the establishments that HE opened are now closed…FOR GOOD!!!"

Trentino bristled instantly. Turning towards the altar, he wagged his finger at the priest, shouting, "Prepare to meet your God, Savonarola."

"What do you know of God?" he replied angrily. "Your God is money…your money…his Holy Father's money! That's not the God I worship. Go back and tell him that. Tell him I will not make money for him or anyone."

Some stood and applauded the man for taking a stand against the church's corruption. Trentino reached the last row of pews when Savonarola screamed, "Tell Alexander that if he wants me, he will have to come get me."

Trentino sighed impatiently then whispered into a man's ear that was standing guard by the doors of the church. "Is everyone ready?"

"Everything is just as Alexander asked us to do." The man's eyes did not leave Trentino's face.

"Good," the visiting bishop said. "Tell them to start and then have the Vatican guards come and get him."

Opening the enormous doors, the signal was given to the planned rioters. Loud cries filled the air as violence rained against the corrupt and the innocent. Savonarola's promise of closing down its taverns and gambling houses irritated the angry mob which spilled out into the streets of the city. Savonarola jumped from his altar and forced his way outside to witness the fighting and destruction. His pulse was thundering when he raised his face towards the heavens and screamed, "Almighty God, cast these sinners to hell."

In a public display of arrogance, he prayed loudly in the street when he was struck from behind with the butt end of a sword, dropping his body hard onto the stone steps of Il Duomo. A shock ripped through Savonarola's body making his heart seize inside his chest. Gasping for air, he cried out weakly for his heavenly Father to end his life. Lying on the steps, Savonarola thought it cruel that God did not grant his request. Looking up to the heavens, he mumbled for God to exercise justice on the city as he did Sodom and Gomorrah.

Wincing in pain, he summoned all his strength and stumbled his way back into the church. Able to dodge the heavy blows from the fights inside, he made it into his chambers. His badly wounded body crashed down into his chair with a loud thud. After what just happened, he hung his head in disappointment. His grief was like flaming fire. Savonarola sat back in his chair until his rage exploded in a cry of pain, drowning out the violence that was all around him.

Retribution was coming…whether from the church, from Pope Alexander or from God himself was yet to be determined.

Chapter Twenty-Four

Savonarola felt hollow hours after the revolt in the city. Numb, he turned to face the giant cross that silently hung behind the altar in the empty church. He offered a prayer to God asking for forgiveness and direction for what just happened. He wasn't sure whether to feel relieved or disappointed that God spared his life. Scanning the walls of the church, Savonarola's eyes fell upon one of Sandro Botticelli's frescoes. The expression of the woman in the painting conveyed love and humanity, something he felt was missing now. He stared at the painting in amazement for a while, wondering why the people of his city have acted in such a barbaric way. Savonarola stepped forward and eased into his usual red chair that sat center of the altar. His shoulders slumped as he rapped his knuckles on the large wooden armrest wondering, did Alexander try to kill me? His gaze caught the roughly carved figure hanging on the cross in front of him. His eyes and the eyes of Jesus were locked in a visual duel. Savonarola did not blink and was unaware of the dark shadow looming from behind. The flickering soft glow of candlelight captured his attention when suddenly the intense searing pain around his neck caught him off guard. Fighting for air, his fingers struggled to find any space between the rope and the cutting flesh of his neck. The intruder planted his feet, putting all the weight on his back legs and giving one more strong pull. Savonarola's lungs strained for oxygen as an overwhelming sense of terror took over. His heart beat wildly as he struggled for life. Savonarola put leverage on his legs and lifted himself off the chair, letting a small wisp of air sneak in.

"ENOUGH!" a deep ominous voice cut the air from the last pew in the church.

The intruder gave slack on the rope forcing Savonarola to collapse back into the seat. Gasping for air, he repositioned his body to overcome the darkness his brain was feeling. His fingers clawed and pulled at the rope, giving much needed space from the large gash. His fingers, which instinctively reached for the wound, were smeared with his blood. Savonarola's eyes darted back and forth in terror, looking for his assailants.

"Who…who are you?" he choked. "What do you want?"

Silence.

Savonarola's words returned no answer.

"What gives you…?" he gasped. "What gives you the right to come into my Father's hou---?"

"AGAIN!" the voice cut Savonarola off.

A sudden wave of panic rose in Savonarola as his body was viciously pulled back into the chair. His trembling hands pulled on the rope repeatedly in a vain attempt to free himself from death. Filled with desperation, he extended his arms in a final plea for mercy.

"ENOUGH!" the voice growled from the back of the church.

The rope slacked, sending Savonarola crashing to the floor with a thud.

A long moment passed. Two massive hands lifted his body and threw him back into the chair, snapping his head back then forward, his eyes staring at the floor. His body was barely clinging to life. *Am I in hell?* he wondered. *God, why have you forsaken me?*

Savonarola lifted his head slightly and squinted at the carving of Jesus looking down at him. Anger growled in his hoarse voice. "Answer me…why have you forsaken me?"

Something was wrong…it was too quiet. Within minutes, the sound of a low murmuring prayer moved closer. Prayers were all too familiar to him and should have been a comfort, but something was different about these. Within seconds, a slow rhythmic tapping sound of heeled boots on marble worked its way closer to him. Tap…tap…tap. Savonarola's body shook as the sounds inched closer towards him when suddenly it stopped.

His eyes barely open, Savonarola stared at the pair of polished black boots in his line of sight. "Please," he choked, struggling to get the words out, "Please…stop."

"Savonarola," the low sounding voice called. "Savonarola, look at me."

The helpless priest lacked the strength to lift his head and look at the man. The stranger grabbed a handful of Savonarola's long, sweat-soaked hair and yanked his head up. Savonarola's eyes were like narrow slits. He glanced at the ominous figure in front of him. In seconds, he whispered, "I know you."

A perverse smile appeared on the stranger's face. "Very good, my son…very good. You should know me. Years ago, I played a big influence in your life." The man's image was overpowering. Tall, thin with a ghost-like appearance of grayish pale skin and long greasy hair. His black robe matched his expressionless black eyes, resembling death. "Savonarola…I was your teacher."

Savonarola's eyes widened, "Fra… Greco?" he gasped.

His old instructor stood in the dim light of the church as he nodded his head. "It's Cardinal Greco now."

Savonarola's lips twitched. Instantly, the breath went out of him. "Yes," he answered slowly, "I remember you." Barely able to believe his eyes, he asked, "I have done you no wrong… why are you doing this to me?"

Greco was stunned. "You don't know?" Greco chuckled. "Savonarola, my old pupil, you do amuse me greatly. Perhaps I can explain by posing a simple question." The tall man leaned over and gazed into Savonarola's weary eyes.

He shook his head and whispered. "Why must you be so stubborn? You are not God and you cannot pretend to be God. Savonarola… stop fighting against us."

"Us?" he moaned. A sudden feeling of nausea came over him. The mere thought that his old instructor would betray his own faith was crushing. Angered by Greco's words, Savonarola mumbled loudly, "Alexander is a murderer…you're all murderers! No one is clean in the eyes of God, do you hear me…NO ONE!"

"My, my, you do seem to have a little fight left in you," Greco said softly, his fingers raking through the priest's hair. "Savonarola, I'm going to give you a chance to live. If you listen to my words very carefully and obey… you shall live."

Savonarola closed his eyes, ignoring Greco's words. The silence infuriated the Cardinal enough that he grabbed Savonarola by the hair and screamed, "You stupid fool…listen to me!" Lowering his voice, Greco tried a softer approach. "My dear friend, I am the only one who can save you now. Savonarola, I always liked you. You were a good student. One of my finest.

Please… please reconsider your actions. You and I are men of God and I'm sure we can come to some form of agreement."

"YOU…A MAN OF GOD?" he gasped. "Greco, I respected you years ago. Today, you're unfit to wear that robe."

Savonarola spit at Greco's feet. "You are worthless in God's eyes. Punish me if you have to, but God will avenge my death when he sends you to hell. Mark my words. You will end up there."

Greco closed his eyes and released a heavy sigh. "Take him!"

Defiant, Savonarola taunted, "Is your plan to kill me here, in the house of my God? You evil man of lawlessness…kill a man of God in his…his sacred house?"

"You would like that, wouldn't you? To be a great martyr to God himself. Look at me!" Greco screamed. "I'm the great Savonarola!" he jeered. "Savonarola, my friend, I will decide where and when you die, but first there is something that I need from you."

Savonarola was appalled by his request. "Something from me? You'll get nothing!"

After a long pause, he smiled. "Well, we'll see about that, won't we? Take him back across the street to his cell. Put him with those other two animals, Silvestro and da Pescia."

Greco glanced up at the hanging cross bearing the body of Jesus Christ, then back down to the priest and smiled. "I have a little surprise waiting for you, my friend…soon, soon you'll see it!"

"Once that fool is dead, Florence won't know what to do," Pope Alexander laughed. "People either love him or hate him, but because of him, they fear God. With Savonarola dead, we'll take over Florence and soon control the country."

His fist pounded angrily on the table as Alexander raised his voice.

"Power and wealth will be mine…will be yours! With Medici dead and soon, Savonarola will be out of our way, nothing will stop us!"

A few moments later, Alexander dismissed his men. In a secluded room, away from the pontiff's chambers, a knowing groan escaped Fra Del Veccio lips. "He's lost his mind…we're all going to get killed if he goes through with this madness."

"Shhh, be quiet!" pleaded Fra Stasi.

"No I won't," Del Veccio charged. "This is not what the church is supposed to be about. We serve God, not kill the ones who serve him."

"Keep your thoughts to yourself," Stasi said angrily.

"I won't…something has to be done about it. He's gone insane!"

"What would you recommend? We just can't kill the man."

Del Veccio arched a single eyebrow. "You're right, but I know someone in his family who will."

Stasi's heart pounded. "What are you talking about?"

"Alexander's son…Don Cesare. He was voicing his displeasure about his father the other day."

"Cesare… the bastard son of the Pope?" Stasi asked curiously. "Go on."

"He despises his father," Del Veccio grinned.

Stasi's eyebrows arched high with intrigue. "And what does Don Cesare plan to do?"

"To get rid of the man who has made his life miserable. His father…Pope Alexander."

Stunned, Stasi paused for a moment then whispered, "Is he serious?"

"Very! Alexander treated the boy horribly since the day he was born. He despises him and his mother."

Stasi tried to focus, "But it's his son!"

Del Veccio was silent a long moment. "Follow me," he whispered. "We need to discuss this in private."

Del Veccio dabbed a bead of sweat from his forehead as he led the way down the long corridor to a single door leading outside.

Savonarola awoke in pain, his muscles felt like stone…tight and brittle. On his back, he was able to turn his head slightly to the side when it first appeared. Though his vision was blurry, he saw what seemed to be a ghost…a faint glowing outline standing not far from him. Savonarola's face was gaunt and bruised from the beating he took at the hands of Greco's men. Focusing on his surroundings, he realized he was lying on a table in a room with iron bars, but where? Is this my jail cell? His eyelids fluttered, trying to sharpen his vision in the poorly lit room. His mouth was dry and swollen. Creating saliva proved unsuccessful as his tongue eagerly searched his mouth for liquid.

"Water…water. Please, I beg you," he mumbled.

"Good…you're awake," Greco said in a low growl. "You've slept enough."

"Please…show me mercy, I need water," Savonarola groaned.

"Mercy? You wish mercy?" Greco looked at the man without emotion. "Tell me why, Savonarola? What makes you special in my eyes?"

Savonarola shuddered.

Greco turned a glare on the prone Savonarola. "Alright…I'll make a deal with you. I will give you some wine but first, you must do something for me."

Savonarola's tongue brushed over his cracked lips, tasting dried blood from his beating. "What?" he whispered. "Do what…?" his voice trailed off.

Greco picked up a small cup of wine and traced his fingers across its rim in a circular motion, smiling at the unfortunate Savonarola.

"Is this what you want? It's not water, my friend, but wine…the very best wine. It is the blood of the Christ. Will this suffice?"

Nodding his head, tears formed in Savonarola's eyes. "Thank you," he whispered.

Greco's finger dipped lightly into the cup and slowly pulled upward, letting Savonarola see the small droplets fall from the tip of his finger back into the cup. "Is this what you want, my friend? This will make you feel better, won't it?"

Trembling, Savonarola's tongue sought moisture for his lips. "Yes, this will make you feel much better."

Again, he dipped into the wine and placed his finger gently onto Savonarola's bloodied lips, letting the liquid ooze into his cracks. "Better?" he asked. "Your throat must be so dry…would you like this cup for yourself?"

Savonarola's eyes were glued to the cup.

"This can be yours, old friend, but again, I need you to do something for me. Do it…and I shall replenish your body with the very best wine and hot food."

His breaking point reached, the weary priest whispered, "Anything."

Greco smiled, pulling a rolled parchment from beneath his robe. "Sign this paper admitting your guilt for crimes against the church, and all this evil will go away. You can go home to Ferrara, go live your days in the countryside, drinking and eating the fruits of your labor."

"But…but I've committed no crime," Savonarola whispered hoarsely. "I cannot sign that…I will not sign it."

"Nonsense!" Greco snapped. "You can sign it. No one shall know anything about it."

Persecuted to excess, Savonarola's dark eyes suddenly filled with rage. "God will know!"

"Yes…yes you're right, God will know. But under these circumstances, I assure you that you will be forgiven. Savonarola, one last time…sign this and I will release you immediately."

"NO!!!" Savonarola gasped. "I said NO!"

Furious, Greco threw the cup to the ground. Running his finger down the length of the table that Savonarola was chained to, his eyes showed little compassion. "Don't be a martyr, my friend," he whispered. "Nobody cares if you live or die. Silvestro and da Pescia already signed, and now it's your turn. Sign it and gain life. Refuse…and you shall die!"

Savonarola clenched his eyes shut, refusing the cardinal's command. Greco cursed under his breath and with a simple nod of his head, a man turned a large wooden crank attached to the chains on Savonarola's arms. The sound of ligaments tearing made a sickening noise as Savonarola's left arm was being torn from its socket.

"Sign it now and I promise you, it will be all over," Greco urged again. "There is no shame. Sign it and I promise you, the torture, the pain…and eventual death will stop on my command." The sound of bone snapping made Greco grimace. "I don't want to rip your body apart, but you are giving me no choice."

With another nod of Greco's head, Savonarola felt the intense searing pain rip through his body. The sadistic cardinal slowly waved the paper in his face tempting him to sign it.

One more crank of the wheel sent horrific screams of pain that broke the peacefulness of the night. Greco felt a warm anticipation spreading through his body. His eyes glistened as once more, he took the rolled confession paper and this time, ran it slowly down the length of Savonarola's body.

"Cardinal," asked the man administering the torture, "shall we pull it out cleanly?"

"No, no, my son," Greco laughed. "Not yet. If you do, how will this poor misguided man sign it? We will need that arm and hand to remain intact so he can admit his guilt."

"Never," Savonarola's voice mumbled.

Greco sighed heavily. "You and I serve God in different ways." Greco stood silent for a moment, studying the man. "It's over, Savonarola. You have lost everything. His Holiness has already ex-communicated you from the church…yes, your beloved church. Now what will you do? You're no longer welcome here…no longer wanted here."

Savonarola couldn't believe his ears. God does not want me? he wondered. No, that's a lie. Mustering up enough energy, he screamed, "God knows I did no wrong. It is YOU who are the guilty one! I've done nothing wrong."

"Nothing?" Greco laughed loudly. "Do you realize that His Holiness has charged you, along with da Pescia and Silvestro with heresy, uttering prophecies, sedition, and other religious crimes? You've done quite a lot, my friend…quite a lot. At least da Pescia and Silvestro admitted to their crimes. They'll pay with their lives, but they won't have to endure this torture."

"I've done nothing, I tell you…nothing wrong…nothing wrong…." Savonarola muttered, slipping in and out of consciousness.

"Please believe me, my son, whatever is left of the Medici guard will soon be dissolved. I will eliminate them one by one. That pawn of the Medici's, Captain Rafael sentenced the three of you to burn on a torture stake in the piazza. That fool, made my assignment that much easier, so the truth is the city of Florence will kill you, not the church."

Greco nodded his head once more.

Savonarola's excruciating screams intensified, reverberating through the building. A few cells away, da Pescia and Silvestro cringed in the darkness hearing Savonarola's agonizing cries. Quivering in fear, da Pescia's voice broke, "We were betrayed. Alexander used us and now he's betrayed us."

"Shut your mouth!" Silvestro yelled. "You knew what you were getting involved in…I did too. If it is God's will, then death is our fate."

Greco looked down at his old student. "This is your last chance. Admit your crimes in front of God and I will stop this torture. If not," Greco frowned, "I will be forced to pull your body apart, piece by piece and trust me…at this point God doesn't care if you sign it."

Savonarola opened his eyes slowly, fearful his eyelids would inflict more pain to his body. Opening his mouth, he whispered, "Sign----"

Greco placed a piece of charcoal in Savonarola's hand and smiled as the beaten priest signed the document. Greco placed his hands on the fallen priest's head. "You are wise, my son. This would have been a horrible way to die. Unfortunately," Greco bemoaned, "you still must pay for the crimes that you have committed."

Savonarola's blood ran cold as he was given this death sentence. "You lied?" his voice cracked. "You said if I signed, you..." he gasped, "you would release me."

Greco ignored Savonarola's words. Raising his head to the heavens, he prayed loudly over his body.

"O Lord Jesus Christ, our Redeemer and Savior.
Forgive these lost souls of their sins.

May God the Father bless us, and may the blood of Christ save us.

Please commit these evildoers to their eternal damnation in hell.

Yours is the divine power and glory for all eternity.

…AMEN."

Greco drew a deep breath. "Girolamo Savonarola, for your crimes against the church and your crimes against God himself, you, along with Fra Domenico da Pescia and Fra Silvestro, will be burned alive in the Piazza della Signoria."

Greco took his thumb and made the sign of the cross over Savonarola's forehead.

"I'm innocent… innocent," Savonarola moaned.

"Really?" Greco asked. "Well make sure you tell that to God when you see him."

Chapter Twenty-Five

Cesare Borgia pounded his fist on the table. "NO! This can't go on any longer. You all agree that my father has to be stopped but you're afraid of him. You won't stop his madness…so I will."

Fed up by the whispers directed at him and his mother, Cesare wanted his father to stop hiding behind the papacy and put an end to his corruption and brutality.

A young man of twenty-two years of age, Cesare is tall and lean with long brown hair down to his shoulders. A straight-boned nose sloped down from his broad forehead showing a hint of thin hair under his nose. The hatred of his father coursed through his Italian blood, causing him to be unafraid of breaking one of God's most sacred commandments, Thou shall not kill, to end his father's evil rule.

Pacing the floor of an abandoned dungeon below the ornate halls of the Vatican, Cesare Borgia took a deep breath as he spoke to a few men of the church. "This dungeon hasn't been used since the war some years ago. No one ever comes down here but me."

"*Signore* Borgia," an older cardinal whose voice simmered with anger bellowed. "You have no desire to enter the priesthood, but yet, you call all of us down here for this secret meeting. Our time is precious, boy…this better be important."

Cesare smiled, "Do you consider the murder of a Pope important or do wish to see his reign of madness continue?"

Chapter Twenty-Five

"Lower your voice, boy!" growled Fra Del Veccio. "You'll get us all killed."

"I told you, nobody ever comes down here," he replied, easing their fears. "To get away from my father, this is where I come to think…to dream…to plan."

"Plan?" one cardinal curiously asked.

"Yes, I do have a plan. Do I now have your attention?"

The handful of men nodded in agreement. "Ever since I was a child, my father has hated me. He's hated my mother! I've seen him beat her, call her a whore and parade women around in front of both of us. I know of men…good men, whom he had killed for whatever riches he wanted. Upstairs, in those holy walls above us, I've seen his hypocrisy…I've heard him plan murders. A few years ago, he threatened me when I confronted him with his lies." Borgia shook his head in disgust. "I'm only twenty-two years of age but I've seen enough."

"Young man," Stasi argued. "Think of what you're proposing…murdering the Holy Father."

"Holy Father? My father is Rodrigo Borgia, the murderer. He just hides behind the name Alexander. Like I said…from down here, I can hear his plans. Lately, a Cardinal Greco has been visiting him."

"Greco?" Stasi shuddered. "I've talked to him a few times. There's something in his eyes…I can't explain it, but I see evil in them."

"*Signori*, I overheard some of what they were saying," Cesare said. "Greco has been in Florence and I believe that he is involved in a plot to kill the priest Savonarola."

Stasi froze for an instant then let out a hushed gasp.

"Don't play dumb!" Del Veccio barked at his friend. "You know all about Alexander's evilness."

"I know." Stasi lowered his head and confessed, "Still…he's our…our ruler. He's God on earth. He's ----"

"He's sadistic!" Cesare shouted, interrupting the frightened Stasi. "Both he and Greco are, and if they're not stopped, then no one is safe. Any one of us could be next. I don't trust either of them and I suggest none of you here do the same."

Stasi glanced at the young Borgia. "So tell us, just how do we stop the most powerful ruler?"

"With a plan, my friends…with a plan. And I won't put your lives in danger. I will be the one who will stop him."

Most of the older men were totally unprepared for the young Cesare's reply.

"Really?" Del Veccio chuckled. "Stop your father? Stop Greco? Tell me, young man, what plan have you devised that can outwit those men?"

The younger Borgia paused a long moment. Suddenly, from under his garments, he produced a razor sharp dagger. "You stop violence with violence."

Stasi's eyes widened at the sight of the weapon. "You're very young, my friend, but what could you possibly know about killing? This is sacred life we're talking about. He's your own flesh and blood…your father!"

A slow grin creased Borgia's face. "You're a fool!"

Standing beside a few of his stunned colleagues, an elderly cardinal from the rear of the room strode to the front to address the small group of men. "*Signori*…brothers. I have heard what young Borgia is proposing to do and yet while I abhor murder, I cannot escape my own conscience by letting His Eminence continue in his evil course. He must be stopped any way he can and if it means the death of he and Greco, then I am giving my full support and most importantly, my blessing."

Silence.

Arguing developed among those who were divided on the plan.

Cesare's face flooded with fury. "In these sacred hallowed walls of the Vatican, a dark, evil figure prowls looking for prey. Right now, it's Savonarola, next time, who's to say that it's not one of us?"

"Stasi's right," Del Veccio grinned. "You are a fool. A soon to be dead fool!"

"*Signori*, I think you severely underestimate me," Borgia said firmly.

He poured himself a glass of wine and threw it down his throat, then poured another one.

"I know that I've hated him for as long as I can remember. I feel no guilt for what I am about to do. I will kill him before he kills me but I will need two of you to help with my plan. You are supposed to be godly men and godly men stand up for what is right…even in the face of death."

Fra Del Veccio felt a pang of truth in that statement.

"WHAT?" Fra Stasi roared. "Your arrogance will lead to your death, young man! We ARE men of God and we will not help you in this insidious plan."

Cesare's face was white with fury, his lips pressed into a thin line. "Fine, I thought you might consider doing the right thing. I will go about this myself."

"You don't understand!" a voice bellowed.

Cesare looked in the direction of the voice.

"I understand enough!" He glared as he headed to leave the room.

"No, you don't. He's a man of God!"

Cesare turned back towards the men. "*Signori*, my father is having one of your own killed and for some strange reason, he also claims to be a man of God."

Turning once again to leave, Del Veccio shouted, "WAIT! Come back!"

Stasi's eyes went wide in fear. "You're actually considering this? If we get involved in this, we'll reap havoc."

"Maybe…but he's right. Something needs to be done." Turning towards Borgia, Del Veccio asked, "So, do you really have a plan or are you just going to walk up to him and kill him?"

Cesare crossed his arms, letting his body sag somewhat. "I would only need help from two of you. Fra Del Veccio, Fra Stasi, my father trusts both of you. Stasi, didn't my father give you the responsibility of engineering the Vatican roads?"

Stasi gulped hard. "Yes, but it's a responsibility I would like to keep, instead of my neck dangling in some noose."

Cesare rubbed his hand on the back of his neck, a sense of urgency in his voice, "My plan is simple. Stasi, you get my father up to the rooftop where he can get a full overall view of the city's roads. I know what to do from there. We need to act immediately or eventually, he'll kill us all…trust me."

"So, the plan is to…to kill Greco and your father?" Stasi asked, frozen in terror.

Cesare nodded. "Greco will be back in a few days from Florence. Whatever he's doing, I'm sure it involves the death of Savonarola."

The three men stepped out of the room and out a secret doorway leading outside. Gulping the cool, fresh mid-afternoon air, Cesare stared hard at the men. "Be ready!"

Chapter Twenty-Six

"I'm here to see the Holy Father…it's imperative that I see him now!" Wearily, Captain Rafael pleaded with one of the Vatican guards at the front gates of the Vatican.

"His Eminence sees worshipers by invitation only, so you must -----"

"I'm not here to worship him," he interrupted. "Look, I need to see Pope Alexander now. It's of grave importance. A man's life is at stake." Rafael's pulse thundered. "You must listen to me!"

"I'm sorry, but tell me who you are and I will arrange a meeting at a later date. His Holy Father is extremely busy. Just give me your ----"

Fury surged through Rafael's veins. "One of your priests is going to be executed in my city and I need Alexander to stop this killing…the man is innocent!"

The guard's soft brown eyes studied Rafael suspiciously. "Tell me, what city do you come from?"

"Florence…I come from Florence," he blurted out. "We need to hurry. Like I said, a man's life, a priest's life, is to be ended soon!"

Rafael's loud commotion caught the attention of one of the Pope's cardinals to investigate.

"What is all this disturbance about?" he barked.

Chapter Twenty-Six

The young guard's face reflected a mixture of fear and confusion. "This man said that an innocent priest in Florence is going to be wrongly put to death!"

The cardinal's fingers scratched at his chin. "A priest in Florence, you say?" His eyes narrowed down into small, tiny slits. "This priest you are talking about…does he have a name?"

"Savonarola," Rafael urged. "But he's innocent! Please…we must hurry."

"Savonarola, you say? Yes, yes, I have heard of him…Girolamo Savonarola. As a matter of fact, I've heard quite a lot about the man." The cardinal gave a dismissive wave of hand to the guard. "You may go back to your business, and I'll take our guest to see his Holy Father. Now tell me, *Signore*, who can I tell His Holiness is here to see him?"

"Rafael…Captain Rafael of the Medici guards," he blurted.

"Medici guards, you say? Hmmm, please…follow me, *Signore*, and I will take you to His Eminence right away."

Exhausted from his long trip, Rafael needed sleep but sleep was the last thing on his mind. *Signora* Medici's words played over and over. *Savonarola is innocent*!

Captivated by his new surroundings, Rafael could barely believe the sight now coming into view…the Vatican Palace.

Studying the captain, the cardinal remained curious. "So tell me, my son, how did you get involved with Savonarola? Are you in trouble?"

Rafael remained silent. His steely glare honed in on the massive doors that they were approaching. The cardinal led the way past the guards as they walked into the circular courtyard. "My son, I asked you if you were in trouble." the cardinal probed.

"My business here is for Pope Alexander only," Rafael replied curtly.

The cardinal sighed impatiently. "Oh…I see." His voice tinged with anger.

Entering the massive foyer, his eyes were riveted on the huge marble staircase that they began to climb. Step after step, they walked up until they reached an expansive hallway filled with paintings and statues. "You may wait in here, captain. I'll let His Eminence know that you wish to speak with him in a matter of urgency."

Rafael looked around the room in awe as he heard the door being locked from the outside. The captain glared at the lock. His first instinct was to pull on the knob, to get out of the room. His fists pounded on the door a few times, then he stopped abruptly. Realizing he was probably worrying for nothing, he laughed to himself, *I am in God's house…I am safe here.* Rafael moved from painting to painting along the wall. He found it intriguing to find a beautiful portrait of Pope Sixtus and signed on the bottom was the signature of "Botticelli." He smiled knowing he had met the artist a few times and always admired his work, even though the Medici boys hated him. The captain stared blankly at the next few paintings along the wall. Dabbing the sweat from his brow, the tired man spotted a comfortable looking chair to sit in and admire the other pieces of art while he awaited Alexander.

"The fool!" Alexander whispered into the cardinal's ear. "This captain came here to have me spare Savonarola's life? What would possess him to do that?"

Chapter Twenty-Six

"It was *Signora* Medici, Eminence. She told the captain that Savonarola had no involvement with her son's murder. The captain wants him freed."

"Troublesome woman." Alexander sighed angrily, "So where is this Medici guard?

"The captain is waiting for you down the hall, Your Holiness."

Alexander stared deeply into the cardinal's eyes. "You know what to do. Buy time then get him in here. I want this whole mess including the executions tomorrow morning…all over. Is that understood?"

After some time, Rafael heard the door unlock. Jumping to his feet, he met the cardinal at the door. "Sorry, we've kept you waiting, my son." The cardinal explained, "His Holiness was in the middle of an urgent matter but he's finished now and should be here shortly. He asked me to give you his sincerest apologies and asked you to be patient a few minutes longer."

The captain nodded. "I understand. I came unannounced."

The cardinal walked into the room with Rafael close behind. "Here, this is some of the finest wine you will find here in Rome. It's Pope Alexander's favorite. Let me pour you a cup while you wait."

"Thank you and please tell His Eminence that I appreciate his kindness to meet with me on such last minute notice." Rafael put his lips to the cup and slowly drank the wine. After finishing, he licked his lips. "The Holy Father has very good taste in wine…this is delicious."

"Please…have more. The Holy Father will be pleased. He likes to know what people think of him."

"Him?" the captain asked, taking another gulp of the wine.

"His offerings…his hospitality…his generosity. He likes to know. He will be pleased with your comments."

While Rafael was pre-occupied with his wine, he failed to notice the dark shadow that entered into the room behind him.

"It should only be a few minutes more, my son. I will leave you now. Enjoy your visit with His Holiness."

The wine relaxed Captain Rafael as he walked around the large room, admiring more paintings that hung on the wall. The warmth of the afternoon sunshine streaming in through the large windows felt good on his face. Rafael pushed aside one side of the large hanging draperies framing the windows. Looking out, he was awed with all that he saw. His head turned sharply to the left where a large statue of the Madonna stood erect. Her beauty captured perfectly in plaster by one of the masters was impressive. Our blessed mother Mary was etched on the base of the statue. Taking another gulp of the wine, Rafael took a few steps backwards, garnering a better view of the artwork in the room, when he bumped into something that moved. Rafael was stunned. He instantly felt a loathing horror as he was hit in the back of his head, crashing him to the floor. Behind him stood a large hulking figure dressed in a black robe and a hood that covered most of his face. The only thing that Rafael could make out was two black slits where eyes should be. The captain quickly regained his senses and jumped to his feet when the attacker charged him like a raging bull. The force of the brutish man sent Rafael stumbling backwards against the marble balcony, high above the gardens. The attacker's massive hands were snapping Rafael's windpipe. Gasping for air, the captain looked down from over the balcony and thought he was going to be thrown from this height to his death. In desperation, Rafael pulled the dagger from his belt and was able to slash at the stranger, ripping the man's flesh across his forearm. The attacker took a step back and smiled. Rafael stood momentarily paralyzed, trying to breathe when the brute, screaming with rage, suddenly lunged again, grabbing Rafael's jacket and throwing him back into the room. Tumbling forward, he fell into the statue of Mary. His eyes made instant contact with hers. Her warm, inviting eyes were glued to his when the pain shot through his body. His scream seemed to echo throughout the Vatican. Rafael felt an upsurge of dread, as blackness seemed to overtake his vision.

There was a dark, widening stain spreading across his jacket as fresh blood spread across his back. His life's blood glazed over the marble floor and the patterned rug beneath his feet. Rafael didn't want to believe that he was going to die here…in the chamber of His Holiness, Pope Alexander VI.

Grabbing one of the edges of the heavy drapery, he held on for seconds. Not being able to stand on wobbly knees any longer, his body crashed hard to the floor. The images all around him began to blur. Rafael looked up to see the eyes of the Madonna staring down at him. Her warm, caring, inviting eyes were looking over him but could not protect him…only watch him silently die.

His eyes began to close when he caught sight of an inscription on the wall above the statue of Mary. From the Psalms:

Deliver me from my enemies, oh my God.
From those rising up against me, may you protect me.

Everything went black.

Chapter Twenty-Seven

Hammering was heard throughout the Piazza della Signoria on this twenty-third morning of May. Workers were furiously finishing building a platform in the piazza for the execution of Girolamo Savonarola, Fra Silvestro and Fra Domenico da Pescia at noon.

In his small, cramped cell, Savonarola quietly worked on his final written meditation, *Infelix ego*. Under extreme stress, he displayed an unusual air of calmness. His hand, still badly bruised from his torture, scribbled the first words across the parchment, *Alas…wretch that I am.*

Through the dim light, Silvestro looked over into Savonarola's cell. A morbid chill raced through his body as he studied Savonarola. "What are you writing now?" His voice was troubled.

Savonarola drew a deep breath and straightened his back. "I am pleading with God for mercy."

"Mercy?" Silvestro chuckled softly. "Why should you receive mercy? You're no different than da Pescia and myself."

Savonarola stopped writing and squinted into the dimness of the room. "I'm asking him to forgive me."

"Forgive you? Why should he? You're as guilty as we are."

"I ask him to forgive me because of my physical weakness. Because unlike the two of you, I was tortured into confessing to crimes that I didn't commit." Lowering his head back to his writing, Savonarola mumbled, "Both of you are the murderers. This is what you deserve."

Da Pescia lay on the cold floor in agony. From their underground cell, small amounts of sunlight crept through the bars securing the window. Da Pescia momentarily looked up and was confused as an eerie silence filled the piazza.

Maybe the Pope has spared us, he thought.

Sensing the gravity of what was soon to come, he lowered his head in silent prayer. Without warning, the sound of wooden stakes being pounded into the ground resumed. As the piazza began to get filled with people, some prayed, some wept and others screamed obscenities while they waited for the execution.

Cowering in his cell, da Pescia's heart pounded wildly as the roar of the crowd was deafening.

Cardinal Greco watched from across the piazza, his lip curled into a monstrous grin. The last of the construction was being finished when the piazza clock tower struck ten.

Greco smiled, knowing the time was fast approaching…knowing the Holy Father would be very pleased. Over the threatening sounds of the crowds, he shouted down to the workers, "Bring the wood and place it around the poles."

"Excuse me, cardinal," a guard approached Greco from behind. "Captain Rafael is nowhere to be found…do you wish us to have nooses ready?"

Silence.

Greco's eyes were glued to the execution platform, oblivious to the young guard's question. This is the final blow to Florence, he thought. With Savonarola gone and no more Medici's, our plan will now come to fruition.

"Cardinal." The guard cleared his throat and asked again, "Cardinal Greco?"

Chapter Twenty-Seven

Terror blazed across the young guard's face when Greco wheeled quickly and pulled out a dagger from inside his long red vestment. Horrified, the young man saw his reflection in the steel of the blade. Greco turned the knife over and held it against the guard's throat. The icy metal gave the man chills.

"What is it that you want, boy?" Greco's deep voice growled.

"Do…do you wish us to ready the nooses?" the frightened guard nervously asked. "I was going to ask Captain Rafael but I haven't been able to find him. It is the godly thing to do…having them die by rope before burning them."

Greco's deadly eyes were keen, like a man with lucid determination as he held the guard at bay, the knife pressed firmly into his flesh.

Grave concern was etched on the man's face as the edge of the blade penetrated deeper into his neck. "Your captain is dead," Greco hissed. "Your orders come from me now. The rest of the guards will do the same. If you disobey, you will have the same fate as Rafael. Do you understand?"

After a slight nod of his head, Greco dropped the dagger away from the guard's flesh. With brutish force, Greco pushed the young guard to the ground. "Use rope for two only," he commanded.

"Two?" the guard feebly replied.

"TWO! There will be no rope for Savonarola. He is to burn to death, not hang." Greco's eyes turned black with dread. "The three poles there…there are large amounts of brushwood under them. Take some away! I want only little amounts under each, then, we will add as we need it."

"Please forgive me," the trembling guard asked, "but with a larger fire, they would die quicker from the smoke. Isn't that what you want? A more merciful death?"

The knife left Greco's hand in a blur, tumbling end over end. Tearing through the air, it landed only inches from the prone guard's body. "EXCUSE ME, BOY!" Greco screamed. "There is no mercy for them because these three are men of God." Greco's pulse thundered. "Don't tell me what my views on mercy should be! You have no idea what these men did. Now obey my orders or there will be a noose for you as well."

The guard's heart raced furiously. Without another word, he got to his feet and ran from the irate Greco.

The cardinal watched as the finishing touches on the rough scaffolding was being completed around the poles. An evil grin grew across Greco's face as he laughed out loud, clearly enjoying the events leading up to the public execution. "I want the fire hot, hotter than the flames of hell. I want them to roast slowly," he cried out, a warm anticipation spreading throughout his body. "First their feet, then their thighs, hands and torso, all of their bodies will burn." Looking upwards to the heavens, he stretched his arms out and prayed loudly. "Oh great God…let these murderers burn as you wish. All those who murder, shall be murdered. Let them burn till they are no more!"

Greco's sinister prayer echoed its way into the dungeon cells below. Ignoring the sounds coming in from the street above, Savonarola took a deep breath and turned his attention back to his work. Lowering his head, he began to read aloud the few words that he had written, Alas wretch that I am. Content, he painfully placed his right hand back to the parchment again to write.

Destitute of all help, who have offended heaven and earth, where shall I go? Whither shall I turn myself? To whom shall I fly? Who will take pity on me? To heaven I dare not lift up my eyes, for I have deeply sinned against it; on earth I find no refuge, for I have been an offense to it. What therefore shall I do? Shall I despair? Far from it for my God is merciful, my savior is most loving. God alone therefore is my refuge.

The large clock in the piazza chimed eleven times. Savonarola stopped only for a moment to look up at the ceiling and close his eyes in a moment of meditation. Knowing that his time on earth was quickly drawing to a close, he looked across into the cell of Silvestro and da Pescia. The two fallen men of God were sealed behind ancient iron bars in their stone jail cell. From his knees, da Pescia was grieved as he confessed his sins to God, including the murder of Lorrenzo Medici.

Through mumbling undertones, he prayed feverishly…then again…and yet again.

Silvestro's life was about to be ended, cruelly and abruptly. He felt the stark reality of his actions now closing in on him. He breathed deeply as ghastly images of his imminent execution raced through his mind. Terrified, he watched as da Pescia prayed and wondered if God was listening. Maybe this is a good time to start praying, he thought. The putrid smell of death permeated throughout the air as the three men awaited their fate.

From the murkiness of their cells, Silvestro and da Pescia trembled when the sound of the heavy iron doors opened from upstairs. Da Pescia felt paralyzed as his eyes stared upwards towards the noise coming towards him. The footsteps of the guards produced a loud clanging of chains that they carried. The clock now read eleven forty. Both Silvestro and da Pescia recoiled as the rattling chains came closer towards them.

Through the bars, Savonarola looked seemingly unaware of what was about to happen.

"Fool… they're coming for us now," Silvestro said.

Calmness took over Savonarola's soul as he slowly got down on his knees and offered up a silent prayer.

Silvestro and da Pescia's door was opened first as Silvestro dove for the guards' legs, sending the man to the floor, crashing his head onto the stone slab. Resisting their captors, they fought with the guards but after a few moments, the clutching and clawing stopped. The two were subdued and shackled with chains and dragged to their feet. They walked one by one out of the cell, their chains dragging the stone floor. Stopping outside of Savonarola's cell door, the guards were amazed as the doomed priest quietly stood and held out his arms out for the men to place the chains on them and his feet. With the three prisoners readied, the guards led them on their last journey up the dark steps. With each agonizing stride, the chains smacked into each other as well as the stone steps, creating a loud crash.

Silvestro and da Pescia clutched their crosses and softly muttered their prayers to God. From behind, Savonarola heard the faint murmur of their voices. "Whoever it is you're praying to, I hope that he is listening," he said.

Reaching the top of the steps, they walked down a long corridor until they were suddenly immersed into the blinding mid-day sun. Standing in the piazza, their eyes witnessed the horror of seeing thousands of people from Florence and surrounding towns jeering wildly to see the church execute their own religious leaders.

Savonarola entered the Piazza della Signoria slowly, regally even. His eyes widened in curiosity, observing the construction for their execution. Up till now, he had only heard the sounds of what was being erected, but now…it stood before him. A scaffold, connected by a wooden bridge with the magistrate's platform on top, had been built on the very spot where Savonarola burned books and paintings almost a year earlier. His eyes caught sight of the three large wooden stakes placed in front of the platform with a large wooden cross, taken from the church, hanging in front. Brushwood was placed around each wooden pole. Clad in their vestments, the three prisoners took their first steps onto the newly constructed bridge amidst fanatical screams from the villagers. Within moments, searing pain shot into the soles of their feet. Young altar boys, hiding under the bridge, thrust sharp sticks between the planks, wounding the feet of the three condemned men thus preventing them from adjusting their bodies higher on the pole in order to escape the impending flames. Savonarola hesitated a long moment, then continued across the bridge until he made it to the platform. Refuse pelted the three as they stood before the execution poles. Using the last few precious moments of his life, Savonarola stood with his head held high before the crazed mob while Silvestro and da Pescia lowered theirs in shame.

The frightening presence of Cardinal Greco as he walked onto the platform sent the crowds into frenzy, cheering for blood. Dressed in his ceremonial robe, Greco played to the crowd as he stopped in front of the prisoners. Rotted fruits and vegetables as well as excrement were still being hurled at the three.

Over the screams for blood, Greco turned and faced the accused, his voice deep. "In front of God Almighty, I am very sorry to have to do this to you, my sons."

Savonarola felt his muscles tighten in anger. "You are sorry?" he asked. "You should be frightened, not sorry."

"Frightened?" Greco snapped, eyeing Savonarola closely. "Whatever should I be frightened for?"

Savonarola snarled. "Because you know that I've done absolutely nothing to inherit this fate. It is you and Alexander who should be very frightened. You two will have to stand before God with my blood on your hands."

"You arrogant fool," Greco shouted at the priest. "It's a pity you will never realize the power that I wield and how that power could have saved your miserable, wretched life."

Greco raised his hands to silence the delirious crowds and out of frustration, spit in the face of his prized prisoner, humiliating the man before the crowd. "Heretics!" he screamed, pointing to the three behind him. "These three heretics are corrupt sinners…they are liars, claiming to be men of God. You do not deserve to wear these." Greco wheeled, and stripped the men of their clerical vestments.

Savonarola's heart practically stopped when Greco ripped the large gold cross that was dangling around his neck.

"Savonarola, may God have mercy on your soul."

Lifting up the gold cross with both hands to show the bloodthirsty crowd, he began the execution by yelling above the jeering crowd. "I separate thee from the church militant and from the church triumphant."

Greco turned to take a last look at Savonarola and whispered in his ear, "It's over, my son. God has disowned you. He has disowned all three of you."

A slight grin appeared on Savonarola's face. "You're wrong, Greco."

"Wrong?" he chuckled. "Please, Savonarola, tell me how in God's name am I wrong?"

"It's not from the church triumphant," Savonarola said. "That is beyond your power."

Greco's lips tightened in anger as he nodded his head, signaling the execution to begin. Three guards attached the chains to the posts and carefully placed a noose around the necks of Fra Silvestro and Fra da Pescia, sending the crowd into hysteria.

Church of Ognissanti," Ernesto said. "Almost there. This will leads us right into the Piazza della Signoria."

Ernesto looked at his surroundings closely. "The last time the road was this empty, we ran into that burning in the piazza."

"Shhh, be quiet," Fioretta whispered. "Listen."

Antonio gazed at her, "Listen to what?"

"That sound," Fioretta said. "It's like people are cheering."

"More books?" Antonio frowned. "Why would they do it again?"

Ernesto shrugged and focused his attention back on the wild cheers. "I'm not sure, but we'll find out in a few minutes."

The rope was wrapped tightly around the necks of the two priests. Savonarola was stationed between the two men and eyed them carefully as the guards chained their feet in place so they could not pull themselves up. A loud crack of the executioner's whip sent the horses moving forward, pulling on the rope alongside of the stakes that the two priests were hanging on. The crowds cheered wildly as they witnessed the power of the horses. With each forward stride of the horses, the struggling bodies of the priests were writhing in pain. Savonarola's eyes were glued to the horror that surrounded him. Often, he looked away to the stone's curvature of the piazza, the religious artifacts that people were holding up. He looked at both the cheering and the pained faces of those who came out to watch.

Savonarola's eyes met da Pescia's briefly, seeing the choking man's neck stretched further and further as the reaction of the bloodthirsty crowd grew in intensity.

Savonarola quickly closed his eyes and began to pray for forgiveness. The executioner cracked his whip once more on the back of the horses. Their nostrils flared as they pulled the ropes violently one final time, twisting the bodies of Silvestro and da Pescia, gasping for air.

It took a few minutes, but suddenly their bodies went limp…their necks snapped.

Chapter Twenty-Seven

Wasting no more time, Cardinal Greco ordered the guards to bind the arms of the two dead men to the pole, cutting the rope that was connected to the horses.

"Savonarola!" the bloodthirsty crowd screamed, "We want Savonarola."

Not wanting to disappoint, Greco showed his penchant for cruelty by intentionally making Savonarola the last to suffer. With a simple nod of the cardinal's head, two guards approached Savonarola and lifted his body up. A third guard climbed the pole to secure his arms into the iron loop so that his body would not move.

"I'm sorry, Father Savonarola," the guard whispered into his ear.

The crowd hushed as Cardinal Greco again walked across the platform. "For your disobedience to the church…your disobedience to his Holy Father… your disobedience to God Almighty himself and for the murders of Giuliano and Lorrenzo Medici, I summon the flames of hell to swallow your body for all eternity."

Running into the piazza, their eyes were drawn to the platform and the man speaking. "Lorrenzo murdered?" Ernesto shouted to the others. Pushing their way through the throngs of the people, the three were unrecognizable as their dark brown hoods concealed their faces. Ernesto's eyes quickly scanned the balconies around the piazza to see if his enemy was lurking in the shadows. It's impossible…Lorrenzo dead? he wondered. It must be a trap.

"Who is that man?" Fioretta whispered.

"I don't know, but if what he said is true…then we're…we're free," he said in disbelief.

Squeezing their way closer to the platform for a better view, Fioretta screamed in horror. "Ernesto…look! That's Savonarola…they're killing Savonarola!"

Their discovery was quickly silenced by the thunderous voice of Cardinal Greco. "It is customary to give a dying man an opportunity to speak. Savonarola, my son, are you ready to publicly declare your guilt in front of God? In front of all these witnesses?"

Savonarola remained silent to Greco's question.

"This is your last chance," he growled. "Do you wish to confess your guilt to the crowd?"

Blocking the pain and the fear, Savonarola summoned an inner strength as his voice shook with rage. "Should I not die willingly for him who suffered so much for me?"

Startled, Greco whirled around and with a dismissive wave, he motioned the command to place the brushwood under the pole and light it. When the crowds saw the wood being lit by the torches, they began to cheer wildly.

Ernesto felt paralyzed looking upward. Savonarola's arms were spread out, chained at the wrists on a makeshift wooden cross. His terrified eyes met Ernesto's as he gazed down in a silent plea for help. The flames climbed higher, circling around Savonarola's legs as he let out a piercing scream. A breeze rushed in as a sudden surge of flames shot higher around his body. The skin on the priest was blistering as his body was being roasted alive.

In his last few moments of consciousness, Savonarola saw the blackened skin on his body begin to peel away. Summoning all the strength that he had left, he let out one final gasp. "God will be my avenger…my ----"

The crowd cheered viciously as his last words seemed to ignite the flames in an all out assault on his body.

Horrified, Fioretta buried her face into her husband's shoulder. "I can't watch anymore!" she screamed.

Ernesto stared at the final moments of Savonarola's life.

"Ernesto, please," she cried. "Please take me out of here." Fioretta's teary eyes locked on her husband's. "I'm begging you!"

Moments later, Ernesto's pulse raced as he grabbed her arm. "We're going to Sandro's. Antonio, follow us!" he shouted as they ran through the crazed mob.

An hour after the blaze began, onlookers still cheered every time a flame crackled higher into the air, consuming not only Savonarola but the bodies of Silvestro and da Pescia as well. Through the remaining billowing smoke, Cardinal Greco watched with satisfaction at the horrific site. The intense heat made Savonarola's chained arms and legs drop off into the fire. Hours later, body parts that were clinging to the chains, were knocked off by the stone-throwing mob. People cheered when the executioner broke apart the men's remains and mixed it in with the brushwood.

Giving his nod of approval, Greco told a lone guard still watching, "I must return to His Holiness. When the fire dwindles down, I want you to take the ashes and toss them into the Arno River. I want nothing left of their bodies. Is that understood?"

Leaving the city, Greco watched from the Papal carriage, supporters of Savonarola on their knees crying and praying to God for his soul. Suddenly, a feeble high-pitched cry from a group of women, drifted to his ears. He had the driver stop the carriage as he sat there amazed by the sight before him.

"Old woman," he called out. "Do you really think your prayers are going to help him now?"

The woman with tears in her eyes looked up and scowled. "We're not praying for him anymore. God has him."

"God has disowned him. Your Savonarola is with the father of the lie now, so stop that annoying wailing."

The woman briefly met Greco's eyes then returned her gaze looking up to the heavens praying loudly.

"I said stop praying for his soul!" he screamed.

"I'm praying for your soul now, *Signore*," she growled. "God will punish you worse that what you did here today! Trust me…you will suffer a horrific death!"

Greco remained silent, staring bitterly at them. He then turned and stormed away.

Chapter Twenty-Eight

Gisella Mangini gave the woman at her door a silencing glare. Her aged brown eyes sent a clear message.

What do you want here?

The blistering memory of Ernesto's death was still raw. To *Signora*'s surprise, the visiting woman looked nervous, stuttering to find the right words. There was pure sadness in her eyes.

"I…I know you think of me as the enemy, but I'm not. Please…you must believe me."

Signora's eyes hardened, "Why should I?"

The woman weighed her words carefully, "I realize that you believe that my Giuliano killed Ernesto, but please be assured that he----"

"What do you want from me, *Signora* Medici?" Gisella's tired and angry body cried.

The woman took a deep breath, "I understand your grief. I just came to see how *Signore* Botticelli was. I heard that his condition was grave. I mean to cause you no pain."

Gisella's jaw tightened speaking through clenched teeth. "I should spit on you."

Signora Medici gave a stiff nod and turned to leave.

"Wait," Gisella mumbled, thinking of her words. "I doubt he will make it through the night. I know he liked you and Lord Medici. I will watch my tongue…come in and pay your respects."

Signora Medici offered a crooked smile and walked in. Her eyes were instantly drawn to the floor. Rows of canvas paintings, ones that she had never seen were lined against the wall. She slowly moved over to the bed where Sandro was. The fond memories of the artist and her husband caused the woman a pang of sadness. She pulled a clean cloth and gently dabbed it to her eyes. Running her fingers slowly through his hair, she remembered when he painted portraits for her family. "It was just yesterday…just yesterday," she whispered softly. "Thank you, Alessandro."

Ernesto let out his breath slowly and whispered. "I was right, it is the Medici carriage. It was a trick…he's here!"

Antonio's chest heaved with anger. Hiding in the shadow of the carriage, Antonio kept his voice low, "My God, what is he doing here?"

"He's after Sandro…I know it! He's always hated him!"

"Keep quiet," Fioretta hissed, her eyes peering into a small window. "I see *Signora* Medici but no one else." Fioretta crouched behind the Medici wagon, her body dissolving into the darkness of night. As she got up slowly, she crept closer to the window for a better view. "Wait!" she exclaimed. "There's someone lying in bed." Trying to keep out of sight, she was shocked to see the woman praying over the person. Fioretta spun, her face grim. "Something's wrong!"

Chapter Twenty-Eight

The paintings on the floor roused *Signora* Medici's curiosity. Her eyes widened in amazement as she flipped the canvas between her fingers. Trying not to draw attention to herself, she nervously smiled at Gisella who was preoccupied making a broth. The unexpected knock on the door startled both women. The blackness of night made it difficult to make out the hooded ghostly figure standing in her doorway.

"*Signora* Mangini?" the stranger whispered. "Please, I need to speak to you…It's a matter of life or death."

Signora stared at the hooded individual for several moments but sensed urgency in the soft voice. Cautiously, she opened the door allowing the stranger to step inside. Turning to the side, *Signora* Medici was visible to the stranger, prompting a whisper. "We need to speak in private."

Gisella's eyebrows arched with intrigue. "What is this all about?"

"Please…in private," the voice said softly.

Gisella nodded as they both turned to look at *Signora* Medici.

Sensing her presence was not wanted, Medici walked across the room and stopped at the door. Forcing a smile, Medici stared at the stranger in the robe for several seconds. Realizing the stranger had feminine features, she tried to peer closer but the stranger quickly lowered her head as not to be seen.

After a long moment, Medici turned back to Gisella. "He's in God's hands now. I'll pray for his soul tonight."

Soul? Pray for whose soul? The stranger spun quickly to see the body of Alessandro Botticelli on the bed.

Signora Medici's lips twitched in a slight smile and she nodded her head to Gisella, and then walked out the door.

When the door closed, the strange woman's voice gasped, "Sandro!"

As she ran to the bed, Gisella grabbed the robe and pulled back. "Who are you and what do you want?" Gisella demanded. Within seconds, the stranger removed the hood revealing her identity.

"*Signora*...you know who I am. Please, you have to trust me."

Shocked, Gisella's body weakened by what she saw. "No...no, this is impossible. I stood with Sandro and watched them pull a bloodied body...it...it was you! Your dress, soaked in blood being loaded onto a cart. You were killed that night...I saw it, I swear I did!"

The old woman dropped to her knees, crying. "You...you were kidnapped by the Medici guards. They killed you...that's what we were told."

Incredulous, Gisella realized that they were all lied to. Someone took Fioretta and hid her from danger, but who? From her knees, *Signora* stared at the beautiful young woman standing before her, trying to make sense of everything. Fioretta's green eyes sparkled, the way that *Signora* remembered them. Gisella reached out and clutched a portion of Fioretta's wool robe, squeezing it between her fingers as she tried to ease her sense of fear and confusion. "Oh my child...we all thought you were dead. Your parents are heartbroken."

Chapter Twenty-Eight

"*Signora*, dry your eyes, my parents know that I'm alive. They know we both are."

"Both? Fioretta, who else is with you…who took care of you?"

Ignoring the woman's question, Fioretta looked to the bed in the corner of the room.

"*Signora*, what's going on here? What's wrong with *Signore* Botticelli?"

Heartbroken, she whispered, "Oh my dear…he's near death."

Fioretta rushed to the bed and gently ran her fingers across his cheek. His love and kindness to both her and Ernesto was etched on her mind. Softly, she whispered in his ear, "Don't die yet, *Signore*, Ernesto is alive…he's with me. Please hold on a little longer."

Seeing *Signora* still on the floor, Fioretta helped her to her feet. "Is Lorrenzo dead or alive?" she asked, her voice hollow.

The woman sighed, "Dead. Poisoned by someone in the church."

"And his father, Lord Medici?"

"Dead…all the Medici men are dead. Why are you a----?"

"Why was *Signora* Medici here?" Fioretta pressed.

Signora frowned, "She came to pay her last respects to Sandro."

Fioretta remained silent for a moment, and then slowly, she untied the rope sash securing her robe, revealing her already swollen belly.

Signora's eyes grew wide as she ran her fingers across the new life growing inside of Fioretta's womb. Shocked, frightened, curious, the old woman gasped, "Whose child are you carrying?"

"*Signora*…it's Ernesto's," she whispered. "I am carrying his child."

"NO!" *Signora* choked. "That's impossible. You're lying to me."

Fioretta shook her head, seeing the shock in the woman's eyes. "No *Signora*, I'm not lying. Please believe me."

"No," she gasped. "How is this possible? He's dead. He's been dead for some time now. Fioretta," the woman pleaded, "please tell me what has happened? How did you get here?"

"*Signora*, listen to me. Please, for Sandro's sake, wait here."

The old woman stood dumbfounded at Fioretta's response. Running outside the door, Fioretta felt free…like a gigantic weight had been lifted off of her shoulders. "They're dead…all of them…dead," she shouted. "We don't have much time! Hurry, get up and follow me."

Startled, Ernesto looked up at his wife. "Who's dead? What are you talking about?

"You and Antonio come with me!" Fioretta urged. "Hurry!"

"Medici's are dead? Is that what you're saying?" Antonio asked forcefully.

"Just come with me!"

Antonio felt a cold sweat break across his forehead. "Go see your teacher, I have to do something."

"What? Where are you going?" Ernesto whispered.

Antonio sighed heavily and raised his eyes to meet Ernesto's. "You're home and now I'm going home. I'm going to my father." Antonio whirled around and in an instant he slipped away quickly and quietly into the night.

Chapter Twenty-Eight

Ernesto's hands began to tremble as he followed Fioretta into the house. Knowing *Signora* Medici was here and not understanding Fioretta's words, Ernesto remained cautious. Waves of emotions swelled through his entire body. *This is where I live. My teacher's house…I'm home,* he thought.

He cocked his head and continued looking around the room, his memories coming back to him. The handsome features of his youth had been replaced by the weariness of his plight for over a year. He touched the lines in his forehead, ran his hands through his long scraggly hair and felt the stubble on his chin. His eyes welled up with tears.

My sketches…Sandro kept them!

His mouth dropped open in shock thinking back when suddenly, his eyes focused to the other corner of the room. Lit candles casted a soft glow around his teacher's bed. "Oh my God…SANDRO!" he shouted, running towards the bed.

Signora eyed the man suspiciously. Suddenly, she wheeled, anger brimming, "You stay away from him!"

"No, *Signora*, it's alright!" Fioretta shouted, grabbing the old woman's arm.

"Teacher, I'm home," he cried, tears streaming down his cheeks. "I'm home…wake up!"

Gisella Mangini's eyes were menacing. "I said leave him!" she shrieked. With one big tug on his robe, she spun Ernesto around, so that she was face to face with him.

Signora's body went rigid. Staring into the eyes of the intruder, her initial revulsion gave way to anger. "No," she screamed. "You're not Ernesto. I saw him burning in the fire. I looked into that burning pit where his charred body was. I found clumps of his hair that they cut and left in this house. I saw blood...his blood, splattered all over this very floor. And I saw his face in that fire. Please don't lie to me like this. I'm an old woman and my heart cannot take this trickery."

It took a few minutes for her mind to register that this might be Ernesto. Her thoughts went back to the days when she would watch him run and play when he was a skinny little boy.

Could it be...is this possible?

She felt slightly lightheaded from this shock. After Sandro was gone, she would be alone with no one to care for her. Ernesto was like her son. Her legs were wobbly as she swayed from this sudden news.

Fioretta grabbed the grieving woman's arm and held her upright. "*Signora*, Ernesto was not killed...this really is him," she said, removing his hood. "And he is the father of my child."

Gisella's fingers cautiously wove through his hair and beard, down to his weathered rough skin. She couldn't tear her eyes away from the young man before her.

"*Signora*," Fioretta pleaded, "please, let him see Sandro."

Gisella's attention snapped back to him for a moment then she stepped aside, letting Ernesto get to Sandro's bedside.

His eyes filled with emotion as he ran his fingers through the dying man's hair. "I'm here, Teacher," he said softly. "I'm back. You have to live. I have so much to tell you." Ernesto knelt at the bedside, laying his body onto Sandro's, cradling his dear friend.

Gisella stood next to Fioretta, watching Ernesto and whispered, "This is a miracle from God. Is it really him?"

Chapter Twenty-Eight

Caught up in the emotion, Fioretta smiled as tears ran down her face.

"My God!" Gisella gasped softly. "Where have you been?"

"We've been hiding in the forest. Ernesto, myself and a group of men, Antonio included."

"Antonio? I spoke to his father just a few weeks ago. He assumed that he and his cousin were also killed by the Medici guards."

"No, they stayed with Ernesto. They helped him."

"Helped him? Helped him do what?" The old woman raised an eyebrow. "Fioretta, is there something that you're not telling me?"

Fioretta ignored her question as she watched her husband tenderly kiss the cheek of his teacher.

Realizing Sandro's breathing had slowed, he bowed his head in silent prayer for his friend. His long, messy hair fell in front of his face, as he watched in silence. After a few moments, Ernesto's voice trembled. "He's not waking up."

"He won't wake anymore," Gisella whispered. "He is near death now."

The old woman shook her head and raised her voice in anger. "Why didn't you tell us that you were alive? Sandro was so distraught that he wanted to die…don't you understand?"

"*Signora*!" Ernesto's voice rose, "If you and Sandro knew, then both your lives would have been in danger. Lorrenzo would have killed anyone to find out where we were. His guards have been after us since Giuliano was killed."

"Giuliano?" she asked, her brow furrowed. "What do you know about his death?"

Ignoring *Signora*'s question, Ernesto turned his attention back towards Sandro. Gently, he leaned and whispered, "Teacher, it's me. Please, wake up. Please Sandro, I beg you. Hear my voice. It's me, Ernesto."

Signora reached towards the back of Ernesto's head and pulled his long unkempt hair to the side, exposing the back of his neck. *Signora*'s eyes moved across his skin when she was drawn to something. "Hmm…I believe this is it."

An odd look came across Fioretta face. "*Signora*? What are you looking for?"

"When they were young, Ernesto and Giuliano looked so much alike, it's almost as if they were twins. Sandro and I would laugh watching the two boys run and play out in the fields." Sighing aloud, she frowned. "Jealousy crept into the heart of Giuliano." Her hands moved a bit more of his unkempt hair. "Yes, this is definitely it. Look…it's his birthmark. Sandro first showed it to me after Ernesto was beaten badly by Giuliano. Now I know it's really you!" Wrapping her arms around him from behind, he quickly turned as she hugged him.

"How do you know it was jealousy?" he asked.

"When *Signora* Medici talked to Sandro after her husband died, she complained about Giuliano's horrible jealousy. He wanted power for himself and he would do anything to get it. He was even jealous of his own father." *Signora* frowned. "You were a threat to him. When you both got older, that's when he wanted you dead. He would not share attention with anyone. You became the enemy simply by looking like him."

Ernesto gazed around him. The room seemed larger now but everything was still there. His bed, a small table where he sketched years ago. A slight grin appeared on his face, remembering his time with Sandro. "Then what happened, *Signora*?"

"When Sandro came back from Rome that day, he was so excited to see you but…but…" she said, getting misty- eyed, "that's when we saw you…saw it. We saw the blood and then the body smoldering in the fire. Of course, we thought it was you." She closed her eyes in pain. "Ernesto, our hearts were broken. We loved you and it killed Sandro. He's never been the same."

Ernesto's eyes never left *Signora*'s when a slight moan from Sandro quickly cut their conversation short. Holding his breath, Ernesto gently placed his hand on the artist's forehead, as Sandro was stirring in bed.

"Ernesto," *Signora* asked. "If that wasn't your body in that fire, then whose was it?"

Fioretta had a pained expression. "A Medici guard. *Signora* please, we needn't speak about this anymore. He's home…we're home!"

"SANDRO!" Ernesto's excited voice filled the room. Very slightly, Sandro opened his eyes just enough to see who was with him.

The corners of Sandro's lips turned upwards. "Piccolo…" he moaned.

Ernesto's pulse was thundering. "Yes," he shouted! "Yes, it's me. It's me…your Piccolo. I'm here with you for good. I'm back, Sandro, and I have news for you! Fioretta and I are married and we are having a baby! Isn't that wonderful?"

Lowering his head, Ernesto tenderly kissed Sandro on the forehead. "I'm home, Father," he softly whispered into Sandro's ear. "I'll never leave you again."

Mustering all his strength, Sandro slowly raised his limp, withered arm and touched Ernesto's cheek as his body trembled, "Piccolo…my son."

Ernesto grasped his teacher's hand. "Sandro…I love you. Please don't leave me."

The crooked smile on Sandro's face turned flat in seconds. His vision blurred and his body began to shake violently.

"Sandro?" Ernesto screamed. "Sandro…what's wrong?" Ernesto's eyes grew wide in fear. "NO!!! Not now. Please, you can't leave me. Sandro, I'm home. We're going to be a family again…all of us. Please Sandro, please!"

A haunting chill tore through Ernesto. In despair, he buried his face onto Sandro's chest, wanting a miracle but getting none.

Sandro's eyes met Ernesto's for his last few seconds of life. "Er…Ernesto." Sandro's final words were a forced whisper, "I…I love you."

The great artist, Alessandro Botticelli took his last breath of life and then fell silent. His body collapsed motionless. All his physical pain gone, he was comforted knowing that Ernesto was home…he was safe and he was loved.

Shocked and both physically and mentally exhausted from taking care of her dear friend, *Signora* slumped into a chair and stared at his body in silence.

"I've had four great loves in my life," she said, her tone flat. "My husband Donatello and my son Massimo. I loved Donatello the first time I laid eyes on him. He was so handsome and strong. I miss him terribly, even after all these years. Massimo died alongside his father in the great earthquake. My other loves?" she asked, her voice cracking, "you, boy, you. From the moment I met you, I was in love with you. You were so scrawny. When Sandro found you, you were so helpless, and now look at you."

Signora formed a weak smile and groped for the right words. "My last love? Sandro…it was Sandro. We hated each other but learned to love and rely on each other. My God, I won't know what to do now that he's gone. At least he's at peace, no more pain." The woman's eyes scanned the entire room of her small house. "This was a pigsty. I met him when he was a young artist. He had so much talent but he wasted it on too much wine." *Signora*'s eyes got misty. "It's because of you, Ernesto, that this place looks like a home. You made this possible. When he found you in the street, he instantly fell in love with you. I was so angry that he brought you, a little child, into the filth, but you changed him Ernesto…you did this. We both drew closer caring for you. His heart was broken thinking you died, but I know he fell asleep in death knowing that you were here, his little Piccolo," she said, dabbing the tears from her eyes. "I can honestly say, I loved Alessandro Botticelli very much and I will miss him terribly."

"*Signora*," Ernesto whispered, drying his tears. "Where will Sandro be buried?"

A sad weariness hung in the woman's voice, "He had money that we used to help him get better, but without the use of his hands, he couldn't paint anymore. I guess I was going to bury his body out in the meadows. You remember…where he took you to sketch when you were young."

"I do remember it," Ernesto sighed. "*Signora*, I promise you that after all is settled, I will personally see to it that he is given a grand burial, the grandest ever seen in Florence! He was one of the world's greatest artists. I know where I will bury him. It's what he would have wanted."

Signora stared deep into Ernesto's eyes, "How would you know that?"

"Let's just say I saw him go to a certain place and I'm convinced it's what he would want. Please *Signora*, don't worry about a thing. I will take care of this and also I will take care of you."

"Me?" *Signora* let the tears flow. "Ernesto, I have been taking care of myself for years as well as taking care of others. I have a little money left. I will be fine."

They stood in silence for a moment. Ernesto dried his tears and smiled. "After my mother died, you were there for me, took care of me. When Giuliano and Lorrenzo beat me in the fields, you nursed me back to health. *Signora*, we will take care of you. You will want for nothing."

All three stared motionless, gazing down at Sandro's body. The expression on Ernesto's and Fioretta's faces was one of overwhelming dread. The taking of lives weighed heavily on their consciences. There was no turning back the hands of time, no pardon, and no negation for their sins. Fioretta sensed she was starting to come unhinged; her sin was too heavy to bear. Ernesto's head ached, feeling this immense loss. To make it home just to see Sandro die was too much for him. He knew his friend must have suffered in his illness but for the brief last moment that he saw him, it was quick…silence…then heaven.

Feeling bone weary, *Signora* closed her eyes and thought a moment about her friend. "He was a beautiful soul. I know he's with God now."

Chapter Twenty-Eight

The soft rap on the door took her away from her words. *Signora* rose from her chair and slowly walked to answer. Opening it a crack, she seemed surprised, transfixed by the visitor. After a brief interchange of words, she took a package carefully into her hands. She offered the visitor a slight nod and mouthed silently the words, *Thank you.*

Her eyes shining with hope, she thought, This should help. A warm smile came across her tired face as she placed a book into Ernesto's lap.

"What's this?"

"Somebody wants you to have this," *Signora* answered.

"Who? Who wants me to have this? Everybody thinks I'm dead."

"Not everybody," she said softly. "*Signora* Medici wants you to have this."

"Medici?" Ernesto scowled with resolved hatred.

"But how? How did she know we were here?" Fioretta asked. "Did she recognize me?"

The woman paused for a moment. "When she left, she had a hunch. After she pulled away in her wagon, she hid behind some trees and saw you calling Ernesto. As soon as she knew it was you, she went to the palace for this. It's something you must read."

"Why? Why should I read it? It's from the Medici's. I hate them…all of them!"

Signora's eyes were awash with emotion. "No, Ernesto, don't hate. This is how all of this started, because of hate…Giuliano's hate! Please, just read it. Sandro read it and shared it with me. Ernesto…it's your future."

"My future?" he asked. Looking at Botticelli's body, for a brief moment, Ernesto thought he heard Sandro's voice. Ernesto nodded, a faraway look in his eye. *I hear you, Teacher...I hear you.*

Chapter Twenty-Nine

"It's been over two months," Fioretta frowned. "Are you ever going to read this book?"

Ernesto's eyes hardened. "I don't know."

"You don't know?" she barked. "You promised *Signora*, you promised me, and now you don't know?"

"No," he fired back, tired and frustrated. "I don't."

In the past months, memories had haunted Ernesto. Kill or be killed. Tomasso's dying last words, replayed in Ernesto's mind daily, making his muscles tighten in anger. The once little scrawny young boy as *Signora* called him was now a powerful young man, a powerful man who has killed. In town, he heard passers-by mutter under their breath, he's a murderer…no better than Medici. He feels dead, like a ghost, just floating through life.

Why did Sandro have to die? he thought. Still brooding over his hatred of the Medici's, at night he still wakes from nightmares of being beat by the two brothers. Full of hatred, a pain gnawed in the pit of his stomach. *They're dead…Tomasso's dead and now Sandro. I need to be ----.*

"Ernesto! Are you listening to me?" Fioretta demanded angrily.

Ernesto jumped to his feet. "WHAT? No…it's our souls that I'm worried about," he shouted. "Yours, the baby's and mine. I don't want us to burn in hell. Savonarola condemned all murderers. Fioretta…we murdered!"

Ernesto felt anger boil in his stomach. "I've wanted to speak to Antonio…to see how he is coping, but his father said he left and he didn't know where he went." Ernesto's face reddened with fury. "We're home two months and he's gone? It's been weeks now and he hasn't said a thing."

Fioretta didn't wait to hear his last words. Her green eyes blazed with anger. "Enough of this…take the book!"

Fioretta's hands stroked her huge belly continuously as if trying to comfort the baby inside. At eight months pregnant, the baby had dropped quite low, a sure sign that birth was imminent. She shifted out of her seat uncomfortably and dropped the book in Ernesto's lap.

"I'm sorry," he told her, frowning.

Fioretta drew a deep breath. "I know you are. I go through these same feelings too. In my dreams, Lippi is following me and when I scream for help, nothing comes out. I killed him and now I can't get him out of my mind. We've been running for our lives and now that we're free, I don't feel I have any freedom. I feel like I'm a prisoner, no…I feel like a caged animal."

Ernesto hesitated slightly. "You're right. For me…these last few weeks, I haven't been myself. I just…you know. I miss him. I miss Sandro."

"I know you do, but at least you had the chance to say goodbye. That's more than others get. He loved you and at the end, he knew that you were safe. There's nothing more we could have done."

Book in hand, Ernesto stood and opened his arms for his wife. She leaned forward and kissed his lips. Their bodies came together. When she pulled away, the book slipped from his hands. Looking down, she noticed papers that fell from the book.

"Ernesto, I don't feel well."

Her breathing heavy, she sat down in the chair and her eyes quickly scanned the papers.

"OH MY GOODNESS" she screamed, clutching her stomach.

Ernesto's eyes went wide in fear. "What's wrong? Are you alright?"

"My stomach. I think the baby is coming!" she bellowed. "I think the baby is coming…NOW!" Doubled over in pain, Fioretta took the papers and slipped them near her breast.

Chapter Thirty

"More wine I said!" Turning to a bottle, Antonio's memories of fear and hatred surfaced.

The tavern owner was livid, glaring at Antonio in disgust. "*Signore*, you've had enough…go home."

Antonio said flatly, "I have no home…not anymore."

Over the course of three months, Antonio had wandered throughout the countryside of Rome. Trying to gain some normalcy back in his life, he returned to work for his father in the tanner business, but soon troubles set in. His sleep was restless. Feelings of guilt over Tomasso's death festered in him. His sins of murder haunted him endlessly. With nowhere to turn, Antonio left Florence, not telling a soul…he just disappeared.

The owner, a short, thin man, gave an irritated huff and wondered if Antonio understood his words. Angered, he growled, "I said, get out…NOW!"

Antonio's slurred speech lowered to a guttural rumble. "Have I told you that I killed men? Do you understand that? Me…I actually killed, with these very hands, and make no mistake, *Signore*, I will kill again...now I said get me more wine!"

A chill rose from the man's flesh as took away his cup. Sitting at a round wooden table, Antonio's blurred vision had him disoriented. "Where am I?" he shouted, his voice sounded hollow.

"Bacco," the man growled.

"What…what's Bacco?"

"You fool!" he sneered. "Bacco is the Roman God of wine. It's the name of my tavern." Clutching the material of Antonio's coat, he began to shake him. "I've never seen you here before. Where do you come from?"

Dumbfounded, Antonio stared at the man. "I don't remember." Banging his fists on the table, he belligerently yelled, "Stop talking to me. Go and get me more wine, I said!"

The tavern owner was resolute. He stood over Antonio and demanded, "Get out…get out NOW or I'll kill you myself."

In a fit of anger, Antonio overturned the table screaming, "Don't tell me what to do! My whole life people told me what to do!"

The man sputtered in shock, "What are you doing to my place? Leave!"

Antonio's slurred words echoed throughout the tavern. "Have I told you that I killed men with my hands? Just for the fun of it. WELL? HAVE I?" Antonio managed a brief, crooked smile. "Don't anger me, friend, or you will be next!"

The owner's son gave a disgusted snort. Coming from behind the bar, he marched up to Antonio and pulled him to his feet. "Let me kill him, Papa. He's nothing but a drunken fool!"

Antonio laughed. "Kill me? You can't kill me. Do you know who I am?"

"I don't care," the young man answered. "Look, it's simple. You leave, and I won't have to put a knife in your heart. Understood?"

Antonio spit on the floor. "Then I'll kill you!"

Everyone froze. In an instant, Antonio felt the young man's arm clamp around his neck as he was being dragged out. "It was me, Tomasso and the Pazzi's," he bellowed. "We saved Ernesto Palazzo from those damn Medici's. We saved him and killed the others."

Skirting the edge of consciousness, Antonio broke free of the young man's grip, screaming, "They're all dead, do you hear me…DEAD! And it's my fault, the church's fault…Alexander's fault. He left us out there to die. My cousin is dead because of him! ALEXANDER SHOULD DIE!"

At a table a few feet away, an old man sat stunned, his wide eyes drawn to Antonio. The mysterious rant of Antonio had him thinking. *He's no ordinary visitor to Rome. He knows things…seen things.* The old man suspected something odd when Antonio shouted complaints against the church and His Eminence, Pope Alexander VI.

The tavern's heavy wooden door opened and Antonio's body was sent flying out, the door slamming behind him. Cheers suddenly erupted from all the patrons except one. The old man's heart was racing, his wide eyes staring at the overturned table of Antonio's. Not wanting to draw any undue attention to himself, he waited a few moments then quietly snuck out.

The old man was on a mission. His great fear drove his legs faster. Rounding the corner from the tavern, the man heard a slight moan.

Puzzled, he looked around, when laughter rose from his throat. In the corner, behind two horses, he found Antonio passed out, face first in a pile of fresh manure.

The old man gave an inward smile.

"*Signore*!" he whispered. "*Signore*, wake up."

Glancing around to ensure no one was watching, he began to filter through Antonio's jacket for any belongings. *This is it?* he thought, *a dagger and a few Florins?*

Quickly slipping the dagger into his own pocket, the old man fled silently into the darkness.

Across the city, the old man stood at the doorway of an old, abandoned home. Out of breath, he pounded on the door, hoping someone would answer. His brow furrowed as slowly the door opened a crack. Large black eyes peered at him from behind the door. A middle-aged manservant appeared almost ghostlike in the shadow of the flickering candle that he carried.

"Tell him I need to see him immediately," the old man demanded, sounding unusually anxious.

"It's late and he's very busy, *Signore.* Come back another time," the servant replied.

"Busy with what? My time is valuable," the old man growled.

"He's with men of the church."

The old man ignored him. "You need to take me to him now…he'll want to hear what I have to say. You know me; I've been here many times. Have I ever lied?"

The servant sensed the importance in the man's voice. "Wait here…I'll get him."

After a few moments, a set of menacing eyes stared at the old man standing in the doorway. Cesare Borgia was livid, glaring at the old man in disbelief. "I told you before that you're not welcome here anymore. You'd sell your own mother for a few Florins."

"You don't frighten me, Borgia," the old man said, his tone dangerously defiant. "I believe I've found what you need."

Borgia was silent a long moment, studying the man. "Really? And just what do you think I need?"

"Someone who hates your father more than you do."

Stunned, Cesare's blood went cold, his steely eyes cut right through the man. "Bring him to me. I have certain men here that he needs to meet." Borgia felt a pulse of excitement. "I believe I can make him a very wealthy man."

As the door closed, the old man quickly stuck his foot in its path.

"Ahem…perhaps you've forgotten something?" Borgia watched as the man pulled out the lining in his pants pocket, displaying its emptiness.

Borgia drew a seething inhalation. "Bring him to me, then we'll talk about your compensation."

Taking a long swig from the bottle, the old man stood over the prone body of Antonio and began to pour the blood red wine on the back of his head, soaking his hair. Antonio awoke with a start. He had no idea who woke him or of his surroundings. Rubbing the grogginess from his eyes, he looked around, *where am I?* he thought. He gazed down the murky corridor that he lay in.

A sinister laugh behind him drew a startled breath. Antonio glanced up to see the old man's eyes upon him.

"Let's go, boy…get to your feet."

Chilled by the coldness of the stone floor, Antonio groaned in pain. "My head!" Holding his hands to his head, he sat up. "Who are you? What do you want from me?"

"Never mind who I am, I know who you are. Now follow me," the man demanded. "Someone wants to meet you."

Those words seemed to strike a nerve from his Antonio's past. "Don't tell me what to do, just leave me alone," he yelled. Antonio's legs wobbled slightly as he tried to gain his bearings.

The man's anger rang sharply. "I said FOLLOW ME!"

Antonio ignored the words until the stranger came from behind and placed the tip of his sword onto his back, directly behind his heart. Antonio felt his muscles tighten in fear. "What do you want, old man?" he hissed.

The smile on the man's face was almost obscene. "Just you…and a pocketful of Florins."

Antonio's heart turned grave as the point of the sword led him forward into the darkened streets. With each step, he heard the faint murmur of the man's voice over and over…Florins.

Ernesto stood alone in front of the small house where he and Sandro lived. The sounds of crying babies and joyful laughter brought a content smile to his face.

"You slipped out quietly," *Signora*'s tired voice startled him.

"It seems like yesterday, I ran through these fields with Giuliano and Lorrenzo. I would take long walks with Sandro and now look at me…I'm a father."

Signora smiled warmly and hugged him. "You picked beautiful names."

"Giulio, named for Fioretta's grandfather and ----"

"Alessandro," she cut him off. "Named after the man who found and raised you…Sandro."

Ernesto and *Signora* walked in to join his new family. While the two newborns nestled upon their mother's breasts, Ernesto looked at his wife and then at his sons, his eyes awash with emotion. "I promise, you both will grow up to be good, strong men. You will make a difference in this world."

Ernesto gave a tired smile and sat while Fioretta fed the babies. Seeing the book that *Signora* had left him, he thought it a good time to read it.

His eyes traveled the length of the pages when a sudden upwelling of fear raced through him. Ernesto dropped to his knees in horror.

"This can't be!" he gasped. "It's impossible…it can't be true. My father? My brothers?"

The papers floated gently to the floor as he gazed upward towards the heavens.

"MEDICI!"

Chapter Thirty-One

Emerging from the shadows, the two men stood at what looked like an abandoned building. The house was dark except for an ominous glow coming from an upstairs window. A stiff breeze blew in, sending a chill through Antonio. Two strong knocks echoed loudly. After a long pause, the door creaked open.

"Welcome, we've been expecting you," a lone priest whispered.

Antonio cautiously stepped forward but the old man remained at the doorway with his palm extended out, clearing his throat. "I believe we had a deal?" he asked.

The priest whispered something inaudible when from across the room, Borgia raised his voice enough to be heard without shouting. "Pay him!"

The old man tipped his head and scurried back off into the direction of the tavern.

"Please, my friend, come in," Borgia said.

The room was shaped in a large square, dark and gloomy. Old linens were draped over chairs and tables. In the corner, a tall iron candleholder held a single stick of wax that provided a small flickering light.

"Welcome. Please come forward."

Taking a few steps, Antonio peered through the dimly lit room to see who was speaking. After a moment, shapes of two men standing around a table came into focus.

"Please accept my apologies for having summoned you at this late of an hour but I've been anxious to meet you."

"I don't understand." Antonio moved a little closer to look into the man's eyes. "Do I know you?"

His voice was apologetic. "I'm sorry, my name is Cesare Borgia, please sit down."

Antonio's head still throbbed from his excess of wine. He looked tense as he stared at his unwanted host. "What do you want with me?" he asked uneasily.

"Just to talk, my friend. Just talk." Borgia smiled. "So, tell me…what is your name?"

"Antonio Solasso, and again…why am I here?"

"That man who brought you here, earlier he mentioned that he overheard you telling a story. A story that I find very interesting and could be helpful to me."

"Story? I didn't tell a story," Antonio barked. "I don't know what you're talking about."

Borgia walked to the end of the table and sat across from Antonio. With his hands clasped together, he rested his chin in them. "Tell me, what do you know about the Pazzi's?"

"Pazzi? What about it…it just means crazy, that's all."

"Hmm, that man said you were with the Pazzi's. He also said you helped kill the Medici's. Why would he say something like that?"

Antonio stared at the man, remaining silent.

"So *Signore* Solasso, was this a story or not?"

Antonio's eyes traced the man sitting before him. Cesare Borgia had a slender build with long, sloping shoulders. His dark brown hair fell straight down from his square framed face. As he stared at Antonio, Borgia's dark eyes seemed to penetrate Antonio's soul. Below his mustache, a pencil thin strip of hair turned into a full beard.

"*Signore* Solasso...Antonio. I have the means to make you a very wealthy man. You and I appear to be close in age; I think you'll understand why I had you brought here. Apparently, you took part in the Medici assassination in Florence. You helped the Pazzi's and I'm guessing there were more who were with you. Would you care to tell me about it?"

Antonio remained silent.

Borgia sighed impatiently. "Fine...so, tell me about this friend of yours, Ernesto Palazzo."

"You leave him out of this!" Antonio screamed.

"Oh," Borgia smiled, "you do know the man."

Startled to find Borgia standing in front of him, Antonio stood from his chair and did likewise.

"I do know him. He's my closest friend, but how do you know his name?"

"Ahhh *Signore*, people given to a lot of wine tend to talk way too much." Sitting back in his chair, Borgia lowered his voice to a soft whisper, "Look my friend, I mean you no harm, but I am in a position, almost like you were and I need help to carry it through...your help."

Antonio was silent. Despite the soft glow of the candlelight, he was able to look into Cesare Borgia's dark eyes. He paused a long moment, reflecting on the man's curious request. "You say your name is Borgia? That's a famous name."

Borgia replied in a steely tone. "It is and I have a famous father…and therein lies my dilemma. So, would you care to tell me what happened to you and the others?"

Antonio's face reflected a mixture of fear and confusion. The wine began to wear off, his vision becoming sharper. "Who are they?" he asked, his words strangled in his throat. Out from the darkness of the room, two men walked towards the table.

"These men are from the Vatican. They serve as cardinals for my father. This is Fra Del Veccio and Fra Stasi. These men are helping to rid me of this dilemma."

A chill raked Antonio's flesh. "And just what is your dilemma?"

"Murder."

Antonio openly cringed at Borgia's callous words. "M…murder? Murder who?"

Cesare paused a long moment. "My father, Pope Alexander VI."

Borgia's words sent a shiver down Antonio's spine. "You want to murder your own father? Are you insane?"

"In a single word? Yes!" Borgia grinned.

Antonio's voice was tinged with anger. "Why in God's name would you ask me to help you in this…this murder?"

"Look my friend, if your words are true, then my father had something to do with the murder of a family member of yours. Granted, it was the Medici guards, but I believe my father was behind all of it. Am I correct?"

Antonio never took his eyes off of Borgia's face. Suddenly, he bolted from his chair and headed for the door. "We're done here," he shouted.

"Please listen to me. If my father is not stopped now, what he did in Florence, he will do throughout Italy. Who's to say that your family…your friend Palazzo, won't be the next to suffer at his hands?"

Antonio lowered his head and took a deep breath. He was surprised how little emotion Cesare Borgia had for his father. Antonio's head swung around, his eyes narrowed into small, thin slits. "Why do you hate your father so much?"

Borgia became irritated. "Because my father hates me. He hates me; he hates my mother and hates most men in Rome. All he cares about is power…he cares about greed. He has the blood of thousands on his hands and now is the time to stop his madness before countless others die."

Antonio eyed Cesare Borgia a long while. His last haunting words made him immediately think of Tomasso. *He was right; Alexander was behind it the whole time. All the lies, all the murders could have been prevented, and who might be next?* he thought.

Antonio knew Borgia's story went deeper. More horror would come from the hands of this madman who was veiling himself behind the guise of Almighty God. Antonio contemplated his future actions as he walked back across the room and took his seat across from Borgia. The two cardinals, Fra Del Veccio and Fra Stasi joined them. Antonio felt an unexpected sadness at the realization that he would be doing the one thing that had been troubling him for months.

Kill or be killed. Tomasso's words still echoed in his mind. A knot was growing in his throat. "I'm sorry, but I…I cannot bring myself to kill the Pope."

"You're not," Borgia replied. "I am."

"Then why do you need me?"

Cesare Borgia's voice fell to a whisper. "Sit and listen. This is what we're going to do........."

Chapter Thirty-Two

"Where's Stasi?" Alexander demanded, walking up the dark winding stairwell.

There were one hundred and twenty steps to the roof, and each time he stepped on one, the ancient muscles in his legs trembled as though they would betray him and buckle. Short and extremely overweight, Alexander's breathing was heavy and labored. After a long pause, he grumbled, "Why in God's name does Stasi want to see me this early in the morning?"

Saying the words required the Pope to inhale deeply as the chilly, morning air filled his lungs to the point that he thought they were going to explode. Alexander was fighting the urge to ask for help to make the climb, but he succumbed, grabbing his chest and grimacing. Wheezing heavily, the obese Pope reached out and grabbed hold of the much younger Cardinal Greco.

Greco glanced back to see the pain riddled face of Alexander. The cardinal chuckled to himself when he turned back to see the seemingly endless steps. Not surprising, Greco thought. Maybe if his Holiness didn't eat so much.

A smile touched his lips as they continued to climb higher. Reaching the rooftop, the exhausted Pope Alexander hardly noticed the strong wind rustling through his loose-fitting cassock.

The rooftop of the church and all around was deserted at this hour of the morning. Seeing Fra Del Veccio waiting for him, Alexander shouted, "Will someone please tell me what this is all about?"

Swallowing hard, Del Veccio shouted over the howling winds, "Your Eminence, I apologize but Stasi needed to show you his plan for the city."

"This early in the morning? It's ridiculous," he yelled.

Del Veccio found himself being quickly intimidated. Observing the morning light creeping across the rooftop, Del Veccio pursed his thin lips and cleared his throat. "Umm, we apologize for the early hour, but this is the only time to see the city when it's not crowded with people."

Alexander's eyes were black, lacking any compassion. "Nonsense," he snapped looking out at the slumbering city. "I could see fine from down below. I am tired. You woke me early for nothing! Now I'm going back down."

Del Veccio's voice dropped. "If you please, Your Holiness, you wouldn't have the perspective that you have from this elevation. Just give us a few minutes."

Del Veccio saw the Pontiff's jaw muscles tighten, knowing his anger was building.

"Fine…just show me now," he barked. "And where is Stasi? Wasn't this his idea?"

"Yes…yes, please accept our apologies, but this needed to be done early to see what options we have."

Grabbing the Pontiff's arm, Del Veccio led him towards the edge of the roof. He lowered his voice to a whisper. "Stasi is down below waiting to show you. Be careful and stay close to me."

When they approached the edge, Alexander screamed down to the road below. "Stasi," his tone cold, "you have one minute to tell me why I am freezing on this roof!"

Chapter Thirty-Two

Del Veccio's face turned ghostly white, his heart pounded wildly. "Here…grab my arm. You need to lean over more. With these winds, Stasi can't hear us."

From the very edge of the roof, Alexander leaned over and shouted, "Stasi, answer me! What in God's name am I looking at?"

Standing over one hundred feet below, Stasi pointed to the distance, yelling into the wind. "I need you to look down this road, Your Eminence! DOWN THERE!"

Alexander grew more impatient, hearing only a faint murmur of Stasi's voice. He turned his head and let out a guttural roar of rage to Greco and Del Veccio. "This cursed wind…I can't hear him at all!"

"Father, I need to speak to you," Borgia's voice came out of nowhere.

Startled, Alexander spun his head and looked down at his son from the elevated area on which he stood. "What do you want here, boy?"

Stepping from the shadows, Cesare Borgia's voice penetrated the wind, which caught Cardinal Greco off guard. "Father, I really need to speak to you."

Alexander's obese body wheeled, his anger brimming. Dumbstruck, he shouted, "What do you want here?"

"I said, I need to speak with you…NOW!" Cesare snapped.

Shouting over the wind, Alexander demanded, "Get away from me. Can't you see that we're busy?"

"But my mother is ill. Father please, she needs you. I need you to go to her."

"You are in no position to make demands. Now leave me!" he exclaimed. "Go back to your whore mother! Dying would be the best thing for her."

Alexander's memories of hatred towards the woman immediately surfaced like a monster. He remembered the night Vannozza dei Cattanei got him intoxicated and tricked him into having relations with her. Pregnant, she forced Rodrigo Borgia into marrying her…a marriage that he did not want. Every glance at his son Cesare, reminded him of his hatred for his wife.

"FATHER!!!" the young Borgia screamed. "Please, Mother needs you!"

Alexander's dark eyes settled on him once more. "Go tend to that whore yourself!" Turning his back on the boy, a thought raced through him as he quickly spun around. "Wait! How did you know to look up here?"

"The guards told me you were here."

With a dismissive wave of his hand, Alexander hissed, "Very well…leave us."

Greco momentarily froze in panic. "Guards? What guards? No one knows we're up here."

Before Greco could voice alarm, Cesare sprang at his father, as if a demon controlled his body. Without a word, he pulled a steel blade from beneath his coat and plunged it deep into Alexander's back.

Cesare moved with lightening speed to pull his knife out and plunge with brutal force, tearing through his flesh. Alexander's kidneys burst as the knife ripped apart his insides.

Greco watched in horror, unable to move…unable to scream. Silent.

Chapter Thirty-Two

Alexander felt as if his body were on fire. He let out a deafening groan. Within seconds, his son pulled out the murderous steel device, then, in sheer brutality, plunged it deeper into his father's upper back. The knife tore into Alexander's lungs with such force that he projectile vomited blood through his mouth.

Greco never took his eyes off of Alexander's face.

"What's the matter, Greco? Are you frightened?"

Greco shifted his eyes to the boy and slowly reached out a hand towards Cesare in a gesture of surrender. Greco noticed Cesare's eyes turning red like fire. Years of abuse and neglect had sent Cesare past the breaking point. Displaying a lust for blood, he screamed out, "Greco…hell is calling our names. Are you ready?"

Greco swallowed hard. Shocked in disbelief, Greco's voice trembled, "Boy, what in God's name have you done?"

Cesare shot the cardinal an intense stare. Pulling the knife from his father's back, a loud sucking noise was evident as the young man felt a surge of adrenaline. Whirling around, he turned the bloodied knife on Greco. "What have I done?" he screamed. "Something that you and others should have done already… put an end to his madness."

Greco briefly closed his eyes out of dread. Cesare lunged at him, forcing the cardinal back a few steps. Cesare's scowl deepened as he held Greco at bay.

Within seconds, the loud gurgling sound from Alexander's throat quickly turned Cesare's attention to his father. Alexander's thick, wobbly legs buckled under the weight of his fat frame. A large pool of fresh blood formed around his feet, trickling over the ledge to the ground below. A cold dread settled over Alexander as he swayed back and forth precariously on the edge of the roof. Cesare took a step closer to his father, his bloodstained eyes gleaming in the satisfaction of finally putting an end to everyone's misery. Greco watched in horror as the young Borgia spun his body and planted his foot squarely onto the back of his father's blood stained cassock. With a powerful thrust of his leg, Cesare sent the lifeless body of his father over the ledge.

From the ground, Stasi looked up to see the hurtling mass fall from the roof, plummeting to the ground with powerful speed. Stasi looked away as Alexander's body smashed the earth with such force that it burst upon impact.

Without a word, Greco spun on his heels, backing away from Borgia.

The howling winds picked up as Borgia stalked the cardinal. Turning quickly, the terror stricken Greco screamed, "Cesare…is this what you wanted? You just killed God's chosen agent on earth in front of two witnesses."

Cesare hesitated slightly. "God's chosen agent?" he sneered. "He was a murderer…like you. God turned his back on him long ago."

A brief smile fitted across Greco's face. "Congratulations boy, you just signed your own death sentence."

"My death sentence?" Cesare asked, his words dripping with sarcasm. "I think you're mistaken, Cardinal Greco. I think you're sadly mistaken." Cesare grinned broadly.

The young man's tone made Greco uncomfortable. "Cesare, I realize your father treated you cruelly. I promise I will never do that. I was next in line to be elected Holy Father. We had it worked out that way. We can continue what we started. I can use you, Cesare."

Greco's request brought a smirk to Cesare's face. Like a lion hunting his prey, Cesare wiped the blood off the knife and moved in closer toward Greco. "What could you possibly use me for?"

"I…uh, I would need some…uh…help…yes, I would need some help," Greco stammered.

A slow grin creased Cesare's face. "Help? I heard what happened to Bishop Felice. My father threw him out of the window to his death, for what? Couldn't he have helped you?"

Greco's eyes widened in fear as Cesare moved closer…stalking him.

"Well, answer me? Did Felice help anyone? Tell me, Greco…why did he have to die?"

Backing away slowly, Greco growled, "God will have no mercy on you, Borgia. God will punish you to an everlasting fiery torment."

"Do you care to enlighten me, cardinal? Trust me…I think you severely underestimate God's mercy."

"What do you know of God?" Greco screamed.

"My mother was called a whore. My mother loved God. She taught me that Jesus spoke of peace, not violence. He spoke of love. What you and my father have done is betray that message. You've betrayed the Christ. You may feel that you know God, but Greco…I don't think he knows YOU!"

Borgia's face was white with fury, his lips quivering in anger. "I should kill you right now."

"Your father was right. Your mother is a whore. I'll have you tied up and butchered outside these gates for all to see…especially your mother."

Cesare lunged at Greco wrapping his fingers around the cardinal's throat. The powerful strength of Cesare's hands began to crush Greco's windpipe, leaving him gasping for air.

Cesare felt a warm anticipation spread throughout his body. Justified killings, he thought. Seconds later, the sound of popping cartilage came from Greco's neck.

Cesare let go and pushed the injured cardinal to the stone flooring of the rooftop.

Greco lay there for a moment, rubbing his hands over his neck. "Boy, think of what you are doing," he said, his voice hoarse. "I can offer you life… a better life." Slowly, Greco got to his feet. "I am poised to take over all of the cities in our country. Florence was just the beginning. Savonarola was just the beginning. All who stand in opposition of our way of ruling will suffer the same fate. Boy, this was your father's vision. It's my vision…I need you."

"WHY SHOULD HE HELP YOU?" Del Veccio's voice cut through the wind.

Startled, Greco's head sharply turned to the side. "Don't be stupid, Del Veccio. Alexander's dead. I am now in control. Help me…NOW!"

"Why? Why should I help you?" Del Veccio's voice echoed in the winds of the rooftop. "You're a murderer, just like Alexander."

Greco snarled, "YOU FOOL! So you side with him? The man who murdered his Holy Father!"

Chapter Thirty-Two

The young Borgia's eyes never left the face of Greco as he again stalked the cardinal on the rooftop, forcing him into a corner.

Looking left to right, Greco realized he was nearing the doorway leading down from the roof. He grinned as he angled his body towards his only escape.

Cesare's eyes sharpened as he moved closer to his prey.

Fumbling for the door behind him, he smiled when his hands felt the heavy frame of the doorway. "You're not going to kill me, are you, boy?" he scoffed. "Oh, I know you want to, but you won't...you can't."

Cesare smiled back, prompting an odd look from Greco. A few feet more and he forced Greco further back into a small opening of the door. Undetected, a dark figure lurked in the shadows. In the small alcove hid a menacing figure. Despite the cold wind, under his dark wool hooded robe, Antonio sweated profusely. He was silent, except for his pounding heartbeat, which he feared Greco could hear.

Antonio prayed to God for strength. *Should I put down my weapon and beg for my life to be spared?* The thought of it was almost irresistible. He gazed blankly at the floor, waiting to strike.

With a coward's cockiness, Greco taunted, "Come on, boy. I'm waiting. Are you going to kill me?"

Dragging haunting memories of death and suffering from his soul, Antonio lunged out screaming. "NO...I AM!"

Greco's head snapped back viciously when Antonio's hand clamped over Greco's mouth. Panic spread through him as the cold tip of Antonio's razor sharp knife rested against the front of his neck, piercing through the thin, fleshy part of his skin. In breathless silence, Greco watched as Borgia walked closer towards him framing a sadistic smile.

Trembling, Greco closed his eyes and exhaled.

In the blink of an eye, Antonio's knife quickly crosscut into the soft flesh with ease.

Greco clenched his eyes tightly, not wanting Borgia to be the last image he saw. The swelling in Greco's throat came instantly as the taste of vomit mixed with blood filled his mouth. He let out a muted scream while Antonio watched his last desperate moments of life.

Visions of Tomasso's death at the hands of the Medici guards fueled his anger. Ernesto's savage beating and seeing the horrible murder of Savonarola spurred his bloody actions even more.

I am not a killer…a sinner…this is divine intervention. Antonio repeated these words in his head as he watched Greco slowly die. In an instant, a sneer grew across Antonio's face as he moved with lightening speed and thrust the dagger into Greco's neck, twisting the handle deeper into his flesh. The blade was removed with a gurgling sound as Greco slipped to his knees, his dead eyes open, staring up at Antonio.

Antonio threw the blade to the floor. His heart was filled with rage. The words *kill or be killed*, raced through his mind. "I can't believe I did this," he said, his voice heavy with emotion. He looked back down at Greco's body then into the heavens. A feeling of wariness came over him, expecting something more to happen but it didn't. A slow stream of tears rolled down his cheeks as he stared at the body.

Seconds passed.

Chapter Thirty-Two

A peaceful calm came across the rooftop. The sounds of playing children rose high in the air over the whistling winds.

Fra Del Veccio stood silent, feeling the gravity of what he had just witnessed. Turning his eyes towards the body, he felt the sudden urge to ask God for forgiveness. His conscience weighed heavy due to his part in these mercy killings.

Borgia came up behind Del Veccio. "I know you are a good man," he whispered. "There are many like you. Please…please, if there is any way…find a good man to hold the office of Holy Father so this never happens again." Cesare Borgia's smile was tired but calm. "You were never here, do you hear me? You and Stasi have been in Florence the last few days calming the people down after what Greco did."

Several moments passed. Del Veccio nodded his head and slowly walked away.

High atop the church, Antonio stood still a long time, gazing outside the Vatican walls, alone in his thoughts. Outside was quiet; people were just beginning to fill the city roads.

Alexander's body, he dolefully thought. *It's a good time to start praying.*

Antonio scanned the rooftop and strode slowly to where Borgia was standing. Cesare's dark eyes studied Antonio a long moment. A heavy silence fell between them. The son of Pope Alexander VI displayed an eerie poise. Two murders in a matter of minutes, and the man looked incredibly calm.

He pulled a small sack from under his coat and placed it into Antonio's hand.

"What's this?" he asked, perplexed.

"I told you that you would be a wealthy man if you did something for me, and you have. I'm keeping my promise."

Antonio looked totally lost as he peered into the sack. "Gold?" he gasped. "From where?"

"It was his. Most of everything that he has was stolen...he stole from God. It didn't matter to him." Cesare shrugged. "He deserved to die. I'm just sorry that it wasn't done long ago."

"Now what?" Antonio asked. "People will find the bodies and ----"

"Bodies?" Borgia interrupted. "What bodies?"

Antonio looked stunned. "Your father's body? Greco's?"

"I have no clue what you're talking about. Show me the bodies."

Spinning on his heels, Antonio's jaw dropped when he saw that Greco's body had disappeared. "That's impossible!" he whispered. Running to the edge of the roof, he looked down into the courtyard and gasped, "Your father...Alexander. He's gone!"

Cesare looked up to the sun coming across the sky. "I believe by this time his body should be at the bottom of the Tiber River," he whispered.

"What will you say when people start looking for him?"

"My father had many, many enemies. Knowing him, he had a bad night with a prostitute and disappeared. Trust me...he won't be missed."

Antonio nodded. "And Greco?"

"My father sent him to an alliance meeting with the bishops of France to try and end the war. Poor man, he was ambushed along the way, never to be heard from again." Borgia grinned.

Chapter Thirty-Two

There was something about Antonio's expression that changed, a hardness in his eyes that wasn't there before. He was mentally and physically exhausted and had to remind himself why he was there.

Antonio swallowed hard as he wiped some of Greco's smeared blood off his face. "My God! What do I do now?" he mumbled.

"You go on and live your life, Antonio. I know that killing is wrong, but if you and I didn't act…scores of others would have lost their lives. You have to understand what you did and why you did it." He offered a crooked smile. "Will your newfound wealth ease your conscience some?"

"No," he sighed. "I've killed for the last time. God will deal with me in his own way, in his own time, but for now I have to leave."

"For home?" Borgia asked.

"No…no more. I have no home, no family."

Antonio walked away, his conscience pained. He summoned all his strength to live the remaining years of his life shamed before God Almighty. To live every day with that weight was a burden of unimaginable guilt.

Leaving the rooftop, the wind was playing tricks on him. Stopping for a second, he closed his eyes and looked upward to the heavens. The warmth of the sun felt good on his skin when he thought he heard something.

His eyes opened wide as he looked around.

No one.

Through the rustling winds, he swore he heard Tomasso's voice crying out…

Kill or be killed....

Stay alive!.....................

Live your life!.....................

Chapter Thirty-Three

Seasons change, winter to spring, summer to fall and the city of Florence changes with them. What once was a city held captive by the tyranny that the church and the politics of the day held over them, a new Florence was born; these were the days of artistic enlightenment. Masters of the arts wielded their craft much to the enjoyment of the world. The days of assassins trained to kill the Medici family were over. No more did priests, bishops or cardinals take lives for the advancement of the church. The war that raged for years against France had ended. It was a time of peace and prosperity, a time for young love to blossom, and a time to raise children. It had been five years since the deaths of Savonarola, the evil Pope Alexander and his counterpart, Cardinal Greco. An older, kind man named Francesco Todeschini Piccolomini was elected to the office of Pontiff and went by the name, Pope Pius III. His reign stayed within the boundaries of the church. Long gone were the days that Italy's populace had suffered at the hands of the church.

In Florence, a new Republic had been formed and a new Gonfaloniere of Justice had just been elected. Ernesto Palazzo stood poised to take on this new role. Piero di Cosimo de Medici, Ernesto's natural father, held that office for years. Although a fair man, Medici was also a hated man. Ernesto knew that and vowed that that would never happen to him.

The crisp air whipped through the Tuscan mountains as night was beginning to fall. Glorious hues of yellows and reds lit up the sky, painting a beautiful canvas, sumptuous for the eyes.

Ernesto held his five-year old son, Alessandro, as he stood at the heavy wooden doors at the Church of Ognissanti. Fioretta and their other son, Giulio, stood beside him.

Gazing at the doors, he remembered when he followed Sandro into this church. From that day on, he knew where his teacher needed to be.

"Father," Giulio's tiny voice asked, "why are we here?"

"We're here to visit my old teacher," Ernesto replied.

Little Giulio, standing behind his father asked, "But Father, I see my teacher in school and this is a church. Will he be in here?"

Ernesto gave a tired smile, "People live all over, son. Remember how we sketched the fish? They live in the water and my old teacher lives in here."

The two young boys stood next to their mother while Ernesto told them the story of the man who became like his father.

"On the day that you boys were born, my teacher had left," Ernesto explained in a voice choked with sadness. "He was a very famous man named Alessandro Botticelli and he gave the world such beauty with his art. He found me in the street begging for food one cold winter's day."

"Where were your mother and father?" Giulio asked.

"My mother died when I was very young and I never knew my father. This man who's buried here raised me. He taught me how to draw, how to live, how to love, and how to be loved."

Fioretta sighed and began walking through the large doors.

"Let's go visit Sandro," she whispered.

Chapter Thirty-Three

Each holding one of the boy's hands, they started up the main aisle of the darkened church. Ernesto felt his eyes reaching across the sanctuary, taking it all in. A year had passed since he was last here. A soft glow of the remaining sunlight was coming in through the stained glass windows. His two young sons keenly followed every move that their father made, they followed him as he turned into a smaller outer chapel off to the side, when they came across a row of lit candles giving the room a faint golden heavenly aura. Fioretta held her husband's hand as she looked at what Ernesto had engraved on the tomb.

Simonetta "*La bella* Simonetta" Vespucci, and Alessandro "Sandro" Botticelli lie here, entombed for all eternity in love.

In their small hands, each boy held a single rose and gently placed them on the base of the tomb, just as Sandro did for his beloved Simonetta.

"He would be very proud of you." Fioretta leaned forward and kissed Ernesto on the cheek. Their bodies came together while they stood in respect. "Since his death," she whispered, "you always, said where his final resting place would be. You did it…you took care of him and *Signora*."

Ernesto's eyes welled up with tears. "I owe both of them my life. They were my family. When *Signora*'s husband and son died in that earthquake, they never had a proper resting place. Now they all can be at peace…together."

He could not help but feel a deep sense of loss at his teacher's death. The image of the boisterous Sandro flashed in his mind. He looked down at his sons, forcing the picture from his mind. He gently kissed his finger and dabbed it on the engraved nameplate on Sandro's tomb whispering, "Goodnight, my friend. I'll be back soon."

Night had fallen as the sky lit its glorious spectrum of colors of purples and grays.

A few steps from the church, a sizeable plot with a large obelisk grave marker read:

Mangini:
Donatello, Gisella and Massimo

He and Fioretta placed a few roses at the foot of the tomb. A smile weakly grew on his face. "Thank you for everything, *Signora.* Rest now with your family," he whispered.

"May I bow down before you, my lord?"

The familiar voice garnered Ernesto's attention, taking him away from his paperwork, to see the man standing in the open doorway.

"Ernesto Palazzo…the Gonfaloniere of Justice? Hard to imagine. So remind me, my friend, just how many times did I have to save you?"

Stunned, Ernesto gasped, "Oh my God!"

The two men warmly embraced.

"Let me have a look at you. Hmm, you've gotten a little older looking, even some gray hair."

Chapter Thirty-Three

Ernesto eyed his friend for a long moment then furrowed his brow. His voice turned serious, "Antonio…where have you been? You just vanished without saying a word."

Antonio Solasso had long flowing hair, with a hint of silver on its sides. His brown eyes, at one time so fresh and innocent seemed weary, as if carrying the weight of the world on his shoulders. He wore a black silk jacket on top of an expensive fitted shirt and pants. A beautiful gold ring on his third finger shone in the sunlight coming in through the window. Antonio stammered for a moment and suddenly gave an awkward smile. "Well, while you've been stuck here in Florence, I've been exploring the world."

Ernesto's bushy eyebrows arched with excitement.

"The world? I want to hear everything."

Sitting on a large velvet red chair perched next to Ernesto's desk, he told him of his adventures of faraway lands and of exotic women. Ernesto's mouth dropped in astonishment. The hours they spent talking flew by quickly. Soon, the conversation turned serious.

"Right after we got back, you left," Ernesto said. "Nobody knew what became of you…not even your father. No letters…nothing. My children were born, and you weren't here with me! Sure, you saw the world, but what really happened?"

Antonio glanced at his friend and gave a soft nod. "I was mistaken for somebody else," he sighed.

"Mistaken?" he asked. "Mistaken for whom?"

"A killer."

"Antonio…what are you talking about? What did you do?"

Antonio stared at Ernesto a while, and then whispered, "It had to do with the killing of Pope Alexander."

"Alexander? They said his body was found outside one of the houses of prostitution…his throat cut. You killed the Pope?" Ernesto gasped. "But, I …I don't underst---."

"No." He cut his friend off mid-sentence. "Not him…his son did that." Antonio lowered his head in disgrace and mumbled, "I killed Cardinal Greco."

Ernesto looked overwhelmed. "I don't understand. Why did you do it?"

"Revenge!" Antonio shouted.

The word surprised Ernesto, his eyes narrowed into slits. "Revenge for what?" he gasped.

"Revenge for what happened to you…to us…for Tomasso!" Antonio lowered his head, gazing at the floor. "I was paid a king's ransom for doing it."

"You did it for money?" Ernesto shouted.

"NO! Not only that," he explained. "They had a greater plan for all of Italy. They were going to come back here and garner control over everything while they pocketed riches from our friends and families right here. They would have gotten you. There would be no Gonfaloniere. We would have to give so much and get nothing in return. They needed to be stopped."

He was still talking when Ernesto's voice blurted, "And how did you get involved?"

Antonio felt himself hesitate, uncertain if he should continue. After a long wait, Ernesto's gruff tone startled him. "Well?"

"I was alone…I felt lost. You had Fioretta and *Signora* to lean on. Who did I have? My father was angry at first, for not telling him. Tomasso's death was too much for him to bear. When my uncle died, my father sent for Tomasso to come live with us and he raised him like he was my own brother. When I told him how he died, it ripped a hole in my father's heart." Tears welled in Antonio's eyes. "Ernesto, I couldn't live with that guilt anymore."

Ernesto's voice softened. "It wasn't your fault, Antonio. If it weren't for me, he would be alive today."

Those words surprised Antonio. "No, my friend, you're wrong. We went into this together. We thought we were something that we weren't. Killers! We were too blind to see what the whole Medici involvement would bring…pain and death."

Ernesto waited a moment while Antonio gathered himself.

"It was all our fault. We killed to survive and we are paying for that now. I'm troubled every day. So is Fioretta. It's like a bad nightmare that we can't awaken from."

Antonio nodded. "The guilt got to me so I left. I left for Rome, to forget. I vaguely recall what was said as I went from tavern to tavern, getting drunk every day, trying to forget my pain…or at least trying to drink it away. One night, I found myself screaming about how Tomasso was killed. I told everyone that I fought with the Pazzi's and how Alexander and the church betrayed us. The next thing I know, I'm standing in front of a few men with a plan."

"To kill Alexander?" Ernesto asked.

"And Greco!"

The words hung in the large office. A chill raked Ernesto's flesh. Numb, he whispered, "How did you do it?"

The question was met with stunned silence.

The edges of Antonio's lips tried in vain to curl upward for a resemblance of a smile, to no avail. "Like I said, I was given riches for doing that one thing. Blood money! That's what it was and I drank and wandered, depressed for five years. I thought I could run from my problems, but I can't. I can't run anymore, so I'm here…I'm home."

"To stay?" Ernesto asked.

Antonio swallowed hard, his voice resolved, "To stay. I'm going to try and make amends with my father and then find work."

"What a coincidence. I just happen to be looking for a good man to help me here in Florence. A good, brave man who I can trust."

Antonio's eyes got misty. You would hire…" he paused, swallowing the emotion, "a killer? You would trust me?"

Ernesto's dark eyes studied the man who he had known for years. "Of course I trust you. If I recall, you saved my life twice." A smile formed on Ernesto's lips. "You're a good man, Antonio. Remember that. No matter what our past is, you're a good man."

Several hours passed. Finally when it was getting late, Antonio ran his fingers through his long hair and asked, "My lord, what is the first thing you wish me to do?"

Suddenly, Ernesto's voice grew stern. "Never call me lord. We're brothers, you and I. We've lived, fought and almost died together. We'll be together till we die. Is that understood?"

Antonio felt tears welling as he nodded to the new Gonfaloniere of Justice.

As he was leaving for the night, Ernesto stopped him. "I need to ask you something." Ernesto stared at a painting of the previous Gonfaloniere, Lord Medici. His thoughts seemed far away. Looking at his friend, there seemed to be an uncertainty about him. "Antonio, what is my surname?"

"What?" Antonio chuckled, "what kind of question is that? Palazzo, of course."

"What would you say if I told you my real name is Ernesto…Medici?"

"WHAT?" Antonio gasped. "Medici? That's impossible!"

Feeling weary, Ernesto closed his eyes while thoughts of guilt and shame flooded his memory. He hated the Medici's for years, but even though they tried to kill him, Ernesto felt a strong bond to family.

My blood is their blood, raced through his thoughts.

"Lord Medici is my natural father. I have the letters that he wrote to my mother. He tried to hide it but his wife found out, so he abandoned us." His voice trailed off. After a few moments, he wiped his eyes and struggled for his next words. "Antonio, I buried the dagger deep into my brother's chest, possibly his heart."

"Ernesto, you didn't kill him. The Pazzi's did, Bracciolini did…we saw it."

"Yes, but my dagger could have been the deadly blow." Tears continued filling Ernesto's eyes. "I guess I'll never find out. My brother's face…my face, that's what I see…me, plunging that dagger into his body. It's strange, but when I was young, I would go into Il Duomo with no problem, but since then, I can't bring myself to walk in that church. Even for Sandro and *Signora*'s funeral, I stayed outside."

A heavy silence fell between them. "Maybe it's for the best, I guess. You and I have tormented souls. Hopefully one day, we will be at peace with ourselves."

"One day we will, my friend," Antonio promised. "One day we will. I'll leave you to your family now. Goodnight, Ernesto."

Sitting back in his chair, Ernesto thought of his conversation with Antonio. Joyful that his old friend had returned safe, he also knew that they both needed to settle matters. Settle first with themselves and finally, settle with God.

But for Ernesto, he now needed to settle matters with the dead.

Chapter Thirty-Four

"*Signora* Medici, thank you for inviting me in at this time of night." Standing in the doorway, Ernesto looked into the eyes of a woman who carried the name Medici…the name he had despised for years. The weathered lines across her forehead gave evidence of the pain she had been living with for over five years. The smell of fresh baked bread carried through the palace.

"Lord Palazzo," the woman hesitated, "please…"

"No, please," Ernesto said, "please don't call me that. It is to you that I should offer my highest respect."

A warm smile broke across the woman's face. "Please, Ernesto. Do come in and share a meal with me."

The woman had long, luxuriant silver hair that fell down her slender back. Her sad eyes were filled with painful memories as she peered at Ernesto and saw her own Giuliano in him.

"I can't. Not this time, *Signora*, but perhaps in the future." Clearing his throat, he stammered on his words. "This, um…this is very awkward for me to be here, but I need to do this."

"I understand." The old woman placed her hands on Ernesto's shoulders and marveled at the young man. "Ernesto, you have the title of Gonfaloniere, the title that my husband held for many years."

As he listened to the woman, he realized that her husband and her two sons had something in common with himself.

Ernesto felt the power of the Medici blood coursing through his veins…the blood they shared.

"My goodness," she said as tears rolled down her cheeks. "I was going to call you dear boy, but look at you. All grown and with a beautiful family of your own. I have something that I must confess to you." She paused a long moment until she composed herself. "I knew who you were when I first laid eyes on you. One could not deny the resemblance. Out of respect for my husband though, I never let on that I knew. Ernesto, at first, I was torn. Knowing where you came from, I was angry. Angry at Piero, angry with your mother, angry with you and finally, angry with myself for letting this happen. When I looked at you, I saw a beautiful young child, innocent and sweet, and when I saw you playing with my children, your brothers and sisters, I was happy and the anger seemed to eventually fade."

Ernesto glanced at the floor uneasily. "*Signora*, I…I hold nothing against you or Lord Medici."

"I know you don't." She paused for a moment to sigh. "Something went very wrong in Giuliano's soul, an evil jealousy came over him. I blame my husband and myself for spoiling those children to the point that they believed themselves better than others. Ernesto, it broke my heart how my sons treated you. Piero never let on about it, but I could tell in his eyes that you were being hurt…his son, and it was crushing him. This is why he loved *Signore* Botticelli so much, because of how he cared for you and loved you. Loved you the way he wanted to."

"*Signora*, please," Ernesto tried to explain in a voice choked with pain, "I am here to apologize for taking a part in killing Giuliano...my brother."

The woman threw her arms around Ernesto, tears running down her face. "I know you are. I found out that they both tried to kill you as well, more than once." Clutching him tightly, she sobbed, "I forgive you, Ernesto, I forgive you. None of it was your fault." She kissed the young man's forehead and whispered, "Ernesto, I think it's time that you learn the truth about the Medici family…your family."

For hours they reminisced about their past, stories of her children, his brothers and sisters. Stories about Sandro, and how Ernesto, Fioretta and others hid in the wilderness out of fear of Lorrenzo. Finally, they spoke of healing. The night was growing cooler; a stiff breeze blew in front of her residence. As he was about to leave, he turned to look at the woman with whom he just formed a bond. She stood in the doorway, the darkened skies above lit up its glory by the brilliantly blazing stars. Her silver hair shimmering in the night, she reached out and touched Ernesto's cheek. "Thank you, Ernesto. Thank you so much for this evening."

Ernesto's eyes were awash with deep emotion. All these years, since his mother's death, he felt so alone. Even with Sandro, *Signora* Mangini, Fioretta, Antonio and Tomasso, he felt alone. Finally somehow, in the company of a woman he at one time despised, in the palace where he was abused as a child…at last he felt that he was home.

As he walked away from the door, he stopped for a moment to think. Turning back to the woman, he smiled. "*Signora*, I'm going to visit with my father and brothers tomorrow morning."

Chapter Thirty-Five

Ernesto felt a gnawing in the pit of his stomach as he walked through the deserted cemetery at dawn. He carefully inspected the large, somewhat gaudy tombstones, each one calling attention to who they were. Looking ahead, he remained motionless for a moment. Not far up ahead loomed a large obelisk with the name MEDICI engraved across the top. With a surge of energy, he ran towards it. Breathless, he dropped to his knees and slowly raised his eyes to the enormous stone in front of him. Taking his finger, he brushed it across the names engraved on the stone.

Piero the Gonfaloniere
Lorrenzo
Giuliano
REST IN GOD'S LOVING ARMS

Looking at the ground, he ran his fingers through the coarse dirt and picked up a handful and let it trickle between his fingers back to the earth. "Father," he whispered. "I'm so sorry. I'm sorry for what happened between us, between you and my mother. She loved you very much. I know it must have hurt you, seeing me with your children…my brothers and sisters." Ernesto fell silent for a moment, formulating his next words. "I guess we're all born with a form of evilness. Giuliano and I looked alike, and for that I suffered…no, we all suffered. Father, I beg your forgiveness for what I have done to my brother. I know he lies beside you, but if I could, I would take his place in death. None of this can be changed, so all I can beg for is your forgiveness."

Ernesto lay on the ground, looking up at the Medici name on the obelisk. His eyes felt sleepy. After a few minutes, the letters of the name got blurry until they disappeared.

"Ernesto, wake up. Are you alright?" Fioretta's voice startled him.

Ernesto awoke with a start. His heart pounding, he fumbled to gain his senses. Embarrassed, he realized that dawn was just breaking when he arrived and now the sun was crossing overhead.

"I was so worried. You've been here for hours. Please…come home now."

Getting to his feet, his body felt warm and content.

"Are you sure you're alright?"

A grin appeared across his face. "I am now. I'm going to be just fine. I spoke to my father. I still need to talk to my brothers though. Not today…but one day I will." Ernesto felt himself awaken fully now as Fioretta grabbed hold of his arm and they walked out of the cemetery.

After walking several minutes, Fioretta stopped and faced her husband. "I have something to tell you," she whispered. "It's important."

Ernesto's eyes traced the outline of Fioretta's face. Her beautiful green eyes looked so full of promise and hope as they did when he first laid eyes on her.

"Is it serious? Are you alright? The children?"

Fioretta sucked in a deep breath and held it for a moment. "You're going to be a father again!" she exclaimed.

Ernesto reeled for a moment, lost in her eyes. Thinking that she was toying with him, he smiled. "Really?"

Fioretta reached out and placed her soft hand on the side of his face. Leaning forward, she kissed him tenderly on the lips. "Really," she said with a smile. "Let's go home…we have a lot to do."

Chapter Thirty-Six

"Lord Palazzo, I insist," the servant groaned. "Please sir, let me help you with the last few buttons."

"Nonsense, Claudio. I can still dress myself."

With a wave of his hand, Ernesto dismissed his servant. Wincing in pain, his fingers clumsily tried to finish buttoning his shirt with no success.

Turning his gaze to the mirror, he stared at himself a long while. Ernesto's hands slid through his now thinned, silver gray hair. What happened to me? he wondered. Where is that young boy? Turning slightly to view different angles of how he looked, Ernesto sighed, remembering when he was as thin as a stick with long flowing brown curly hair. His reflection showed that the thirty-eight years of being the Gonfaloniere of Justice had taken its toll on him.

While his cloudy brown eyes peered deeper into the mirror, his mind wandered to his haunting memories of Il Duomo. He pictured his two murdered brothers and the part he played in Giuliano's death. Beads of sweat formed on his brow, realizing that he would soon be standing on the very same floor where both his brothers died. *I can't go through with this*, he thought. At fifty-six years old, he was a prisoner trapped in his own thoughts.

I have to find a way, he told himself. The man gave a dire sigh. *Will it ever end?* Pounding both fists on a dressing table he pursed his lips, whispering, "Will it ever end?"

Sliding his jacket on, he used the blue velvet material of his sleeve to wipe his drenched brow.

"Are you ready?" Antonio's voice shook Ernesto from his thoughts. "The door was open. I hope you don't mind."

Ernesto took a deep breath, mumbling, "No…it's fine. I don't know if I'll ever be ready. I haven't stepped foot in Il Duomo or any other church in over forty years. Antonio, I'm frightened, but…it's my son and I know that I have to do it."

Antonio's dark eyes settled on his friend. "Ernesto, put your demons behind you. I've been tormented for years by my memories but that's all they are, memories. I can't go back and right my wrongs."

Ernesto stared blankly at his friend, a gnawing pain in his gut. "I know…it's hard though."

"Of course it is!" Antonio snapped. "Do you remember that I was there with you?" Antonio's expression turned to one of deepening concern. "Hell, I know what you're going through. Tomasso died saving your wife! Ernesto, it was a long time ago, leave it in the past."

Ernesto gave a bleak smile. He studied his friend for several moments. Antonio's words jogged his memory. He thought of Tomasso, Jacopo and of Silvio and immediately his memories of Sandro rushed in. The sound of his teacher's voice echoed throughout the room, reverberating into his body. He remembered what his teacher taught him, of love and beauty and being a good man. When he finished, he remained quiet in his thoughts a few seconds. A knowing smile appeared on his lips. "I'll try, I promise I will," he said softly. "Thank you, my friend."

Chapter Thirty-Six

The laughter of children reached the upstairs of the Palace di' Palazzo.

"Let's go. They're all waiting for you downstairs."

"Wait," Ernesto said as he fumbled with the last button of his shirt. "I hate these things. They're too small to see."

Antonio laughed loudly. "Unfortunately, that's the first sign of old age, my lord."

"Hmm, is that so? I do believe that you are a bit older than me, am I correct? My daughter, Eugenia, would always button these for me. She looks so much like my mother." Ernesto recalled fondly.

"And your son, Alessandro, looks too much like you! Now hurry or you'll be late. It's not every man that can say that one of his sons is going to be the new Holy Father."

Ernesto burst out into laughter. "Hold on. Let's not rush it...he's the newly elected Pope. The Papal Coronation comes in a few months."

"From priest to bishop to cardinal in a short time and now this? It's special, Ernesto. The boy has been in Rome for fifteen years. It's nice that he can give the Easter Sunday Mass here, in front of you and Fioretta. In front of all of us who have seen him grow up." Antonio finished with the last button. "There, all done. Now if you please, my lord...we have to leave."

A floorboard squeaked loudly as Ernesto and Antonio made their way down the spiraling staircase. Fioretta turned slowly and looked up. Her gaze never wavered as she stared at her husband, her green eyes dazzling like they did when they first met. Fioretta placed her hands on her husband's shoulders and gazed at him. "It's a special day for our family, but just because he's our son, doesn't mean we can be late." She smiled and placed a tender kiss on his lips.

"Grandfather!" children's voices shrilled throughout the palace as they ran to Ernesto, taking turns jumping into his arms.

A woman's soft voice from behind quickly grabbed Ernesto's attention. "Hello, Father."

As he spun around, a big smile appeared on his face. "Eugenia," he said surprised. "It's so good to have you here."

"I've missed you, Father. Six months is too long to be away."

"Do you miss me too, Father?" Alessandro laughed from behind, wrapping his strong arms around his father.

"I do, son. I'm just not sure about my shoulders though."

Ernesto's eyes got misty as he scanned the room to see his son and his daughter along with his grandchildren. With a mischievous grin, he laughed, "Which of my grandchildren wants to ride with grandmother and myself in my carriage?"

In unison, all six grandchildren squealed loudly, "WE DO, WE DO!"

While the grandchildren ran out to the waiting carriage, his face grew serious. "Your mother and I will meet you there," he said to his son and daughter. "We have a few stops to make first."

"Stops?" Fioretta's eyebrows turned upward. "Ernesto, I told you…we can't be late."

The two carriages separated soon after they left the palace. A few miles away, they passed through a small wooded valley that led them into the Piazza Santa Croce. An old woman selling flowers in the piazza caught Ernesto's attention.

"*Buongiorno, Signora.*"

Chapter Thirty-Six

The woman gazed upward and saw the Gonfaloniere. She respectfully bowed before him. "Lord Palazzo, I will be at the church today to watch your son."

"Thank you, *Signora.* Please give me some of your finest roses. It is a special day for our family."

"Has he picked a name for himself?" she asked, handing him the flowers.

"Clement. His new name will be Pope Clement the seventh."

"Just a little bit farther," he whispered to Fioretta, holding her hand as the carriage began to slow. In the distance, a small cemetery came into view.

Slowly, Fioretta let her eyes trace the outlines of the church that they were approaching. "Ognissanti…I figured that's where we were going."

Ernesto smiled as he climbed from the rear seat of the carriage. Helping Fioretta and his grandchildren out, they quietly followed him into the small church. Standing before the tomb, Ernesto dropped to his knees and whispered, "Sandro, I'm here. I always will be here. Soon, when I die, I will be buried on these grounds not far from you."

Watching from a short distance away, one of the children mumbled under his breath. "Is this where our great-grandfather is?"

Fioretta nodded.

The children watched as Ernesto laid two roses down in front of the tomb. Copying their grandfather, they likewise put some of the flowers down besides his. From his knee, he turned and gave an approving smile as he got back to his feet. "This is your great-grandfather Alessandro. He was the most famous of all the artists in Italy! Tonight, before you go to bed, I will tell you the stories about him."

Closing the doors of the church behind them, they stopped at the grave of *Signora* Mangini. Ernesto gently placed three roses at the base of the large monument that he had bought for her. He looked down and whispered, "Thank you, *Signora*."

"Grandmother," the young girl asked, "who is grandfather talking to?"

"After your great-grandmother Eugenia died, this woman took care of grandfather."

"Eugenia?" the young girl shouted, not being able to contain her excitement. "That's my mother's name."

The shadow casting its light on the sundial outside the church told Ernesto that it was almost noon. "We have to go. It's going to start soon."

The sweet spring air filled the morning as they passed beautiful Mediterranean Cypress trees. The carriage slowed down as it came upon a large cemetery. The children saw the large stones that rose high in the sky. Climbing out of the carriage, they slowly walked through the cemetery. One of the children spelled out the name that was written on the very large obelisk monument that rose high in the air. "M.E.D.I.C.I." the young boy proudly said. "That spells Medici."

"That's right!" Fioretta exclaimed.

"Grandmother," the child asked. "Who is Medici?"

"Oh, they were old friends of your grandfather." Distracting the children, she asked, "So, do you want me to tell you my stories about Great-grandfather Alessandro?"

"Yes!" all the children shouted.

"Well, his nickname was Sandro, and everyone loved him............"

Ernesto slowly made his way to the large monument. He felt tears welling as he realized that it had been years since he was last at this grave.

Piero the Gonfaloniere

"I know you gave me my life," he whispered, "and for that, I am eternally grateful. In my heart, I will always respect you for giving me a chance to live."

He turned slightly to the other names on the tombstone. "Giuliano and Lorrenzo...my brothers." At this moment in time, he felt the power of family, of unity, of the same Medici blood coursing through his veins...the blood he now fully realized that he shared. "Today, my son is speaking in the same church where both of you died." Ernesto gave a tired smile, thinking of his childhood. "I wish we could have stayed children. We would have had so much fun...like we did. Remember when we played together all day long without any cares or hatred."

Bowing his head, he placed flowers on the grave and offered up a silent prayer. "I'm sorry," he gently whispered.

After a long moment, he turned on his heels without saying another word. *The past is dead. Live...live your life.*

"Are you alright?" Fioretta asked as he made his way back into the carriage.

Leaning over, he kissed his wife tenderly on the cheek and handed her a single rose that he had in his hand. "I am now. Let's go see our son."

The slow, leisurely pace of the carriage gave the children time to enjoy the beautiful Tuscan countryside.

Enjoying the warmth of the sun across his face, Ernesto felt his eyes drawn to Fioretta's. They still had that brilliant sparkle after all these years. "You are still so beautiful…beautiful as when I first saw you on the steps of Il Duomo."

Fioretta gave her husband a knowing smile as she enjoyed the glorious scenery around her. The gorgeous landscape stretched into the horizon. Approaching the city walls, the gentle breeze blowing through the wheat brought Ernesto back as he remembered running with the Medici boys. He reflected on happier times when all they knew was friendship, before growing up got in the way.

Getting close, they felt the vibration in their bodies as their carriage went from dirt to stone. Ernesto's eyes narrowed into tiny slits when he stared at the very spot where Sandro found him sitting in the street…cold and hungry, so many years ago. A lump grew in his throat, as he offered a silent prayer of thanks in his heart.

The horses lightly trotted into the Piazza della Signoria. Ernesto's memory was lucid as he relived the events that had happened here. Seeing Fioretta for the first time, Savonarola's mass burning of art and then, his execution.

Chapter Thirty-Six

The carriage stopped in front of the church as he felt a burning knot in his stomach. This would be the first time since the assassination of his brother Giuliano, that he would be stepping foot in this church.

"Sandro always laughed about going to church. He once told me going was like going to jail," he whispered to his wife.

Fioretta smiled quietly, sensing his anxiety. Leaning over, she whispered, "Thank you."

Ernesto remained silent.

"From the bottom of my heart, thank you."

"For?"

Fioretta reached out and placed her soft, delicate hand on Ernesto's check. "For saving me…for saving my life all those years ago. I've never told you, but you rescued me from a life that I would have hated. A life that would have been miserable for me. And I probably would have been dead by now. You saved me from Giuliano and at the same time, saved me from myself." Ernesto was taken back momentarily. "You've given me a life full of love and adventure."

As she stood to leave the carriage, she leaned over and tenderly kissed her husband on the lips. "I love you more than you'll ever know."

Slowly, Ernesto, Fioretta and their six grandchildren walked up the steps leading into the church as his hands began to tremble.

"So," she asked, distracting him, "you say that this is where you first fell in love with me?"

Ernesto smiled playfully. "Right over there. That's where I was sitting and you were walking up these steps, just like we are now."

He held on tightly to her smooth, calming hand as they walked through the large doors of Il Duomo.

Tremulous, Ernesto walked in and stopped in the center aisle. His eyes darted back and forth. His heart felt like it was bursting through his chest.

As he walked past the spot where Giuliano died, he felt as if he was crossing into another world, a guiltless world. One that once was a heavy burden, but now that burden had been lifted. Ernesto felt alive, he felt himself awaken fully when his eyes quickly focused on familiar images. Alive with wonder, he saw that the ancient stone walls of the church were still covered in the frescos that Sandro painted so long ago. He raised his eyes as old memories washed over him.

His emotions were coming in waves now. Ernesto smiled broadly as he remembered helping his teacher with these paintings. As they reached their seats, Ernesto sat back and opened up the small booklet that was placed in front of him while he waited for his son to begin the Mass.

The powerful aroma of Florence's sweet flowers and fragrant trees blew in through the huge doors of Il Duomo, filling Ernesto's nostrils. He looked around and Sandro was everywhere. He gave a reassuring smile to Fioretta and leaned his head back.

A stiff rushing wind whipped up the aisle and blew the pages from his booklet back and forth. With his hand securely in Fioretta's, their son, the new Pope Clement, strode across the grand altar to begin.

Raising his eyes past the ceiling and into the heavens, Ernesto closed them and whispered, "I've come home."

For a brief moment, over all the noise, he thought he heard Sandro's voice whispering back, echoing throughout the ancient church………..

Yes, you have, son…welcome home.

Chapter Thirty-Seven

The wind outside the famous Paris library, Bibliotheque de Paris, had picked up. The pages of the book that Yvette Dufour was reading danced in the breeze. Startled, her eyes opened wide. As her vision began to adjust to the morning light seeping in through the dingy basement windows, she realized where she was.

Yvette lifted her head up from the desk that she was sitting at all night. The cool morning Paris air blowing in through the window, replaced the stale, musty air that hung in the ancient library. Her eyes scanned her surroundings as she tried to come to terms with what she just saw. *Was it all just a dream?* she thought to herself.

Loud snoring quickly garnered her attention as she looked over and saw Jacques' head down on the desk, sleeping soundly.

"Jacques! Wake up," she screamed enthusiastically. "I've found them!" Despite dark rings under her eyes, Yvette was full of energy. "Come on, Jacques…wake up!" She shook the older gentleman.

"What?" the tired man questioned. "Who did you find? What are you talking about?"

"Botticelli…Alessandro Botticelli. His nickname is Sandro. I've found them, I've found them all," she screamed.

"Yvette!" Jacques bellowed. "Have you been drinking?"

Flushed with embarrassment, the Parisian beauty countered, "No…I haven't been drinking. I've seen them! I've seen their lives."

"Alright," he said wiping the sleep from his eyes. "Take a few breaths and try to calm down."

Not being able to contain her excitement, she paced back and forth mumbling loudly that she saw them.

"Please Yvette, sit down and tell me whose lives are you talking about? Who did you see?"

"Ernesto! I found him, Jacques," she blurted.

"Who? Who in the world is Ernesto?" Jacques asked, lowering his voice to calm the excited woman.

"Botticelli kept a boy. Remember? What Savonarola said about Sandro. Ernesto was the boy. It's all there. All those books I read tell about them. They're real, Jacques! Ernesto fought the Medici's. He saved Fioretta. Antonio and Tomasso fought with him."

"Okay." The cantankerous old man leaned in closer to smell her breath.

"Please stop. I haven't been drinking. Just listen to me!"

"I will, Yvette, I will. Just sit down and calm yourself before you pass out."

Yvette, still trembling, forced herself to sit back down in the chair. Jacques brought her a small glass of water.

"Maybe it was just a bad dream."

"Dream? No, it wasn't a dream, it was real. I saw it with my own eyes," she shouted loudly, echoing through the basement.

"Alright…alright, I apologize."

"Please, Jacques…please believe me. I saw their lives. It was beautiful! Sandro was a beautiful, caring man."

"Sandro?" His eyebrows rose curiously. "Ohhh, that's right, Botticelli. You know, Yvette, the more I thought about it last night, since we couldn't find any good information about him, I was just going to write a generic article."

"WHAT?" Yvette shouted. "No, you can't! You mustn't!"

Confused, Jacques shook his head. "Sure I can. I'll just mention a few of his paintings and----"

"NO," she shot back. "Jacques, please listen to me. There's so much more to their lives."

He shrugged and looked curiously into her eyes. "You're serious about this, aren't you? Listening to you, you actually make it sound like you've met them."

"I have, Jacques…I have. They're real and they are wonderful. The Medici's, the Pazzi's, Antonio and Tomasso and…"

"Medici's? Pazzi's? Oh, alright, I guess I can add a little something more to the article, but you're going to have to tell me all about your meeting with these people."

"I will," she promised. "It was real. Please believe me. I'm not crazy."

"Yvette, it was all a dream…made up. This article has to be real, not that anybody will ever know. Wait, who am I joking?" he asked. "My credibility is on the line and if I-----"

"No, Jacques!" she interrupted, her heart pounding wildly. "No dream. They lived… my God, how they lived."

Jacques pursed his lips and remained quiet a long moment.

"Please, I beg you. Please believe me."

Chapter Thirty-Seven

Jacques' eyes hardened as he inhaled deeply and let out a slow deliberate burst of air. "Okay," he said, humoring her. "Let's have it…I'm listening."

"Here? No… not here…I'm famished."

Jacques' jaw tightened as he spoke through clenched teeth. "WHAT? What do you mean not here?"

"*Monsieur* Mesnil," Yvette countered with a sparkle in her eye, "please don't tell me that you're reverting back to your grumpy old habits again."

Learning to control his anger, the edges of Jacques Mesnil's lips began to turn upward. His mind raced to their conversation the night before and how their initial conversation went. His rudeness was very apparent but he finally met someone who would not put up with his obnoxious behavior. Yvette was just as intelligent, energetic and sophisticated as he was but all the while, she showed grace and elegance, that of a Parisian woman. Seeing his smile, she noticed that his rude demeanor quickly melted.

"Now isn't this so much better? I will tell you all about Sandro, Ernesto, Fioretta and their friends over breakfast. That is if you are taking me, *Monsieur* Mesnil?"

Jacques sighed, wanting nothing more. "*Mademoiselle* Dufour, it would be my honor."

Gently taking her small delicate hand in his, they began climbing up the steps together from the dark basement. Stopping for a moment he asked, "Won't the library be opening soon?"

"Opening?" She smiled playfully. "Jacques, this is Sunday. Today we are closed."

Yvette reached forward and kissed Jacques on the cheek. Together, they climbed the steps from the basement. Jacques turned for a moment to look back down into the underground room. He smiled, thinking to himself, *Down there, I've found my story, but more importantly…I believe I've found love.*

He felt an unexpected sadness leaving the basement, but was excited for this new chapter of his life. He smiled as he switched off the light behind them. Yvette and Jacques walked hand in hand through the quiet, empty aisles of the majestic Bibliotheque de Paris. As they passed rows of history, Jacques felt somewhat humbled. Understanding the importance of what these people in his article had accomplished in their lives, he was invigorated to do something about his.

They both smiled at each other as they approached the solid wooden doors exiting the library. As Jacques opened the door for Yvette, they both took one last look into the deserted building. Jacques quickly realized what the last twenty-four hours meant to him and how it changed his life. Remembering what his professor told him over forty years ago gave him hope for the future.

All that a man does with his life, the good as well as the bad, can be changed in an instant. Never dwell on your past. Never lack humility or be proud enough to change your life course. A man can conquer evil…move forward. Move forward with love and compassion…never look back...live your life.

After Yvette locked the door to the library, they both turned to see Paris greet them to a new morning. Their sense of smell was given a treat from the aroma of freshly baked bread that lingered around them. The sweet fragrance of freshly cut flowers hung in the air as the two watched a young woman push her cart of brilliantly colored flowers. An old man was setting up his organ as he was dressing his trained monkey in a cute costume.

Music was playing, people were singing, even at this early time of the day.

Jacques looked over to Yvette. Her eyes closed for a moment, her lips relaxed in a contented smile. "Yvette? Do you know where you would like to eat?"

Slowly, she opened her eyes and turned to him. Her face was radiant in the new morning light. "I do. When my husband was alive, we would go to that one café that I told you about last night. If it's alright with you, I would love to go there."

A sweet smile formed across Jacques' face as the two walked in silence, taking in the sights, smells and sounds of Paris. Walking hand in hand, a gentle morning breeze cooled their faces. "So now tell me," he said, "tell me all about Botticelli and his boy, Ernesto."

Finito

About the Author

Vincent F. Porzio, is an engaging debut writer entering the literary world. Born and raised in New Jersey, he graduated with a degree in art history. Yearning to see the world, he found himself among people from all walks of life, learning from them throughout the continental United States. His travels took him worldwide where he roamed dark dingy basements throughout ancient churches in the U.S. and in Europe, studying architecture and historic art forms of long ago civilizations such as the ancient Romans and Etruscans. His travels enabled him to not only study people, but to observe their struggles, triumphs, loves and passions. As a result, creativity and passion for the written page was born.

Vincent has also written skits for cable network shows and has written and produced a short film.

Keeping his two passions alive, he currently works in the art industry as a graphic artist, and always has his eyes open and his vivid imagination ready to capture a moment that will allow him to write from an artistic perspective.

He enjoys visiting his family in the beautiful Tuscan region of Italy where he never takes for granted the beauty that is all around.

Vincent is also a powerful and engaging motivational speaker. He has given public lectures on art, and still finds himself quite comfortable in public speaking arenas, giving lectures for an audience that ranges in the thousands.

However, his passion for writing still remains a constant reminder of the beauty that the written page offers. For him, writing is home.

Having raised two girls, he now resides in a small country suburb of Atlanta, Georgia, with his wife.

Other books by Author V.F. Porzio

Sandro: The Forsaken World

Part One

Available on:
Kindle
Amazonc.om
Barnes & Noble
Nook
Bookstores Nationwide

Author's Website:
www.authorvfporzio.com

21211921R00222

Made in the USA
Charleston, SC
09 August 2013